SAVAGE PRINCE
RUTHLESS HEIRS

SIENNA CROSS

Copyright © 2025 by Sienna Cross

All rights reserved.

No part of this book may be reproduced in any form or by any electronic or mechanical means, including information storage and retrieval systems, without written permission from the author, except for the use of brief quotations in a book review.

Paperback ISBN: 9798314699621

Cover Design: Covers by Juan

Interior Art: Samaiya Art

❀ Created with Vellum

To all the women who find it perfectly acceptable to fall for the gorgeous Italian mob boss keeping them hostage…
~ Sienna Cross

PLEASE NOTE

This is a dark romance novel with scenes that may be triggering and sexually explicit in nature, specifically but not limited to SA, violence and torture.

Savage Prince

SIENNA CROSS

CONTENTS

1. A Hot Stranger — 1
2. Fashionista — 6
3. The Cousin Crew — 13
4. Somewhere Private — 19
5. Consumed with Revenge — 25
6. Cuore Mio — 31
7. A Puttana — 38
8. How to Catch a Mafia Princess — 45
9. Mine Now — 52
10. A Good Little Hostage — 59
11. Something Hard — 66
12. Hurled Back in Time — 72
13. A Valuable Prize — 78
14. See Something You Like? — 84
15. Escape — 91
16. Ransom — 98
17. Last Beautiful Thing — 104
18. Terror — 111
19. Too Soft — 118
20. Complicated — 124
21. Ghosts — 131
22. He Stayed — 137
23. A Picnic — 144
24. A Little Tipsy — 150
25. An Inferno — 156
26. A Moral Dilemma — 163
27. A Slow Agonizing Death — 169
28. The Ugly Truth — 175
29. A Coincidence — 181
30. A Good Man — 186
31. Don't Stop — 194
32. Lost Causes — 201
33. Inexplicable Feelings — 208
34. So Long Suckers — 214
35. Tastes Like Mine — 221

36. A Sucker	228
37. Afraid of the Truth	234
38. Grand Theft Auto	241
39. Powerless	247
40. A Lot of Fines	255
41. Make It Good	261
42. Villains	267
43. Under Different Stars	274
44. Wreckage	281
45. Before You Were Mine	289
46. Bliss	295
47. The Best Nurse Maid	301
48. The L-Word	307
49. Almost Home	314
50. Traitor	322
51. You Saved Me	328
52. Imperfectly Perfect	334
53. Dante Valentino	340
Epilogue	350
Also by Sienna Cross	359
Acknowledgments	361
About the Author	363

CHAPTER 1
A HOT STRANGER

S*erena*

I will not cry. I will not cry.

Blinking quickly, I force back the tears as I jab my finger into the elevator button but keep my gaze pinned on my cousin and best friend, Bella, who still stands in the doorway of the penthouse watching me leave. Her new boyfriend tucks her into his side as she brushes away a tear that's spilled over. Her bottom lip trembles when I step into the elevator with one last wave, and Raf presses a sweet kiss to her forehead.

So what if we'll be living an entire ocean away from each other with my new job in Milano? And who cares if she's met the man of her dreams? We're blood. And have been best friends for two decades. Nothing will ever change that.

I exhale a sigh of relief once the doors glide closed, convincing myself I'm overreacting as I lean against the sleek metal wall. When your father is Dante Valentino, the enforcer and brother to the *capo* of the ruthless Kings, the most notorious crime syndicate in all of Manhattan, there's nothing more important than blood and loyalty. As a result, I don't have many female friends, but with Bella I never needed one.

The past few months in Milano have been tough without her and our cousin crew, the Valentinos and Rossi's. But I love it there, and I'm finally thriving.

My phone vibrates, and I draw in a breath as I fish it out of my purse, brushing the Glock 42 I take everywhere.

New message from Italian_Stallion69.

He was the guy I'd swiped right on before leaving my cousin's welcome home party earlier this evening. Black hoodie with sunglasses, face covered in shadows, there was just something dark and mysterious about him. I have to stop it with these dating apps. My finger hovers over the *View* button for an endless minute. I should just go home and get some rest, right? Or I could drown all my anxieties and fears with a hot stranger and just forget for one night...

Fuck it.

I press the button and the message pops up.

Italian_Stallion69: Meet me for a drink?

This guy doesn't waste any time. I like that.

Me: Where?

Italian_Stallion69: You pick. I'm not from here.

Oh, a tourist. Even better. Then there's no chance we'll awkwardly meet up a few months from now. And luckily, there's the perfect bar down the block from here.

The elevator doors slide open, and I cross through the elegant lobby of my uncle's modern building before I find my driver parked out front. One of the perks of being a mafia princess, no need to hail cabs in the typical congestion of New York City. He opens the door, but I wave him off. "I'm not going home yet, Nicky. The night is still young and hot, like me." I toss him a wink. "I'll text you when I'm ready."

"Yes, Miss Valentino." He dips his head and slides back into the front seat of the Audi SUV. "Take your time."

I don't know what I'd do if *Papà* were as controlling as Uncle Luca who forces an entire security team on Bella. I would lose my shit to have someone following me every second of the day. The Valentinos and my dad's half-brothers, the Rossi's, may have found peace, but that doesn't mean every other criminal association in New York City doesn't want our parents dead.

As the daughters of the notorious Valentino brothers, and heiresses to the King's throne, Bella and I, along with our cousins, have grown up surrounded by guards, trapped in gilded cages of our fathers' makings.

Or at least that's what they tried to do…

When I turned eighteen, six years ago now, I sat *Papà* down and told him I'd had enough. Luckily, my mom is awesome, and she had my back. After a lot of yelling, crying and cursing, we'd come to an understanding, and I'd been allowed to move into my own apartment with a minimal security team attached. I attended the Fashion Institute in Manhattan, graduated and got a job, and what do you know? I've survived just fine.

Now after a summer in Milano working for Dolce & Gabbana, I've been offered a full-time position. It's more than I ever could have wanted. The only downside is being so far away from Bella and our cousin crew.

With a quick wave goodbye to Nicky, I continue down Fifth Avenue toward the Pierre Hotel. It's sophisticated and luxurious, the perfect spot to wow a tourist, plus if things don't work out with the Italian Stallion, I won't have to worry about getting harassed by dirtbags.

Not that that's ever a major issue with Dolce around. My fingers tighten around my new Prada purse, home to my beloved weapon I affectionately named after my favorite designer. Pa insisted I learned my way around a gun at the ripe old age of twelve. The shooting range quickly became my favorite place to go with him, and now my aim is as sharp as my tongue. Target practice was our bonding time, a safe place for both of us to get out some aggression.

Some members of our family think I have a wild streak just like him. They're not wrong, but they keep it to themselves unless they want their head bitten off by *Papà*. I'm still his only child and little princess.

The grand façade of the elegant Pierre Hotel is just ahead, and I pick up the pace, an odd stillness across Fifth Avenue. Most of the stores are closed at this hour, the sidewalks barren. A limo pulls up alongside me, likely going to The Pierre or the St. Regis nearby. It slows, and the hair on the back of my neck rises.

After years raised in a family like ours, I've developed a sixth sense, an innate awareness for self-preservation. I slow my footsteps, internally grumbling at my choice of stilettos. Fabulous but not ideal for running.

The black stretch limousine stops just a few yards in front of me, and the back door whips open. The distinctive gilded canopy of The Pierre next block is so close it's taunting. I almost make a run for it, but he's too damned fast. A man in all black leaps out of the car, reaching for me. I try to jerk back, but I stumble on my damned high heels, and my heart catapults up my throat as an arm curls around me. I wiggle and squirm and kick, but the steel band around my torso only tightens, squeezing the air from my lungs.

"Let go of me!" I scream as I try to slide my purse from under my arm into my hand. Either my phone or Dolce would do right now. The asshole wrenches my clutch from my fingertips, and I hiss out a curse as it clatters to the sidewalk.

"Let me go!" I shout again.

He tosses me into the backseat of the limo before I can shriek out a second string of expletives. Icy fear streaks up my spine as my face hits the soft leather. I search the dimly lit back seat, heart kicking against my ribs. Another man sits on the far seat wearing a black hoodie, smoldering velvety eyes locked on me.

Shit. Tinder guy, really?

He's completely still, jaw locked in a hard line.

"Do you have any idea who I am?" I shout as the guy who

just nabbed me dives into the car and shoves me down. "When my father finds out I'm gone he will paint the city in your blood," I hiss.

The man in the back slides to the edge of the seat and pushes back the dark hood. The overhead light reveals the harsh contours of his savagely handsome face. "Do you have any idea who *I* am, *tesoro*?"

My stomach drops, a tight knot twisting my insides. "Fuck," I grit out.

Antonio Ferrara.

CHAPTER 2
FASHIONISTA

S*erena - One Month Earlier*

Hopping off the tram at *The Duomo*, I throw the driver a wink and race across the street to the *piazza*. The towering spires of the grand gothic cathedral spiral up to the cloudless sky, overlooking a crowded square filled with pesky tourists and peskier pigeons. The damned rats with wings followed me all the way from Manhattan. Ignoring the flying pests and countless tourists snapping photos in front of the white church's jagged spiked peaks, my footsteps quicken. It's a perfect summer evening, which means *aperitivo*, or the typical Milanese happy hour at my favorite rooftop bar with sprawling views of the historic site.

Strutting through Galleria Vittorio Emanuele, one of the world's oldest shopping malls, I pause beneath the glass-vaulted dome to peek through the window of Prada. I've had my eye on a cross-shoulder bag that would be perfect for running around the city for weeks now. Once I get my next paycheck, it's mine. After living in Milano for two months now, I've managed to save up a little bit of money to fund my extravagant lifestyle. Between epic nights out and my measly internship salary, it's been a struggle, but I prefer it a hundred times over dipping into my trust fund.

At twenty-two, *Papà* handed over my share of the Valentino family fortune and it's a shit ton of money. There are definite perks to the only child thing, but all that money also comes with strings. Which was why I leapt at the chance to get a job in fashion and make my own mark without having to rely on Daddy's fortune.

"I see you eye-fucking that Prada, girl. What are you waiting for, just make your move." Santi strolls up, looking fabulous as always in frayed D&G jeans and a tight leopard-print button down. He bends down to offer me the traditional Italian double-cheeked kiss before joining me beside the window. Santiago and I met the first day I started at Dolce & Gabbana and have been inseparable ever since. We're the most promising fashion design interns according to Bianca, our boss.

"Just a couple more weeks and I'll be strutting around Via Montenapoleone rubbing shoulders with all the fashionistas with that bad girl."

"Aren't you filthy rich, Serena? Why the unnecessary restraint?" His dark brow arches, amber flecks illuminating his warm hazel eyes.

"I'm not filthy rich, my family is. And I'm trying to prove to my dad that I can get along just fine without him or his money."

"What a waste." He smirks before swinging his arm around my shoulder. "If I came from the kind of money that you do, I would be living it up here."

"I think we're doing just fine, don't you? I didn't see you complaining the other night when I got us into Armani Privé with a private table." The elegant club is a staple in Milano, designed by the iconic Giorgio Armani himself. Luckily, I made friends with the bouncer my first week here and have been enjoying free admission ever since.

"Your fuck buddy bouncer got us into the club."

"Semantics." I shrug as I lead us across the intricate tile mosaics of the galleria. Dmitri has proven invaluable over the past two months, and he's a decent lay, so it's a win-win really.

Tucked between Savini Café and Prada is a secret staircase that leads to a quaint rooftop bar. Only the locals know of its existence, and it's become one of my favorite summer happy hour spots.

Once we reach the fourth floor, Santi opens the graffitied door which leads to the open-air *terrazzo*. Shimmering lights are hung across graceful arcs, setting the spires of the grand Duomo alight in an ethereal glow. I draw in a breath as I take it all in. Even though I come here at least once a week, it's still a breathtaking sight.

The cute hostess greets us with a smile before motioning for us to seat ourselves. There are only about a dozen tables across the rooftop and more than half are already full. I weave my way to the edge of the *terrazzo* which overlooks the *piazza* below and flop onto the wrought iron chair.

"Damn, do I need a drink."

"Same, girl. The usual?" He tosses his head of light brown curls back, tucking a few wayward locks behind his aviators.

"Of course. I was drinking Aperol Spritz long before it became a thing."

The waiter appears, flashing a smile, and a tumble of dark hair falls over his brow. He looks oddly familiar. I'm fairly certain I hooked up with him a few weeks ago after an all-nighter at Hollywood, another famous club in Milano teeming with celebrities and amazing parties.

"*Due* Aperol Spritz," says Santi in his best Italian accent, holding up two fingers.

A few more months and he'll sound like a local. His adoptive mom was Puerto Rican, so having arrived already speaking Spanish definitely gave him an edge over the other interns. Still, I'm impressed by how good he's gotten all the same. I was lucky enough to have been taught Italian by *Papà* and *Nonna* as a child. My grandma was adamant I learned at a young age, just like all of us Valentino and Rossi cousins. We may not all speak it often, but we know more than enough to get by, not to mention all the good curses.

When the waiter saunters away, Santi turns his mischievous gaze on me. "He's gorgeous, and he looked like he wanted to fuck you."

"Been there, done that."

"Seriously? Are there any hot, single men in Milano you've yet to screw?"

"Yes, you." I offer him a wink, and his head falls back as he cackles. With deep mocha skin and a model-like physique, my friend is beyond good looking. He's tall with lean muscles, and a heart-stopping smile that has both women and men swooning at the sight of his Afro-Latino ass.

"Trust me, if I were into pussy, there would be nothing to keep me away, girl."

"Oh, I know. Not only am I gorgeous, smart and funny, I'm also fantastic in bed."

His cackles only get louder, showcasing his blindingly white, perfect teeth. "I bet you are." He finally straightens and takes a sip of water as the fit subsides.

The waiter returns just in time with our bubbly Aperol Spritzes. After placing Santi's bright orange drink down, he leans in as he delivers mine. "*Ciao, Serena, tutto bene?*"

"*Si, grazie,* all good." For the life of me, I can't remember his name and he's not wearing a nametag. I glance down at the napkin, trying to avoid his questioning gaze, and a scrawled phone number catches my eye. No name though.

"Call me sometime. I'd like to take you on a date. I had fun the other night."

I stare up at him, slack-jawed for a long moment before he shoots me a wink and saunters away.

A low whistle purses Santi's lips, and I jab my elbow into his side. "Don't start."

"What? He likes you… why don't you give the man a chance?"

"I don't date, I don't do relationships. I already told you."

"But why?" He drags the last word out for a long whiny moment.

"I don't know. It's just not in me." My shoulders slowly lift. "Actually, none of my best friends back home do."

"Oh, you mean the notorious cousin crew?" He grins like he's actually met the rest of my family. What I haven't told him yet is that they're coming to visit in a few days. It's Alessandro and Alessia's birthdays so they decided to make a trip of it and the whole crew is meeting up. I'm weirdly protective about my relationship with my cousins, and I don't like to share them. I fully realize how insane that sounds, but as the oldest, being the protector has always been my role. Even though the twins are barely a year younger than me, I've always considered myself the mother hen. Which is weird because I don't have a maternal bone in my body. I'm pretty sure I don't even want kids.

"Actually, they're coming to visit on Friday."

"Your cousins, all the way from Manhattan?" His dark brow lifts.

"Well, Bella is still interning in Rome, but yeah, the rest are flying in on the jet from home."

"On the jet? Of course they are." A hint of hurt flashes across his expressive irises.

"I'm sorry I didn't tell you, I just wanted to keep them all to myself while they're here, I guess. I haven't seen them in months and—"

He raises a dismissive hand. "Nah, I get it, it's fine. They're you're family."

But he still looks genuinely hurt. And now I feel like a shitty friend. He's the one person I've really connected with since I moved here, and I don't want to jeopardize our friendship.

"We'll all go out one night, okay? Bella is only here for two nights because she has to get back to her medical internship in Rome so let's do an aperitivo on Friday."

"I'm not sure if I can make it, but I'll let you know." He picks up his glass and takes a long pull from the straw.

An uncomfortable silence lingers over the table, and now I just wish I could take it all back. Why didn't I just tell him sooner?

I gulp down my drink, then scoot my chair back, the metal legs scraping against the terracotta tile. "Bathroom break, be right back, then we can plan for Friday, okay?"

He nods, a half-smile lifting the corner of his lip.

Clutching my purse under my arm, I scoot around the crowded rooftop, a pang of regret weighing me down. I'm such an idiot. Santi didn't grow up with a big, loving, albeit sometimes dysfunctional family like I did. He was raised by his adoptive single mom who did the best she could to keep a roof over their heads in the super expensive L.A. area.

As I trudge down the long, quiet corridor to the bathroom, I resolve to make sure he's included in all the cousin events while they're in town. I'm so preoccupied I must pass the restrooms all together because I end up in some maintenance hallway with the steady thrum of an HVAC unit vibrating the narrow space. Spinning around, I return in the direction I came from and nearly crash into a wall of muscles behind a black trench coat. Piercing midnight eyes peer down at me through an ornate Venetian mask.

"*Scusi.*" The voice is low and guttural and has the hair on the back of my neck rising. His hands come up, but before he can make contact with my bare skin, I duck under his arm and race by.

Glancing over my shoulder as I jog down the hallway in my heels, I find the stranger standing perfectly still just where I left him, dark eyes glaring through that creepy mask fixed in my direction.

What the actual hell?

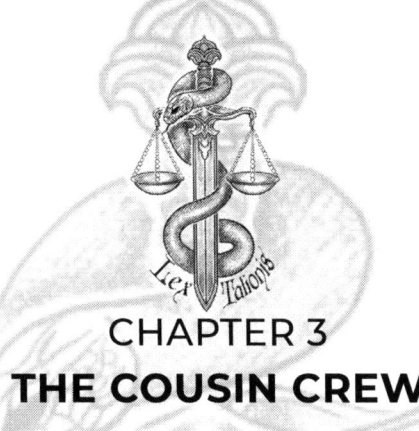

CHAPTER 3
THE COUSIN CREW

S*erena*

"Eek! I'm so glad you're here, Bella!" I launch myself at my cousin, barreling through the entryway of my apartment.

Her bodyguard, Raf, glares down at me as if I might accidentally crush his precious client by squeezing her too tight. Okay, he's not just her bodyguard, but I refuse to believe my baby cousin is actually in a committed relationship.

"Me too!" she squeals right back as we spin in a circle like we did when we were kids excited about our parents taking us to the movies or the zoo at Central Park.

Once we're both dizzy, I finally release her and tug her into my apartment. Raf grabs their luggage and trails behind, something like annoyance carved into his ruthlessly handsome face. I still can't believe I was the one who'd insisted she pick the hot bodyguard all those months ago. Really, Raf should be kissing my feet right now for getting them together in the first place.

"Where should I put the luggage?" Her grumpy guard scans

the apartment, eyes narrowed, as if a sniper could jump out from behind one of the velvet curtains at any moment.

"*Your* room is the second one on the right down the hall." I reach for my cousin and tuck her into my side. "But Bella here will be sleeping with me in my room."

"I don't think so," he growls, dropping the luggage and stalking closer.

"Don't you dare growl at me, Raffaele Ferrara." I jab my finger into his ridiculously hard chest. "You get her every day in Rome. I only have my favorite cousin and best friend for two measly days. Who knows when they'll let her have another weekend off from that hospital."

"Sere is right, *amore*. It's only two nights." Bella rewards him with a sappy smile, and to my shock, the big beast actually backs down. "I promise I'll make it up to you when we get home."

"I'm going to hold you to that, *principessa*." A silly grin curls the corners of his lips, but he still releases a huff of irritation as he picks up the suitcases and trudges down the hallway to the guest room.

"Impressive, Bella," I whisper as soon as he turns into the bedroom. "You've really got that man pussy-whipped, don't you?"

"Oh, stop." She laughs, but I can't help noticing the way her eyes sparkle in Raf's presence, the bright blue, a mirror of my own, sparkling in intensity. I've never seen her so happy.

"So everything's okay now after the kidnapping and all?"

She nods slowly, her dark hair falling across her shoulders in gentle waves. "It's been quiet for the past few weeks, but Raf still hasn't heard a word from his brother, Antonio."

My thoughts swirl back to my visit to Rome a few weeks ago. We ran into Raf's brothers coming out of a nightclub. Before then, we had no idea who they were, or what they were involved in. Much like Raffaele, the elder Ferrara brothers were gorgeous, especially Antonio. Of course after what happened in Rome, I'd been sworn away from the entire family.

A pair of piercing, velvety irises flicker across my mind. The heat that came from that man's gaze should have been illegal. Even now, after all these weeks, Antonio Ferrara haunts me. Figures, I'd be attracted to a monster.

Forcing the inappropriate memories to the far corners of my mind, I refocus on the present. "Does Raf think Antonio could be a threat?"

Bella shakes her head. "He's not sure. Antonio is the only family he has left, and I don't think he wants to believe he'd come after me for revenge, but who knows? Raf's always on high alert."

Approaching footsteps turn my attention to her faithful bodyguard, and I'm not the only one who notices his return. Isabella moves toward him like a magnet, pulled into his orbit without the faintest persuading. She wraps her arm around his waist and curls into his side like the curves of her body naturally fit against the hard planes of his.

"So what's the plan for tonight?" Raf turns his dark gaze on me. "I'll need to have all locations vetted prior to our arrival. My security team is ready to go so just give me the names." He sweeps a lock of Bella's hair behind her ear, the move so sweet for the big hulking guard, my head snaps back in shock. "I've been asking Isa for the information since we found out we were coming last week, but she insists I'm being overly paranoid."

"You are," I retort. "Your precious Isa is more than safe here in Milano."

Raf lets out a grunt, tightening his hold around Bella. "I'll be the one to determine that."

"Anyway," Bella interrupts, prying herself free from his possessive hold, "I can't wait to see Milano, the shopping, the food, I want it all!"

"Now that's what I'm talking about." I throw her overbearing guard a smirk. "Matteo and the twins should be arriving in the next hour or so, then we'll go to dinner at DG Martini, followed by a pop-up night club in Parco Sempione. There's a hot new DJ performing that I've been dying to see."

"In the middle of a park?" Raf snaps. "It's going to be very difficult to maintain the perimeter in that enormous area."

"Relax, *amore*." Isabella squeezes his hand and flashes another nauseatingly sweet smile. "Andrew will be in charge of the team tonight. You're off duty, remember?"

His eyes lock on hers, and this weirdly intense moment passes between them. Like I'm tempted to leave them alone before they jump each other. "I'm never off duty when it comes to protecting you."

"I know… but please try for tonight, okay? I just want my boyfriend, not my bodyguard. We're supposed to be on vacation."

"Fine, I'll try," he grumbles.

I flutter over to the two lovebirds and pat the big brute on the back. "It's going to be perfect, you'll see."

I can't help the stupid grin that stretches across my face as I watch Alessandro and Alessia bickering over the merits of a vodka or gin martini while Matteo and Bella gush over the zebra print couches and crimson damask wallpapering the elegant lounge. All of us together again feels so normal, as if not a minute has passed since we've seen each other. Raf sits stiffly beside Bella, his eyes searching every velvet curtained corner of the restaurant for threats.

Ignoring him, I refocus on the conversation. "Vodka all the way." I pick up my dirty martini and clink the glass against Alessia's. "I don't care if it isn't the original."

"You're both barbarians," Alessandro grumbles. My cousin owns The Velvet Vault in Manhattan, one of the hottest new clubs in the Meatpacking District. He thinks he's the end all, be all of cocktails now.

"So should we move to the dining room?" I tick my head toward the archway that leads to the elaborate interior with sleek black contemporary furnishings and opulent gilded touches.

"One more drink," Bella replies. "I have a feeling once dinner arrives, I'll find myself in a food coma before long."

"She's not wrong." Raf glances down at her adoringly. "This girl loves her pasta."

"Oh, *Dio*, Bella, I almost forgot to tell you. They have the most amazing Nutella calzone!"

My cousin licks her lips, excitement lighting up her lively blue eyes. She picks up her champagne flute and downs it in one huge gulp. "On second thought, let's get this dinner going."

Matteo laughs, bringing his cocktail to his lips. "Slow down, Bells. We've got a long night ahead of us."

"Don't make it sound like I'm forcing you to go out and have fun, Matty."

"Not at all, Sere. I'm thrilled to have my wingwomen back." He casts a glance at Bella who's wedged beside Raf, hands intertwined, and frowns. "Well, at least I have you."

"Hey!" Isabella swats at his arm, her lips twisting into a pout. "I can still be your wingwoman. Just because Raf's here doesn't mean I can't have fun."

"Right…"

"Oh, I can be fun." The big bodyguard rises and pulls Bella up with him. "Come on, *amore*, let's dance."

"There's no dancefloor," she squeals as he tugs her into his arms and begins to sway to a slow beat which is in sharp contrast to the pulsing rhythm of the background music.

I scoot closer to Matteo, rolling my eyes. "Drink with me, Matty. I'm going to need to be good and drunk to survive the night with those two."

He chuckles, revealing the dimple that has all the girls back in Manhattan dropping their panties for. "You should be happy for Bells."

"I am."

"You don't look it."

"Why can't I be happy and still cautiously suspicious?" I watch Raf and Bella, giggling and whispering as they dance. "I just don't want her falling for the first guy she fucked. And what do we really know about him anyway?"

"You know Uncle Luca had her guard meticulously vetted before he hired him."

"And still he missed all that shit about the Ferrara family."

Matteo shrugs. "I guess even the great Luca Valentino isn't completely infallible."

"Right. How are your parents by the way? Your five hundred siblings?"

With a grin, he takes another sip before answering. "They're fine overall. *Papà* and Uncle Marco have been on Alessandro and me about taking over the Geminis. Technically as eldest, it should fall on Ale, but he loves the club and wants nothing to do with Gemini Corp."

"And you?"

His shoulders lift again, accentuating the tight fit of his jacket. Damn, Matteo has been working out. And it looks good on him. Too bad we're related. "I don't know. I've gone into the office a few days a week over the summer since you and Bells abandoned me for Italy. I've been working with Sam in the cyber security department. That part I like, but CEO? I'm not sure about that."

"Once a hacker, always a hacker."

"Exactly." He shoots me a grin over the rim of his glass.

A waiter appears dressed in a leopard floral print shirt I recognize from the latest collection at D&G. "Excuse me, your table is ready."

"Yes!" Bella pulls free of her guard and bounces on her stilettos. "Let's eat!"

CHAPTER 4
SOMEWHERE PRIVATE

S*erena*

Neon lights are strung between ancient trees, painting everything in a surreal glow. The peaceful Parco Sempione is transformed into a vibrant, beating heart of music and movement. I move to the rhythm, the bass resonating through the ground, mirroring the heartbeat of the gathered masses. It's a freeing escape; all the usual shit that gathers around my shoulders dissolving into the night.

Tonight is the first night since I arrived in Milano that I feel free to just be me. With my family surrounding me, I don't have to be Serena Valentino, heiress and aspiring fashion designer. I can just have fun and let loose and not think about a damned thing. Most would have no idea the burden of responsibility I feel, which is why I do my best to drown it out with a life of partying and meaningless sex.

My therapist says it's normal given my rather particular upbringing, so we're still working on it. My phone vibrates in my purse, and I fish it out, the flash of the shiny metal of my gun glinting beneath the lights. Finally, a response from Santi. I'd been texting him all night to come meet up with us.

Santi: I think I'm going to stay in tonight.
Me: Are you serious? Since when do you miss a Friday night out?
Santi: It'll be good for you to spend time with your family.
Me: Come on! I really want you here.

I wait for the telltale sign of blue bubbles that he's typing a response, but I see nothing. A second later the annoying *Santi has notifications silenced* pops up. Damn it.

"Everything okay?" Isabella shimmies her way closer, sipping her cocktail from a bright pink straw.

"Yeah, it's just my friend Santi. He was supposed to come meet up with us and he cancelled."

"Oh, that sucks. I was looking forward to meeting him. He sounds like a lot of fun from all your tales of wild nights out."

"He's the best."

"What's wrong with you two?" Matteo asks.

Alessandro and Alessia saunter up behind him, the twins impeccably dressed as always in their mom's designs. My aunt Jia has her own fashion label with her flagship store in Manhattan. She's the one who got me the internship with Dolce & Gabbana and has been my inspiration for years.

"Nothing is wrong, right, Sere?" Bella grabs my hand and spins me in a circle.

"Nothing at all." I give my cousins a smile as I give into the beat of the pounding bass, and I'm squeezed between Ale and Alessia in a twin sandwich.

"Happy birthday to the twins!" Isabella raises her glass, and we all clink our cocktails against it, the sharp clank echoing over the booming music.

The hours fly by, the enveloping beats captivating me in their hypnotic rhythm. A few guys have attempted to approach, but most are chased away by Raf and Alessandro's intimidating glares. I sure as hell wouldn't come near with those two surrounding us.

Matteo, on the other hand, has already danced with multiple females, and if I'm not mistaken fucked one behind the encircling trees. I have a nose for sex, and that man looks like someone who's just been screwed. In the good way.

If I have any hopes of getting laid tonight, I need to lose these scary ass males surrounding me. Dancing over to Alessia, I whisper, "Let's go to the bar."

She eyes my nearly full glass, her dark brows furrowing.

"We're surrounded by cock blockers, Alessia," I hiss, eyeing her brother and Raffaele. "Don't you want to have some fun tonight? It's your twenty-fourth birthday, damn it."

Her dark eyes light up, and she tosses her drink back, her bleached blonde hair cascading down her bare shoulders. "We'll be right back." She wiggles her fingers at her twin before weaving her arm through mine.

Alessia and I have never been super close. Somehow, we never clicked like Bella and me, but now that my baby cousin has a man, I'll need a new partner in crime when—if—I return to Manhattan. I haven't told anyone yet, but my boss Bianca told me I have a real shot at getting a full-time job. I'll know for sure in the next few weeks. I'm excited and nervous as all hell about it.

Alessia pushes her way through the mass of bodies and finds a spot at the bar. With her exotic Asian Italian mix, the guys are putty in her hands. Two attractive men squeeze closer together just to let her stand beside them.

"*Grazie.*" She smiles, flashing them perfect white teeth.

Both men watch her in awe as she orders our drinks in perfect Italian. The craziest part about the twins is that not only are they fluent in their father's native language, but they also understand quite a bit of Mandarin from their mom's side.

Once the bartender hands her our cocktails, one of the guys

makes a move. He's cute with wavy, dark hair and light hazel eyes. Alessia would devour him.

His friend inches closer to me, an easy smile stretched across a scruffy jaw. "*Ciao, sono Giancarlo.*"

"*Ciao*, I'm Serena." Though I can get by in Italian, I'm still more comfortable flirting in English.

"You are beautiful." His accent is thick and rich, and I can already picture him moaning my name as I ride his cock in the backseat of his car. "Would you like to dance?"

"*Certo.*" I offer a smile before he ticks his head at his friend who's already whisper-shouting to Alessia over the music.

He tries to lead me back to the crowded dancefloor, but the last thing I need is Giancarlo getting a peek at one of the overprotective men dancing just a few yards away. Ale gets crazy when any man comes near his sister, and I'm not in the mood for that drama tonight. "Let's go somewhere more private." I tick my head toward a thick copse of trees just past the bar.

Giancarlo calls out to his friend and the four of us make our way around the crowd of people huddled at the bar. We're just beyond the main dancing area, but still well within range of the DJ's intoxicating beats. I start to dance, and Giancarlo moves behind me, hands gripping my hips. He's rubbing his dick against my ass and after a few seconds, he's already hard.

As I lose myself in the music and the pleasant heat growing between my legs, the time blurs by. While I dance, I cast an occasional glance in Alessia's direction then swivel to the rest of my cousins in the middle of the jam-packed dancefloor. Thankfully, Raf is enormous and easy to pick out of the crowd.

I throw my head back, resting it on Giancarlo's shoulder and catch a glimpse of the stars peeking through the thick canopy of trees overhead. I was right, it was a perfect night. Giancarlo's hand slips from my hip and drops to the hem of my tight dress. I rock my hips, urging him on and his fingers slide beneath the clingy fabric and run across my silk panties.

A groan vibrates his throat, and he presses his cock harder

against my ass. "Can I?" he whispers against my ear, his finger sliding closer to the waistband. Alessia is only a few yards away, making out with her guy under the shade of an enormous oak.

I'm horny as fuck and fiery heat is streaking down my core.

"Yes," I murmur, spreading my legs.

His finger slides beneath my panties, and glides between my wet folds. I rock against his finger, urging him inside me. He takes the hint, filling me up with one finger while the other circles my clit.

"Mmm, yes," I moan.

"Let's go back to my place?" he pants against my ear.

I'm not going home with anyone tonight, not with my cousins in town. "Do you have a car?"

"No, I took the tram."

"Shit," I mutter, my hips still grinding against his palm. I glance at the woods to our right. It's dark and everyone is entranced by the DJ and free-flowing alcohol. No one would notice. I tick my head toward the encroaching forest. "Over there."

His light eyes blaze in excitement as he pulls his finger out, and I lead him into the murky shadows. The moment we're cloaked beneath the canopy of trees, his mouth captures mine as he backs me against an enormous trunk. One hand is on my breast which he's freed from my dress, his fingers teasing my nipple into a sharp point. "Mmm, yes, that feels good," I groan. Then, I slip my panties off and get to work on his zipper as his lips burn a scorching trail down my neck.

His fingers are working me again, pumping in and out in a steadily intoxicating rhythm. I let out another moan when he pushes a second finger inside me and my pussy stretches around his skilled digits.

"Condom?" I whisper against his lips.

He pulls one from his wallet with his unoccupied hand as I free his cock. He's hard as hell, cum already glistening on the tip as I stroke his shaft.

The sharp crackle of a twig snapping sends my eyes leaping over his shoulder.

"What was that?" He drops the condom on the ground and mutters a curse.

"I'm sure it's nothing." Still, I scan the darkness, in search of what I have no idea. "It's probably just another couple hooking up."

He glances over his shoulder, eyes wide. "Maybe we shouldn't…"

"Are you serious?" I release his cock and glare up at him.

Another crackle, closer now. A hint of unease sparks low in my spine, and I reach for my purse. Luckily, Dolce is always ready.

"I'm married," he blurts as he stuffs his dick back into his jeans.

"Oh, for fuck's sake," I hiss.

"*Mi dispiace.*" He takes off through the woods, racing toward the sound of the music.

"Yeah, I'm sorry too, *coglione.*" Tugging up my panties with one hand, I keep the other tight around my purse. Gun laws in Italy aren't as lax as they are in the U.S., and I don't want to risk just anyone seeing me swinging my Glock around.

Narrowing my eyes, I scan the darkness once more, but all I can make out is a whole bunch of nothing. Heaving out a breath, I turn toward the clearing. I just hope Alessia had better luck than I did.

CHAPTER 5
CONSUMED WITH REVENGE

A*ntonio*

"*Cazzo, merda, porca puttana!*" Every hissed curse only intensifies the burning rage as I stumble around in the darkness. The pounding bass thrumming through the woods worsens the oncoming headache, but I have no choice except to move toward the sound. I came all the way to fucking Milano, trailing after my traitorous brother and his little mafia princess in hopes of catching them off guard.

But damned Raffa, he never leaves Isabella's side.

Not to mention the army of security he's amassed around her. Attempting to infiltrate his defenses would be like trying to penetrate the damned Vatican in Rome.

Merda, I should have sent one of my men instead of coming myself. My trip to the city last week had proven fruitless, trailing Serena Valentino to gather intel. The only thing I'd determined was that Isabella and her cousins would be here this weekend. That and the blonde heiress was still as beautiful as I'd remembered. When she caught me following her at the rooftop bar by the Duomo, I'd been so tempted to snatch her on the spot. But that was not the plan...

If I had any hopes of this working, I had to play it smart, but it was nearly impossible to keep the emotions out and focus on the logical. No, not when this was so personal. I must have revenge at my own hands. It's the only way to extinguish the burning hatred devouring my soul.

My vision begins to darken, and the acrid scent of smoke fills my nostrils. Squeezing my eyes closed in a vain attempt to drive back the grisly memories, I stagger forward and stumble into a tree. Leaning against the rough bark, I'm pulled into the past despite my best efforts.

Flames roar around me, a beast uncaged, devouring everything in its path. I push through the smoke, my breath ragged, my eyes stinging. The heat sears my skin, but I can't stop; not yet. I'm looking for him — my father, the man who built this empire from the ground up. The villa, our family home, is collapsing around me, timber and memories falling to ashes.

I find him in his study, the place where he made his most ruthless decisions. The flames haven't reached him yet, but it's too late. He's slumped over his desk, laying in a pool of his own blood, a still figure in the chaos. My heart clenches — relief, pain, a twisted grief that has no name. He's gone, truly gone. I reach for him, my skin blistering as I pull him into my arms, trying to feel the pulse of a heartbeat I know I won't find.

Papà is — was not a good man. Even I am not blind enough not to see it, but he was still my father. And he did not deserve this... A dark voices leeches through my muddled thoughts. *Didn't he though? After everything he did?* I grit my teeth, ignoring the traitorous musings. *What he did to Raf was to teach him a lesson, much like he's done for me. He taught me everything, how to not only survive but also thrive in this cruel world.*

The fire licks at my back, greedy and unrelenting. I'm burned, my skin a map of pain, but I can't feel it — not really. It's the weight of

Papà's *stillness that crushes me. We need to get out, both of us, or be lost to the flames. I stagger toward the exit, his weight in my arms a heavy reminder of everything we've been through. The heat is unbearable, a hellfire that consumes all it touches.*

I carry him out of the study, the flames engulfing the hallway. Thick smoke curls in every corner, devouring our home. My lungs are so tight I can barely breath, but I continue on, my feet moving on autopilot. I cannot see an inch beyond my nose the smoke is so dense and suffocating.

Somehow, I make it out. The cool night air hits my charred skin, a harsh contrast to the inferno behind me. I collapse, the ground hard and unforgiving, my father's body beside me. I've escaped, but at what cost? The villa is nothing but a fiery skeleton, a tomb for my father's sins and sacrifices.

And I, the son of a fallen capo, am left with the ashes of an empire, burned but not yet broken.

I blink quickly, chasing away the dark memories, the pungent odor of smoke still infiltrating my senses. Pushing myself off the trunk of the old oak, I weave through the thick copse of trees with renewed purpose. "I will have my vengeance, *Papà*, I swear it."

Ahead, the strobe lights of the dance party pulse in a hypnotic rhythm. There must be hundreds of people at this damned event. I pat the gun at my hip, my finger itching to wrap around the trigger. First, I'll kill Isabella so I can enjoy watching Raffaele break as he stands by unable to save his beloved *principessa*. Then I'll put him out of his misery.

A twinge of unease streaks through my chest as vivid images of the Valentino heiresses flit through my mind. It was the first time I'd met them in person that night outside of my nightclub in Rome, when Giuseppe and I accidentally crossed paths with Raffa and his new charge. I've done many questionable things in my thirty-four years on this planet, but I've never executed an unarmed woman. Just the idea of it doesn't sit right…

Perhaps after all these years, a sliver of *Mamma*'s heart still breathes life into my dark one. *Dio*, the damned cancer took her from us when she was so young, when *we* were too young. Was it enough time to leave a lasting impression on a vulnerable, hurt boy? Her pale, gaunt face surges to the surface, and I can almost see her look of disappointment. *Did I raise you like that, Tonio?* No, she didn't get to raise me at all because the brain tumor stole her from us on my tenth birthday. The pain of the past floods in, threatening to swallow me whole.

She never would have wanted me to turn out like this. After she died, everything changed. *Papà's* restaurant couldn't cut it anymore, and he dove deeper into debt until he borrowed from the wrong man. From there, it was a downward spiral for all of us. He never set out to create a criminal empire, and I never intended on fulfilling my role as heir but once you start down that dark path, it sucks you into oblivion. One that's impossible to escape.

I must have my revenge. It's the only way to survive for now, then maybe I can finally do the impossible and leave this life behind for good.

Then I hear it, the unmistakable sound of a woman moaning in pleasure.

All the dark thoughts fade back into my subconscious, to the far corners where I keep them locked up tight. My feet propel me toward the hypnotic sound. That voice… sexy and sensual, and *cazzo*, it has my cock leaping up in attention for the first time in months.

"Mmm, yes."

I follow the siren's call, my feet moving of their own accord. All thoughts of Raffaele, of his girl, of revenge fly right out of my mind. My heart slams against my chest, my cock hardening with every step closer. The moans grow louder, and I move faster. Now, only a few yards away, I see them through the encroaching darkness. A man backs a blonde against a tree. I dart behind an ancient oak, the trunk big enough to conceal my entire body. I peer around the corner, my pulse skyrocketing.

"Mmm, yes, that feels good," she groans, head tipped back as he fondles her breast. Her hand is curled around the back of his neck, long, delicate fingers tangling in his hair. The guy's head is in my way, obscuring her features. I only get an occasional glance of the top of her head, her mouth, her bare breast. It's a milky white, the peaked bud a perfect rosy pink. I imagine licking it, drawing my teeth across the sensitive tip until she cries out my name.

The woman's bottom lip is trapped between her teeth, keeping the moans at bay as the guy fingers her, or at least I assume that's what he's doing. I can't quite see where his other hand is from this distance, but judging by her moans, it's a fair assumption. I wonder what her pussy feels like. Is she wet? Tight?

Her panties fall to the ground, and I hear the unmistakable sound of a zipper being dragged down.

"Condom?" she whispers.

Fiery heat races to my dick at the sound of that voice. There's something oddly familiar about it, but I can't quite place it with the haze of lust blanketing all logical thought. My breaths are coming hard and fast as I imagine my own cock freed from its tight constraints.

Dio, when was the last time I had sex?

I've been so consumed with rage and thoughts of revenge, I ended things with my girlfriend, Stefania, right after *Papà* was killed. And even before that, we weren't having sex often. My head simply wasn't in it. I can't even remember the last time I jacked off or even wanted to. Now I'm so fucking hard I'm certain I'll explode if I don't come.

Papà. My thoughts refocus for an instant. *Merda*, what the hell am I doing? I'm supposed to be trailing Raf, finding his girlfriend and putting an end to this. But all I can think about is that voice, the curtain of wavy blonde hair, and that pouty lip trapped between perfect white teeth.

Dio, I've never felt such an intense, instinctual pull toward a woman, especially one I've yet to meet up close.

A groan builds in my throat, the need for release overpowering all common sense. *Fuck it.* My hand dives beneath the waistband of my slacks, my fingers wrapping around my cock. I close my eyes and imagine those pouty pink lips on it as I start to stroke myself.

The woman's moans are a symphony in the background, the perfect backdrop to my fantasy. I get so worked up, my shaft slick with precum, I stagger an inch, and my shoe crushes a twig beside a delicate sprig of violets. My eyes snap open, the sound reverberating across the sudden stillness. Through the inky darkness, I meet a pair of familiar blue eyes. The blonde is glancing over the guy's shoulder, scanning the woods, and for the first time, I catch a good glimpse of her entire face.

Wavy blonde hair, the perfect bow of pink lips, lively, darting eyes...

No...

My stomach drops, and I yank my hand out of my pants.

Cazzo, Serena Valentino.

CHAPTER 6
CUORE MIO

S*erena*

I glance up at the clock from my desk and mutter a curse when I notice it's just past seven. I'm supposed to meet *Papà* at my apartment in less than an hour. Like always, I got sucked into the work and lost all track of time. There isn't one thing about this internship I don't love. From assisting in the design process, from concept to development, including sketching, sourcing fabrics, and helping with fittings, every second has been amazing.

"I'm out, girl." Santi's head of dark hair pops up over the cubicle, and he releases a dramatic yawn. "I've been working like a dog all day. It's *aperitivo* time for me."

"Lucky you." I watch only slightly jealously as he throws his satchel across his shoulder. "Have an Aperol Spritz for me."

"No need to twist my arm." He gives me a smile, and I'm relieved things are back to normal again.

Once my cousins left, I took my fashion bestie out for a drink to make up for my less than stellar behavior. I don't know what comes over me when I'm around my family. I'm like a different person. I miss them already, but I bury the twinge of sadness and remind myself I'll see them in a few weeks back in Manhattan.

"*A domani.*" Santi drops a kiss on my forehead and sashays out.

"See you tomorrow."

Once he's gone, I run my fingers across the delicate petals of the violet bloom that sits on the corner of my desk before I refocus on my latest sketch, a bright floral pattern with smatterings of zebra and leopard print. I'm a total whore for animal motifs mixed with brilliant, obnoxious pops of color.

Which is why I'm a great fit for D&G. I'm lost for a few more minutes, my brain completely immersed in the drawing and my pencil moving on autopilot. If I could do this for the rest of my life, I'd be happy. Who needs a man when you love your career, right? I may have still been a little salty about that encounter the other night. No man ever says no to me... especially not seconds from sex. Even if it was for a good reason.

A married man? That would have been a new low for me.

"You're still here?" Bianca's voice sends my head spinning over my shoulder.

"Yes, I was just finishing up on this design." I hold up the colorful sketch, and my boss rewards me with a smile.

She walks closer, bringing the glasses perched on her head down to her nose. Squinting, she scans the design, and I find myself holding my breath. There's not much in this world that flusters me, but this woman's word means everything. She's the difference between a permanent position at Dolce & Gabbana and a one-way ticket back to Manhattan. Not that my life in the city wasn't great, but these past few months in Milano, the fashion capital of the world, have been a dream.

"It's excellent, Serena." She pushes the chic glasses up to sit atop her neatly gelled chignon. "Your work in the last month has been exceptional honestly. I've never seen someone advance so quickly. It seems Milano is good for your soul."

"I couldn't have said it better myself."

Her dark eyes sparkle with excitement, and her red-stained lips curve into a smile. "In fact, I'm supposed to wait until the end of the month to tell you, but if you promise to keep it between us..."

My pulse accelerates, the enthusiasm in her gaze leeching into my skin. "Yes, of course, anything."

"The partners and I have spoken, and we'd like to offer you a permanent position as a design assistant. It's an entry-level job, but you'll be assisting the more senior designers with their tasks, conducting research, creating sketches, and learning about garment construction. It's a great opportunity to gain valuable industry experience, develop skills, and begin building your career in fashion design."

"Damn, that sounds amazing!" I press my lips into a tight line before I start cursing like a sailor.

"I am pleased that you are interested."

"I'm more than interested, I'm ecstatic." I can't believe this is finally happening.

"Very well, now you must keep the news to yourself. We have decided only to keep one intern, and we wouldn't want the others to hear before the end of the program."

My happy heart sinks when Santi's face materializes in my mind. He's going to be so disappointed he didn't get it.

My Apple watch vibrates, the reminder popping up on the screen. *Merda*, dinner with Dad. I shove all the papers scattered across my desk into the drawer and jump up. "Thank you so much, Bianca. This is going to be amazing, and I promise to keep the news to myself until it's time."

"Yes, I believe it will, Serena. I'm looking forward to watching you grow within the Dolce & Gabbana family."

"I'm sorry, but I have to run. I'm meeting my father in ten minutes across town."

"Of course, please give Dante my regards."

My eyes widen, and I'm certain they look cartoon-character ridiculous. "Oh, you know *Papà*?"

It was my Aunt Jia's connections who'd gotten me into this internship, but I had no idea Bianca knew my father too.

"Yes, we met a few times prior to your arrival." The light in her eyes darken, and a pit of dread sinks to the bottom of my gut. Did *Papà* threaten her? Am I only getting this job because of my scary-ass father?

Throwing my bag over my shoulder, I offer her an uneasy smile. "*Grazie* again. I'll see you tomorrow, then?"

"*Si*, enjoy your night out."

I've never raced out of the office so quickly as a swirl of anger brewed in my gut. Nothing should surprise me about Dante Valentino, but if he went behind my back and bought my way into this job, he was going to be in so much trouble.

I glare at my father from across the table at the quaint restaurant along the canal. The picturesque district of the Navigli is another one of my favorites, but unlike the trendy areas I'd brought my cousins, this one has a bohemian flair with a charming array of boutiques and art galleries offering local crafts and artworks. It's nothing like the grand canals of Venezia, but it's cute and the polar opposite of the hectic nightlife of downtown.

Papà stares at me like I've grown a second head. Like it's perfectly natural to offer bribes to advance my career.

"You can't just butt into my life like that, Pa."

"What? I was only trying to help. Bribery is the local language in Italy."

"*Merda*," I mumble. The man has spent his entire life surviving in the shadows and has no concept of what it's like to live a normal existence.

"Serena Valentino," he growls.

"Oh, fuck off, Dad. I know you've heard much worse."

He slams his hand on the table and the old wood creaks in protest. "It doesn't mean I have to like that foul language coming from my only daughter's lips."

"Then you shouldn't have interfered in my life!"

"Excuse me for caring." He pouts, crossing his arms over his chest like an overgrown baby. I honestly don't know how my mother puts up with him.

"First thing tomorrow morning, you call Bianca and take back whatever you offered her. I want to earn this job on my own merits. *Capisci?*" I shoot him a narrowed glare.

"*Si*, of course, whatever you want, *cuore mio*."

My heart. The childhood nickname hits, and the scowl entrenched across my jaw falters. Now, he's really laying it on thick.

"So you're actually flying back to Manhattan tonight?" I push the remains of the risotto Milanese across my plate, the vibrant golden color of the typical dish from Milano has become one of my staples. For a second, I'd lost my appetite, but now, it's starting to return. I may just have to spring for my favorite post-dinner *gelato* after all.

He nods. "I only came for a quick meeting this afternoon in Rome. Now I must return before Luca misses me."

I laugh. "Yeah, right. I bet he's thrilled you're out of his hair."

"Don't be too upset, Sere, I'll see you back in Manhattan in just a few weeks, no?"

I nod quickly, remembering I promised to return at the end of the summer. Now it'll only be to pack up my things for the permanent move, assuming I still get the job. At least I'll get a chance to see Bella and the cousin crew before I leave for good.

"Does Uncle Luca even know you're here?"

He ignores my question and takes a long sip of his wine, delaying his answer.

My dad and uncle haven't exactly had the best relationship,

especially not when they were young. Now they seem to have come to an understanding. Luca is the ruthless businessman, smart and level-headed while *Papà* is the enforcer with zero impulse control, but he'll do anything to get the job done.

Together, they make a formidable pair.

Papà's phone vibrates on the table as I pick at the final bites of risotto. "*Cazzo*," he mutters before continuing on a tirade in Italian.

Once I've finished off the risotto, I wash it down with a healthy sip of *Barolo*. After he's done yelling at Aldo across the phone, he shoves his cell in his pocket and reaches for his own glass of red wine. Gulping down the rest in a big swallow, he hisses another curse.

"What's wrong?"

"*Mi dispiace*, but I'm going to have to go. Something has come up that I should handle while I'm in town."

An odd flicker of loneliness settles low in my chest. Now that the anger has past maybe I just need to fill the void with something. Or maybe it was seeing Bella and the rest of the crew and then their quick departure. "You're sorry? But I barely saw you and we didn't even get the *gelato*." *Nocciola* is my dad's favorite, the unique hazelnut flavor not one that's easily found back home. I'd chosen this restaurant because there's an artisanal *gelato* shop just around the corner along the canal.

"What can I say, Serena? I must speak to this associate, and it's essential I do so in person."

"Then, I'll go with you."

"Serena..." While Uncle Luca has always encouraged Bella and her younger brother Vinny to be involved in the family business—the legitimate parts anyway—*Papà* has taken the opposite approach. Maybe it's because while Luca deals with the lawful real estate development and construction side of the corporation, my father has always preferred the dark, underground dealings.

"No arguing, *Papà*. I'll go with you to this meeting and wait in the car. I owe you a gelato."

He smirks, the playful smile lighting up his dark irises. "I can never say no to you, *cuore mio*."

CHAPTER 7
A PUTTANA

S*erena*

"I thought you said you would wait in the car," *Papà* growls as I hop out of the Alfa Romeo.

"I lied." I throw him a smirk and curl my arm around his before tipping my head back to admire the enormous villa. The gleaming white façade is practically glowing beneath the pale streetlights of the luxurious *Brera* district. "Besides, there's no way I'm missing out on seeing this gorgeous home up close and personal."

"Serena…"

"I promise I'll keep my mouth shut. I won't say a word."

"But—"

"But what? You said this was an associate of yours, right? So it's not like I'm going to be in danger." More than the normal amount that comes along with my last name. Here in Milano, I've enjoyed the anonymity of it all, but I have to admit, it's also gotten kind of boring. The Valentino name may come with some risks, but there are also countless perks. I've missed out on enjoying the luxurious aspects of the life.

"He's a new associate," *Papà* grits out, returning my wandering thoughts to the conversation. "And you know I don't trust anyone."

"So don't tell him I'm your daughter. Just say I'm a *puttana* you picked up off the streets."

"Serena!" His eyes grow impossibly wide. "I would never do such a thing to your mother. I could never even pretend. And *cazzo*, you're my daughter... Just the idea of it—" His lips screw in disgust, and a tremor races across his broad shoulders.

Okay, maybe I'd gone too far with that idea, but anything is better than being babysat in the car by Aldo for the next hour. "I'll say whatever you want, okay?"

"Say nothing."

I slam my jaw closed, the crack of my teeth vibrating across the still air. As he leads me up the stone walkway, through the perfectly manicured gardens complete with intricate topiaries and marble fountains with chubby cherubs, I can't help a smile from curling my lips. Everyone always said my mom was the only person who could wrap *Papà* around her finger. She was. Until I came along.

"So who is this guy anyway?" I whisper before we reach the guards stationed at the front steps of the sprawling villa. Four beefy men in all black remind me of smaller, less intense versions of Bella's bodyguard.

"His name is Enrico Sartori. He's a big player in Rome and a key partner for the Kings in our growing Italian ventures. His son, Federico, is being primed to take over the Sartori syndicate, and he felt it was imperative I meet him in person since I'm in town."

"Interesting... I wonder if he's good looking."

"Serena..." he snarls my name like a curse.

"I'm kidding, relax, Pa." Only partially. I've never gone for the good boys—dark, broody, fucked up, now that's my type.

"I'm not here to arrange your damned wedding."

Now I'm the one cringing. "Hell, no. I would kill you if you ever tried such a thing."

A dark chuckle bursts from my father's lips. "Oh, I know."

We reach the front door, and one of the guards dips his head and motions us through the grand foyer. "Welcome, *Signor* Valentino and *signorina*." An icy chill races up my spine as we cross the threshold. My heels click on the silver-veined marble, my head tilted back to take in the vibrant frescoes painted across the ceiling. It's like walking through the Sistine Chapel at St. Peter's Basilica.

The hulking guard leads us into a large study with dark mahogany paneling. A thick silence descends over the room as we walk in. A massive desk sits in the center with an imposing male perched in a high-backed leather chair, the smooth caramel coloring reminding me of a well-aged scotch.

"*Signor Valentino…*" The man's dark eyes chase to mine. With wavy, salt and pepper hair and a strong Roman nose, he must have been attractive when he was young. I stiffen my spine and offer a tight smile. I've grown up surrounded by powerful men my entire life, and very few have ever made me tremble in fear. Sartori is no exception. "I expected you to come alone."

"Yes, well, you caught me a bit off guard, and I was at dinner." *Papà* shifts his gaze in my direction but never introduces me, neither as his daughter nor his whore as I'd suggested.

Another man walks in a moment later with a guard at his side. *Papà* visibly stiffens and I instinctively clutch my purse tighter at my side. If I need to pull Dolce out, I'm ready.

"I thought this meeting was to meet your son, Enrico… who the fuck is that?" Dante growls. "He looks like he could be your father."

The male who just entered offers a smile, wisps of silver hair barely covering his scalp. "Excuse me for the intrusion." He extends his hand, but *Papà* eyes it warily, glare unflinching. "Michele Salerno, a fellow businessman."

"I hope you don't mind," Enrico interjects. For a second, the air thickens, the tension in the room palpable.

"And if I said I do?" My father's eyes narrow at the two men before a smile slides in. "Fuck it, I don't have time for this. Let's get on with it already."

When the men move past the preliminary introductions, I'm relieved to just stand there in anonymity as they begin to discuss the tedious details of their new agreement. At some point in the conversation, the guard who escorted us in, reappears with another man. This one I'm more interested in.

With bright green eyes that sparkle like the finest emeralds and a strong, square jaw, he flashes me a smile. "Excuse the delay." With his gaze still pinned in my direction, he offers *Papà* a hand. "Federico Sartori."

Pa is not as interested in the newcomer as I am. "Let's move this along. I have a jet home to catch."

"Of course." Federico finally peels his gaze from mine and the four men gather around the enormous desk, while I'm left to wander the study. Rows of bookshelves line the back wall, so I entertain myself by reading the spines. I've never been a big reader, not like Bella who spends hours with her nose buried in the pages of a good romance novel. I'd rather be living my own smutty fantasies in real life.

"…Antonio Ferrara…"

My head spins at the familiar name on the lips of a male voice. Antonio Ferrara is Raf's brother, the new head of the Ferrara crime organization. Bella's bodyguard never wanted anything to do with the family business and after everything went to hell last month during her internship in Rome, his eldest brother, Antonio, assumed the role of *capo*.

I turn toward the four men and find Enrico speaking. Inching closer, I strain to make out bits of the conversation without being overly obvious. *Papà* did say he'd been in Rome. He isn't working with Antonio, is he? It's not possible after everything Bella went through...

Unless Uncle Luca doesn't know, and my crazy-ass father is working on something on the side. I vow to get the truth out of him before he steps foot on that jet back to New York. With Bella still living in Rome, I have to make sure she's safe. She's my baby cousin, and I don't care that her boyfriend thinks he's the most lethal bodyguard that ever lived.

"The Ferrara empire will be no more within months. The pieces have already begun to crumble." Federico smiles, not the kind that has heat unfurling between my legs, but rather a calculating, cold-blooded one. "With the Kings, Sartoris and Salernos working together, they will be forced out."

"And you're certain Antonio Ferrara won't be a problem?" *Papà*. His back is to me, so I can't see much from the corner of my eye as I continue to pretend to peruse the bookshelves.

"I will make sure of it," Federico whispers. "Though my father has moved his permanent residence here to Milano, I will remain in Roma and see to it that the Ferraras are destroyed."

"And if they attempt to retaliate?"

"Antonio is weak; he's not cut out for the cutthroat role. He's new to leadership, and his men cannot possibly be that loyal yet. It takes time to rebuild an organization like theirs. He's on the brink of destruction as it is, and we will be sure to push him over the edge."

"I'm counting on you, Sartori," says *Papà*. "If my niece gets caught in the crossfire, I will hold your son personally responsible."

My breath hitches, and I barely restrain the gasp from seeping out.

"Federico insists he has everything in control, and I trust him."

"*Bene.*"

The conversation takes a turn to logistics, and I lose interest once there's no further mention of Antonio. As soon as I talk to

Pa, I have to warn Bella. Raf needs to know what's happening so he can take the necessary precautions.

An hour later and *Papà* and I are back on the *Navigli* enjoying our *gelato* and the warm night air. He's tense despite the heaping spoonful's of *nocciola* ice cream he shovels into his mouth.

"Does Luca know what you're doing?" I finally ask. I hoped he would offer the information, but it's late and he hasn't said a word. In less than an hour, he'll be on his way back to Manhattan.

"What are you talking about?" He dips the spoon into the *gelato* once more, staring at the creamy treat.

"With the Ferraras... You know very well that's Raf's family."

He rolls his eyes, a rueful grin tugging at his gelato-smeared lips. "His ex-family from what I understand."

"It doesn't matter. Bella is still in Rome and if Luca knew what you were up to, he'd rip you a new one."

"Both the Sartori's and Salernos assured me they could handle Antonio without any collateral damage."

"And if they can't?"

"Nothing will happen to Isabella, trust me. Antonio Ferrara will have enough to worry about without going after his brother's girl."

"I hope you're right, *Papà*, or I'll be the one ripping you a new one." I give him a sweet smile before finishing off my gelato and licking the last remnants of *fragola* from the spoon. Bella's always been a chocolate girl, but for me, there's nothing like strawberry ice cream. In fact, I'm kind of addicted to the scent and practically bathe in it between my hair products, bath gels and body moisturizers.

Besides, it's better if people think I'm sweet when they first meet me. The scent is innocent yet alluring, and it hides the tougher side of me just long enough to get the upper hand. In the world I grew up in, you must have an edge if you want to survive, and if mine comes wrapped in a strawberry scent, so be it.

CHAPTER 8
HOW TO CATCH A MAFIA PRINCESS

A*ntonio*

"It's impossible, *capo*." My righthand man and quite possibly my closest friend, Pietro, cowers behind the chair across my—no, *Papà*'s desk as he breaks the news. I still don't feel quite comfortable in this seat, as if I haven't earned my place here. I stiffen, playing the part of *capo* as I have been for the past month.

"Raffaele's security team is impenetrable," he continues. "There are zero chances we'll be able to get to Isabella Valentino before her return to Manhattan tomorrow."

A flood of anger surges across my insides as I glare across the mahogany desk at my enforcer. After my own failed attempt in Milano, I passed the mission onto Pietro. Perhaps it was cowardice, or something else entirely, but I wanted to wash my hands of the whole situation.

I wanted my brother to pay for what he did to our father, to our family. But every single attempt at retribution was thwarted.

Dio is punishing you for your cowardice. Shame on you, Antonio

Ferrara, for targeting a woman. Mamma's voice sails through my thoughts, her disappointment like a shot to the heart.

"I'm doing this for our family," I shout out loud, my voice echoing across sophisticated space my father created. Everything about his office was designed to impress and intimidate in equal measure.

Pietro's eyes narrow as he regards me. "I know that, *capo.*"

Perfetto, now he's going to think I've lost my goddamned mind.

"I'm sorry, we tried everything. There is simply no way around Raffaele and his team. Maybe in Manhattan—"

"No," I hiss. "If you think getting to Isabella Valentino was difficult in Rome, you'll have zero chance once she's home. Not only will she have my brother and his team, but the entire force of the Kings."

I drag my hand through my hair, pulling at the dark strands. I'm on the brink of losing everything my father built. Fucking Dante Valentino brokered a deal with our long-time enemy, Enrico Sartori and now, half of the Ferrara territory has been taken over by the Kings. As if it wasn't bad enough before… The other half is about to fall at the hands of the Sartoris and whatever they don't take, the Salernos are more than happy to pick off. It wasn't enough to kill my father, his enemies want to see his entire empire crumble. My gaze flickers over my shoulder to the backdrop of floor-to-ceiling windows that frame a panoramic view of the bustling city below. My city. Or at least it should have been until *Papà* was killed and his dreams of grandeur destroyed.

And now, I'll go with it.

Swinging around to face Pietro once again, I bark, "What's the status with the new restaurant deal?"

"The owner is refusing to sell to us. No doubt the Salernos got to him first. The capo has been requesting a meeting with you for weeks. Why do you keep blowing him off?"

"Because I can't deal with another fucking rival family, Pietro!"

"You know how this works, *capo*. When the others scent blood, they'll be circling like sharks."

I heave out a frustrated breath, cursing *Papà* for leaving me with this disaster. "How the fuck am I supposed to launder our money without legitimate businesses to run it through?" I growl.

"I—I don't know."

"Well, you better fucking figure it out. You're all *deficienti*, one more worthless than the other." *Cazzo*, I can't believe this is happening. In a matter of a few months, everything my father built over the past two decades is teetering on a knife's edge.

First, it was the Salernos, then Enrico and now Dante. They're like bloodthirsty vultures, scavenging for the Ferrara's carcasses. *Your father never should have gone after Enrico's daughter... Mamma's* voice echoes through my mind.

She's not wrong, but there is nothing I can do about the past. Now, I'm forced to pay for my father's sins.

"What about Enrico's son, Federico? Isn't he poised to take over?"

Pietro nods. "That's the rumor."

"Maybe he'll be more reasonable than his old man. See if you can arrange a meeting."

"I can try, *capo*, but Laura was his sister…"

Cazzo. Why did my father have to kill that poor woman? "I know very well who she was to him. I didn't ask for your opinion." I slam my fist on the desk, the polished mahogany trembling beneath my fury. "Go, now!"

"Yes, *capo*. I'll see what I can do." He spins on his heel and races out of my office, his damned tail between his legs. *Dio*, I miss Giuseppe. "Thanks for leaving me to handle all this *merda*, brother." I glance skyward and my fingers instinctively move to the gold cross at my chest. I stopped believing in God a long time ago, but still I wear the chain my mother gave me for my first communion. It was the last gift before—

Squeezing my eyes closed, I chase away the dark memories. God, heaven, hell, none of it exists. If it did, *Dio* would've never taken away my precious mother, leaving three young boys in the inept hands of our father.

And if hell does exist, I suppose I'll find myself there soon enough. Because this is not how my story ends. If I can't get to Isabella, there must be another way to bring the Kings to their knees.

My thoughts flicker back in time to the night in the woods in Milano, to a pair of lively blue eyes and wild, blonde hair. To the feel of Serena Valentino when she ran into me in the hallway of that rooftop bar in Milano. To the sound of her sultry voice, echoing through the park that night. There are two Valentino mafia princesses, and if I can't have one, then I'll simply have to steal the other.

Present Time

Hidden behind the airplane hangar, I watch intently as the Kings' private jet roars across the runway. I'd been forced to hire my own jet to secure access to the area. Luckily, I'd timed our arrival almost perfectly, and within seconds, Raffaele and his *principessa* should be deplaning.

The past few days before my arrival to Manhattan had been disastrous. I finally met with Michele Salerno who refused my new restaurant deal. Without it, I'm fucked. Then Federico Sartori denied me the chance to even meet to discuss an equitable way to carve out our territories.

Now I'm left with no other options.

I keep my eyes trained on the airplane now lumbering closer, then my gaze lifts upward to the sky. Pressing my finger to the com in my ear, a sharp hiss explodes across my eardrum, and I mutter a curse. "Pietro, can you hear me?"

"Yes, *capo*, loud and clear."

"Is the bird in the air?"

"Ready and waiting."

Reaching for the binoculars, I search the clear sky for the new drone I purchased from an old friend of mine. Its top-of-the-line technology boasts complete radar invisibility, even against top security measures. I suppose we're about to find out how good it really is.

A roar of applause and whoops and shouts draws my gaze from the sky to the jet door. It finally opens and the happy couple descends the steps to another chorus of cheers. Raffaele walks beside Isabella, or rather drapes his enormous form over her body, while a second bodyguard flanks her exposed side.

My fingers itch for my gun, but it's not strapped to my hip like always. Instead, I was forced to keep it hidden in my carry-on. Even if I did have it, the likelihood of a clear shot would've been infinitesimal. As much shit as I liked to give Pietro for his incompetency, I've seen my brother at work firsthand, and as a bodyguard, he's second to none.

A head of blonde hair zips through the crowd, pushing her way to greet Isabella. Serena practically throws herself at her cousin, wrapping her arms around the girl's petite form. Even from this distance, I can feel my brother bristling.

The man is a Pitbull when it comes to his clients and now that Isabella has become more, I can only imagine his level of obsession. My gaze pivots from my brother to Serena and a lick of heat surges all the way down to my dick as memories of the last time I saw her rush to the surface.

Her sexy moans have been a constant companion the last few lonely nights. I'd never admit it to anyone, but I finally found the release I so desperately needed stroking my cock to memories of the other Valentino princess in the woods. Those sounds... *Dio*, I could come from them alone.

Blinking quickly, I force the completely inappropriate thoughts to the far corners of my mind. You're here for revenge, *coglione*. You're supposed to be planning how to kidnap Serena Valentino, not fuck her.

Yes, Mamma would be proud. I've altered my plan from straight up murder to kidnapping for ransom, perhaps some torture to satisfy the bloodthirsty monster within. Unlike Isabella, Dante's daughter travels with minimum security, if any at all. If I get my hands on Serena Valentino, I can force her father and the Kings out of my territory. Better still, I can compel the Kings to take my side and coerce the Sartoris out of my lands for good.

A crackle across the com focuses my attention. "The drone audio is coming through now," Pietro confirms.

Another hiss and the voice on the other line switches to a decidedly more pleasant one.

"Finally, you made it back." Serena's sensual timbre invades my eardrums, and a shudder races up my spine.

I peer around the corner so I can steal a glance at the face that goes with that unforgettable voice. Serena still hugs her cousin, but now Raffaele has moved from her side. Only her second bodyguard remains. I scan the other hangar and catch a glimpse of my brother inside with the one and only Luca Valentino.

Serena, on the other hand, has no guardian pressed to her side. None even within striking distance. According to Pietro, she arrived at the airport with a driver and that was it.

"Of course I'll be at the party at your parents' tonight." Serena's voice snaps my attention back to the two females. "I came all this way just to see you."

"I thought your internship was over." Isabella's dark brows pucker as she eyes her cousin.

"Not quite. There are a few more things I need to do before I return."

Return? According to my intel, Serena had been offered a permanent position at Dolce & Gabbana where she interned for the summer. It perfectly played into my new plan.

"Okay, you'll have to tell me all about it tonight."

"Absolutely." She smiles, but it seems forced. "There's not

much to tell anyway. I want to hear about you and Raf and all the amazing sex you've been having."

My stomach churns at the comment. I may hate the *bastardo*, but he's still my younger brother and I do not need to hear about his sex life.

"Please, I know you, Sere, I'm sure you're having just as much sex if not more than us. Just with more of a variety of guys. You're still on Tinder, aren't you?"

A wicked grin curls her lips. "I just can't stay away."

And just like that, I know exactly how to catch this mafia princess.

CHAPTER 9
MINE NOW

Serena – Present Time

The limo speeds down Fifth Avenue and for once in my life, I wish we were stuck in the typical traffic of Manhattan. Instead, we zip eastward, the quiet streets blurring by through the tinted windows. My heart is a mad drumbeat in my chest, but I ignore it, breathing slowly to force the calm.

"Get your fucking goon off me!" The guy who just shoved me into the car yanks my arms behind my back, and I grind my molars to keep from crying out. That motherfucker is trying to break my damned arm.

"Say please, *tesoro*, and I'll think about it."

Tesoro? Treasure, really?

"Fuck you, Antonio."

He slides to the end of the seat, nods at the guy holding me down and the asshole releases me. A feral smile kicks up the corners of his lips. "Oh, good, you remember me, then?"

I snap my jaw shut, pressing my lips into a hard line. Like I'd ever admit that dark gaze has starred in more than a few naughty dreams. Well, that's the end of that. "Sure, you're the less attractive Ferrara brother."

That smirk flips upside down, and the groove between his dark brows deepens. "Ah, so of the Kings' heiresses, you're the funny one?"

"Among other things." I'm also lethal as fuck.

"Put on your seatbelt," he hisses.

"So kind of you to care." I pull the strap across my shoulder as I search the floor, praying for some miracle that the guy who snagged me grabbed my purse before jumping into the car behind me. No such luck. I almost cry at the thought of losing Dolce. I hazard another quick peek out the window. We're on the FDR now, heading out of the city. That's not good. "So what the hell do you want from me? Or are you really just looking for a quick fuck?" I suck my bottom lip between my teeth and bat my lashes, offering a sexy smile. My gun isn't my only weapon, and I'm more than willing to use whatever it takes to get out of this situation. "If you promise to bring me home, I might be willing to overlook the kidnapping and give you a night you'll never forget."

A dark chuckle parts his lips, and he seems as surprised by the warm sound as I am. "I wish it were that easy."

"It can be. I've been told I'm a sure thing." I slide to the end of the supple leather seat and cross my legs. My sexy romper hikes up my thigh. *Thanks, Mom and the endless hours of yoga, for the killer legs.*

His piercing gaze traces down my body, over the plunging neckline revealing my cleavage and scorching a fiery trail until it reaches the scandalous hem of the shorts. "If only we'd met under different circumstances, I would have been more than happy to take you up on the offer. You shouldn't have run off so quickly the first time we met. Perhaps things would have turned out differently between us."

The man beside me shifts, and I catch his hungry gaze on my upper thigh.

A beastly growl vibrates Antonio's throat as his eyes follow the man's gaze. "*Smettila di guardarla così o ti cavero gli occhi.*"

Wow. Possessive much? *Stop looking at her like that or I'll gouge your eyes out...* Damn, someone doesn't like anyone else playing with his toys. I play dumb, pretending I don't understand a word. Taking on the role of ditzy blonde has proven invaluable more times than I can count.

"Anyway, who says we can't make up our own rules?" I offer.

"I'll be the only one making the rules, *tesoro.*"

That's what you think. "So what's the play here?" I glance out the tinted windows as the city grows farther away. A hint of nerves scrapes at my insides, but I ignore the sensation. Freaking out won't help anything. I have to stay calm and come up with a plan. Clearly, he doesn't want me dead, or I'd already be nothing more than a blood splatter on Fifth Avenue.

This is a hostage situation.

The question is: what does Antonio Ferrara want?

As if he's read my mind, he finally responds, "You'll find out soon enough. For now, just sit back and enjoy the ride."

I pretend to follow his commands and slide as far away from the guard sitting beside me as possible until I'm pressed up against the door. He has a gun at his hip, and I fully intend to snatch it from him as soon as I figure out a plan. A complete bar is stretched out in front of me, crystal tumblers and every top shelf liquor one could ask for. Alessandro would be in heaven with all the alcohol.

I tick my head toward the bottle of Grey Goose, impressed by my coolness despite the turn we just took onto Grand Central Parkway. I took this exact drive yesterday. We're heading toward the airport and nothing good can come of that. "May I?"

"*Prego.*" He motions to the thug next to me. "Otto, make her a drink."

"I'd rather make it myself, thanks. I don't need your hired help slipping something in my beverage."

"I'm insulted you think so little of me."

"Well, you did resort to kidnapping so there's that…"

With an exaggerated eyeroll, I unbuckle my belt, lean forward and grab a tumbler, slowly filling it with ice. The tongs have pointy tips and in a second, I'm going to jab them into Otto's eyes. But before that, I need to solidify my next move. The slider between the front and back seats is closed, and in my experience, generally pretty soundproof. The limo slows, pulling toward the off ramp to LaGuardia, and I thank *Dio* for the perfect timing. *Seems like someone up there is looking out for me.*

Here goes everything. I drop the tumbler, and glass shatters across the floor. The next part happens so quickly, it's nothing but a blur. With both men distracted, I whirl around and stab Otto in the face with the tongs. He lets out a shriek when the jagged end scrapes across his eyeballs, and I lunge for his gun.

Before Antonio can release his weapon from inside his jacket, I have the muzzle pointed at his head. "Now, I'm in charge, *bastardo*. Tell your driver to unlock the door."

Otto is whimpering beside me covering his eyes and cursing up a storm. From my periphery, I can see the blood dribbling down his face.

"Do it!" I shout at Antonio, who's staring at me wide-eyed. "Or I'll shoot you in the face."

"We're on the highway, you can't just jump out of the car."

"We're not actually." I tick my head at the street ahead. Not only is there a stoplight but also a narrow sidewalk I can sprint down if I can just get the asshole to unlock the door.

He slides to the edge of the seat, and my finger tightens around the trigger. "Not an inch closer, *Signor* Ferrara. I'd hate for Raf to become an only child." I throw him a cheeky grin. "Now, tell the driver to unlock the damned door," I growl.

His eyes narrow as he regards me for a long moment before

his knuckles tap the divider. It slides open, and he hisses at the man upfront. "Unlock the back doors."

"But—"

"Just do it," he roars.

The unmistakable click ignites a flare of hope, and my smile grows wider. With my fingers closing around the door handle, I twist my head over my shoulder. Antonio's glare is murderous, and I barely restrain a giggle. "Next time my profile pops up on Tinder, do me a favor, and don't swipe right."

I jerk the door open and leap out with the limo still moving. As sure of myself as I sounded, I've never actually jumped out of a moving vehicle, and I did not account for the intense momentum from the car, even going less than thirty miles per hour.

I hit the asphalt and my right ankle twists, sending shooting pain up my leg. "Fuck!" I grit out as I attempt to run across the street to the sidewalk in my sky-high heels. Adrenaline from the blinding pain courses through my veins, compelling my legs to keep moving. The sharp blasts of horns and angry shouts provide a steady symphony, but I ignore them all and weave between the vehicles.

I pause in front of a beat-up old van and wave wildly. "Help!" The man, who looks shadier than shit, drops his gaze and presses his foot on the gas, nearly running me over as he weaves around my stumbling form. *Son of a bitch*! The light turns green, and I'm shit out of luck as not a single car stops to help me. Which isn't entirely surprising since it's almost one o'clock in the morning and definitely not the best part of town. With this outfit, these drivers probably think I'm a freaking *puttana* looking for a lift.

The slap of heavy footfalls behind me only escalates my pulse. I stagger between two more fleeing cars and finally hit the safety of the sidewalk. Hazarding a quick glance over my shoulder, I find Antonio racing after me, on two good legs. Dammit. I should have just shot him when I had the chance. I clutch the gun in my fist, but it's not like I can just turn around and shoot the guy in the middle of the streets. Or should I?

The moment of indecision costs me valuable seconds, and by the time I start running, or more like, hobbling, he's almost on me. My breath comes in ragged gasps, the balmy night air squeezing my lungs as I push myself into a sprint.

The sound of Antonio's rushed footfalls echoes behind me, a haunting rhythm to the chaotic pounding of my heart. I glance back; he's too close. Fear propels me forward, my mind racing as fast as my feet. I need to find cover, disappear into the shadows before he can reach me.

Merda! There's nowhere to go. Only trees line the streets, stretching endlessly ahead, the sidewalk dotted with closed shops and darkened windows. With every step my ankle throbs in protest, but I can't stop. Not now. Not when my freedom is just within reach.

I can feel Antonio's presence looming behind me, his ragged breaths nearly at the back of my neck.

"There's nowhere to go, *tesoro*." His shout is taunting, a hint of amusement in his tone.

I'm sure I look ridiculous, limping along the street in my stilettos. There's nowhere to go, nowhere to hide, but I have to keep moving. The pain in my ankle is becoming excruciating. I grit my teeth, biting my tongue not to scream with each step.

I'm hobbling now, nowhere near a jog even, and his footfalls slow, growing ever closer. The hair on the back of my neck rises, every sense on high alert.

"If you keep trying to run, you could break that ankle."

"What the fuck do you care?" I shout back over my shoulder.

"It would be a shame to retire those red heels. They're sexy as hell."

An odd mix between a laugh and a sob bursts through my clenched teeth. I whirl around, clutching the gun in my fist, my finger on the trigger. "Too bad you'll never get to see them again."

I level the muzzle at his head and at this distance, just over a yard, I know I won't miss. Velvety midnight orbs sear to mine, the piercing intensity just as powerful as the first night we met outside his nightclub in Rome. A tiny pang of regret squirms its way into my chest as my finger skims the trigger.

And I squeeze.

My heart stops as I wait for the earsplitting bang, for his body to crumple, for the crimson bullet wound to bloom across his forehead. Only none of that happens. Instead, he simply stares at me, a savage grin curling the corners of his lips.

It wasn't loaded...

"You were never going to get away, *tesoro*. Don't you see? You're mine now."

CHAPTER 10
A GOOD LITTLE HOSTAGE

A*ntonio*

The familiar scent of leather and polished wood greets me as I step onto the private jet I hired for this little excursion. It's likely an extravagance I shouldn't have indulged in given the precarious state of the business, but with my prized *tesoro* in tow, I didn't have any other option.

Even with a sprained or possibly broken ankle, not to mention the handcuffs I was forced to use to restrain her, Serena doesn't stop fighting. I find it oddly endearing. The woman has fire, and a mouth that would seem more appropriate on a *puttana* on the streets of Napoli. I watch my new hostage as Ottavio, whose eye is still bleeding, drags her onto the plane. She's kicking and scratching him, more feral animal than female.

And fuck, if it doesn't make my dick hard.

What is it about this woman?

I sink into the plush leather seats across from the polished mahogany tables which shine under soft ambient lighting. The hum of luxury and relaxation is shattered by the screams and curses coming from my newest guest.

I huff out a breath and drag my fingers through my hair. "There's no point in fighting him, Serena. You'll only hurt yourself."

Her eyes are wild, the brilliant sapphire ablaze with fury. "Oh, I don't know. I think I did a damned good job hurting good old Otto." She twists her head back and tosses my scowling colleague a shit-eating grin. His bloody left eye is bandaged, the right one bruised but still functioning.

She's not wrong. The man may lose his eye from those lethal tongs. At least now, I've learned never to underestimate Serena Valentino.

With a growl, Otto shoves her toward the seat beside me. She trips, her bad ankle faltering and she barely gets her hands out in time before her face slams into the back of the seat.

A jab of unexpected fury lances through my insides as I see her fall. "Enough, *bastardo*," I snarl as I leap up and curl my fingers around his throat. "That's the last time you lay a hand on her."

"But, *capo*—"

"I don't want to hear it. She is to be treated with the respect a woman deserves. From now on, no one touches her but me. *Capisci?*"

My fingers tighten until he finally nods reluctantly. I release him and stalk back to my seat. Serena is curled into the supple leather, her gaze shooting daggers as I slide past to sit beside her.

Once I'm settled in, I pivot to face my new captive. "Let me see your ankle." At least I could wrap it, like I did Otto's eye.

"*Vaffanculo*," she hisses, folding her arms around her legs and turning so that her back faces me. *Go fuck yourself.*

"I see that went well." Pietro appears from the back of the jet, and a woman scurries out behind him. His dark curly hair falls in messy tangles across his forehead, and the redheaded flight attendant has that just-been-fucked look about her. She lowers her gaze as she zips by and disappears behind the curtain to the cockpit.

My righthand man saunters down the aisle, stopping just in front of Serena, a stupid smile on his face.

"Do you really think *that*"—I tick my head toward the cockpit— "was the best use of your time and mine?"

"Sorry, *capo*. You took longer than I expected—" His words fall away as his gaze wanders toward Otto. "What the hell happened to you?"

"I happened," Serena grits out. "And you'll be next if your *capo* doesn't release me at once!"

A deep chuckle vibrates Pietro's barrel chest. "She seems feisty. Maybe we should have stuck with the original target."

Serena's head whips in my direction, her eyes smoldering with rage. "The original target?" she hisses.

"Oh, for fuck's sake, Pietro, *state zitto*! Can't you keep your mouth shut?"

"Who?" Serena glares at me, eyes narrowed, fingers clutching the armrest between us.

I see it the moment she realizes the answer. All the fight in her eyes vanishes, her entire body deflating.

"Isabella..." she whispers. "You were going to take my cousin."

"This isn't about you," I grumble, unsure why I feel the necessity to explain. "It's about my family business, my father's honor and the way my brother pissed all over it for *her*."

"Let's just go," she mutters. "I swear I'll be a good little hostage. Get the plane in the air or whatever the hell your plan is. You've got me, so now let's get the hell out of here so we can get the negotiations rolling." She reaches for the folded-up blanket on the seat and drapes it across her scandalous romper.

I gape at her for a long moment, caught completely off guard by this sudden change in demeanor. What happened to the feisty, spirited woman jabbing tongs at my men and jumping out of moving vehicles?

"You heard her," I bark at Pietro. "Tell the captain we're ready for departure."

Despite the metal cuffs and Serena's reassurances, I don't dare close my eyes the entire flight. She sleeps beside me, chair stretched out so that it lays totally flat. Her breaths come in soft, measured intervals, her chest slowly rising and falling. Apparently, someone is completely at ease in my presence. I'm not certain if I should be insulted or flattered.

I should be content. In the grand scheme of things, my mission was a success. I have Serena and, in a few hours, once we land, I'll contact Dante and if everything I've heard about the man and his love for his daughter is true, I should have the Ferrara territory whole once again within the week.

Then why the fuck does the victory feel hollow?

Serena murmurs something in her sleep, and I inch closer, that voice, even now, waking something raw and primal deep within my core. "No," she whimpers, her expression darkening. "Not Bella... anyone but her." Tears fall, stealing down her cheeks, and my insides twist. "Take me instead, just leave her alone."

She continues to whisper, to plead and with every passing moment, that guilt squeezes my gut tighter. I'd always heard the Valentinos were close, but to prefer to give up her own life for her cousin? It's completely unexpected.

They're not even sisters...

My thoughts whirl back to a time when I had two *fratelli*, two brothers that I would do anything for. When the hell had our relationship gotten so fucked up?

Papà.

The answer comes from that dark voice in the furthest recesses of my mind, the one I refuse to accept. Our father had broken our bond long ago. Even Giuseppe and I weren't close, not really, not when it counted.

Serena shifts beside me, drawing my attention away from my muddled past. Her eyes slowly open, meeting mine. The moment of shock passes quickly, the haze of sleep vanishing as she takes in her surroundings. *Papà* often pitted us against each other, dangling the business' fortune over our heads. Though I was his enforcer, his heir, he often insinuated given the right circumstances Giuseppe could steal it all from my grasp.

Now I often found myself wishing my brother was still here. I'd hand it all over to him happily.

"Dammit, I was hoping it was all a bad dream," she mutters, drawing me away from thoughts of the past.

"Hate to disappoint you, *tesoro*." My lips slide into a smile, unbidden.

Her bound hands pop up from beneath the blanket as she runs slender fingers through her disheveled hair, revealing angry red skin ringing her wrists beneath the metal. Another twinge of guilt rears up. I could uncuff her… There's nowhere to go here and given her familiarity with guns, she wouldn't be stupid enough to start a midair shootout.

"I have to pee." She presses the button on the leather seat, and it adjusts until she's sitting upright, matching my pose. "Are hostages allowed bathroom time or what?"

I nod and slowly rise, my legs stiff after six hours of little movement. "This way." I tick my head toward the door in the back which boasts a full bedroom and second bathroom. I can't explain why I don't take her to the bathroom in the front, which everyone else uses. I tell myself it's because it's too close to the cockpit, and I'm afraid she'll try something desperate.

Even though it's only now I'm beginning to truly understand her sudden compliance. She wanted me far away from her precious Isabella. What the hell is it about that girl? First my brother and now this…

She trails behind me, moving slowly even though she's shed

those sexy heels, and from the corner of my eye, I note she barely puts any weight on her right foot. *Cazzo*, I hope it's not broken. Dealing with Dante will be difficult enough, but explaining a broken ankle? I have no intention of torturing the girl, not that I haven't done it to men before, but the idea of physically hurting a woman makes me sick to my stomach.

"You don't trust me to pee by myself?" Serena's bright eyes lift to mine as I motion through the mahogany doors into the bedroom.

"I'm not going in with you, *tesoro*. I'll simply wait outside."

She eyes the bed, the lavish sheets and her eyes darken for an instant. That look alone has a direct link to my cock. Clearing my throat and my mind of the completely inappropriate thoughts, I open the bathroom door.

She hobbles inside before spinning around with a grunt and flashing me her handcuffs. "I can't exactly unzip the back of my romper with these sparkling bangles." She twirls around, and I catch a quick glimpse of the zipper. "So can you take these off if I promise to be a good girl?" She flashes me a flirty grin, and I remind myself *she's playing you, you* coglione.

"No," I grind out. "But I can help you with that zipper."

With a frustrated groan, she twirls around again and lifts her hair off her back, revealing more skin. I creep closer, my fingers closing around the tab and a spark of electricity thickens the air. I succeed in getting it down about an inch before it catches on something. I place my free hand on her shoulder, attempting to get some leverage on the damned zipper and she startles at my touch. She staggers back, her ass grinding against my already hardening cock. She must clearly feel it because a hiss of air escapes through the perfect bow of her lips.

Fuck.

She pauses for an instant, frozen against me, as if she's debating whether to take advantage of this clear moment of weakness on my end. Then she peels her body free of mine and wraps her hand around the door handle, steadying herself. "Can you hurry? I really have to go." Does her voice sound breathier than normal or have I lost my damned mind?

"I'm trying, *tesoro*," I mutter, and I'm certain my breathing has become more ragged. I finally get it past the trouble spot and the rest of it glides down easily, revealing a black lace bra and… no panties. *Cazzo*, this hostage situation will be the death of me.

My hand lingers at the perfect swell of her ass, the tab of the zipper in a death grip between my fingers. I can't help but stare at the miles of exposed, perfectly tanned flesh.

"Done?"

Clearing my throat, I inhale a deep breath, and her sweet scent of ripe strawberries and spiced vanilla invades my nostrils. "Yes," I grumble, prying my hands from her back.

She darts inside, moving surprisingly quickly considering her ankle and slams the door behind her.

The moment she's gone, I slump down on the bed and mumble a curse. This is not at all how this was supposed to go.

CHAPTER 11
SOMETHING HARD

S*erena*

I brace myself against the sink in the tiny bathroom and stare at my weary reflection in the mirror for an endless moment. I look like absolute garbage. *Get your shit together, Serena*! Who cares what you look like? According to the captain's announcement, we'll be landing in Milano soon, and I need to figure out if I should run and risk Isabella's safety or just stay put and wait this thing out.

This is all *Papà*'s fault. If he hadn't made that deal with the Sartori's it wouldn't have pushed Antonio to make such a rash decision. Kidnapping *me*, seriously? My father is going to rip the guy's spleen from his throat and dance on his eviscerated entrails. Just because I don't have a security entourage like Bella's doesn't mean I'm not valuable.

And Antonio is about to have all hell rain down on him.

A smirk spreads my lips as I consider it. The asshole deserves it.

Still, my traitorous cheeks flush at the thought of his hands on my back as he tried to unzip my dress and his stiffening cock against my ass... I slam down on the completely insane thoughts and bury them in the dark corners of my mind.

Antonio Ferrara just kidnapped you, and he's holding you hostage. How the hell are you turned on by this?

Two sharp knocks on the door jerk me from my mental monologue. "Serena, are you almost finished? The pilot has informed me that we must return to our seats."

"I'm coming in a sec," I mumble.

Heaving in a deep breath, I spin around, hand closing around the knob. I jerk the door open and find Antonio at the foot of the bed. For a bedroom on a jet, it's surprisingly large, a king maybe. I take a step forward on my good foot. The other one hurts like hell and I'm already regretting denying his request to wrap it, and the jet dips. All my weight falls on my bad ankle, and I stumble forward, right into Antonio's arms.

"Shit!" I hiss as arms and legs fly.

Antonio falls back on the sleek gray comforter, and I land on top of him in an awkward straddle. I scramble to get my cuffed hands unpinned from between us. His arms curl around my waist, firm fingers secure at my hips.

"I've got you," he whispers, and the tone is so soft I barely recognize it as the mobster who just kidnapped me.

Our eyes meet and hold for a never-ending minute. Those pits of smoldering darkness burn with some unreadable emotion as he regards me. His chest doesn't move beneath me, and I'm fairly certain he's stopped breathing. Interesting...

Before I can think on it further, the inside of my thigh grazes something hard. Not his cock which is wedged against my pussy and also thickening. No, this is another type of hardness I quickly recognize.

His gun.

And it's wedged between my leg and his pocket.

With the damned handcuffs, I can't move as fast as I'd like

and somehow, he reads my mind. I get one hand in his pocket, but he lunges for the second one, hanging from the silver chains.

"Don't you dare," he hisses. His gaze scans the oval windows on either side of the unusually bright room. "If you hit the glass, do you have any idea what would happen?"

"A violent rush of wind would engulf the cabin resulting in a sharp pressure drop and loss of oxygen. Depending on the sturdiness of your jet, it could strain the fuselage, and we could potentially plummet to our deaths."

He watches me with eyes wide as I spit out the words of the scenario my father had forced me to play out countless times as a child. I know very well the consequences of shooting a gun midair. "Very good," he murmurs. "Then I suggest you take your hand off my gun." My hold only tightens around the handle.

"And I suggest you remove these damned handcuffs." His grip around my wrist constricts until its punishing.

"That's not happening, *tesoro*."

"Why not?"

"Because even handcuffed and with a sprained ankle you cannot be trusted." His piercing gaze dips to my hand stuffed into his pocket.

"What do you expect me to do? Just sit here like an obedient little captive?"

"Yes!"

"Is that what you would do?"

He grits his teeth, jaw grinding.

"I didn't think so." I shift my weight across his hips with a sigh, and my clit accidentally rubs against the hard ridge of his cock. Even through his slacks, it sends a jolt of awareness all the way up my spine.

He must notice my reaction because a wicked grin melts across his stupidly attractive face.

"What are you smirking about? You're the one whose dick is

hard when I'm moments away from shooting that smile right off."

"I think you're smarter than that."

"Shows how little you know me." I flash him a sneer.

The jet lurches, and my stomach climbs up my throat as we begin the descent.

"You know what that means, *tesoro*. It's time to return to our seats and buckle our safety belts."

"Thank you, Captain Ferrara. If I'm a good little girl, will you give me my own pilot wings pin?"

He squirms beneath me, grimacing, rubbing his hard-ass cock against my center. "At this point, I'll give you anything you want if you just get off me."

"Handcuffs off?" I bat my lashes and shoot him my most angelic smile.

"Fine," he grits out. "But you understand that if you try to escape, I will go after your precious little cousin instead?"

"Stay the fuck away from Isabella," I snarl.

"I swear to it, as long as you keep your word."

I squeeze out a frustrated breath and release my hold on his gun, slowly withdrawing it from his pocket.

Antonio heaves out a sigh as I slide off his lap and scoot to the edge of the bed. I would stand, but my damned ankle hurts too badly.

He shoves his hand into the opposite pocket and fishes out a small set of metal keys. Damn, I was so close to finding my own freedom. "Give me your hands."

I flash them within an inch of his nose, and his head whips back.

"So that we're clear," he grumbles, "just because I'm removing these doesn't mean I trust you."

"Same here, buddy."

Antonio slides the key into the hole, and the sound of the satisfying click has a swirl of hope rising. I'll play the role of good little captive for now, but the second I have a chance to escape I will. Somehow, I'll find a way to send word to Bella, and Raf will make her disappear before this *coglione* can get anywhere near her. At least with her all the way across the Atlantic in Manhattan, some of the pressure is off. She should be moderately safe.

Or at least that's what I'm banking on.

Once the cuffs are off, I rub my sore wrists. Angry red marks crisscross my flesh, but I've endured worse.

He rises and motions toward the main cabin. "After you…"

I push myself up and immediately my ankle falters. *Shit.*

Antonio's wary gaze flicks to mine, and a flash of something that looks an awful lot like empathy crosses those stormy eyes. But I must be hallucinating because this is Antonio Ferrara, the man who stood by and allowed his father to do unforgivable things to his own brother.

"You should have let me wrap it," he mutters as I attempt to walk past him, holding onto the wood-paneled walls.

"I don't want anything from you but my freedom." Without sparing him another glance, I hobble back to our seats.

The other guy, Pietro, eyes me as I limp by and sink into the cushy chair. Then his amused gaze pivots to Antonio behind me. "I thought you two got lost back there, *capo.*"

"*Zitto,*" he hisses.

The man's smile evaporates, and he leans his head against the headrest. "By the way, I just heard from Salerno's righthand man, he said if you can keep Sartori away from his territory, he's ready to talk about an investment in the new restaurant complex."

Wonderful, at least something has gone right today. If the rumors are true and Dante and Enrico have brokered a deal, now that I have Serena, I could force him to break it, weakening the Sartoris in the process.

The flight attendant appears, flashing a smile. "We'll be landing in twenty minutes, *signori.*"

"Good." I pivot my gaze to Pietro. "Is Nero already waiting at the airport?"

His head dips.

"Send him a message to call for Elena. We'll require her services this evening upon our arrival at the estate."

"Will do."

I listen to their exchange with my eyes closed, pretending to zone out. Estate? There aren't many of those in the city center of Milano. Where the hell is Antonio taking me? An escape from a city I know well is one thing, but from some small town in the periphery… that was another story all together.

CHAPTER 12
HURLED BACK IN TIME

A ntonio

I spend the entire car ride watching Serena as she regards me with a bored expression. I underestimated her before, and it wouldn't happen again. I thought that sprained ankle would slow her down, or perhaps the blatant warning about her beloved cousin would make her more tractable but she's proven otherwise.

Now I've made the threat official, and I only hope she'll behave. Somehow, I'm certain that won't be the case.

Which is why I spend the nearly two-hour trip to our summer home in Lago di Como with one eye on her despite the ever-looming presence of my guard, Otto. Pietro rides up front with my driver Nero, and his obnoxiously loud snores infiltrate the backseat. Otto keeps his good eye on her despite the pain each blink clearly costs him.

He's a good man, and I regret that he got caught in the middle of this mess. He's been with our family for as long as I can remember and is no stranger to the risks of our world but losing an eye would require him to step down. It would be regrettable, indeed.

We turn the corner of the cobbled street lined with towering cypresses, and our family villa takes shape silhouetted by the warm glow of the setting sun. For the first time in hours, I take my eyes off Serena to take in the home I haven't visited since *Mamma's* passing. It didn't belong to the Ferraras, it was passed down from my mother's side of the family, the Domenicos. As such, few know of my tie to the property which is what makes it the perfect spot to hide the lovely Serena Valentino until my demands have been met.

Nero maneuvers the limo up the drive, delicate olive trees framing the property, and I'm instantly transported to my youth. To running with my brothers through the orchard, picking lemons and oranges from the groves behind the house.

The pastel-colored villa sits along the edge of the lake, sprawling terraces overlooking the sparkling waters and Alps in the distance. I'd forgotten how beautiful it is. My breath catches as I take it all in, at the onslaught of memories that exist only within the parameters of this property.

All the hate, the anger, the thirst for revenge begins to wane at the sight.

"Nice place." Serena presses her nose to the tinted window. "I hope I get a lake front room."

A rueful chuckle builds in the back of my throat, but I'm hesitant to release it. I should keep her in the basement. It would be the most secure location for a hostage. I tell myself it's the guilt from that twisted ankle that's making me reconsider her accommodations for the next few days.

The limo pulls to a stop in front of the marble fountain my mother chose. A trio of rotund marble cherubs spouting water from puckered lips. She said it reminded her of her three sons.

Dio, she'd be so disappointed.

Nero slides open the partition between the front and back seats. "Ready, *capo*?"

"Just a minute." I uncross my legs and move to the opposite bench between Otto and Serena. Turning to my beautiful captive, I don the mask of the savage prince, the new heir to the Ferrara empire. "Before Nero unlocks the doors, I simply want to remind you of our deal, *tesoro*. If you try to escape, your cousin's life will be forfeit. *Capisci*?"

"I already said I agreed on the plane," she hisses.

"Good girl. Now, just so that we're very clear, be aware that there is nowhere for you to run. The closest villa is half a mile away and with that ankle, you won't get more than a few meters before I catch up to you."

"I got it," she grits out.

"Very good girl."

She snags her bottom lip between her teeth as she regards me with furious, narrowed eyes.

My hand snakes out, fingers clamping around her chin before I can think better of it. Giving it a gentle tug, I free her swollen lip. "Don't do that, *tesoro*, I have little restraint when it comes to a beautiful woman pouting."

Her shoulders tremble, and I'm certain it's not from fear. No, Serena Valentino isn't the slightest bit afraid of me. Which is oddly exciting.

I tip my head at Nero and the lock disengages. Serena throws the door open and jumps out of the car, or at least she tries, until she's thwarted by that ankle.

"Can we go inside already?" Goose bumps pebble her skin as the cool evening air drifts off the lake.

She's still in that scandalous romper, and I only hope I can find something of mine for her to wear until I can send Mariuccia into town in the morning for more suitable clothing. I should have thought about it sooner. When I called the housekeeper to ready the villa for our arrival, I hadn't considered women's clothing. I'm sure I had something of my ex's in my apartment in Roma.

Otto trudges by Serena then climbs the steps to the front door, his good eye locked on her now freed hands. He wasn't pleased by the development, but he knows better than to question me. He has the door unlocked and swung open in seconds, holding it ajar for us to enter. Serena limps forward and judging by the wincing, her ankle appears even worse than before.

"Is Elena on her way?" I snap at Pietro over my shoulder. He's at the trunk of the car removing our measly luggage.

"*Si, capo,* she should be here within the hour."

I glance at my watch, and a scowl twists my lips. It's nearly midnight in Manhattan already. I had hoped to speak with Dante tonight, but perhaps I should wait. He may take the news of his daughter's capture better and be more amenable to negotiations after a good night's sleep.

Marching between the towering columns on the front landing, I barrel by Otto and follow Serena into the foyer. A wave of nostalgia surges over me as the familiar sights and smells of the old villa overpower me.

How could a room possibly still smell like *her* after all these years?

The light powder scent fills my nostrils, and I'm instantly hurled back in time to our last visit here. *Papà* thought the fresh air would help combat the debilitating effects of the chemo. It didn't. She died days after we returned to Roma. A piercing ache assaults my insides, claws of pain tearing at my heart, no, at the heart of a young boy who lost his mother.

"Is this you?" Serena's voice propels me back to the present. She stands in the middle of the foyer, pointing at an ornate gilded frame hung on the wall. Five strangers stare back at me, smiling, eyes filled with so much hope I barely recognize that version of my family.

Tearing my gaze away from the painful past, I meet her

curious eyes. "That hasn't been me for a long time now," I mutter.

Her lips twist, but she doesn't say a word as she takes another unsteady step into the living room and continues to scan the opulent surroundings. Unlike *Papà*, my mother had come from money, but my father was much too proud to take any of it. He insisted he would rather live in poverty than take a penny from the Domenicos. We did at first, until the business began to flourish, but *Mamma* was dead by then and the success felt hollow.

Quick footsteps echo down the hallway, and a familiar figure appears from the shadows. Mariuccia's pale gray eyes light up when they find me. She gasps, her hand resting across her heart. *"Non lo posso credere."*

I can't quite believe it myself. I never thought I'd return to this home, let alone to find the woman who had been our nanny all those years ago still living in the area. I wrote to her for years when I was a kid after Mamma passed. She was like a second mother to me. Then after everything went to hell with Raffaele and *Papà*, I sent one final letter. I just didn't have it in me anymore.

"Tonio!" She springs for me and wraps her warm, substantial arms around my stiffening form. I can't remember the last time someone hugged me. The feeling is awkward and comforting in the same instant. I can't seem to push her away, not when I can feel the joy in her embrace. The last time she saw me I was just a boy.

Mariuccia chatters on in Italian, never quite releasing me as she catches me up on thirty years of her life. All the while Serena watches, her gaze heavy on me from the corner of my eye. I have to put a stop to this, or she'll lose even the tiniest bit of fear she may have of me.

I finally push free of my former nanny's embrace and stiffen my jaw. "Thank you for coming in such short notice."

"Anything for you, Tonio." She pinches my cheek, and I

barely restrain from wincing. Serena does nothing to suppress the eruption of laughter.

I spin on her, shooting a narrowed glare and my best scowl. It does nothing to tame the wild cackles. *Merda*. As if this woman wasn't proving to be enough of a problem.

Pivoting back to Mariuccia, I decide to dispense with the pleasantries. "This is Serena Valentino, she is our guest, but she is not permitted to leave the property, do you understand?"

Her silvery brows furrow, but she nods all the same. "*Certo, signore.*" Word of the infamous Ferrara family stretches across the peninsula of Italy. Surely, she must know who I've become and what I'm capable of.

"Please accompany her to one of the guest bedrooms."

"Lakeside, *per piacere*," Serena interjects.

This time, I don't suppress the eyeroll.

"I'll be right behind you," I warn in my most severe tone. "Don't try anything."

"Of course not, I'll be a perfect little captive." She shoots me a grin, and as I'm shaking my head, I meet Mariuccia's disapproving glare.

Wonderful, just what I need. Another *rompicoglione*, another woman to bust my balls.

CHAPTER 13
A VALUABLE PRIZE

S*erena*

I follow the housekeeper, Mariuccia, through the winding halls of the grand estate, switching between admiring the decadent artwork on the pastel walls and analyzing the scene in the foyer. Clearly, the man this woman remembers is nothing like the monster he's become.

Still, he was kind to her, warm and caring even. Shocking.

I struggle to accept the huge disparity between the image I have of the cold, cruel Antonio Ferrara and the little boy in that family portrait. A knot of emotion tightens my chest, a tangle of anxiety, anger and an unexpected twinge of sympathy. What happened to that young boy to create the man Raf warned us about, the one who kidnapped me today?

Mariuccia stops in front of a pale lemon door, the hue matching the orchard filled with citrus trees surrounding the villa. She turns and offers a quick smile. "I'm sure you will be comfortable here, *signorina*."

"I hope so."

She twists the antique crystal knob, revealing an expansive bedroom. I step inside and I can't settle on where to look. The entire chamber is tranquil and luxurious, reflecting the villa's elegance and warmth. It's completely different from my modern apartment in the city and not at all what I ever thought I would like. An enormous canopied king-size bed, draped in fine linens lines the far wall, the canopy decorated with sheer, flowing fabrics that catch the gentle breeze from the open balcony doors.

I move toward the *terrazzo*, the breathtaking view of the lake beyond calling to me. The large space is adorned with vibrant flowers and elegant wrought-iron railings and a small table and chair to admire the sparkling waters and jagged mountains beyond.

"I think I'm in love." The words accidentally erupt out loud.

"It is truly a beautiful sight, isn't it?" Mariuccia sneaks up behind me, her gray eyes twinkling as she admires the lake.

"It is. I guess as far as prison cells go, it's a damned good option."

Her brows crinkle, just like they did when Antonio alluded to my imprisonment downstairs. I guess she had no idea what she was getting into when her old employer summoned her to the villa.

Maybe I could get her to help me.

I open my mouth to ask, but the shuffle of approaching footsteps clamps my jaw shut. From over my shoulder and through the wispy linen curtains, I can just make out Antonio stalking toward us.

"This room, really, Mariuccia?" he growls.

Her shoulders lift innocently, a knowing smile on her weathered face. "It has the best view of the lake."

"This isn't a fucking hotel. Serena is my pr—" He snaps his jaw shut as the housekeeper's eyes widen in horror.

"*Scusi*," he mutters, gaze cast down to the marble floor.

"Antonio Ferrara, your mother would be appalled by that language and this poor girl—"

He lifts his hand. "Enough. Perhaps I made a mistake having Nero call you here. I'm not the same little boy you knew all those years ago, Mariuccia." His icy stare flickers in my direction before returning to the woman. "Serena Valentino is the key to salvaging what *Papà* spent years building, and I won't let anyone derail me from achieving my goal."

The elderly woman glances between Antonio and me, the pity in her expression palpable. But was it for me or the little boy she once knew?

"Now, should I have Nero return you to your home?"

She shakes her head, calmly, resolutely. "No, Tonio. I owe it to your mother to stay. After all that she did for me and my family, it is the least I can do."

His head dips, jaw tense. "We won't remain here for long. If all goes as planned, Serena's father will agree to my terms in the morning and all of this ugly business will be over in a few days."

"*Bene.*" Mariuccia's chin dips. "There are fresh towels in the bathroom as instructed. Is there anything else I can get you, *signore*?" Her tone is frostier than his.

"No," he mutters. "Elena should be arriving shortly. Will you please see to it that she is escorted to Serena's room upon her arrival?"

"To this room?" I interject.

He eyes me as if he's forgotten I was here.

"Yes, fine, you can stay in the master suite."

I can't help the satisfied smile from crawling across my lips. No wonder he's so pissy. This was supposed to be his room. And just like that I'm absolutely loving Mariuccia.

He marches back into the bedroom and swings his gaze toward a door along the far wall. "I'll take the adjoining room."

"Adjoining?" I splutter.

"You didn't think I'd let you stay by yourself, now, did you, *tesoro*? Such a valuable prize must be protected at all costs."

His fathomless, obsidian eyes heat, and I hate how my body reacts to that look. An ember ignites, faint at first but with the potential to burn down an entire village.

Mariuccia must feel the intense shift in the atmosphere because she lowers her head and makes a beeline toward the door. "I'll have your luggage brought up," she calls out over her shoulder.

Once we're alone, Antonio steps closer and I mirror his move backwards. His eyes lock on mine and a flash of something indecipherable streaks across the endless night of those piercing orbs. As if he's finally realized what he's done, he heaves in a breath and knots his arms across his chest.

"It's too late to call your father tonight. I'll see to it first thing in the morning."

"Yeah, we sure wouldn't want Pa cranky when you tell him you've stolen his only child."

"I already told you, this isn't about you. Dante did this. He conspired with my enemy, the Sartoris, to dismantle my father's entire organization. This is all his doing."

Shit. I knew that deal with Enrico Sartori was going to come back and bite us in the ass. Only I thought it would be Isabella to pay the price. Uncle Luca is going to be furious with my dad, and he deserves every ounce of his wrath.

"Wait a second, Isabella said something about your father making moves in King territory in Manhattan. Wasn't he the one that started all of this?"

"He only did that in response to Dante's encroachment in our territory in Roma," he growls.

Okay, that's believable. My dad is always looking for ways to expand the King's sphere of influence. But why'd he choose to do it in a city where Bella had been living? *Idiot.* If it had been Isabella instead of me, I'd find myself a fatherless orphan. *Papà* and Luca didn't exactly have the most stable relationship as it was. Maybe it is a good thing I was the one nabbed after all.

"Okay, I get it," I hiss. "It's all my father's fault. That still doesn't excuse you kidnapping me, so don't try to pretend you're some chivalrous guy just because you're keeping me captive in a beautiful estate."

The hint of a smile tips up the corners of his lips, and the word beautiful vibrates across my skull. "I'm glad you think it's beautiful. It was my mother's greatest masterpiece." He pauses for a long moment before whispering, "Besides my brothers and me." A rueful chuckle slips out. "And look how well we all turned out."

A charged silence fills the room once his jaw snaps shut, as if he hadn't intended to divulge that little bit of personal history. From what I'd heard from Bella, Raf and Antonio had lost their mom to cancer when they were just kids. Raf barely mentioned her but given their age difference, Antonio probably remembered more of his mother than his younger brother did.

My mind wanders back to my mom and every childhood memory that she stars in. I couldn't imagine what life would've been like without her. Again, that twinge of pity rears up. I shove it far down as I continue this weird game of chicken. Neither of us looks away as the tension in the room only escalates.

"She's right this way." Mariuccia's voice echoes down the hallway, along with her footsteps.

"I hope it is only a sprain," says the other female voice. "If what you said is true and the girl has been walking on it for hours, she could have done irreparable damage."

My head snaps toward the door where the housekeeper and a second woman, this one at least a decade younger than Mariuccia's sixties, if I had to guess. She's holding a big leather bag, nearly limping from the additional weight on her small frame.

"*Dottoressa* Bergamaschi." Antonio dips his head at the new arrival. "Thank you for coming so quickly."

"I didn't do it for you, Tonio. It was only in your mother's memory." She pushes the wire-rimmed glasses up her nose and drops the bag on the bed, then turns to me. "*Signorina*, take a seat so I can look at that ankle."

I stare at the woman wide-eyed, then my gaze pivots to find Antonio's again. He called a doctor in for me? He must really be scared of returning me broken to my father. He makes a move in my direction like he's going to help me to the bed before he stops in his tracks and clears his throat.

Instead, Mariuccia closes the distance between us and weaves an arm through mine. "Come, Serena, Elena will take good care of you." Shooting a scowl at her employer, she gently guides me to the bed.

The doctor starts poking and prodding at my ankle, and I can't help wincing at each touch. Antonio watches every move, a tendon in his jaw tweaking at each of my grimaces. His lips are set in a grim line, the flutter at the pulse in his neck so powerful its visible over the collar of his shirt.

Finally, a long minute later, the woman's kind eyes lift to mine. "It's not broken, but it is badly sprained. I will stabilize it with a bandage, so the muscle has time to heal. You must try to keep off it as much as possible for the next two weeks. I'll have crutches delivered in the morning."

I groan internally, all the while keeping a smile plastered across my face. Wonderful, so much for my plan of a great escape.

CHAPTER 14
SEE SOMETHING YOU LIKE?

A*ntonio*

After escorting the *dottoressa* to the door and being forced to endure her veiled glares and muttered insults, I turn back to the immense double stairway that leads to the second floor. It's absurd, but I hate that Serena is out of my sight even for a few minutes. Everything is riding on her. Pietro left, his presence necessary in Roma to run the daily operations in my absence. I would have preferred he remain here as an extra guard, but my choices are limited at this point. Otto is standing guard outside her door, a new bandage on his wounded eye thanks to Elena and a dozen other guards line the property. There's no way she can escape, nowhere for her to run, and still, I need to see that she's under this roof with my own eyes.

Just over twenty-four hours with this woman, and I've completely *impazitto*. I've lost my damned mind.

I drag my hand through my hair and pause on the first step. *Cazzo, be the man you were groomed to be, damn it. Papà* named you his enforcer, then his heir for a reason. Doubt encircles my lungs, squeezing until I can barely breathe. My gaze travels the foyer, searching for that portrait, the one of the five of us before our life began to crumble.

My eyes linger on the image of the little boy with smiling eyes and wild tumbles of dark hair. He clings onto *Mamma*'s side as if somehow, he knew she was going to be ripped from his arms too soon. That boy was not built for this life.

And still, somehow, I forced it upon him.

Or rather *Papà* did.

I was the eldest, born to take over the Ferrara empire. My father trained me, spent countless hours preparing me for the inevitable day when I would become king. And I failed. Only months after his death and his precious kingdom is crumbling.

The worst part: I'm starting to realize I don't honestly give a damn.

"*Signore*..." Mariuccia appears around the corner, her hands folded across her rounded midsection. She looks at me like I'm a stranger. Gone is the warmth that filled her gaze when she first laid eyes on me less than an hour ago.

"*Signore* was my father, Antonio is fine."

She shakes her head, eyes cast down. "It doesn't feel right."

It's all I can do not to beg for her to call me Tonio once again. Anything to bring back memories of a sweeter time.

"The cook has left dinner on the table for you and the *signorina*," she continues. "Is there anything else I can do before I retire for the evening?"

"*Si*. Serena will need clothes for her stay. Can you pick something up in the morning?"

She glances at her wristwatch and begins to move toward the door. "The shops in town are still open for another hour. I can go tonight. She shouldn't have to sleep in those indecent scraps of fabric she's wearing."

I barely restrain a chuckle and the urge to hug the woman. For my own sanity, a less revealing outfit would do wonders.

"*Grazie*, Mariuccia. I mean it."

With a tight smile, she marches the rest of the way to the door. Her hand closes around the knob, then she turns to me, her expression conflicted. "Perhaps it is not my place to say, but I wouldn't forgive myself for not speaking up. I don't pretend to know about your life or what has happened over the last two decades to turn the sweet, kind boy I knew into a cowardly, heartless man who would kidnap a woman. This is not who you are, Antonio Ferrara. Maybe *Dio* brought you here for a reason. Maybe here, in this home, you will remember the man your mother bore, not the monster your father raised."

I stare at her, my jaw hanging open, as she spins toward the door and walks out, slamming the old timber behind her for good measure. I can't remember the last time anyone dared speak to me like that or when truer words were spoken.

Instead of continuing up the stairs, I just stand there for an endless moment like a complete *coglione*. A part of me rages at the idea of being talked to like that, that's the new me, while the old me can't help another rueful smile from breaking through.

Mariuccia is right. My mother would be disgusted by the man I've become. By the man who just stood by and watched when *Papà* took out his thirst for revenge on Raf's innocent girlfriend, when he banished my youngest brother from the family for no good reason. I was a complete and utter coward, just like my former nanny claimed.

But how can I go back now?

After years spent crafting the monster, how can I possibly banish the darkness I'd nurtured within myself? I wasn't sure there was anything left of that little boy in the gilded frame.

The savory scent of garlic and herbs wafts down the hall, filling my nostrils and distracting me from this completely unexpected moral dilemma. *Get a hold of yourself, Antonio.* Some things have to be done despite the unpleasant consequences. My feet instinctively turn toward the kitchen, and I follow them in search of the delicious scent, anything to get my mind off the past.

Balancing the tray of food in my hands, I tick my head at Otto to open the door of the master bedroom. The grand chamber that should have been mine. Then again, maybe my parents' old bedroom would be filled with too many ghosts, and Serena has actually done me a favor by claiming it.

The door swings open and I march through, only to barrel into a naked, wet form. The tray crashes to the ground, the food splattering across the marble, and a hiss escapes through my clenched teeth as I take in all of Serena. Miles of perfectly tanned flesh gleams before me, tiny droplets of water dripping down her shoulders. I trail one of the glistening beads that traces a path from a lock of blonde hair over the perfect swell of her breast, winding around the peaked pink nipple, then diving lower across her abdomen. Somehow, by the sheer will of *Dio*, I force my eyes up before they delve lower to ogle the hollow between her thighs.

Finding a pair of amused sapphire orbs watching me stare at her, a smirk quirks up the corners of Serena's lips. "See something you like, Ferrara?"

Squeezing my eyes closed, I grit out a curse before spinning around. Otto stands in the doorway gawking at the still naked Serena, who hasn't even made a move to cover herself. *Cazzo.* A wave of unexpected irritation crashes over me, and I take it out on the gaping guard.

"*Smetti di fissarla e vattene da qui,*" I growl at Otto. *Stop staring and get the hell out of here.*

With one final glance at Serena's perfect form, and a smile that says he's memorizing every delicious inch of her, he whirls around and starts to retreat.

"And have Fabi come up here and clean up this mess," I shout.

"Yes, *capo.*" He marches out, slamming the door behind him.

My fingers tighten into fists, nails digging into the flesh of my palms. The idea of him, of any man, seeing her bare has unexpected rage consuming my insides.

"Get dressed," I hiss and crouch down to toss her the discarded towel, ignoring the splatter of ravioli and cream sauce across the floor.

She barely wraps it around herself before her eyes meet mine, taunting. "In case you forgot, I don't exactly have anything to change into. I've been wearing that romper for more than twenty-four hours, and it's starting to chafe."

I heave out a frustrated groan and march across the space to the door that connects my room to hers. Until Mariuccia returns, I'd rather have her in one of my shirts and a pair of boxers than a measly towel. "Follow me."

I'm surprised when she does, the soft pitter patter of her feet on the marble echoing over the suddenly escalated thrumming of my pulse. I scan the smaller room, still fitted with a king size bed and find my suitcase nestled beside the armoire. Picking it up and splaying it out on the bed, I rifle through its paltry contents. I didn't exactly plan for a lengthy stay at the villa so my options are limited.

Serena peers over my shoulder, eyeing the random assortment and lingering on the compartment that holds my boxer briefs. Grabbing one, I toss it to her then reach for the first shirt I find. "Here. This should suffice for now. Mariuccia has gone into town to buy you something suitable for tomorrow."

"Really?" Her voice rises a few octaves. "You're buying me clothes?"

"Well, I can't exactly have you running around naked in my house. My guards will lose complete focus."

She cackles, her head tipping back and locks of damp blonde hair fall across her eyes. "Just the guards?"

Her grin grows wicked.

"Yes," I hiss.

"Maybe that's my plan."

"It would probably work."

She sucks her bottom lip between her teeth, batting those dark lashes and burning need zips down to my cock. Fuck, what is it about this woman? I've heard about love at first sight but lust at first kidnapping? I'm a complete *stronzo*.

Dropping the towel, which barely covers anything, she presses the shirt to her chest and her nostrils flare. "What cologne do you use? I like it."

Heat rises up my neck, and I clear my throat awkwardly. "I don't wear any," I mutter. Not unless it's a special occasion, but I don't find it necessary to clarify.

"Hmm, interesting." She continues to watch me from beneath waves of damp hair, clutching my shirt and boxers in her hands, and *merda*, seeing her naked like that holding my clothes has my stupid cock thickening.

"Put on the clothes," I bark.

"Okay, okay."

I turn away, focusing on the terrace on the opposite side of the room and the setting sun's reflection on the lake. It may not have been as grand as the master *terrazzo* but at least I'll have a place to sit outside and stew tonight.

Who knows what tomorrow will bring once I deliver the news of his daughter's abduction?

This could be my last sunset…

The thought is oddly comforting.

Thirty-five years and already I find myself looking forward to the quiet peace of oblivion. *Mamma*'s passing was anything but peaceful. When my time comes, I long for a quick bullet to the head.

"You can turn around now. I'm decent."

Serena's voice has the dismal thoughts waning and my head

spinning over my shoulder. "*Cazzo*," I rasp out through gritted teeth.

Serena's even more tempting in *my* clothes.

The black dress shirt is barely buttoned high enough to conceal the sensual swell of her breasts and her long, sexy legs peer out from beneath the hem. I can't even see my boxers under there, but I can imagine the soft material cradling her ass, caressing her pussy…

Dammit, stop that.

"You should go to bed," I murmur, my voice rough.

"Right. Busy day of hostaging tomorrow."

"Serena…" Her name comes out as a needy rumble.

She moves toward the adjoining door before spinning back. "You're not sleeping?"

Of course not. I won't be able to sleep knowing my precious *tesoro* could be trying to escape. "Not tired."

"Right." A sigh parts her lips, and she pads out of my room. "Night."

CHAPTER 15
ESCAPE

Serena

Rolling around in bed, even the tranquil sounds of the waves below do nothing to lull me back to sleep. Damned jet lag. I squeeze my eyes closed and try for the tenth time to force my spinning thoughts to quiet.

It's no use though, I'm freaking wide awake. And hungry…

My stomach rumbles, reminding me I never had dinner since it ended up on the floor thanks to my current captor. That look on his face when he walked in on me naked made it all worth it though. Almost.

Maybe if I'd eaten I wouldn't find myself up at—I glance at the clock on the nightstand—three o'clock in the morning. Well, I refuse to spend another minute tossing and turning in bed. Shoving the silky coverlet off, I slide to the edge of the mattress. The full moon peeking in through the open doors of the balcony sweeps into the room, bathing it in a beautiful silver glow. A breeze blows in, raising the tiny hairs along my arms.

Standing, I wrap my arms across my chest, reveling in the soft fabric of Antonio's dress shirt. I draw in a breath, my lungs hungry for that enticing scent of his. It's a warm amber mixed with cool shadows and dark secrets. *Ugh, stop it.* Shaking the stupid out of my head, I eye the door to my right then the one across the way. The main door, I already know is locked, and being guarded by Otto the pirate with his one good eye, and the other one leads to Antonio's room.

Maybe that one is open...

I creep across the room, trying to shift my weight so most of it is on my good ankle. Even wrapped by the kind doctor, it still hurts like hell when I walk. A shiver skates up my spine as I pass the open balcony doors, and pause at Antonio's, pressing my ear to the timber. Nothing but silence on the other side. Holding my breath, I twist the knob, and it opens.

The creak of the hinges sends my pulse skyrocketing, and I freeze in the doorway, gaze pinned to the unmade bed.

The empty bed. Where is my handsome captor?

Without wasting time to consider, I stagger across the room and find another door, presumably the one that leads to the hallway. My pulse quickens, indecision warring through my insides. Whipping it open, I find the corridor empty, with the exception of a snoring one-eyed guard. Otto is slumped against my door, his haggard breaths filling the passageway.

This is my chance.

I tiptoe down the hall, cursing the fact that my only pair of shoes are stilettos which there's no way I can manage in my current state, so I'm stuck attempting an escape barefoot and limping. Beggars can't be choosers.

I'll be damned if I don't take the opportunity anyway.

Finding my way to the grand spiraling double staircase, I clutch onto the banister for support and hobble down. Pausing at the landing, I scan the dimly lit first floor. All quiet. I skulk down the last few steps, my heart battering my ribcage as hope floods my chest. I'm already making plans to hitchhike to the center of town and beg a kind stranger for a ride back to Milano by the time I reach the front door. I can do this. I can escape. And find a way to warn Isabella before Antonio can make good on his vow.

My heart races as I peer through the villa's ornate French doors, my gaze scanning the sprawling estate bathed in moonlight. The lush gardens glisten with dew, shadows cast by the olive trees offering patches of darkness to move through undetected.

Closing my fingers around the antique handle, I glance over my shoulder one last time. That portrait of the Ferraras stares at me from across the foyer. That little boy with the dark eyes glances at me, almost pleading. Shit, I've lost my damned mind.

With a quick flick of my wrist, I yank the door open and creep out into the brisk night. I immediately regret not snagging a jacket of some sort on my way out. Too late now. Making my way around the edge of the grand estate while avoiding the guards in the utter darkness with only the moon as a guide is more difficult than I expected. Not to mention the whole limping thing.

In only a few hours at the villa, I've learned the guards' routines—two at the front, one patrolling the back, and another by the gate. Timing is everything.

With a deep, steadying breath, I slip across the *terrazzo*, my feet whispering against the cool stone tiles. The scent of jasmine hangs heavy in the air, a stark contrast to the adrenaline surging through my veins. I keep close to the flowering hedges surrounding the veranda, my eyes locked on the silhouette of the gate guard, illuminated by a flickering lantern. As he turns away, I dash for the gate across the driveway, my heart pounding in my ears.

The gravel crunches softly under my feet, a sound impossibly loud in the silence of the night. I'm almost there, just a few more steps. I spy one of the guards on the eastern corner, staring out into the rippling lake. I hold my breath as I tiptoe past him along the pathway. With my eyes on him, I round a sprawling olive tree and barrel into a wall. Muttering a curse, I look up as steel bands close around me and a pair of raging midnight eyes meet mine.

Merda. Definitely not a wall.

Antonio's jaw ticks, a tendon jumping beneath the shadow of his dark scruff. His body presses into me, that amber scent invading my nostrils. "Serena, you swore to me…"

"What?" I giggle awkwardly. "Oh, you thought I was trying to escape?" I slap him playfully on the bare chest, ignoring the perfect dips and valleys of his torso. "I was just looking for the kitchen and the beautiful moon-lit lake caught my eye. So I decided to go for a little walk. You know, it's a funny story really. I woke up starving and—"

"Enough!" he growls, his firm hands pinning mine behind my back. He shoves me until I hit the tree trunk and let out a squeal.

"Watch it, *bastardo!*" I hiss.

"You promised me you wouldn't run. I told you what would happen if you did, your cousin would be the one to pay."

Fear strikes me, sharp and true. "Please, no, Antonio, not Isabella. I'm sorry, okay?"

He glares down at me, fury streaking across the endless abyss of his sinister gaze. He shoves his knee between my legs pinning me against the rough bark. "*Cazzo,* why must you make me a monster? I'm trying—" He bites back the last word.

"I'm sorry, I am." I tip my chin up, fixing my eyes to his and try for my most sincere expression. "I really was hungry and then I found you gone and Otto asleep, what would you have done in my position?"

"That doesn't matter."

"Yes, it does!" I try to squirm free of his hold, but it only tightens so my breasts are pressed more tightly against his bare chest. His knee rubs against my apex, and fuck me, if tiny sparks don't ignite at my core. "You and me grew up in the same world, damn it," I rasp. "We're survivors. You have to be to make it this far in life."

His dark brows furrow, his eyes widening ever so faintly.

I'm right, and he knows it. "What would you have done?" I hiss.

A long silence lingers between us, the sound of my ragged breaths creating a steady symphony against the light crashing of waves beyond.

"I would have run," he finally grits out. His hold around my wrists relaxes but he still has me pinned against the tree. He runs his hand through his hair and draws in a ragged breath. "I will give you one last chance, Serena, a chance my own father would never have given me."

The line between his brows deepens, lips parting as if he hadn't meant for the final words to fall out.

"Thank you," I whisper and attempt to wriggle free.

But his body is an immoveable force.

"Can you let me go now?"

"I don't think I can." His jaw slams shut, the crack reverberating across the quiet stillness of the night. He spins around and trudges back toward the pathway that leads into the villa, a warm glow lighting the trail. Before he enters, he swivels his head back toward me, eyes smoldering. "Come inside, and I'll give you something to eat."

Dipping my head, I slowly limp after him. I can't keep risking Bella's life. How many more chances will I really get with this man? With my shoulders rounding, I stagger the rest of the way back into my new beautiful prison.

I sit across the table from my brooding captor, slowly chewing on the ridiculously delicious *spaghetti al pomodoro* Antonio just whipped up. It's everything I can do not to moan as the savory flavors of vine-ripened tomatoes and roasted garlic roll around my tongue.

The craziest part is that he made it all from scratch in a manner of minutes. As if creating the best pasta I've ever tasted outside of my *Nonna*'s kitchen, *Dio* rest her soul, is a daily occurrence. Maybe I seriously do need to reconsider my attempts at escape.

He watches me, that piercing gaze boring a hole into my forehead. But I don't look up, I keep my head down and focus on shoving as much pasta into my mouth as I can fit without choking.

Damn, when was the last time I ate? It had been the longest forty-eight hours of my life.

I slurp up the final strand of spaghetti and the savory sauce splashes my chin. Before I can swallow, Antonio leans across the table with a napkin and dabs at the tomato splatter.

Wow, that's embarrassing, but also, "Boundaries!"

He jerks his hand back, crumpling the paper napkin. "I didn't want it to fall on my shirt," he snaps.

Oh, right. I almost forget I'm still wearing it. His warm amber scent covers me like second skin. After only half a night wearing it, I've already become accustomed to his natural fragrance.

"Right, tomato sauce is a bitch to get out of clothes."

His lip twitches, but he doesn't fully give in to the smile.

"How did you learn to cook like that? I didn't think mob bosses had time to master the culinary arts."

A long beat of silence passes, and I'm certain he's going to ignore my question when his mouth starts to move. "My mother was an excellent cook, and when I was young I would spend hours following her around the kitchen." The words tumble out, slowly at first before picking up speed. "After she died, *Papà* was left with three boys and little skills in the kitchen." He shrugs. "I helped as much as I could."

"How old were you?" I whisper.

"Ten."

A twinge of sympathy fills my chest as I regard the man staring intently at me from across the table. I picture that little boy from the painting again and the ache intensifies. "*Dio*, that's awful. You were so young." My eyes widen. "Also, you learned to do all this at the age of ten?" I'm twenty-four and still can't cook a decent meal to save my life.

"Necessity is the mother of invention." His head cocks to the side as he scrutinizes me. The momentary vulnerability vanishes, replaced by the icy mask I've come to recognize. "Do you cook?"

"Absolutely not, so if you're looking for a hostage-slash-home cook you took the wrong Valentino princess." I throw him a smirk before I realize what I've said. "Not that Bella is any better so don't get any ideas."

"Relax, I have no intention of keeping you longer than absolutely necessary. And I have my own cook." Something dark flashes across his face, the ominous streak vanishing before I can fixate on it. "If you've eaten enough, I'll escort you back to your room." He stands, looming over me, his jaw hardening. "And I urge you to stay put this time, *tesoro*. I'm cranky when I don't sleep, and as it is, tomorrow will be a difficult day."

I pop out of my seat before my ankle reminds me that moves like that are *not* a good idea. Wincing, I grip the chair and glance up at him, flashing my sweetest smile. "I promise to be on my best behavior."

CHAPTER 16
RANSOM

A *ntonio*

As if the discussion with Dante isn't going to be painful enough, I had to deal with Otto's utter ineptitude last night. How does a guard fall asleep the first night on the job and nearly allow my most valuable hostage to escape? He would lose a week's pay for his incompetence. If it happens again, he'll lose something more vital. If Serena had gotten away, everything I'd fought so hard to hold onto would have slipped right through my fingertips.

I will not make the same mistake again.

On the bright side, upon Pietro's return trip to Rome he managed to secure a deal with the Salernos for the new restaurant complex. At least one good thing to come of the past few days. Of course, it's all riding on Dante agreeing to my terms.

Staring out onto the tranquil lake with streaks of morning light glittering on the glassy surface, I attempt to still my racing pulse. For some goddamned reason I can't seem to find the nerve to pick up the phone. What the hell is going on with me? This woman falls into my life, and I'm a fucking mess.

I left the adjoining door between Serena and me ajar and kept my eyes on her all night. My gaze flickers to the bed she's still sprawled across through the opening in the door. I hadn't slept for the second night in a row now. Raking my hands over my face, I heave in a breath. If all goes according to plan, Dante will concede to my demands and the blonde beauty would be out of my life by tomorrow. So I could finally sleep...

A hint of sadness? Regret? What the *cazzo* is that? Some inconvenient feeling I can't quite name squirms its way into my chest at the thought of resuming my solitary existence.

Maybe I'll reach out to Stefania again once all of this is settled. With the Ferrara empire back on track, I could afford the time to devote to a real relationship. But do I even want one with her? Can I see Stefania as the mother of my children? I'm not even certain I want any. Not after seeing how easily a father can fuck up their kids' lives.

And with the one I had as a role model, I don't have high hopes for my own parental skills.

A hint of movement through the crack in the door draws my attention away from the lake and the muddle of thoughts to *her*. Serena rolls over, then groans, before pushing the comforter back. She slides to the edge of the mattress, blonde locks tussled and wild, and slips out of bed. Her shirt—no, my shirt—rides up, revealing her long, perfectly muscled legs in my boxers.

My stupid cock twitches at the sight. Last time I saw Stefania, I felt nothing. It must be a reverse Stockholm's Syndrome or something illogical like that. My gaze follows her like a starving man as she disappears into the bathroom.

Blinking quickly to chase away her tantalizing lingering image, I reach for the phone in my pocket. Pietro assures me the signal has been scrambled, and the call to Dante will be completely untraceable. I suppose we'll see because it's time.

With purposeful strides, I march into Serena's bedroom and

find a shopping bag filled with clothes wedged in the doorway. I pick up the bag with a quick glance at Otto stationed outside the door once more and drag it to the unmade bed. How long does Mariuccia think she'll be staying? There are enough garments here to clothe the girl for a few weeks. As I rifle through the collection of sundresses, blouses and skirts, I find a lacy array of underthings. I groan. The last thing I need are mental images of Serena's sexy bra and panties engraved in my mind.

The creak of old hinges spins my head over my shoulder. Serena saunters out of the bathroom, her head tipping back on a yawn. "Jet lag sucks," she mutters before she plops back down on the bed. Then her eyes drift to the shopping bag perched at the edge. "Aww, you bought me something? How sweet."

I grunt, shaking my head. "Mariuccia bought you some clothes last night. You should thank her."

"I will. Now gimme, gimme." She reaches for the bag, her eyes alight with excitement.

That look of pure joy is contagious and the ominous feelings roiling around in my gut momentarily ebb. "You work for Dolce & Gabbana, and you're excited by a bag of cheap clothing from H&M?"

"I'm a fashionista, Antonio. I love clothes and don't you dare diss H&M. It's one of my favorites." She holds up a frilly sundress with splatters of bright colors and smiles. "Besides, Mariuccia has great taste, and she nailed my size perfectly."

"I'll be sure to commend her on excellent work." I look down at the phone still clutched in my hand and remind myself why this woman is here. This is not some romantic lakeside retreat, *coglione*. My fingers tighten around the cell, and I bring it up to Serena's face. "It's time to call your father."

"Oh." Her lips screw into a pout, and she drops the colorful assortment of dresses back into the bag. Then she peers up at me, gaze narrowed. "You want me to talk to him?"

"No," I growl. "I will speak to him first and lay out the conditions of your return. I'm sure he'll want to speak to you after."

"Right, proof of life and what not."

My head slowly dips.

Serena leans back on her palms, the picture of calm. "Well, let's get this over with."

"You're not the least bit nervous?"

She shakes her head. "Why should I be? *Papà* will do anything for me. You're the one who should be shitting yourself. He might give you what you want now, but once I'm back safe and sound, there will be hell to pay." She shoots me one of her feral grins, the one that has blood pumping to the wrong head. "No one fucks with Dante Valentino's daughter and lives to tell the tale." Her lips pucker around the last few words, as if she doesn't find the thought of my bloodied corpse sprawled across the *piazza* of the Duomo as appealing as she thought she would. Or maybe I'm imagining it…

Drawing in a steadying breath, I jab my finger at the call button. It rings once, then twice and the pleasant voice of a young woman answers.

"I need to speak to Dante Valentino." I attempt to match her cordial tone, but my voice is clipped and rough from exhaustion.

"I'm sorry he's not in today. Would you like to leave a message?"

"No, I'll call his cell, thanks."

"You won't be able to reach him that way either. I'm afraid he's out of town and will be unreachable for the next week."

I hiss out a curse through clenched teeth. That may be true for business associates, but surely, he'll take a call from his daughter. Too bad I had Otto dump her phone before we took off for Milano. "Fine," I grit out and hang up.

"What happened?" Serena stares up at me with wide, blue eyes.

"Apparently, he's unreachable."

"Not to me." She holds out her hand, palm up. "Give me. I'll call him."

Handing over my phone, I watch as she dials her father's number, brings the phone to her ear and waits...

"How could he not answer?" she snaps.

"Well, he clearly doesn't recognize the number."

"I'll just call my mom."

Again, no answer, but this time she leaves a message, and I'm impressed by the coolness in her tone.

"Damned spam block," she mutters as she drops my phone beside her on the mattress.

"I'm sure she'd return the call if the number wasn't untraceable."

"Oh, right," she grits out. She taps the toes of her good foot on the terracotta tile, her knee bouncing. "Maybe I should just call Isabella—"

"No!" The shout comes out more forcefully than intended. Softening my tone, I continue, "I don't want Raffaele to know about this until it is done."

"Well, he's going to find out. The moment my father knows, word will spread across the King's empire. And as Bella's bodyguard and boyfriend, there's no way he won't hear about it."

"I only hope by the time he does, you'll be on your way back home."

"Why does it matter?"

"Because I don't want my brother involved," I hiss. Which is ironic since only a week ago, I was considering taking his life myself. Only twenty-four hours in this place and the memories of the past have weakened my resolve, turning me into a sentimental fool.

"You think he'll come after you himself?"

"Not if it puts his precious *principessa* in danger." Anger coils around my heart like a poisonous snake. My pulse grows more violent, my fingers curling to distract from the onslaught.

"Are you jealous of Bella?"

"No," I grit out. Aren't I though? Not of her exactly but that my brother has found a love so deep it's worth ruining everything for.

Rolling her eyes at me, she glances down at my phone to the black screen. "So now what do we do?"

"We wait."

CHAPTER 17
LAST BEAUTIFUL THING

S*erena*

An hour later and no call back from my mom. I've left two more messages with the number to the untraceable phone and Antonio even tried *Papà* again, this time leaving a detailed message about my capture. Where the hell could my dad be that he wouldn't answer his phone or at least check the voicemail? A hint of unease rattles in my ribcage, but I shove it down as I tug the brush through my wet hair.

After the shower and the new clothes, I feel almost normal. If I can just ignore the fact that I'm a prisoner and pretend I'm on a weekend getaway, I can trick my heart into pumping as it should, instead of the manic beats from earlier.

I don't doubt that *Papà* will do whatever it takes to get me back, but the fact that he seems unreachable has me on edge. Slowly twisting the knob on the bathroom door, I find my room empty. Both doors are ajar, the one leading to the hallway barely wide enough to make out Otto's form. His good eye peers through the opening, and his lips curl into a snarl when our gazes meet.

That guy is not my biggest fan.

As if the eye gouging thing isn't bad enough, I overheard Antonio ripping him a new one last night after my escape attempt. I think I'll try to avoid him for the near future. Instead, I turn toward the other door, the one which I'm assuming will lead me to a still brooding Antonio.

This kidnapping isn't going as planned and his temper escalated to new heights before he stormed off to shower. Reaching for the crutches which appeared in my room this morning, I hobble toward Antonio's room and pause in the doorway, peeking inside.

The bathroom door is ajar, and I can just make out slivers of tanned flesh blanketed in splotches of dark ink. Even through the crack, I can see the dips and valleys of his muscled torso. *Dio*, I love a man with tattoos.

Said no one ever who was being held hostage by said tattooed man.

Shaking my head of the stupid, I stagger forward, bumping into the doorframe with the unwieldy crutches. Antonio springs out of the bathroom, his eyes wide as he takes me in. But it cannot in any way match the wide-eyed stare I'm ogling him with. He's all endless expanse of carved muscles with only a towel hung around his waist. His body is a canvas of art, both physically innate and fashioned by the intricate patterns adorning his flesh.

Once I've forced my gaping jaw to shut, I attempt to string together a sentence. "Relax, I'm not trying to escape." For some reason, my ankle feels worse today than yesterday. Maybe it's because the pain meds the lovely doctor gave me are starting to wear off.

"Good girl." He smirks before turning to the dresser where all his clothes have now been neatly folded and stacked. He tugs a shirt over his head but leaves the flimsy towel which seems to be holding on by a thread. I force my gaze away from the sharp V that descends beneath the trail of dark hair.

"I was thinking you could try calling Tony. He's Luca's right-hand man. If there's something going on, he would know about it." I also tried calling my Uncle Luca and Aunt Stella in a desperate attempt an hour ago, only to reach more voicemails.

"Very well. Let me finish getting dressed, and we can try him next." He pulls out a pair of boxers from the drawer then turns toward the bathroom. He closes the door behind him, but again a sliver remains open. My curious gaze drifts through the opening, catching a glimpse of the towel hitting the floor.

Stop it, Serena. What is wrong with you?

Ripping my traitorous gaze away before it lands on any naughty bits, I glance out the glass doors to the lake instead. Yesterday, I'd barely had time to take in all the beauty. Now I see a small wooden boat bobbing along the shore.

Too bad we can't take it out for a little ride.

Not on vacation. Hostage! That annoying voice in my head resonates across the crazy.

Antonio reappears, now fully dressed, and I can't help the tiny twinge of disappointment at seeing his beautiful body covered up.

"So you like tattoos?" The question pops out before I can stop it.

"Mmm," he mutters.

"Do they mean anything?"

"Don't they always?" he counters.

"Touchè."

His gaze trails down my body as if he's memorized every inch of my naked form or maybe hoping he could peel away my clothes and figure out if they are concealing any hidden ink. Or weapons. "And you? Any tattoos?"

"Just one." My thoughts flicker to the bouquet of violets inked across my inner thigh. It's ironic because in Italian culture, violets are a symbol of modesty and faithfulness, neither exactly my forte. It was Nonna's best-loved flower, the one of her birth month and coincidentally her favorite color. When she passed away, I was flooded with the pain of her loss. And one night, indulging in too much alcohol, I marched to the nearest tattoo lounge and got it in memory of her.

"Of what?" That piercing gaze razes over me again.

"I'll let you see it when you let me go." I throw him my trademark smirk.

"You said I'd be dead soon after..."

She shrugs. "Maybe it'll be the last beautiful thing you see."

A flash of something unreadable surges across his midnight eyes, softening the hard lines of his jaw. Just when I think he's going to say more, he reaches for the phone on the dresser instead. "Let's make that call to Tony."

I hold Antonio's phone to my ear, my heartbeat escalating with each unanswered ring. I'm embarrassed when that familiar gruff voice resonates across the line, and hot tears spring to my eyes. For a second, I was worried something terrible had happened to all of them. How could no one answer any of my calls?

"Who is this?" Tony grumbles over the phone.

"Tony, it's me!" The humiliating high-pitched sound grates on my own ears.

"Serena, what's going on?"

"Where's *Papà*? He's not answering the phone. Is he okay?"

"Yeah, he's fine, don't worry, kid. He and Luca were pulled away to an emergency meeting with one of their distributors in a remote part of China. Your mom and aunt went with them. I imagine they're still flying."

I heave in a breath of relief.

"What's going on?"

Antonio snatches the phone away, and I throw him a scowl. "I need you to listen well, Tony. My name is Antonio Ferrara, and I have Serena in my possession. She hasn't been harmed and if you'd like to keep it that way, I suggest you have Dante call me the moment that jet lands."

"What the fuck do you mean you *have* Serena?" Tony snarls, the growl so enraged it bounces around the room.

"Just like it sounds." Antonio's voice is calm, icy cool in sharp contrast to Luca's righthand man. "I have some demands I need met before I return the lovely Serena to her father. You have until midnight your time."

"And if I can't reach him by then?"

"Serena's life will be forfeit."

A gasp hisses out as I watch in pure indignation as the asshole who just threatened my life jabs his finger at the call end button. Then he paces the length of the room, his steps growing more agitated with each circle. As if somehow all of this shit is my fault.

"So you're going to kill me if my father doesn't call you back"—I glance at the clock on the nightstand and do the conversion math—"in six hours?"

He cants his head over his shoulder, putting a pause to the manic pacing. "Serena…"

"What? That's what you just said. Are you going to torture me too? If I only have six hours left in this world, I deserve to know. There are things I need to do and—"

He lifts a hand, cutting me off. The towering man steps toward me, the scowl carved into his jaw softening a tad. "I'm not going to kill you…"

Unexpected relief crackles over me. "Yet?" I blurt.

He drags a hand through his hair, the only response. I spend the next few seconds just standing there, leaning on my crutch considering the possibilities. He wouldn't really kill me, right? Logically, it makes no sense. If I'm dead, he'll never get what he wants. *Papà* would destroy him and there'd be nothing left of the Ferrara name but bones and ash.

Consoling myself with the thought, I force myself to turn

around and do my best to stomp out in indignation, which is pretty damned hard on crutches.

"Serena!" His growl echoes into my room which I'm only halfway across because who the hell knew crutches were so hard to navigate?

Ignoring him, I keep moving toward the door which leads out to the hallway. I know Otto stands in front of it, but right now, I'd rather deal with him than the man who just threatened to kill me.

"Serena, wait!" Antonio's voice is close now, but I refuse to turn around.

Instead, I whip the door open and attempt to squirm by Otto, but his meaty hands clamp around my shoulders and slam me against the wall.

"Ow!" I squeal as the back of my head hits stucco and the crutches fall to the tile with a clatter. Damn it, that hurts.

Antonio is beside me a second later, cursing and hissing at Otto in Italian. "*Che cazzo fai?*" He glares down at the man with a look that would have most pissing themselves. Not me because I grew up in my dad's household, but most normal people, nonetheless. "I warned you once, Ottavio, keep your fucking hands off her." His fingers curl around his wrist and he twists it so far back, I wince at the sight. I wait for the pop of bones or at least tendons but Antonio releases his guard at the last minute. A tiny part of me is sorry he didn't finish the job. The asshole deserves it. "That is your final warning," he snarls. "I've been more than lenient with you. The next wrong move will have more permanent consequences."

"But she was trying to run away from you."

"I didn't ask for your excuses," Antonio barks. "Are we clear?"

A hint of satisfaction swirls in my middle at his harsh reaction to the dickhead guard.

Otto's good eye narrows as he regards me, the hatred

pouring out so potent through that one eye, he might as well have had twelve. "*Si, signore,*" he murmurs.

"Serena is mine to handle, *coglione*. How far do you think she possibly could have gotten on those things?" He ticks his head at the crutches splayed on the floor. "Now pick them up, hand them to her and apologize."

Otto stares at him incredulously.

Damn, Antonio's mood swings are making my head spin. One minute he's threatening to kill me and the next he's threatening to maim others or worse for touching me? Someone must be feeling guilty.

"Now," he hisses, that icy cool demeanor back.

With a grunt, Otto bends down and collects my fallen crutches. He hands them to me with a scowl.

"The apology…" Antonio snaps.

"*Scusi, signorina,*" he mutters through clenched teeth.

"Now get out of my sight before I lose my temper." He waves off his guard, and the man's angry footfalls reverberate across the quiet hall.

Gently running my fingers across the back of my head, I search for the bump I'm sure the big beast caused when he slammed me against the wall.

Antonio inches closer. "Are you alright?" The hard set of his jaw has softened but the murderous gleam in his eye remains.

"Why the hell do you care? If you're going to kill me anyway…"

"*Cazzo*, Serena, I'm not going to kill you." He huffs out a breath. "We both know that wouldn't get me anywhere with your father."

My brows furrow as I tip my head back to meet his weary gaze. "Is that the only reason?"

"It has to be."

CHAPTER 18
TERROR

S*erena*

I wander around the villa for the next few hours by myself, Antonio's callous remark to Tony still irritating me. Which I fully realize makes no sense. I'm a hostage, of course death is a possibility. But somehow in the past few days, I've felt like something shifted between us.

Clearly, I'm more deluded than I thought.

I pass through the perfectly manicured gardens and pause at a circle of lounge chairs positioned along the lake. For a house that's been abandoned for twenty-some odd years, everything is still pristine. Why would Antonio spend so much money to preserve the place if he had no plans to ever return here?

"*Buongiorno, signorina.*" Mariuccia appears from beneath a hedge of sweetly perfumed gardenia. She's on her hands and knees, pruning the deep green leaves.

"Buongiorno." I take a few shaky steps on the crutches toward her before she waves a hand.

"Please, sit, *signorina*. I would hate for you to fall on the uneven ground." She rises, shakes the dirt off her gloved hands, and walks toward me.

I wonder if she heard about my attempted escape last night. She's right, the ground is totally uneven and if Antonio hadn't caught me, I probably wouldn't have made it far before I landed on my ass. I plop onto the lounge chair, resting my crutches on the side and draw in a breath of fresh air. Leaning against the lounger, I brush the knot on the back of my head from that asshole Otto and wince.

Maybe I should have agreed to the ice Antonio had offered to lessen the swelling. Too late now.

Mariuccia folds down on the chair beside me, lively gray eyes on the rippling waves of Lago di Como before turning to me. Her gaze trails over my dress, and a smile curls the corners of her mouth.

"Thank you for the clothes, by the way. Antonio mentioned you went out last night to get them. That was very kind of you."

"I'm glad they fit. I had to guess on the size."

"They're perfect and just my style." I give her a warm smile in return. "And you bought me so many. I hope you don't know something I don't. I wasn't planning on being here long enough to use them all."

Her smile falters, and her darkening gaze pivots to the lake. "You know, Antonio wasn't always like this," she whispers a long moment later. "He was a good boy; all the brothers were. His mother's death hit him the hardest. He was the oldest, the one who felt he bore the responsibility." She draws in a shaky breath, pausing. "Alfredo, Tonio's father, wasn't even there when she died. It was only him and the two younger boys to face that terrible moment alone. Can you imagine? To watch your mother die in front of you…"

No, I couldn't. Mom was everything to me. Pain twists through my insides like a scalding blade to the heart. I shouldn't pity the man who is keeping my captive, but I do all the same. What the hell is wrong with me?

"I'm not trying to excuse any of this, *signorina*. What he's doing to you is cowardly and disgraceful. His mother would never forgive him for this. But I only want you to understand what brought him here. His father was not a kind man, and he only grew worse once their mother was gone. Maria Graziella was a joy to this world, a soul much too pure and kind to have ended up with a man like Alfredo." She shrugs, turning her gaze to the water once more.

"Can you help me?" I whisper.

She swivels to face me, sadness steeling into her pale gray eyes. "I wish I could, *signorina*. I'm scared… I have family I must protect, and I'm afraid I don't know the man Antonio has become. The boy I knew never would've gone to these lengths for any reason."

I nod slowly. "I understand." Besides, I've already promised to stay put twice now and risking Bella's life isn't worth my own. And I know *Papà* will come through any minute now, I just have to wait.

"I truly am sorry." She lowers her gaze to the verdant grass between us. "But I pray to *Dio* every day that Antonio will see the error in his ways."

Not likely. From what I've learned growing up with the Valentinos and Rossi's, bad men don't change. They soften, adjust a little for the ones they love, but everyone else can go to hell. Or at least that's been my experience with *Papà* and my uncles.

"I hope you're right," I finally murmur. "Where is my jailer anyway?" Not that I care.

"Tonio left the villa to take care of something in town. He'll be home soon."

I nod, an unexpected pang at hearing of his absence. It's not like he has to inform me of his whereabouts. He probably snuck out of here hoping I'd never find out. Or is this a test of some sort to see if I'll escape?

"Well, I must get back to work." Mariuccia springs up from the chair, collecting her pruning scissors. "Enjoy your afternoon, *signorina*."

"Thanks." I trail her stout form as she weaves between the thick hedges and disappears into the garden. As I sit and watch the lapping waves, my fingers twitch with something to do. Not having a phone or access to the internet makes me feel so disconnected. Not for the first time, I think about Santi. He's probably sitting in the office right now planning this evening's aperitivo. He probably thinks I abandoned him to return to my life in Manhattan. I wish I could talk to him, follow his crazy posts on Instagram. And weirdly enough, there's a certain peace that comes along with completely unplugging from the world that I never expected.

An hour later and the brisk air and huge lunch Fabi, the cook, brought out to me has my lids heavy. I could just take a nap right here beneath the warm sunlight, but maybe my bed would be more comfy.

Forcing myself to sit up, I reach for my crutches and manage to stand without toppling over. *Woohoo!* From running in stilettos to this… how did I fall so far?

By the time I make it up to my room, I'm practically panting. Jumping up that sprawling staircase has my chest heaving and my armpits sore as hell. Maybe I'll just stay up here for the rest of the night. *If I survive that long…* That stupid dark voice echoes across my mind.

I glance at the antique gilded clock on the mantel and internally cringe. Only two more hours until the deadline. Steeling my nerves, I convince myself Tony could have already gotten ahold of Pa by now, and my dad could've already spoken to my captor. In fact, he could be on the way for me as we speak.

Taking a nap will be the perfect distraction. When I wake up, my bags could already be packed and ready to go. I turn the meandering hallway that leads to the master, and I'm shocked when I find the corridor empty. Where's my friendly guard?

There's no way Antonio left me alone in the villa with only Mariuccia, Fabi and the guards stationed outside. Even he must notice his housekeeper's traitorous tendencies. A yawn splits my lips, and I force my weary muscles to keep going just a few more steps. Too bad I don't have it in me to attempt another escape because it seems like the perfect time.

When I finally reach my room, I can't get into bed fast enough. Performing a dainty belly flop, I sink into the plush mattress and a groan slips out. If only Santi could see me now...

With all the kidnapping drama, I completely forgot about the internship at Dolce & Gabbana. Did I get it? Did Santiago? If I ever get out of this mess, I'm going straight to Bianca and begging for my job back. The thought is surprising as it flits through my mind. A part of me just wants to go home to Manhattan and forget all of this ever happened, but the other half doesn't want to give up on my dream of living the life of a fashionista in Milano.

Shaking my head of the pointless thoughts, I draw the comforter up to my chin. I'm not going anywhere but to sleep right now. My heavy lids droop closed almost instantly.

What feels like only minutes later, I'm awoken by a strange prickle up my spine, a sense of awareness I can't quite name. My eyes pop open just as a big hand clamps over my mouth.

Terror rushes my veins as I recognize the bandaged eye over the hand blocking most of my vision. Otto's free hand holds a switchblade, hovering just a few inches above my face. I scream, but it's muffled by his meaty palm.

"Hold still you *maledetta puttana!*"

"Let go!" I grit out but it's nothing but a stifled groan.

"Since Antonio brought you here, you've been nothing but trouble. First, you almost take my eye, then you cost me an entire week's pay and now the capo is threatening physical punishment because of you. What the fuck is it about you?" He moves on top of me, pinning me down to the mattress.

"Get off!" I wriggle and squirm, but the man is just too heavy, his weight crushing me to the bed.

His one good eye narrows. "Are you fucking the boss? Is that why he's so obsessed with you?" He glances at his watch, then at the jagged blade in his hand. "It's already past midnight and you're still alive. I've never seen Antonio falter on a vow, not once in his life." He brings the knife to my throat, and a mixture of raw fury and panic crash over me. "So I'm going to make sure he sticks to his word. But first, I need to see what makes that pussy of yours so phenomenal that in only a few days, I don't even recognize the man who I've known for years."

With his hand still covering my mouth, he balances on one elbow and tugs his pants down, freeing his cock with the switchblade still in his hand.

No. No. No.

This is not happening.

I scream again and try to get my knee up between his legs, but I'm hopelessly trapped. The man is a fucking beast and heavy as all hell.

"I can't wait to slam into that tight pussy and teach you a lesson," he hisses as he runs his dick across my panties.

With his focus on pulling my underwear off with one hand while still juggling the knife, his hold over my mouth loosens just enough so that I can sink my teeth into a finger. He lets out an angry roar as I clamp down so hard, the warm coppery taste of blood fills my mouth.

Oh, *Dio*, disgusting.

"You fucking bitch!" he roars and jerks his hand back before slamming it down full force across my cheek.

The crack echoes over the wild roar of my pulse across my eardrums. I squeeze my eyes closed, dazed from the hit and the knot on the back of my head is throbbing again.

"Now, you're really going to pay." He slices the knife across the waistband of my panties, the sharp bite of the blade digging into my skin.

Another scream peals out as my thong falls away, leaving me exposed.

Pure menace radiates across that one eye as he holds me down and positions himself at my entrance. "I'm going to fuck you until you learn some respect, you spoiled princess."

"No!" The blood curdling shriek explodes from my lips and my eyes slam closed, desperate to escape the sickening reality. "No, please no!"

CHAPTER 19
TOO SOFT

A*ntonio*

Serena's scream echoes across the villa as I step into the foyer. My heart catapults up my throat, and sheer terror rushes my veins. My feet are moving before I can stop them, sprinting up the stairs toward that panicked cry.

"Serena!" I howl.

Mariuccia races in behind me, but I'm barely aware of her shouts.

Who could have possibly gotten to her? A thousand questions swirl through my mind as I turn corridor after corridor in a mad dash to reach her room. When I see her doorway at the end of the hall, I pump my arms faster, desperate to reach her. I'm torn between wanting to shout to her, to tell her I'm coming and keeping my mouth shut to get the drop on her attacker.

I'm going to tear the *bastardo* limb from limb.

I reach the doorway, and red-hot fury burns through my veins. Ottavio pins Serena to the bed, her long legs kicking and writhing beneath him. Otto? Crimson bleeds through my vision, a blinding rage like I've never felt before flooding my system. I trusted that *pezzo di merda* implicitly. I lunge, grabbing the traitor by the back of the neck.

"What the fuck are you doing?" I howl as I yank him off.

The anger only intensifies when I see his cock out and Serena's torn panties. Then my furious gaze lands on the angry red mark across her cheek, and all I see is crimson. He stands at the foot of her bed, hunger in his eyes. A whirlwind of Italian curses explodes from my mouth as I start to process what's happening.

Otto flashes the knife at me, a smattering of blood on the blade, and the monster I keep buried inside surges to the surface. Jagged claws tear at my insides, desperate to shred everything in its path. "How dare you touch what's mine?" I roar and twist his wrist until I hear the satisfying snap of bone, and he drops the blade with a scream. It falls to the tile with a clang.

He stuffs his dick in his pants with his good hand and lowers his gaze to the floor between us. "You said you would kill her—"

"How the fuck do you know what I said? Are you eavesdropping on my conversations?" There's a tremor in my voice, a rage I don't recognize torching through my veins like wildfire.

"I didn't mean to, I just heard, and I thought—"

"I don't pay you to think, *testa di cazzo!*" I lunge again, unable to keep my twitching hands from around his neck. "I pay you to obey my every word, and I told you never to touch her again." I eye the fireplace tool set, desperate to bash his head in with that bronze poker.

He swallows hard, his Adam's apple bobbing beneath my thumbs. I press harder and his eyes bulge, two wild, dark orbs of pure fear. His gaze flickers to the discarded knife, but I kick it out of his reach, burying it beneath the bed. Behind me, a faint whimper escapes Serena's lips and darkness encroaches my vision. "Not only did you touch her, you tried to rape her?" I snarl. "Since when do we do that?"

I slightly release the pressure on his throat so he can speak.

"I don't know, *capo*. Everything's been different with her," he pants, cradling his likely broken wrist. "From the moment you saw her all those months ago outside the club, you haven't been acting right."

"I haven't been acting right?" I barely recognize my own voice. It has a deep, sinister quality unlike my own.

"Yeah. For months, you knew it was Dante pulling the strings in Rome, but you were so fixated on Raf's girl, Isabella, instead of facing the real problem head on. You should have gone for Serena from the start."

"So now you're giving me advice on how to run *my* organization?"

"Yes," he rasps out. "Your father would have killed her by now or at least tortured her to show Dante he meant business. Instead, you coddle her, buy her nice clothes, bring her dinner in bed. I'm only trying to help you, *capo*."

"Help me? Because I need *your* help?" My fingers clamp down tighter from the rage polluting my veins.

"All the heads of households in Rome are just waiting for the Ferraras to crumble to pick off the pieces. The Salernos, Sartoris, they're only the beginning. The rest of your men are too scared to say it. Even Pietro agrees. Your *Papà* was a hard man, a man who knew what he had to do to run an organization like this. You—"

"I what?" I glare at the piece of shit, waiting for him to dare speak the word. I know it's coming. Even Mariuccia who snuck into the room a few minutes ago and lingers at the door knows exactly what this *figlio di puttana* is about to say.

"You're too soft," he spits.

Wrath uncoils in my gut, potent and poisonous as my eyes narrow, drilling into a man who had faithfully served my family for years. "Maybe you're right, Otto." I force my lips to curve into a smile. "Maybe I have been too lenient since taking control of the Ferrara territory. But that changes tonight." I release my hold and take a measured step back, grinning like a psychopath, the smile much too wide considering the rage twisting my insides. "Thank you for bringing this to my attention."

Relief softens his pinched features, and he heaves out a breath. "You're wel—"

Before he can finish, I jab the side of my hand into his throat, cutting off his air supply. Then I kick his leg out from under him, and the big guy hits the floor with a thud, rasping for oxygen.

He lets out a shriek as he slams into the tile, panting and dazed. Muttered gasps echo around me, but I ignore them, focusing only on the *imbecille* who dared lay hands on Serena then had the balls to question me. Dropping over him so he thrashes beneath me, I pull my arm back and let my fist loose. The crunch of bone breaking bone begins to satisfy the thirst for vengeance eating at me. *Lex talionis. An eye for an eye.* I hit him again and again. That darkness sweeps in, blotting out the screaming women and the writhing man beneath me.

Pressing all my weight down on him, my thighs straddling his midsection, I'm an unmovable force. I'm fairly certain he snapped something in his back when he fell because he's not putting up as much of a fight as I'd expected. Soon it's not only the lack of air that's a problem. He's choking on his own damned blood. I finally pause, my knuckles torn and bloodied, and loom over him.

"You think anyone will think I'm soft now, Ottavio?"

His lips are so swollen he doesn't utter a sound. Instead, his head barely turns to the side.

"What do you say I display your head on a pike outside the gates of the villa? Do you think then the others will stop saying I've gone soft, *coglione*?"

Fear sparks across his bloodied, bruised eyes. They're barely open now.

"And then what if I drag your eviscerated entrails across the center of Roma for your betrayal? Do you think then they'll believe I'm just as savage as my father?"

His head slowly dips.

"Good. Then that's exactly what I'll do." I reach for the metal poker by the hearth and hold it high over my head.

A tear streaks down his cheek, clearing a path through the crimson painting his face. "No, please," he murmurs.

"Did Serena beg? Did she ask you not to defile her with your filthy cock?"

His lips go still.

"But you were going to do it anyway. You dared to touch my property, my *tesoro*, not only with your hands but with your fucking cock! Serena is mine, and I will use your gutted, mangled body as a warning for anyone who ever tries to take her away from me again."

Before he can utter another lying, traitorous word, I bring the poker down with all my strength burying the pointed end into his good eye. Screams fill the chamber as he thrashes beneath me for only a second before I drive it in deeper, piercing his skull and reaching the soft, delicate brain tissue.

His muscles tense for an instant before his entire body relaxes beneath me, mouth falling open.

A sudden stillness blankets the room.

I sit there, straddling the dead *bastardo*, my nostrils flaring as I attempt to reel in the rage. The pungent, metallic scent of blood permeates the air, and crimson stains my vision. For an instant, I'm transported back in time to another villa, this one consumed in smoke instead of blood.

Fire licks up my back as I carry *Papà*'s body through the blazing inferno. All I see, all I feel is scorching pain. The flames race across my shirt, then devour my skin, destroying everything in its path. It's a miracle I survive... or at least that's what the doctor says when I emerge from the wreckage.

"Tonio!"

I blink quickly, banishing the grisly thoughts of the past and meet pale gray eyes. Mariuccia stands over me, horror written across her features as her gaze pivots between my own and the poker protruding from Otto's face. It seems as if she's moving and speaking in slow motion. "Tonio, you must get up. I will call Pietro and have him send someone."

She helps me stand and the scene coalesces around me, back to normal speed. I nod slowly at Mariuccia, then watch as she marches out of the room. I finally hazard a glance over my shoulder to face *her*. I promised she'd be okay, told her she would be safe as long as Dante came through. Now her father is MIA and one of my own damned men had tried to rape her.

Her eyes meet mine, the range of emotions streaking through the brilliant sky blue indecipherable. A spiral of rage, fear and something else... something I can't quite pin down surges to the surface. She jerks her shirt down—no, my shirt, she's still sleeping in my shirt, stretching it until it covers her legs.

That *bastardo* tried to rape her while she wore *my* shirt. How the fuck dare he? I wish he was still alive so I could kill him again, more slowly this time so I could savor every second of his agony.

I open my mouth to speak, to say what I have no idea. To apologize?

Cazzo, maybe.

But my phone rings and I jerk it out of my pocket. I don't recognize the number on the screen, but I sure as hell recognize that country code. My eyes flicker to Serena's for an instant before I press the call answer button.

"*Pronto?*"

"Release my daughter immediately, Antonio, or I will rain hell on you and everyone you've ever met. The streets of Rome will run crimson with the blood of the Ferraras, and I will let you live until the end, so that you can watch as I tear you apart limb from limb then beat you to death with your own fucking bones."

CHAPTER 20
COMPLICATED

S*erena*

I'm in shock. I recognize the symptoms, the tremor running through my body, the icy chill surging through my veins despite the comforter I'm curled under, the muffled sounds, the slow movements, all of it.

Antonio's wild gaze lands on mine, and instead of the terror it should bring after that gruesome display, I feel a tiny measure of relief. That dark glare grounds me somehow. Even the blood splattered across his face and dress shirt don't ignite the fear it should. I just watched this man beat another guy to death and not just anyone but his own employee.

Still, I hold his gaze for an agonizing moment until his phone rings.

He rips his eyes from mine, dropping them to the screen. The moment he answers, I know who's on the other line. Only my father could make a man like Antonio Ferrara, one still covered in the blood of his guard, go utterly pale in the span of a second.

Antonio clears his throat, the mask of calm he typically wears falling over his features and his color returns. "There is no need for threats, *Signor* Valentino."

I can just make out muffled shouts from the other end of the line. If I could only get my brain to start functioning, I would ask him to put it on speaker.

"Serena will be returned home safe and sound as soon as my demands are met."

More screaming from the other end.

I can only imagine what *Papà* is threatening to do to my captor. I wish I was in the right state of mind to enjoy it. But right now, all I can think about is what would have happened if Antonio hadn't returned in time.

I tug the comforter up to my chin, trying in vain to dispel the cold that's settled deep in my bones. *Dio*, how could something like sex which I love so much be used against me like this? I feel so completely powerless. I've never felt anything like this my entire life, and I've been held at gunpoint, shot at and chased more times than I care to remember.

But it was nothing like *this*.

"Serena?" Antonio's voice is surprisingly soft as he approaches me. "Your father would like to speak to you."

Panic overwhelms me. He'll know. The minute I talk to him, *Papà* will know something is wrong. And Dio, he can *never* know. I'd take this secret with me to the grave. Serena Valentino cannot be seen as weak, and that man had me at my most frail. Worse, Antonio had witnessed it, too.

He presses the phone into my palm when I don't make a move to take it, eyes searching mine. I shake my head, desperately. Brows knitting, his finger jabs at the mute button, then he folds down onto the bed, remaining at the very edge of the mattress.

"You have to speak to your father," he whispers. "He wants to know you're alive."

"I can't," I hiss.

"Serena, you must. All of this is hinging on you."

I draw in a breath, fully aware of how ridiculous I sound, but *Dio*, I just cannot speak to my father right now. Not so soon after—

Antonio must read the panic in my eyes because he heaves out a breath and unmutes the line, pressing the speaker button. "She's in the shower. I'll have her call you back in the next half hour."

More shouting, and this time I can make out each and every Italian curse that explodes from my father's mouth through the speaker.

"She's fine, trust me."

"I don't have to trust you for shit, Antonio." *Papà*'s furious howls echo across the room. "You took my fucking daughter, you cowardly *pezzo di merda*. If you don't get her on the phone in the next five minutes, I'm going to get on a plane, hunt you down, cut off your cock and shove it down your throat until you choke on your own cum."

Antonio swallows hard, his eyes lifting to mine in a desperate plea.

I lift a finger, signaling for him to wait, and shove the comforter back before dragging myself out of bed. Tugging at the hem of Antonio's shirt, I make sure my ass isn't hanging out. The idea of even looking at the torn panties sends my stomach into somersaults. I force my feet toward the bathroom, then run the water on full force. Through the open door, I motion for Antonio to come in.

Drawing in a steadying breath, I reach for the phone and force my tongue to move. "I'm fine, Pa," I call out over the rushing water.

"*Cazzo*, Serena, how did this happen? I'm going to murder that son of a bitch—"

"I'm okay, *Papà*. Antonio's been the perfect abductor. Just do what he says so I can go home."

"Of course I will, *cuore mio*. It's just that it will take a few days. Your mother and I and Luca and Stella had some business to attend to in Asia. We're a bit isolated here, and it'll require some time to get my men out of his territory."

He's being oddly evasive. For some reason, he doesn't want Antonio to know where he is or what he's doing.

"Just do it quickly, okay? I have to go—"

"Wait, you're sure he hasn't hurt you?"

"No, *Papà*, Antonio hasn't hurt me." My eyes lift to meet the eldest Ferrara brother, lingering in the doorway, and maybe I'm imagining it, but something like regret surges across the dark surface.

Then he reaches for the phone, and I hand it over, eager to end the call with my father. He's always known me too well. And now with the pleasant steam of the shower filling the room, there's nothing I want more than to wash away the feel of Otto's hands on me.

Antonio walks out, my father still yelling in his ear, and I lock the door behind him. Now alone in the safety of the grand, master bathroom, I strip off my clothes and unlock the dam. Tears stream down my cheeks, my entire body shuddering from the stress of keeping the sobs at bay.

My knees give and I drop down to the floor, the cold tile sending another chill up my spine. I bury my head in my hands and allow the tears to fall until there's nothing left. Once I'm good and numb, I crawl toward the claw foot tub, turn off the overhead shower and haul myself into the warm water.

Closing my eyes, I lean my head on the edge of the basin, carefully avoiding the tender bump. A pair of soulless, dark orbs flash across my vision, and fear snaps my eyes open once again. A strong hand holds me down, a sickening warm breath drifting across my face, then another hand runs down to my panties.

No. *Dio*, no.

My pulse skyrockets as vivid images of the attack flood my mind. Attempting to clear my thoughts, I slide down beneath the water until my heartbeat begins to slow. Everything is muffled around me and for a few seconds, there's peace. But my breath is quickly fading, and I'm forced to emerge.

I don't know how long I stay in the tub, but by the time I get out, my fingers are wrinkly and the chill has returned to my bones.

Wrapped in a new robe that just appeared in my bathroom today, I open the door a crack. Antonio sits at the foot of the bed, at the exact same spot I left him. He rises when his eyes find mine, hands twisted into a knot. "I—I wanted to be here if you needed anything."

Ignoring his comment, I eye the bed, then the puddle of blood on the floor. Otto is gone, along with my torn panties, and I can't help but wonder what Antonio did with them. Or was it another one of his goons to dispose of the grisly reminder of the assault? Would I really find the former guard's head on a spike outside the villa? A dark, deeply buried part of me wants to see the asshole pay. I'd enjoyed seeing Antonio beat the shit out of him. I would never admit that out loud, of course.

I draw in a breath, banishing the dark thoughts. I'm not a monster. Not a monster. Just because I have the Valentino name, doesn't mean I have to follow in my family's questionable footsteps. Look at Isabella, she's going to be a doctor.

A weariness sets in as I stand there, after the spiking adrenaline and the relaxing bath. A part of me wants to sink back under the sheets, but the other part is loath to ever sleep in that bed again. So instead, I remain standing, hugging the soft fabric of the terrycloth robe and rubbing my arms to spread the warmth. On the bright side, I re-wrapped my ankle, and it feels a little better.

"What did *Papà* say?"

"He said Tony will begin the negotiations while he's otherwise detained. I've agreed to giving him seventy-two hours before—"

"Before what?" I snap. "Before you kill me?" Anger. Isn't that one of the steps? Yes, anger is good. It's much better than fear or pain. I latch onto it, wafting air onto the growing flames.

"Serena, you know how these things work."

"No, actually I don't. Because no one has ever been stupid enough to take me hostage."

"You know it's not what I wanted…"

"Right, you wanted Isabella, but thanks to Raf, you couldn't get close enough. So I'm your second choice." I pace the room, the fury growing with each staggered step. "So now what? *Papà* is presumably doing exactly what you've asked, so what do I do in the meantime?"

"We wait."

"Wait for another one of your goons to attack me?"

His eyes widen, mouth curving into a capital O like I slapped him. As if I'm the one insulting his integrity.

"Did you not see what I just did to Otto? That man has worked for my family for twenty years. I did that for *you*." His eyes are wild as they regard me. "I made an example of him so that anyone who comes across your path again will think very hard before daring to lay a finger on you, *tesoro*." This time my nickname holds a whole new connotation, one I'm not sure I like any better.

"Of course I saw," I hiss. "It was hard to avoid the blood splatter."

He stands, dragging his hand through his mussed-up dark locks. "*Cazzo*, everything has gone wrong in the past few days. This is not at all how it was supposed to go."

"Did you think kidnapping me would be easy? That my father would simply bend to your will? That *I* would bend to your will?"

"I don't know," he growls. "But I never meant for this to happen." He motions at the bloody pool on the floor. "Or for anyone to *ever* touch you. Not like that…"

"So are you waiting for a thank you?" I snap.

"No!" he grits out. "I only want you to know that I would never have allowed that. That is not the type of man I am."

"Then what type of man are you, Antonio?" I slap my hands on my hips and glare up at him. "Because according to your dead guard you haven't been acting like yourself either."

"This was supposed to be a simple business transaction, that is all."

"And now what? It's gotten complicated?"

"Yes," he hisses. "Otto is right. If it had been my father to have captured you, he would have beaten you bloody by now. He would have sent pictures to Dante, he would have tortured you for information you likely don't have. But I can't—"

"Why?"

He inches closer, those dark orbs searing to mine, wild and chaotic. "I don't know."

"Yes, you do." I narrow my eyes at him, challenging. I've grown up in this world, and I know the dark truths. You must be willing to do anything to get what you want, to succeed and become a savage prince among ruthless royals.

He closes the distance between us, eyes devouring every inch of me. "Because of you," he growls. "And maybe even this damned house. Together, you've done something to me in the past few days. You've forced me to reconsider everything, damn it. You've made me *soft*."

A satisfied smile curls my lips as I regard him. "Good."

CHAPTER 21
GHOSTS

A *ntonio*

A thick tension swirls in the air, the atmosphere oppressive in this once beautiful chamber. I glance across the room at Serena, at the fire in her eyes, despite the obvious trauma she's endured. More than that, she remains standing, shoulders pinned back, even though I can detect the occasional wince when she bears too much weight on her bad ankle.

I've never known a woman like her. She's sharp-witted, with a mouth like a sailor, confident, fearless and of course, gorgeous. Most men I know would've crumbled after the past few days and here she is still staring me down, not a speck of fear in those blazing pools of infinite blue.

She should be lying down or at the very least, sitting. I've never had to comfort someone who's gone through attempted rape, but an assault is an assault, and the resulting feelings must be dealt with or they'll only simmer and grow.

I remind myself that if all goes according to plan in a few

days, she'll be back home with her family. They'll help her deal with the trauma; it's not my responsibility to fix it.

Isn't it though? A voice that sounds terribly like *Mamma*'s echoes through my mind.

"Sit down," I command, my tone harsh in a feeble attempt to mask the guilt eating away at my insides.

Her brow arches as she regards me incredulously.

I never should have admitted how I was feeling. *Soft. Dio, Papà* must be rolling over in his grave. She'll never take me seriously now. I'd only said it in an effort to comfort her, to level the playing field. And it wasn't a lie, however strongly I wish it was.

How can someone turn your world upside down in a matter of minutes?

No… Otto was right. I hadn't been myself since that night I'd first laid eyes on her outside of my club in Roma. Only a few words, some loaded glances, and she'd permanently etched herself into my mind.

Dio, is that why I broke things off with Stefania?

The thought only occurs to me now.

"Serena…" Her name on my tongue is more of a plea than a demand. "The doctor made it clear you had to stay off that ankle."

She crosses her arms over her chest and glares at me defiantly. "I can't," she hisses.

"You can't walk?" I rise, my feet moving toward her with a magnetic pull I can't explain.

"No," she grits out. "I don't want to—" She waves her hand in the direction of the bed and understanding punches me in the gut. *Dio*, I'm a *stronzo*. Of course, she doesn't want to lie in the bed where she was just attacked.

"Right," I mutter, eyes cast down to the floor. Heaving out a breath, I move toward the adjoining door. "My bed then…" As I realize the insinuation, heat races up my neck, settling across my cheeks. Lifting my gaze, I find her wide-eyed one. "You can have my bed," I quickly clarify.

She nods, the move faint but there all the same. She takes a step gingerly, testing her ankle and when it holds, she limps past me, leaving the crutches beside the bed where they lay untouched.

She's wincing, and *Dio* every pucker of her lips is another stab of guilt. Before I can think of all the reasons why I shouldn't, I sweep her off her feet and tuck her against my chest. "Let me help you," I whisper.

She stiffens against me for only a second before she relaxes in my arms. A tear slips down her cheek as I walk the remaining steps into my bedroom, and that fury I tried so hard to bury returns full force.

This woman has been through hell because of me in the past few days. I reach the bed and gently lower her onto the mattress. She immediately curls up in the middle of the sprawling king, tucking the comforter under her chin. She doesn't look at me again, keeping her gaze firmly pinned through the glass doors of the *terrazzo* and the rippling lake beyond.

"Would you like something to eat?" I whisper.

"No, I'm not hungry." Still, her eyes refuse to meet mine.

"Okay, I'll let you rest then." I pivot toward the door, but the rustle of sheets swings my head back over my shoulder. Serena is sitting straight up, eyes glistening orbs of pure sapphire.

"Can you just stay for a little while?" She ticks her head to the foot of the bed. "In case *Papà* calls again or something. I don't want to miss it."

I nod slowly, understanding followed by another stab of guilt wrenching my insides. Of course she won't admit she's frightened to be alone. *Dio*, I'm the *bastardo* that left her by herself with Otto in the first place. This is all my fault.

Sinking onto the edge of the mattress, I watch her watching me. I can almost see her measuring the distance between us, too close or too far away? I can't quite tell.

"Rest, *tesoro*," I whisper. "I will wake you if Dante calls."

"Even if he doesn't... I don't want to sleep for too long, because then I'll never get over this jet lag."

"Your body needs rest after—" I snap my jaw shut when I see the pain encroaching into her features. "Just rest. I'll be here."

Nodding, she lies back down, curling into the down comforter so she's on her side facing the lake again. I only hope the calming ripples of the Como will soothe the turmoil of the day. I watch her for what feels like an eternity, her eyes snapping open a moment after they close. Each time her eyes instinctively search to find mine. Once she's convinced I've remained as promised, they close once again. Multiple times she repeats the torture until she finally gives up the battle, and her lids droop shut for good.

Thank *Dio*.

Once she's asleep, I pull out my phone and shoot off a few messages to Pietro. Hopefully things in Roma are going better than here. I update him on the situation with Dante and warn him to remain on guard. Valentino isn't stupid enough to try anything, not with his precious daughter in my hands.

Lifting my gaze from the screen to the sleeping mafia princess, I allow myself a minute to take her in. Without those darting eyes piercing through to my very soul, I can enjoy the soft pucker of her pink lips, the gentle rise and fall of her chest, the tangle of blonde locks splayed across her pillow like a halo.

She's beautiful when she sleeps... hell, she's beautiful in the most unimaginably awful scenario, kidnapped and nearly raped.

Merda, what did I do?

I inch closer, my hand finding hers. It's as cold as ice. Tangling my warm fingers through hers, I bend over her head and whisper, "Rest, *tesoro*. I swear I'll never let anyone hurt you again." Her sweet strawberry scent reaches my nostrils, and I lean closer, brushing my lips across her forehead. "*Sogni d'oro.*" *Sweet dreams.*

Soft footfalls tear me to the present, and my head spins over my shoulder. Mariuccia tiptoes into the room, carrying a mug of chamomile tea, the sweet fragrance immediately filling the space. "I thought she would be unable to sleep," she whispers.

"It took her awhile, but the exhaustion won out."

She motions to the chair in the corner. "I can stay with her so that you can handle your *business*." She speaks the final word with so much contempt it's like another punch to the gut.

"I've already handled it. A clean-up crew is on its way."

"Still, I can stay—"

"I said no," I bark, the reply coming out harsher than intended. Drawing in a steadying breath, I face the woman who was like a second mother to me. "*Scusi*. Serena isn't the only one exhausted after the past few days. I appreciate the offer, but I will stay with her as I promised."

"Oh." A half-smile tugs at the corner of her lips.

"Don't look at me like that," I mutter.

"Like what, *signore*?" Her eyes sparkle with delight as she sets the cup on the nightstand and turns toward the door.

My only response is a weary eyeroll.

She must see her opening and takes a chance, inching closer. "I know you, Antonio Ferrara." She jabs a wrinkled finger into my chest. "And *this* is not you. There is still time to make it right. Take the girl back to her family."

"I can't," I hiss. "Everything *Papà* built rests on this, on her…"

"Tonio, who cares? Who needs an empire if you don't have real happiness, true love, or a big family to share it with?"

"You don't understand, you simply can't." My fingers curl into fists. "I must do this for *Papà*."

"Your father is dead, Tonio!" Those blazing orbs sear into my own as she regards me. "Ghosts don't need empires either. It is only your pride and your thirst for revenge guiding you now."

I bite my tongue, smothering the building anger, because I know I won't win this argument. Mariuccia doesn't know me, not the man I was forced to become. "It's too late," I finally murmur.

"It's never too late, *figlio mio*." With those final two words, *my son*, she whirls toward the door and steps out as quietly as she'd come in, her words lingering in the air for hours later.

CHAPTER 22
HE STAYED

S*erena*

Shards of brilliant light pierce the translucent curtains, drawing me from a fitful sleep. Muttering a curse, I roll over and pull the comforter up over my head. Wait a second. Morning already?

My eyes snap open and I jolt straight up, a strangling fear squeezing my lungs. A familiar figure is sprawled across the foot of the bed, long legs dangling over the side. With those dark eyes finally closed and that intrusive gaze shuttered, I take a minute to allow myself to trace those dark lashes, defined jaw and masterfully sculpted cheekbones. Those damned Ferrara genes might be ruthless, but damn are they pretty to look at.

Antonio breathes slowly, the softness in his expression at such odds with the typically hard mask he wears. He looks younger, more like the boy in the picture. My heart pinches at the sight of him curled by the footboard, still in his clothes from last night.

He stayed. All night.

Shoving down the unexpected warm and fuzzies, I remind myself it's this asshole's fault that I was assaulted yesterday afternoon. Not to mention the sprained ankle, and the fact that he's still keeping me prisoner.

With the irritation once again alive and burning, I toss a pillow at the slumbering mob boss.

He bolts straight up, reaching for the gun at his hip before his eyes meet mine, and he mutters a curse. "*Cazzo*, Serena. I thought we were under attack."

"Why didn't you wake me up?"

"What?" he groans as he runs his fingers through his sleep-tousled hair.

"You let me sleep all night and now I'll never get over this damned jet lag." I glance at the clock and point. "You see? It's just six o'clock in the morning. No one should be up this early."

"Agreed," he grumbles around a yawn.

Judging by the dark circles lining the soft skin beneath his eyes, I doubt he got the more than fourteen hours of sleep I enjoyed.

Damn, I guess I really was exhausted.

Images of Otto's hands crawling down my leg surge to the forefront of my mind, and a chill rushes up my spine. Blinking quickly, I chase away the disturbing memories. *I'm fine. He tried but failed.*

Thanks to the man who spent the night at my feet.

"I'm getting up," I announce. "Feel free to make yourself comfortable." I motion to the top of the bed as I slide to the edge.

"So kind of you to allow me to sleep in my own bed."

"Yeah, well, you don't look so rested."

"You certainly know how to make a man feel good, *tesoro*." The hint of a smile kicks up the corner of his lips.

"You have no idea, *amico*." For a second, I sound and feel like my old self again. I can do this. I can bury the unwanted tangle of fear, guilt and anger bloating my chest and focus on something more productive. I don't need that single terrible moment to define me. "Did *Papà* call back last night?"

"No, but Tony did. We've begun the negotiations. He assures me that all will be settled in the next day or so."

Again, I can't help but wonder what has my father so tied up that he can't even negotiate his only daughter's release. Not that I'm ready to speak to him yet, but maybe by tomorrow…

Wrapping the robe more tightly around my middle, I place my feet on the floor and test out my ankle. Definite improvement. I push myself out of bed and head toward the bathroom before I remember I'm still not wearing any panties. The idea of going back into that room has nausea clawing up my throat.

Antonio still lies on the bed, watching me from the corner of his eye. It occurs to me that this robe only reaches about mid-thigh and from his angle, he just might be able to see— I move further away from the bed and yank on the hem, making sure it completely covers my ass. Then I turn back at the doorway of the bathroom, steeling my resolve. "Can you grab me some clothes?" I tick my head toward my old bedroom, praying he doesn't question the favor.

Propping his head up on his palm, that piercing stare rakes over me, as if he can somehow read the truth I'm not ready to give. A long minute later, his head dips. Before I disappear into the bathroom, I call out over my shoulder, "Don't forget a bra and panties."

I catch the shock in his expression, his mouth parting, eyes widening, just before I close the door behind me, and it's oddly satisfying. Clearly, this man has never had a live-in girlfriend. That too, I find oddly satisfying.

When I emerge from the bathroom a few minutes later, faced wash and hair slightly less wild, Antonio stands beside the bed staring at a pile of clothes. "I didn't know what you wanted to wear."

"So you just dumped out the entire contents of the closet?"

He shrugs. "*Cazzo*, what the hell do I know?"

Yeah, this man has never had a serious relationship.

On top of the pile is an assortment of lace panties and bras, courtesy of the lovely Mariuccia. He's staring at them like they might attack if he dares look away. Walking slowly so the limp isn't that obvious, I rifle through the pile. Normally, I'd go for the cute, flirty sundresses, but for some reason, today I search for cozy sweats. And come up empty. Understandable, since it's only the first week of September and the chilly autumn weather hasn't quite settled in yet.

"What's wrong?" He eyes me from across the bed.

"I don't know... I just wanted something else."

"I brought you everything Mariuccia bought."

My arms curl around my middle, a sudden chill prickling the tiny hairs on my flesh. "I know, and normally, I'd be all about it. I just don't feel like wearing a dress today, okay?"

Antonio's expression darkens, and something like understanding flashes across those bottomless midnight irises. He spins around and marches toward his closet, then tosses me a sweatshirt. "It'll be a little big on you, but it's warm."

I hug the soft cotton to my chest and the musky scent of amber and fresh lavender fills my nostrils. It's warm and comforting and just what I needed. How the hell did he know?

"I have the sweatpants too, but they'll definitely be too big on you."

"That's okay, I can roll them up."

He eyes me warily before turning back to his closet and pulling the navy sweats off the hangar.

"Bocconi?" I eye the insignia of the university on the sweatshirt.

"Yes. I moved to Milano when I was eighteen and got my business degree there before returning to Roma to learn the family business."

"Impressive." In my short time living in the city, I've already heard about the famous institution. It's like the Harvard of Italy.

"Too bad you didn't use all those brains for good instead of evil."

A chuckle pierces the air between us. "I had little choice, *tesoro*."

"We always have a choice." I shrug before shooing him away so I can change.

"You go in the bathroom, and I'll change out here." He motions toward the closet.

I'd almost forgotten he still wore his dress shirt from yesterday. "Sure," I mumble before returning to the bathroom once more.

Antonio and I eat breakfast in a semi-comfortable silence with the cook, Fabi, already preparing this evening's meal. I've barely eaten since I arrived, and I haven't seen Antonio eat at all except for the night of my escape so I'm not sure why he even bothers having the personal chef here.

But as I shovel the eggs into my mouth, I can feel my appetite returning. It's been too many days and not enough food.

"Eat up, *piccola*. You are too thin!" The middle-aged woman rounds the marble island and pinches my cheek. Then drops a basket of fresh homemade pastries still warm from the oven.

"If you keep feeding me like this, I'll be rolling out of here in a few days."

She laughs, sweeping back strands of silver-streaked hair. "Nonsense, a woman should have curves." She winks, sliding her hands down her hips and sashaying back toward the stove.

Antonio sits across the table, smothering a smile.

Fabi wags a finger at him, the bright pink nail polish glittering beneath the pendant light. "You know it's true, *signore*. Don't you dare try to deny it."

"I'm not denying anything. I love women of all shapes and sizes. I do not discriminate, but I'm also not looking right now. I find myself with more woman than I can handle at the moment." A flirty grin pulls at his lips, and the relaxed look is completely unexpected. Apparently, the key to this man's heart is a conversation around the kitchen table.

"So you set up that Tinder account just for me?" I can't keep the words from spilling out. What is wrong with me? Am I flirting back?

Mariuccia barrels around the corner, her eyes widening as she takes in the weirdly domestic scene. "Good morning, *signorina*. It's so wonderful to see you up and about. You look well."

I scoop another big bite of eggs into my mouth and mumble a good morning to keep my tongue busy.

Mariuccia turns to the windows, glancing outside at the sun-soaked terrazzo overlooking the lake. I follow her gaze to the classic wooden boat which bobs on the current, its polished mahogany hull reflecting the gentle ripples of the lake. Puffy white clouds move slowly overhead, through the glistening sunlight. "It's such a beautiful day, why don't the two of you take the boat out on the lake?"

Antonio clears his throat, then reaches for his cup, drowning his nose in the espresso. He's clearly trying to buy some time just like I had a second ago with the eggs. The woman stares at him expectantly, and I throw a guarded look in his direction.

"We should probably remain near the phone," he finally hedges, "in case Tony or your father call."

I'm about to nod my agreement, reminding myself this isn't a romantic weekend getaway and a boat ride on the lake with my captor should not be on the to-do list, when Mariuccia shakes her head. "The cellular reception is just fine on the lake. I go all the time and have no problem."

Antonio's dark gaze flickers to mine, then back to his housekeeper. The conflict written across his face is undeniable as he looses a frustrated breath. "Serena would you like that?"

I can see the pleading in his eyes. He wants me to say no, to let him off the hook. And only to piss him off, I throw him a smile and my head dips. "Sure, that sounds like the perfect way to kill a few hours."

CHAPTER 23
A PICNIC

*A*ntonio

I'm busy muttering curses as Serena steps onto the classic Riva *Papà* bought for the family over a decade ago. The boat epitomizes Italian craftsmanship and style with its sleek design and glossy finish. A bittersweet smile flits across my lips unbidden as I scan the cream-colored leather seats which sit four with one person standing at the steering wheel. It was just perfect for our family then, and now only two of us remain...

Serena steps over the bench seating and nearly slips on the damp deck. I spin around just in time as she flops into my arms.

"*Attenzione!*" Mariuccia shouts from the dock, a shit-eating grin on her face when I catch Serena. She's pushing a wagon filled with gardening tools and fresh flowers for planting. Her dedication to the villa's flourishing land is all for nothing because I don't plan on remaining here for long. I simply don't have the heart to tell her.

"Damn it, you should have waited until I could help you," I growl into Serena's ear as I attempt to steady her.

She glares up at me, that defiance back in her deep blue gaze, and as irritating as it is, I prefer it a hundred times over to the vacant expression she wore yesterday after Otto—.

Memories of the incident has the blood boiling in my veins, and another wave of fury threatens to erupt. My fingers curl around her hips, and I don't even realize how deeply they dig into her skin until she lets out a squeal and shoves free of my hold.

"Damn it, Toni, I'm not going to jump off the boat to escape. You don't have to manhandle me like that."

Toni? I'm not certain I like the new nickname.

Gritting my teeth, I apologize, but find myself reaching for her, nonetheless. She may not try to jump but with that weak ankle and the slick floorboards from the early morning dew, she could slip overboard anyway.

"I have no intention of going for a swim today so do me a favor and just hold onto something." Guiding her hand to the stern, I finally find her steady enough to focus on the task at hand. I adjust the dashboard's vintage gauges, while keeping one hand on the steering wheel. To be honest, I was surprised the engine started today. Who knew when was the last time anyone used this old thing?

Finding an old rag in the cabinets beneath the seats, I wipe them down then glance up at Serena. "Okay, you can sit now."

"Such a gentleman." She smirks as she slides onto the creamy leather still wearing my sweatshirt from earlier.

The seats have held up surprisingly well all these years. Pushing back the retractable canopy, I glance across the peaceful lake. Mariuccia wasn't wrong. It is the perfect day for a leisurely cruise across the water.

Pivoting back toward the villa, I find my former nanny watching me expectantly. As if this were some sort of date, and she's as nervous as I am. Not am. Would be. If it were a date, which it isn't. Serena is my hostage and what happened to her with Otto has muddled things.

It's ignited some deep-buried, primal need to protect her which is the exact opposite of what should be happening. My gaze flickers from Mariuccia's stupid grin to Serena splayed out across the seat, her legs propped up on the gleaming mahogany of the vintage vessel. She's folded my sweatpants up her long legs, exposing tanned skin below the knee. With the shape of a speed boat, the Riva is built for swift acceleration and quick turns, but there would be none of that today. Not with my prized, injured possession in tow.

"Oh, wait, before you go!" Mariuccia waves frantically from the dock as we start to inch forward. Leaning over the wagon, she pulls out an old wicker basket covered in a floral tablecloth. "I brought you a snack, in case you get hungry along the trip."

"We'll be gone for an hour at most," I call back, irritated. "And we just finished breakfast."

"A snack sounds lovely." Serena sits up, reaching across the few feet of water that separates us from the old dock. "Thank you, that was very thoughtful of you."

Before my *tesoro* falls into the rippling waves, I lunge forward and grab the basket from Mariuccia's hands. "*Grazie,*" I mutter.

"I packed some of your favorites." She beams at me, and suffocating guilt squeezes my lungs. "*Bresaola, taleggio* cheese and fresh bread from the bakery in town. And a little bit of *sbrisolona* with a bottle of *spumante* for a sweet finish."

Oh, for fuck's sake, she's made us a picnic!

I keep my expression calm, despite the turmoil raging inside as Serena lifts the flowery covering and oohs and ahhs at the region's delicacies. "*Grazie, ancora,*" I repeat. "It was very thoughtful of you, Mariuccia, but not necessary."

"Speak for yourself," says Serena as she uncorks the spumante. "Sparkling wine on a boat with this gorgeous scenery is exactly what the doctor ordered after—" Her words fall away, and thick silence descends over the tranquil scene. For a long moment, only the soft lapping waves splashing against the boat's hull fill the air.

"We'll be back soon," I finally call out to Mariuccia to dispel the awkward pause.

"Take your time, Tonio. Enjoy the peaceful moments, the seemingly insignificant ones." She bends closer so that she's on the edge of the dock and reaches a hand to me. Curling her fingers around mine, she squeezes, her wrinkled fingers still strong, grip firm. Her eyes lock on mine, a fierceness in that pale gray now that wasn't there years ago. "Remember, true strength lies not just in power, but in kindness and compassion." Her gaze flickers to Serena before returning to my own. "Nothing lasts forever in this life, but the love you give and receive is what truly endures. Wherever life takes you, whatever dark paths you may walk, never lose sight of the light inside you. That boy who loved so fiercely, laughed so freely, let him guide you back to peace."

I stare at her, jaw unhinged, her words resonating in my darkest depths. Unexpected emotion thickens my throat, making it difficult to swallow. I nod slowly before she releases me with another warm smile and a quick wave.

"Ciao!" Serena calls out over her shoulder.

For an endless moment, I watch Mariuccia as she stands on the dock waving, her words lingering in the air long after. The flutter of the little Italian flag over the rutter catches my attention as it proudly waves in the wind, and I return my attention to the steering wheel. The last thing I need is to crash this damned boat, then this entire grand plan would turn into even more of a disaster.

Once I steer the boat around the bend, I follow the coastline, remaining close to the luxurious villas dotting the shores. Lush, verdant mountains provide a dramatic backdrop to the tranquil lake. *Mamma* had come from money, but *Papà* had refused to accept a penny of it when we were young. With the exception of this house. It was the only extravagant inheritance we were permitted to indulge in. Maybe it was because he knew how much *Mamma* loved it here.

With my thoughts brimming over from memories of the past, I nearly forget about my special passenger. Until a sharp giggle streaks through the dark haze, and I swivel my head over my shoulder. Her full, pink lips are curved around the bottle of *spumante*, the frothy bubbles dribbling down her chin.

And fuck me, if that tantalizing image doesn't race straight down to my cock.

She swallows a big gulp, then another, her gaze drifting across the pastel-hued villas dotting the verdant hills. She licks the rim then tips her head back for another long pull.

Merda... does she have any idea what she's doing to me?

"Take it easy, *tesoro*," I grumble. "Alcohol and the open water don't mix."

"Of course they do." She throws me a rebellious smile and chugs down half the bottle in one go.

"Serena... don't make me take that away from you."

She snorts on a laugh, peeling her lips from the rim. "Who are you, my father?" She shoots me a wicked grin before taking another sip. "I know you've got a few years on me, Antonio, but you're not old enough for that."

"*Dio*, no," I grit out. "That would mean I would have been a father at nine years old." My lips twist at the thought, then my stomach knots. With the sinful thoughts I've had of this woman since the moment I met her, the idea of being her father is nauseating.

Even she looks repulsed as she brings the bottle to her lips once again.

"Serena..." I growl again.

"What? Did you want some?" She dangles the sparkling wine just out of my reach.

Shifting the gears and setting the course due north, I engage the autopilot. Not because I plan on getting drunk with her but because I'm fairly certain I'll need both hands to keep her from falling off once she finishes that bottle.

CHAPTER 24
A LITTLE TIPSY

S*erena*

The light, airy bubbles go straight to my head, which is exactly what I intended when I started to guzzle the sparkling wine. I wanted the numbness, the pleasant tingly sensations to dull the ache that carved into my chest from the night before.

Fuck, I don't know how women do it. How they survive an attack like that... Otto didn't even succeed, and I still feel violated in the most horrific way.

"Serena..." Antonio's growl of frustration tears me from my thoughts to the angry mob boss stalking toward me.

He grabs the bottle of spumante and stares through the dark green glass clearly trying to determine how much I've drank in the last fifteen minutes. The answer is: a lot.

When Mariuccia mentioned it, the idea of a peaceful boat ride along the scenic lake sounded perfect, but now, alone with Antonio in the middle of the rippling waves and unarmed, I'm starting to reconsider this little voyage.

Steeling my spine, I remind myself Tony is already brokering the deal for my release. Antonio has no reason to hurt me.

"You've had enough." He corks the bottle and returns it to the wicker basket, then offers me a chunk of bread. "Eat this."

"No, it'll just sober me up," I squeal.

"Exactly!"

"How do you expect me to enjoy this little cruise if I'm not at least a little tipsy?"

"You were the one that wanted to go out on the boat!" He drags his hand through the waves of dark hair, tugging on the ends.

"I only said that to piss you off because I knew you didn't want to go." I offer a cheeky smile which has less to do with the spumante and more to do with the fact that I love seeing this man flustered.

"So you'd rather torture both of us?"

"Yup." I pop the P just for fun.

He shakes his head, releasing a frustrated breath. "I suppose you think I deserve that."

"Sure as shit."

The hint of a smile kicks up the corner of his mouth as he folds down onto the bench across from me.

"This whole thing has been a fucking disaster." He buries his face in his hands and heaves out a breath. "I just want it all over with."

"Same here, *bastardo*."

"It will be soon. Tony said your father will concede to all my demands."

"Of course he will because he fucking loves me." I cross my arms over my chest triumphantly. When I get home, I'm going to have words with Pa about how long this whole fiasco took.

"How lucky you are…" His words fall away, and a twinge of unwanted sympathy niggles at my chest. After hearing the stories from Bella, I know just what a sick asshole their father was. I hope he's rotting in hell for what he did.

"For what it's worth, you've been a pretty decent kidnapper." I don't know why I still insist on being nice to him.

A deep chuckle vibrates his chest, the warm, rich sound so unexpected I find myself staring. "Just what every man wants to hear."

I shrug, the deep melody of his laughter still echoing on the breeze. "If you don't want to be called out for doing shitty things, don't do shitty things."

"Fair enough."

"Did you really not know what your father did to Raf's first girlfriend?" The question pops out before I can stop it. I'm not sure why it matters but I need to know what kind of man has me hostage. Even if this arrangement should be quickly coming to an end.

He slowly shakes his head, darkness carving into the hard line of his jaw. "Neither Giuseppe nor I knew what really transpired that day. *Papà* told us Raffaele had forsaken his family for Laura, and he made us believe our youngest brother was a traitor." He blows out a breath, his shoulders sagging beneath some invisible weight. "Raffa never reached out, never explained anything. I only discovered the truth after our father was dead. I still can't believe it…"

"But you *do* believe it now?"

His chin dips. "I can think of no other reason why Giuseppe would have interfered the day *Papà* took your cousin. I'm convinced he stood up to our father and gave his life for Raffa and Isabella to make up for his past sins."

"And you?" There's something about the openness in his expression that has me pushing.

"Once this is over, and my father's legacy is reclaimed, I'm done. I don't want my brother or the Valentinos as my enemies. I simply want to be free."

"Good luck with that. Running a criminal empire doesn't allow for much of *this*." I motion at the tranquil scenery surrounding us.

"I never thought I needed *this*." He crosses his leg over his knee, dark gaze intent on the surrounding mountains. "I haven't in the last ten years."

"Maybe you have gone soft in your old age." I toss him a wink before unzipping his sweatshirt and leaning back against the headrest. The oversized thing falls off my shoulders, but the chill has finally passed, and I can enjoy the warmth of the sun's brilliant rays on my shoulders.

"I'm not old, and I'm certainly not soft," he growls. "Or at least I never have been." He mutters the last part under his breath.

"Hey, you're the one that said it…"

He slides to the edge of the seat across from me, the movement so quick I startle and straighten abruptly. "I said *you* made me soft."

"Ah, so you're blaming this on me?"

"Yes," he grits out, tangling his fingers into knots. "I feel responsible for—"

"And you should," I hiss, the flirty banter from a second ago forgotten. "If you hadn't captured me in the first place, then left me with that sick fuck—" I chomp down on my lower lip to keep it from trembling as images from the night before flash in rapid fire. Heat singes the corners of my eyes, but I refuse to let another tear fall in front of fucking Antonio Ferrara. I blink quickly trying to keep the tears at bay, but one traitor escapes, dribbling down my cheek. Before I can lift my hand to erase the damning evidence, Antonio is on his knees in front of me. His touch is surprisingly gentle as his thumb sweeps across my skin.

My gaze drops to his, and a storm of emotions glistens across the dark surface. More tears threaten to spill at the unexpected gesture, at the rage in his eyes. "Dammit, I'm so angry," I howl instead.

"Let it out, *tesoro*. No one can hear you out here."

No one but you. The one person I should fear most. His hand closes around my shoulder, quietly reassuring, as his eyes remain pinned to mine. I throw my head back, my hands curling into fists, and I scream and shout, cursing Otto's name from here to kingdom come. Then I add in a few of my finest Italian curse words with Antonio's name thrown into the mix.

By the time my ranting is over, my chest is heaving, shoulders trembling but at least I'm not crying. And I actually feel better. Antonio's still kneeling, staring at me wide-eyed, a hint of amusement twitching at his lips. "I was right." He smirks. "You've got a mouth like a *puttana*."

"You have no idea." The flirty retort bursts out before I can stop it. The last thing I need is him thinking about my lips on anything.

His gaze heats, and he shifts uncomfortably between my legs where he kneels. His arm brushes the inside of my thigh and despite the layer of clothes between us, a whisper of heat streaks across my core.

Oh, thank gawd.

After what happened, I was convinced I'd feel nothing but numbness down there for the rest of my life. The fact that I felt something, anything, sparks hope in my chest. Sure, I should *not* be turned on by my captor, but semantics...

Clearing his throat, he starts to rise, placing his hands on my thighs to steady himself. A hiss escapes my clenched teeth, and he jerks his hands away so fast he staggers back a step and lands on the opposite bench seat. "*Scusi*," he mutters, holding his hands up.

"It's fine," I mutter. "You just surprised me." I wrap my arms around my middle and curl into his sweatshirt, the warm amber scent bringing a surge of relief that makes absolutely no sense.

Pushing himself up to stand, he turns toward the stern of the boat. "We should probably start heading back."

"Yeah, sure, whatever." I busy my hands, rifling through the picnic basket. I'm not hungry in the least but I need to do something.

We spend the rest of the ride back to the villa in silence, but it's not awkward which is odd. Instead, I alternate between watching the opulent villas nestled in the hillside and my driver. He keeps his gaze intent on the horizon, never deviating in my direction. Watching the muscles across his back bunch and coil beneath his black shirt as he maneuvers the boat is weirdly relaxing too.

"*Cazzo*," he hisses, a sharp gasp pulling my attention from his back to over his shoulder toward the shore.

My heart leaps up my throat as I spot the villa and the raging flames engulfing the entire structure.

CHAPTER 25
AN INFERNO

A*ntonio*

I stare, numb, as the brilliant flames lick up the façade, consuming every inch of the villa *Mamma* adored. The smoke billows, pouring from the terrazzo of the master bedroom and spreads like wild. An inferno shoots up into the blue sky, darkening the clouds and thickening the air.

Mariuccia? Fabi? Fear tears at my insides.

Dio, I hope they got out.

I gun the engine, needing to get closer to see if there is anything or worse, anyone left to salvage.

"What are you doing?" Serena shouts, suddenly standing beside me.

"I have to go back."

"Are you crazy? There's nothing you can do."

"What if Mariuccia and Fabi are still in there?"

Her eyes widen, understanding flickering across her face

before she shakes her head. "You can't just run into a burning building."

"It wouldn't be the first time, *tesoro*, but I sure as fuck hope it's the last."

Her hand curls around my arm, trying to tug the steering wheel off course. "You can't, Antonio. There's something wrong..." Her gaze narrows along the shore as I push closer. "There's no way a fire like that got so out of control so quickly." Then her hand shoots up, pointing at something moving amidst the thickening clouds of ash. "Look!"

I never would have spotted it if it hadn't been for her. The glint of a gun and a figure skulking across the garden. Then another behind the olive tree and another behind the stone wall.

"*Merda*," I grit out. "Who the fuck dared to attack my home?" The Sartoris, the Salernos? Or one of the countless others?

Dante wouldn't... would he? I never thought he would risk his daughter's life like this, but what the hell do I know.

Serena wrenches the steering wheel to the right, jerking it from my grasp. "No idea but now is not the time to find out."

"But Mariuccia—"

Her eyes turn glossy, lips pulling into a pout. "I'm sorry, Antonio, but if she didn't get out..."

"No, I don't accept that." *Cazzo*, this is all my fault. I made Mariuccia come here. I dragged her back to this inferno, to the fucked-up dark world I inhabit. Spinning the boat around, I push the engine to maximum speed and curve around the bend once more until we're out of sight. I only pray no one saw us approaching and with the dense smoke and the chaos of the fire, the probabilities are good.

"Where are you going?" she screeches.

"I'm dropping you off somewhere safe, and I'm going back."

"You can't!" She whips her head back and forth, blonde hair lashing across her face.

"I *have* to." I sear my eyes to hers, forcing my hands at my side to keep them from touching her. "My father was a *pezzo di merda*, and I went back for him. Mariuccia was like a mother to me, and she deserves better. And Fabi... If there is any chance they survived, I have to try."

"Then I'll go with you."

"Absolutely not." I glance down between us at her ankle. Even now as she stands holding onto the stern, she can't put all her weight on it. "I have no idea who is behind this, and there is no way I'm putting your life at risk again. Not when we're so close to an agreement..." *Could Dante have double-crossed me?*

"*Papà.*" Her voice is so low I'm not certain I hear her. "You think it's him, don't you?"

"I never said that."

"But that's what you're thinking. I can see it in your eyes. You really think my father would do that to a house with me in it?"

I shake my head slowly. "I honestly have no idea what to think, *tesoro*. But no one knows about this house."

"So how could my father?"

"Maybe he tracked my phone somehow..."

"I thought you had some sort of untraceable VPN."

"I thought so too, but—"

"No! It's not the Kings. I know my own father and he would never," she grits out the last part as I slow the boat onto the shore.

"Now is not the time to argue." I cut the engine and turn to face her. "Just stay here. I'll be right back."

"You can't be serious?" She glares up at me, eyes narrowed. "You want me to just sit here and wait?"

"Yes, that's exactly what I want." I eye the rope coiled around the metal cleats along the side of the boat. "Don't make me tie you up, Serena."

"You wouldn't dare," she hisses.

I tower over her, my hands clamping around her shoulders. "Give me your word that you won't move."

"And if I don't? You'll tie me up and leave me here knowing there's a very real possibility you won't come back?" Her wild eyes meet mine, and I catch a glimpse of worry. Not just for her, or the situation, but for what she just said, the chance of me not returning.

I loose a frustrated breath, and my hands move to frame her cheeks. I'm surprised she doesn't slap them away. "Just promise me you'll stay."

She clucks her teeth, muttering a curse, then lifts her watch between us, wriggling free of my hold. "You have thirty minutes, Antonio. If you're not back, I'm out of here."

"There's nowhere to go…"

"I'll find a way, hitch a ride, do whatever it takes."

My head dips because I don't doubt her one bit. Even with that sprained ankle, I'm sure she'll find a way out of here. "Thirty minutes," I repeat.

Her eyes lock on mine, and a whirlwind of emotions streak across the typically brilliant blue of her irises. I'm filled with the most overwhelming urge to drag her mouth to mine and devour her lips just one time.

Because she's right and there's a very real probability that I won't make it back. And it would be a sin to die without ever having tasted those lips.

Fuck it.

When this is all over, I'm going straight to hell anyway.

I wrap my hand around the back of her neck and force her mouth to mine. I groan the instant our lips make contact, the sweet strawberry taste more intoxicating than in my wildest dreams. She clenches her teeth for only an instant before her lips part, giving way to my tongue. She gasps as I tilt her head to deepen the kiss and plunder every inch of her mouth. Fire races down to my cock as I imagine that hot, wet mouth not just against my lips but all over me.

Before I lose all common sense, I jerk my mouth off hers and take a measured step back, putting some much-needed space between our heated bodies. My chest heaves, rising and falling in the same erratic pattern as hers.

Her eyes narrow as she regards me, lips parted and panting. Those blazing sapphire orbs rake over me for an instant before a sharp sting registers across my cheek. "Never do that again," she snarls, her hand still raised in the air.

"No promises, *tesoro*."

She opens her mouth likely to hurl a string of curses in my direction, but I leap off the boat before she gets a word out. My shoes sink into the sandy shore, and I'm off running between the thick vegetation of the neighboring villa.

A long minute later, I glance over my shoulder before the boat disappears from view, praying to every god in existence that I'll find her waiting as I asked. And I'm shocked when I can still make out her familiar form is perched on the seat beside the steering wheel.

With her safety confirmed, I pump my arms faster, disappearing into the vegetation. Serena will be fine. I find myself repeating the phrase over and over as I sprint toward the villa, trees lashing at my face in the thickening smoke.

I reach the edge of our property, the wrought iron gate forced open. Rage courses through my veins, and it takes all my self-control to keep it at bay. Who the fuck came for me? Destroyed my family's home? I scan the perimeter for the men we'd seen earlier, but the smoke is too dense. Either they're already gone, or I just can't see them skulking through the clouds of ominous black.

I reach the entry and the door swings open, hanging from burnt hinges. Flames engulf the foyer, each room a cavern of fire and smoke. My gaze immediately leaps to the portrait on the wall, and my heart sinks. The glass is cracked, the image singed and destroyed. The one happy memory of our family is lost forever. Swallowing down the pain, I move past the main hall, coughing, my lungs burning as I search desperately for Mariuccia. The heat is unbearable, the crackling of the fire deafening, but all I can think about is finding her.

"Mariuccia!" I shout, my voice hoarse, barely audible over the roar of the inferno. "Fabi!" I push through the smoke, my eyes stinging, trying to make out either form in the chaos.

The thick, black smoke swirls around me like a living thing, obscuring my vision, choking me. I stumble through the familiar corridors, now transformed into a hellish labyrinth. Each door I fling open reveals another burst of flames, another wave of heat that pushes me back. Desperation claws at me, raw and fierce. I have to find Mariuccia. She's been the only constant in my life, the only reminder of who I once was. I can't let her vanish into the flames; I can't let the fire consume the last piece of my humanity.

Her words from earlier flutter through my mind, her smile as she waved us off from the dock. *Nothing lasts forever in this life, but the love you give and receive is what truly endures. Wherever life takes you, whatever dark paths you may walk, never lose sight of the light inside you. That boy who loved so fiercely, laughed so freely, let him guide you back to peace.*

Those can't be the final words she ever says to me. But how fitting they would be…

I push through the kitchen door, one hand covering my mouth, and sink to the floor when I find her. No, them. Two blackened, scorched forms are splayed out across the tile. All the remaining air in my lungs squeezes out in a pained gasp. I'm too damned late. Just like with *him*.

A burst of flames erupts from behind me as the fire finds the gas stove. *Dio*, there's no time. No way for me to get their remains out. With the blaring heat licking up my spine, I dart across the kitchen to the French doors that lead out to the terrazzo. My hand closes around the antique knob, and the metal burns my flesh.

Merda!

I take a step back and kick at the thick glass panes. It shatters upon impact, glass raining down in glistening shards. Covering my face, I leap through the doorway, my heart a battering ram against my ribs, my lungs burning from lack of oxygen.

I don't stop until I reach the edge of the gardens and finally draw in a careful breath. Ash and soot float on the breeze, the blazing fire raging only a few yards away. My heart aches at the sight, but I push it down, allowing the fury to take its place. I'll find out who dared to murder those poor women, destroy my home, my memories, the one tether to my humanity.

I'll hunt them down and make every last one of those fuckers pay.

The crackle of footfalls on the singed lawn sends my head spinning over my shoulder, but before I can react, a gunshot echoes through the murky air.

CHAPTER 26
A MORAL DILEMMA

S*erena*

Shit. Shit. Fuck.

A thick cloud of smoke billows from the rooftop of the villa, blanketing the serene blue sky in a dark haze. Where the hell is the fire department? If we were in Manhattan, a cacophony of sirens would be blaring by now.

I pace the length of the boat, my movements so quick and erratic I'm making myself dizzy. Why am I still here? I should have run by now. But for some insane reason, my feet are planted to the worn wooden floorboards. Yes, my ankle would be a problem, but it's not like I haven't tried running with it before.

My spinning thoughts whirl back to a half hour ago, to that scorching kiss. My fingers move to my lips, trailing over my skin. Antonio's breath still ghosts over my mouth, the overwhelming fire from that single touch permanently branded in my memory.

But that has nothing to do with why I can't move...

My thoughts swirl to Mariuccia, to the kind woman who tried to make me as comfortable as a prisoner could be, who cared for the estate, and more than that, clearly still cared for Antonio. Possibly the last person left on this planet who does.

Please don't let her be dead. I send the prayer up to the heavens, hoping *Dio* will hear. Not that I've put much stock in religion, but *Nonna* was a fervent believer.

A sharp blast detonates, then the rumble of collapsing concrete rolls through the still afternoon. My head whips in the direction of the villa, and I can't help my heart from sinking. What fell? A tower, a terrazzo? I shouldn't give one shit about Antonio's beautiful home, but I do. It's just a travesty for an architectural masterpiece like that to be destroyed. It has nothing to do with the memories housed within those walls. Or that painting in the foyer.

I glance at my watch, staring at the face as the minutes wind down on the timer. He promised he'd be back. I rise to my tiptoes to see over the dense foliage along the shore. Come on... Two minutes left. I start to mentally prepare for the possibility of escape. If he's not back, I have to go. I'd be insane not to.

How is this even a moral dilemma?

I should absolutely, one hundred percent be attempting to run away from my kidnapper. And still, I'm rooted to the spot, eyeing the thick shrubbery he disappeared through like *my* life depends on it.

The buzzer goes off, the sharp sound sending my heart leaping up my throat. "Son of a bitch," I grit out, my hand on my chest to settle the wild thumping.

Fuck this. I don't owe Antonio anything. He's lucky I waited this long. I stagger toward the edge of the boat and climb up, steading myself on the canopy. It's a good thing he beached the vessel before he left, or I'd be swimming out of here. Instead, I just have to jump a few feet onto the shore. Which with my sprained ankle isn't ideal, but still doable.

But what if he comes back, doesn't find me and goes for Bella instead?

I hover on the ledge, fingers curled around the mahogany siding.

Shit. What do I do?

A gunshot explodes in the distance, and I duck before dropping to the floor. For the hundredth time, I curse the loss of my Dolce. Fucking Antonio. If I had my gun right now, I would not be crouching here defenseless.

More shots pepper the silence, then the rumble of an engine draws my attention around the bend. Peering over the gleaming wood siding, I catch a glimpse of a boat speeding away from the direction of the villa. The roar of the engine grows closer, and I mutter a curse, dropping my stomach to the floor and wedging myself in the tiny space between the bench seat and the stern. Shit. I need a weapon.

Whipping open a cabinet beneath the steering wheel, I rifle through its paltry contents. Life jacket, rope, fire extinguisher, first-aid kit... It's too late for the fire extinguisher, but the first aid kit could have something. The steady rumble grows closer, and my pulse escalates in time with the sound. Unlatching the container, my heart soars at the sight of a little Swiss Army knife nestled within the bandages and alcohol swabs.

I flick it open and find the small blade sharp at least. Throwing a few supplies in my purse, just in case the worst happens, I eye the tiny space built into the stern. I might fit inside it... I don't dare risk another peek over the side of the boat. Drawing in a breath, I crawl into the dark space, just barely getting my legs in and use my foot to close the cabinet door. A pungent, moist odor fills my lungs, and I barely restrain the urge to gag. I bury my nose in Antonio's sweatshirt, his now familiar musky scent an odd comfort to the rising panic. Forcing my lungs to take small, measured breaths, I strain to listen for the approaching boat.

Muffled voices resound over the engine, and I tense, my

fingers curling around the pocketknife. They're still too garbled to determine how many men are aboard the vessel, but any more than two and I'm screwed. I could catch one with the knife using the element of surprise, the second one would be difficult but not impossible to subdue, but a third or more and there's no way I'd be able to fight my way out.

The incessant rumble finally falls away, and gentle waves lap at the hull of my boat from the approaching craft. I hold my breath as they draw closer, and their unintelligible mutters grow more distinct.

"*La barca è abbandonata, vedi?*" A male voice shouts in Italian.

"*Non c'è nessuno.*"

"*E la ragazza?*"

My heart stops. They're looking for a girl. Me?

"*Deve essere scappata. Forse ci ha visti eliminare Antonio, è entrata in panico ed è fuggita.*"

Oh, shit, Antonio. They eliminated him? An unexpected jab of something I refuse to name spears me straight in the ribs. He's dead? My heartbeat races, kicking at my ribs as I attempt to steady its manic pace. I'm sure it's so loud they'll hear and find my hiding spot.

"*Il capo non sarà contento.*"

The boss? Who's your boss, dammit!

"*Bene, attracchiamo la barca più avanti, vicino al centro della città e possiamo cercarla là.*"

"*Va bene.*"

They're going to search the center of town for me? They've killed off Antonio and now they want me? But for what?

My head spins, a desperate tangle of fear and a twinge of that which will remain unnamed. He can't be dead... His musky amber scent still lingers on his clothes. *Dio*, I should be happy if he was. Though now with these guys hunting me down, it looks like I have a whole new set of problems to worry about.

The engine starts up again and I wait, calmly forcing air in and out of my lungs until the sound completely recedes, and I'm convinced whoever torched the villa is gone. Carefully, I hook my good foot onto the interior handle and push the door open.

A part of me is certain I'm going to meet the barrel of a gun once I squirm my way out of this floating coffin.

But I don't…

Once I'm free from the claustrophobic enclosure, I stuff the Swiss Army knife into my pocket, crawl on hands and knees, gulping down semi-fresh air and peer over the siding. No other boat in sight. Dropping down onto my ass, I heave out a breath and search the skyline for the remnants of the villa. From this side of the hill, all I can make out is the dense cloud of smoke.

I have to get closer.

If Antonio really is dead, I need to know.

For Isabella.

Liar. An annoying voice in the dark corners of my mind calls me out. Weirdly enough it sounds a lot like my cousin, Matty. Shoving back the pointless thoughts, I throw my purse packed with first aid supplies over my shoulder and heave myself over the side of the boat.

I land on my good ankle, but still a twinge courses up my leg when the second hits the moist sand a second later. Thank *Dio* I opted for sweatpants today which of course made me choose the sneakers to go with it. At least, I'd have some ankle support for the trek back to the villa.

Which I actually have no idea how to get to.

Luckily, I saw where Antonio had disappeared through the lush greenery, and I start off by simply following his path. From there, it's not hard to track the billowing trail of smoke to the grand estate.

Considering I'm still limping, I make it back to the villa surprisingly quickly, some unknown force guiding my footsteps. The familiar pastel terrazzos appear at a distance, and a gasp parts my lips. The beautiful gardens are aflame, the orchard, the towering pines, all of it, nothing but ashy remains.

Dio, I hope Mariuccia and Fabi made it out.

As I skirt the perimeter of the grounds, I search for any signs of the women. Not only are they nowhere in sight, but also, the guards that prowl the property are missing. They're dead… they must be.

That unnamable feeling returns, my stomach sinking at the thought of Antonio. I should get out of here. There's nothing and no one left. I can't go to the village, but there must be somewhere else I could hide out for a few days. Then I just need to get a hold of Pa, and he'll come for me.

I glance across the swath of destruction, the brilliant flames licking up the sides of the grand villa, and the open wrought iron gate at the edge of the compound. *Go.* It's time to get the hell out of here.

Still, my feet refuse to obey. Just one quick circle around the house.

Mariuccia and Fabi were in the kitchen the last time I saw them. Maybe they got out somehow…

My feet are moving before I can convince myself otherwise. I skirt the outer edge of the property, sticking as far away from the raging flames as possible. Where the hell are the *vigili del fuoco*? It cannot possibly take that long to get firemen out here. I circle the terrazzo where I first chatted with Mariuccia as I sunbathed on the lounger, and my chest tightens. Nothing but charred remnants.

A pit of unease tightens low in my belly. I finally reach the easternmost side of the house and dread coils in my gut. The kitchen windows are blown out, glass shards strewn across the scorched lawn.

A figure catches my eye, splayed out on the ground, just a few yards away from the burning house. My heart catapults up my chest, and I'm sprinting before I realize what a bad idea it is, but the adrenaline numbs the pain.

As I draw closer, that pit of dread only expands. Black shirt, dark jeans and the head of wild midnight hair.

Shit, Antonio.

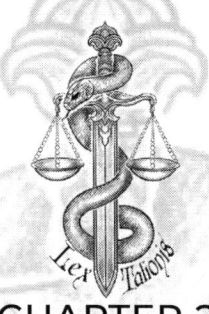

CHAPTER 27
A SLOW AGONIZING DEATH

S*erena*

I slide to my knees by Antonio's side and fear lances through my chest at the deep crimson splotches across the back of his black shirt. He's lying face down in a bed of violets, the scene absurdly beautiful in a chaotic way. Somehow, the fire hasn't reached the flowerbed, but flames crackle across the lawn growing closer every second.

"Antonio!" I shout as I run my hands over his back, and they come away sticky with blood. I can barely make out the faint rise and fall of his ribcage through the back of his shirt. He's still breathing. The amount of relief that courses through me at the discovery is embarrassing. "Antonio, wake up!" I shake him, grabbing his shoulder, and a faint moan parts his lips. "You have to get up!"

Blood warms my icy hand, and I stare at the deep ruby liquid covering my palm. Shit. Where the hell is it coming from? I search his back again, but with the black shirt and the darkening sky, I can't find the damned wound.

"Listen to me, you stubborn, arrogant *coglione*, if you don't move your ass in a second, you're going to be burned alive."

His eyelids flicker open for an instant, and what I could swear is a smile parts his lips. Then he's out again.

"You have to get up!"

"Go." He doesn't open his eyes this time. The word is barely audible over the mad pounding of my heart and the crackle of the roaring fire. "They'll be back…"

"No," I hiss. Then with a big push that has his eyes snapping open, I manage to roll him over onto his back.

A sharp groan purses his lips.

"Who did this?"

"I'm not sure…"

"Look at me!" I shout, clapping my hands on his cheeks, and I can't help my gaze from drifting to his mouth. My thoughts fly back to that kiss… Dark, unfocused eyes finally latch onto mine, and I force the traitorous thoughts away. "Okay, who doesn't really matter right now, but I *do* need you to stand up. Hell, I don't care if you crawl, but we need to get out of here now." The heat of the fire licks up my back as the shrubbery to our right is consumed in flames.

"Go," he rasps out again, clutching his left shoulder. Blood trickles from between his fingers.

"Not without you."

He blinks slowly as if he can't quite follow what I'm saying.

"Whoever did this is coming after me, too, you *stronzo*. They're already headed to the town center to find me. I won't get out of this by myself, and you won't get what you want from *Papà* without me."

His brows furrow as he regards me, and his chest heaves from the effort of lifting his head up. "It's over," he whispers. "You're free."

"I am not free, you stubborn asshole. This is all your fault, and you are the one that's going to get me out of this mess. Now pick your ass up off the ground, and let's get out of here."

That half smile reappears for only an instant before he winces through another pang.

My gaze runs down the length of his jeans. Some blood splatter but looks minimal. "Are your legs okay?"

He nods, then lifts his hand off the wound right below his collarbone, just shy of his heart. "The bullet went through here. It's clean, in and out."

"Good, then you should be able to walk just fine."

His dark eyes settle over my shoulder on the blazing inferno behind me. "It's over. Just let me die here."

"No," I grit out.

"Why not? It's what I deserve, isn't it?"

I shake my head. "No one deserves to be burnt alive, Antonio, regardless of the sins you keep on some mental list to torture yourself. We all have them. Now, let's get the hell out of here and if we survive this and you still want to die, I'd be more than happy to put a bullet in your head." I throw him a smirk. "Clean and easy."

A rueful smile curls the corners of his lips, igniting a spark in those dark eyes more brilliant than the starry sky. "What's your escape plan, *tesoro*?"

"Let's just get to the boat, and then I'll fill you in."

With a frustrated, or maybe pained, sigh, he rolls over again, then pushes himself up to stand. A groan slides through his clenched teeth as he straightens. With my bum ankle, I'm not exactly any help. He grits through the pain, clutching the wound, and we stagger toward the lake and away from the ever-expanding inferno.

"Mariuccia and Fabi?" I whisper once the heat of the flames on my back lessens to a more tolerable level.

"Dead," he whispers.

The pain is sharp and quick. I swallow it down just as fast. "I'm sorry."

"Me too," he mutters.

We stagger through the foliage on the east side of the estate, the part that has miraculously avoided the brunt of the destruction. I lead the way, limping along through the underbrush, the pain in my ankle starting to rush back. Not that the crutches would have been an option in this terrain. At least I still have the bandage keeping the joint in place.

"The boat is secure?" he huffs out once we're clear of the house.

"Yeah. They came to check it out, but luckily, they left me and it alone."

"They who?" He whirls at me, eyes suddenly wide.

"I don't know. I didn't get a chance to look at them."

"How did they not see you?"

"I hid."

"Where?"

"I'm not telling you." I toss him a cheeky grin. "We might be allies for now, but as soon as we're out of here and safe, you're still the man who kidnapped me."

"And you're still my hostage." A smirk flashes for an instant before the darkness descends once again. "I'm going to destroy the motherfucker behind this attack."

I push back a thick branch, letting Antonio go by before I trail after him. The pathway ahead divides and in my mad rush up from the lake, I can't remember exactly where we left the boat. "Who do you think it is?"

"I have a few ideas." His dark gaze rakes over me, a tendon fluttering in his jaw.

"Who?"

"Serena, I know you're not going to want to hear this, but there were only a handful of people who knew where we were. They are my most trusted men."

"Oh, you mean like Otto?"

A scowl carves into his jaw. "Despite his clear lapse in judgement and obvious character flaws, he attacked you in a misguided attempt to help me."

I snort on a laugh. "You've got to be fucking kidding me."

"I'm not excusing his behavior in any way, *tesoro*. And there's not a single part of me that regrets what I did to him. He deserved to die for touching you, but he was never disloyal to me. He never would have leaked our location... none of them would have."

"So what are you saying?"

"Tony and your father—"

I halt midstride and spin at him, anger scorching my veins. "You better stop right there before you say something I'll make you regret."

"I'm only pointing out the obvious—"

"*Papà* would never sacrifice me!" I hiss. "Your dad might have been a fucked-up piece of shit but mine is not. He would *never* risk me getting hurt in that fire."

He heaves out a breath, a twinge of regret in those bottomless eyes. "Then Tony maybe—"

"Nope, also no. Tony is family. He was at the hospital the day I was born. And then again for Isabella and each one of my cousins since. He would never!"

"No one else could have known," he mutters and starts to walk slowly again.

I speed up to his side. "It has to be one of your men... They could have spilled to one of *your* enemies."

He shakes his head, scowling.

"No offense, but you haven't been in charge for long. Maybe someone made your guys a better offer." My thoughts flicker to the past, to the meeting I wasn't supposed to be at in Milano with Pa. "What about that Sartori guy?"

His fist clenches at his side, the tell like a warning bell. "What do you know about Enrico Sartori?"

"Not much, other than he wants you dead."

"That's not news, *tesoro*. But Enrico is old school, he wouldn't pull something underhanded like this." He chews on the inside of his cheek, eyes churning with rage. "These assholes murdered two innocent women in cold blood. That's not the old man's style."

"What about his son?"

His brows furrow. "Federico?"

"He was there, too. He didn't seem too fond of you either."

Antonio slows as the top of the boat's canopy comes into view just over the ridge. Thank *Dio*, we're almost there. "Well, whoever the fuck did it, is going to die a slow, agonizing death."

CHAPTER 28
THE UGLY TRUTH

A *ntonio*

Circling the lake of my childhood home which now sits in a pile of ashes, the anger grows more powerful with each passing minute. Serena stands at the steering wheel, following the route I laid out, skimming the coast but remaining hidden from large ports. That house, Mariuccia, the memories, they were all that was left of my humanity. And some son-of-a-bitch stole that from me.

Worse, they nearly stole *her*.

My eyes flicker to Serena as I stretch across the banquette, useless with this damned bullet wound still spilling blood. She'd offered to patch me up before we hit the water, but my only concern was getting as far from the blazing villa as possible. Her gaze is fixed to the pitch sky, while I can't stop watching her. Neither of us have spoken much the past few hours as we circle endlessly. Whoever is behind this won't linger in Como forever.

We simply must wait them out. Then once I'm certain it's safe, I'll make my next move.

Normally, there would be no question. My gut says this is Dante Valentino; the timing is too perfect for it to be anyone else. And yet, Serena is adamant her father would never do this. In my experience, family, blood and loyalty doesn't mean *merda*. *Papà* turned on Raffaele, Raf turned on *Papà*. I'm not certain exactly how Giuseppe died but it could have been at the hands of my father. Either way, it all proves my point.

My thoughts spin, the anger churning. The arsonists could have just as easily been the Salernos or the Sartoris. Both had motives…

And how can Serena be so sure it isn't the Kings behind this?

Dante is not *il capo*, no matter how hard he pretends to be. That title belongs to his brother, Luca, and if Dante didn't make the call, then it must have been the younger Valentino. That attack was brutal, perfectly organized and left no trace of the culprit.

Once we were at a safe distance, I put the call in to my man at the Como police station. He's kept me abreast of the situation, and as of now, they have nothing. I doubt they'll ever find a single clue. Whoever did this was a professional.

I push myself up, forcing my body into a sitting position, and a groan hisses through my clenched teeth. Serena spins toward me, a look I was certain I would never see on the woman flashing across her face, illuminated by the sliver of moon overhead.

"Are you all right?"

"I'm fine," I grit out, forcing myself to remain upright.

"You are the most stubborn man I've ever met." Cutting the engine so the boat bobs on the faint current, she whirls on me. "You should have let me check your wound. You're of no use to me if you bleed out."

A rueful chuckle slips out, and I barely restrain from crying out as my ribs expand with the laugh, tearing at the wound just above my heart. "*Merda*," I rasp out, pressing the cloth more firmly against my chest.

"That's it. I'm not going anywhere until you let me look at that bullet wound. And if you tell me you're fine one more time, I'm going to throw you overboard."

Before I can respond, she crouches down and rifles through the cabinets beneath the stern. She pops up a moment later with a first-aid kit.

"Lie down," she barks.

I stare up at her wide-eyed as she looms over me. I'm not a man that's used to taking orders.

"Don't make me ask again, Antonio. That crappy cloth that you've been using to staunch the blood is soaked through. The wound needs to be cleaned, stitched up and dressed."

"And you know how to do that?"

"No, you definitely picked the wrong Valentino mafia princess if you needed a surgeon." Her eyes twinkle with a hint of amusement, the first I've seen since we ran from the fire. "But I can at least clean and bandage it. Then we need to get off this boat and find a real doctor." She drops the first-aid kit on the gleaming mahogany, opens it and pulls out alcohol, cotton swabs, and bandages. "What about that doctor that came to the house for my ankle?"

Elena had of course sprung to mind, but after Mariuccia and Fabi... "I don't want to involve *Dottoressa* Bergamaschi," I mutter.

"Then we're going to have to go to the hospital. The bandage will only be a temporary fix."

"No." I shake my head. "That will be the first place they'll look. Whoever is behind this, will have to return to the house to confirm I'm dead. When they don't find my body, they'll search all the medical facilities. Some *bastardo* shot me in the back; that's not something you usually walk away from unscathed."

"In the back?"

I nod, even the faint movement pulling at the torn skin on my chest.

"Coward," she mutters. Then a steely resolve settles across her features, and she reaches for the first-aid kit once more. "Take your shirt off." She pulls out a needle and a spool of thread from her purse, the kind for sewing not surgery.

"Absolutely not." I eye her, my gut churning.

"We don't have butterfly bandages or wound closure strips in here and a regular band-aid just isn't going to cut it at this point. Just cleaning it isn't going to be enough. And sure, there's a risk of infection if you do this, but for now, it's the best option."

"You're really serious about this?"

"Your choice, either you give my sewing skills a chance or we go to the ER right now."

I grit out a curse as I eye the needle she has pinched between her fingertips. If we can buy ourselves twenty-four hours, I can see Elena once the pressure is off. "You can sew?"

"I'm an inspiring fashion designer, Antonio, of course I can sew." She shrugs. "And as you know, Bella is a doctor. We used to practice our stitching together back in college. It's not *that* different."

I nearly choke on a laugh. Am I really going to allow this woman to stitch up my wound with a sewing needle and cotton thread? It's better than dragging Elena into this with arsonists on the loose.

"Fine, just do it." I untuck my shirt, the movement ripping at my torn skin, and a hiss escapes.

"Let me help." She crouches in front of me, fitting herself between my thighs and begins to unfasten the buttons down my shirt. My hand jerks up, wrapping around her wrist. For an insane moment, I don't want her to see the scars on my back. No one has. Though I've had them painstakingly covered with a beautiful canvas, if you look close enough, the ugly truth is hidden just below the inked surface.

"What?" Her eyes meet mine, and I'm scared shitless that

she's going to see the vulnerability that I've tried so hard to mask for all these years.

Though the physical scars are new, the mental ones have been there for a decade.

"Just be careful," I murmur.

Her head dips. My pulse escalates at her proximity, at her hands brushing my skin as she works her way down. Her bottom lip is trapped beneath her teeth and fuck, if I wasn't in so much pain, this would be divine torture.

Once she's gotten the last button undone, she slips her hand beneath my shirt and slowly draws the sleeve down. It's sticky, dirty and bloodied and the sight of those slender fingers coated in my blood, does something to me. There's a slight tremble in her touch, or maybe I'm the one shaking. My heart pounds faster, in time with the pulsating of the festering wound, which is not a good sign.

The shirt falls to the floor, and I lift my wild gaze to meet hers. The bright blue of her eyes has darkened, pupils blown out with… desire? She can't possibly be enjoying this as much as I am, can she?

"Now, lie down," she whispers, a breathy edge to her tone that wasn't there a moment ago.

I stretch out across the seat, the leather sticky with my blood. If she makes me turn around, she'll see the landscape of destroyed skin across my back. "The wound at my back should be fine with the bandage," I blurt quickly. "It's the one at my chest that won't stop bleeding."

She nods, keeping her head down. I watch her intently as she pours alcohol on the cotton swab and gently dabs at the area around the wound, removing the encrusted blood.

"You should have let me do this an hour ago," she murmurs.

"And miss seeing the worry in your eye?"

She snorts on a laugh, nearly swatting at my chest before catching herself. "I'm concerned you'll die on me before getting us out of this mess."

"You're a clever girl, *tesoro*. I have no doubt you could make it back to Milano on your own." And there it is. In the chaos of the fire, I didn't have time to say it or even process her motivations. But the truth hits me harder than the bullet through my chest.

She stayed for me. Saved my life. Why?

Serena doesn't respond to my unspoken question, only keeps her head down, gaze focused on the blood still coating my chest. I have no doubt she's understood my insinuation, but she's chosen to ignore me. Maybe it's what's best for both of us right now.

Once she's satisfied that the wound is clean, she reaches for the needle. I tense for a second, imagining the feel of the sharp tip piercing my flesh.

"I'm not going to lie, it's going to hurt like hell."

"I certainly hope your cousin has a better bedside manner than you."

The corners of her lips quirk, nearly a smile but not quite. "Bella is better than me in every way."

"I find that hard to believe."

She seems as shocked to hear it as I am that the words slipped out.

Still, I continue because apparently the blood loss must have done some serious damage to my brain. "I doubt she would have gone through such lengths to save the life of her captor."

Serena closes her eyes and inhales a deep breath before she stabs the needle into my chest.

CHAPTER 29
A COINCIDENCE

S*erena*

Antonio's scream echoes across the quiet lake as the needle pierces his skin and I drag the thread through the wound, closing the bloody gash. My stomach twists, revolting at the sight of the torn flesh. *Dio*, how does Bella do this every day? Why would she ever want to? I swallow hard to keep down the remainder of the lovely picnic Mariuccia made for us earlier.

"Fuck, Serena, are you trying to kill me?" he growls. "A little warning would've been nice."

"It only would have made it worse. It's better if you don't see it coming. You would've been all tense, and if you tried to fight me, I didn't exactly have anything to hold you down."

He blows out a breath, his skin sallow and beads of perspiration coating his forehead. "Okay, I'm ready, just make it quick." His fingers curl around the edge of the seat, and I'm pretty sure by the time this is all over there will be nail marks in the soft leather.

"I'll try my best." In and out. In and out. The boat rocks steadily as we bob in the middle of the lake under the cover of darkness. With each stitch, I pretend it's a vibrant new fabric I'm sewing together instead of a man's flesh. It's the only thing that keeps me from vomiting or worse, passing out.

To his credit, Antonio barely flinches. After the first shout which took him by surprise, he's been absolutely silent, gritting through what must be excruciating pain. His restraint is impressive. Personally, I'm going to need a hell of a lot of tequila after this.

What feels like a lifetime later, I hazard a peek at my handiwork, the red, inflamed skin forced together by the blood-splattered white thread. It's not pretty and it's going to leave a horrible scar but at least he's not bleeding anymore. To reduce the threat of infection by the far-from-sterile thread, I plan on dousing the area in alcohol hourly until we can see a real doctor. I'm not sure this is sound reasoning but at the moment it's all I can think to do.

"Done…" I whisper once I've covered the newly stitched wound with a bandage.

"Good," he grits out, squeezing his eyes closed.

"You should rest." I rise, stretching out my legs from the cramped position.

"No, I'll be fine." He tries to sit up, but I place a gentle hand on his shoulder to keep him down. His lips twist into a frown, and damn it, if I even find that scowl attractive. What the hell is that? It's this intense situation we've been thrown into. It has my adrenaline pumping and my hormones on overdrive. And that's it.

Refocusing, I clear my throat. "That bullet hole is literally holding on by a thread. The less you move the better."

"You need sleep too. You can't drive the boat in circles all night." He ticks his head at the steering wheel which whirls around lazily.

"Better me than you."

He snorts, shaking his head. "I'm not the only stubborn one here."

"Do you have a better idea?"

"I do, but it's risky."

"I'm all ears, and I love risky." I crouch down beside him once again so he's not straining his neck and the wound to look up at me.

"The house across the lake from the villa belongs to an old friend of my mother's. She passed away a few years ago, and her children have already left for the season. They went back to Milano just before we arrived which was what made the villa so perfect for my needs."

"Okay, so you think we can stay there?"

He nods. "The main home has a security system, but there's a small boathouse by the lake. We can ground the Riva for the night. It's not much but it's shelter, and we can get off the water for a few hours so we can both rest."

"Sounds good to me." After the past few hours, my sea legs are faltering. The idea of being back on solid ground sounds like heaven. And we'd need to get to a doctor in the morning anyway.

"But if anyone sees us, we'll be sitting ducks." He reaches into his pants and pulls out a sleek gun. I'd been so distracted by all the blood, I hadn't even noticed it. Damn it, I'm slipping up left and right.

"Then we take turns sleeping." I shrug. I'll take half a night of good sleep over none at all. I hold out my hand, palm up, eyeing his weapon. "Don't worry I'll take good care of her."

He smirks, a spark lighting up those midnight eyes. "I don't think so, *tesoro*."

"If I wanted you dead, don't you think I would've killed you by now? You're not exactly in any state to fight back."

He looses a frustrated breath, eyes locked on mine. He inches the gun closer, but his wary fingers don't release it into my waiting hand. "Why *did* you come back for me?"

My shoulders lift again, slowly now so I can buy some more time. "I already told you—"

"You're lying. We both know you could've gotten away much faster without me. At this rate, I'll only slow you down."

"You forget I have a sprained ankle, and those arsonist assholes are searching the town looking for me as we speak."

"I have no doubt you could've given them the slip. You had no problem with my guards."

"And yet you caught me."

"Yes, *I* did." His eyes narrow, the sleek obsidian piercing, as if he stares hard enough, he'll be able to tear the truth right out of my soul. "So why did you come for me?"

"I don't know," I grit out. "Clearly, being held captive has fucked with my mind. Isn't that a thing, Stockholm's Syndrome or whatever? Maybe I find you both threatening and weirdly nurturing… especially after what happened with Otto. I guess I thought I owed you or something."

His dark brows furrow, the intense emotion flashing across his face like a brewing storm. His hand reaches out, his rough thumb brushing my cheek. And I *let* him. I don't dare move, I barely breathe. "What happened with Otto was my fault. You don't owe me shit, *tesoro*. I wish I could go back and kill him slower so that I could relish in his suffering, one hour of torture for every minute of pain that he caused you."

He strokes my cheek tenderly and the gentle touch is so at odds with the brutal mob boss who kidnapped me that my brain starts to short circuit, and I lean in. The burn of his lips from earlier today still ghosts over my own, a permanent reminder, a branding. How am I turned on by the idea of him torturing someone?

In all fairness, it's not just anyone, it's the *bastardo* who tried to rape me. And I would enjoy watching Antonio beat the shit out of him again.

He draws in a long breath, then exhales slowly and releases me. "We should go. Are you good to drive?"

"Sure. I'm not the one with the bullet wound."

"How's your ankle after all the walking?"

"It's fine." I jump up and grab the steering wheel, anxious to get the hell out of here. "Plot the course, captain, or whatever the hell you're supposed to say."

Antonio chuckles again, but this time the warm sound is restrained, as if fully giving into it would be painful. "Just skirt the coast, but don't get too close." He points toward an illuminated section of the lake, which I assume must be the center of Como. "Whoever came for us could still be in the vicinity. If I'd been the one to call the hit, I would make sure my guys confirmed all the bodies."

A chill skirts up my spine, a mixture of unease, exhaustion and the breeze churning in the middle of the open water. "What makes you so sure they came for *us*?"

"Because it's too much of a coincidence. I haven't been back at that villa for over ten years. Why now? Why not attack in Roma where I've been for months? I'm not a man who hides, Serena. I've been out in the open living my life since I became the head of the Ferrara syndicate. I attend parties at my nightclubs, a variety of social events, and I even do my own grocery shopping. Coming at me here was no coincidence."

I turn the steering wheel toward the coast, maintaining a low speed to keep the engine from roaring. I steal a quick peek at Antonio over my shoulder. A tendon flutters in his jaw, his dark brows furrowed. "I know what you're thinking, but you're wrong. *Papà* was not behind this. He would never."

"So you say…"

"Yes, I say, and it's true. Same goes for any of the Kings. My father has an iron grip over his men, and none would betray him. They would never be stupid enough."

"I hope you're right, *tesoro*."

CHAPTER 30
A GOOD MAN

A*ntonio*

A musky, earthy odor fills my nostrils as I lead the way, sopping wet, into the old boathouse. We'd been forced to cut off the engine a few yards offshore and drag it in the remainder of the way. Serena walks behind me, her limp more noticeable after today's fiasco. The floorboards creak with each step, escalating my pulse which only worsens the throbbing pain from the wound. Serena was right. I'd waited too long to have it dressed, and the thread was a poor substitute for real stitches. I can almost feel the infection setting in.

Ignoring the bleak thoughts, I reach for my phone and find my pocket empty. *Merda*, I must have dropped it in the damned lake. Can nothing go right for me this week? Muttering curses in my mind, I find a lantern hanging from the wall, and I'm shocked to find it lights up with the flick of a button. It illuminates the old structure, revealing every shadowed nook. Possibly too brightly. A newer version of our old Riva sits in the far corner beneath a large tarp and a variety of other watersports equipment fills the remainder of the space, from kayaks to water skis and tubes, it's well-equipped for the perfect family summer vacation.

"Too bad we can't stay and enjoy the jet ski in the morning." As if she's read my thoughts, her eyes pivot to the sleek wave runner.

"Yes, it is a shame." Not that either of us could ride one in our current states.

I veer to the right, the damp, musty smell following me as I head toward a tower of lounge chairs. It's not a bed, but they'll do just fine. I reach for the one on top and a curse slips out as the move tears at the new stitches.

Serena darts in front of me before throwing me a scowl over her shoulder. "I'll get that. You're supposed to be taking it easy."

"It's a lawn chair. I'm not trying to bench press a car, *tesoro*."

She stands on her tiptoes and hauls the thing down, grabbing some cushions from the top of the pile. Placing it on the ground between the Riva and the jet ski, she arranges the pastel peach pillows and motions for me to sit.

"Let me at least help with the other one."

Serena shakes her head. "Sit your ass down, Antonio."

Normally I'd obey, despite her commanding tone, but the idea of spending the night in wet clothes doesn't sound remotely comfortable. "Do you mind if I…" I signal to my shirt which is already unbuttoned. At least the swim in the river got rid of some of the blood.

"Strip down?" Her brow lifts.

"There must be towels in here somewhere."

"Yeah, that's fine. Nudity doesn't bother me." She yanks at my sweatshirt which is sticking to her wet form. "I'd love to get out of these bad boys, too."

I move toward the row of cabinets along the wall, and just as I'd suspected find a pile of towels. The briny scent of the lake sticks to the cotton, but at least they're dry. I offer two to Serena before taking one for myself and leaving my gun on top of the cabinet.

At this point, Serena could have easily run away multiple times if she wanted, but she hasn't. And if she does, I'd rather her have a weapon. I try not to think on what that means.

Without the buttons fastened, I'm able to shrug out of the shirt unassisted, thank *Dio*. I'm not certain I could resist her unbuttoning my shirt with only towels between us. I get to work on my pants as Serena lifts her arms and peels my sweatshirt off her wet body. Her lace bra leaves nothing to the imagination, her nipples so hard they could cut glass.

Merda. And just like that, I'm hard. Never mind the fact that the wound at my chest feels like it's about to erupt despite the pain meds we found in the first-aid kit. I spin around before my pants drop to the floor, and she gets a front row view of my raging erection. Quickly wrapping the towel around my waist, I try to clear my mind of all lusty thoughts which is pretty damned impossible with Serena now in nothing but panties.

She knots the first towel beneath her arms and the second around her waist. Then she slips her hands beneath the fabric and shimmies out of her panties. The lace hits the floor, and heat races down to my cock.

I barely restrain a groan as she folds down to pick it up, flashing me a tempting view of her cleavage. Focus, *coglione*. Squeezing my eyes closed, I drop down onto the surprisingly comfortable lounger. Propping my feet up, I watch as she struggles to get the second sunbed down, my irritation flaring. I feel completely useless. This is not a sensation I'm familiar with and one that I vow never to revisit again.

Once she has the second sunbed situated beside mine, she folds onto it, placing an extra cushion at the bottom. She props up her bad foot, and my stomach dips at the sight of her ankle. All the heat rushing to my cock evaporates, replaced by icy guilt.

"*Cazzo*, Serena, your ankle is twice the size it was yesterday."

"Did you just call my foot fat?" She narrows her eyes at me, a playful smile parting her lips.

"This isn't a joke." That guilt expands, and I'm drowning in the knowledge that this whole fucking disaster is my fault. If I hadn't kidnapped Serena for the sake of my own selfish vengeance, Mariuccia and Fabi would still be alive, Mamma's beloved villa would still stand, and Serena wouldn't have been caught in the middle of whatever the hell this is. "Fuck," I snarl.

"I don't usually fuck my captors, Toni."

My gaze lifts to hers, that amusement still crinkling the corners of her eyes. Somehow, it tempers the building rage along with the suffocating guilt. "How are you taking this so well?"

She adjusts the towel, tucking it under her arm. "How else can I take it? We're kind of stuck with each other for the next twenty-four hours, aren't we?" She reaches for the lantern on the floor and hides it beneath the lounger, dimming the light. "Once we're back in Milano, we go our separate ways, and this is all over."

I nod slowly as much as I despise it. Dante was ready to pull out of the Ferrara territory as I requested. Or at least that was what Tony claimed. Had it all been an act to lull my suspicions? I thought he'd capitulated too easily…

"Antonio?"

"Hmm?"

She holds her hand out, steady gaze locked on my own. "Is it a deal? We get through this, and you release me?"

I remain silent for a long moment, not because I don't agree with her but because the idea of letting her go makes it hard to breathe again. "Of course, *tesoro*." I offer a tight smile. "It's the least I can do considering everything I've put you through."

My hand envelops hers, and I'm surprised at the tight grip. Someone has taught this woman the proper way to shake a hand. My fingers lace firmly around hers, our eyes locked for an endless moment. I'm reluctant to let go.

She finally releases me and sits back on her lounge chair with a contented sigh. "We should sleep."

"Yes, we should." I reach under her chair and turn off the lantern, bathing the old structure in darkness. As I retreat, my hand brushes her bare leg, and a sharp gasp echoes through the silence. "*Scusi*," I murmur.

"No, it's fine." Her voice rises a few octaves. "Your hand is like ice."

I rub my hands together, noticing the chill for the first time and yet, my body feels like it's on fire. Maybe that ankle hadn't extinguished all the brewing heat between us.

"Do you need another towel?" She's up on her feet again and that damned guilt rises.

"No, I need you to stay off that foot."

"I'm fine," she grits out and grabs another towel from the cabinet before whirling around. "I took the rest of the pain meds in that first-aid kit, so I barely feel a thing." She twirls around on her good foot. "See?"

The towel serving as her top comes undone, gifting me a perfect view of her breasts, despite the encroaching darkness. Bullet wound or not, I jolt straight up so I can—do the polite thing and retrieve her towel from the floor.

Forcing my gaze down, I hand it to her without meeting the eyes I can feel boring into me. Does she want me to look? No, it can't be.

"Thanks." She takes the towel, and only when I'm sure I've given her enough time to cover herself up do I lie back down. "You didn't have to close your eyes. I told you, I'm not embarrassed by nudity, mine or anyone else's."

"Still…" I grind out.

"I appreciate the gentlemanly effort."

"It's the least you deserve." I blow out a breath and force my lids closed. Her soft breaths fill the room, an electric buzz in the air that I just can't ignore. I should be exhausted. I've been shot and nearly burned alive, but the fact that Serena is half-naked beside me has my blood pumping and my cock thickening.

I keep my eyes closed and attempt every trick to force myself to sleep, but it just doesn't come.

"Psst, Toni, are you awake?" Serena leans closer, her sweet strawberry scent replacing the briny smell in the air.

"Yes," I murmur.

"I can't sleep." She rolls over to face me, and I mirror her movement despite the pull at the stitches.

"It's the adrenaline, just try to relax, it should pass soon."

She sits up and slides to the edge of the lounger. "Or I can try the old bottle of Sambuca I found in that cabinet beside the towels."

"Seriously?"

"Yup. Someone must have had a secret stash down here." She's on her feet before I can stop her.

"I don't think that's such a good idea..."

"Don't be such a worrier. We're safe. Who's going to think to look for us here?" Pushing the towels aside, she unearths the hidden gem. After the day we've had, a little alcohol to numb the pain sounds like exactly what I need. But it would be risky and irresponsible. It wouldn't only numb the pain but also my reaction time, and that could be the difference between life and death. For both of us.

She saunters over, her blonde hair cascading across her bare shoulders illuminated by the sliver of moon coming in through the skylight. She holds the bottle out with one hand, the other keeping her towel up. "Come on, just one drink?"

I sit up, wincing through the pain. "I don't know—"

"I think you owe me."

"How will a drink make up for any of the shit I dragged you into?"

Her shoulder lifts slowly before falling. "At least we can end our little kidnapping adventure on a high note."

My brow lifts at the flirtatious gleam in her eye. "How do you know you'd enjoy a night of drinking with me?"

"I don't." She drops down into the sunbed beside me and her knees brush mine. "But I'm curious to meet the old Antonio, and I think with a few drinks, I could coax him out."

I shake my head, inhaling slowly. Even at this distance, her sweet scent invades my nostrils and whispers of heat kindle beneath the towel spread across my legs. "The old Antonio died a long time ago, *tesoro*. You should have let this one burn with his memories."

Her head whips back and forth, lips screwing into a pout, before she brings the bottle to her mouth and takes a deep pull. She swallows, licking her lips, eyes pinned to mine. "I don't agree."

"You know nothing about me."

"You're wrong." She takes another sip, eyes narrowing as she regards me. "I know that you risked your life going back into that fire to save two innocent women, I know that you killed a man who did a despicable thing to your captive, someone who is supposed to be nothing more than a bargaining chip, and I know that you despise this new version of yourself, the one you think you have to be."

Every word spears me in the chest, a direct hit to my blackened heart. I'm a monster, how can she not see it?

My thoughts are a jumbled mess, and I can't seem to extricate a single coherent sentence as she hands me the bottle. "Now have a drink, Toni, and I dare you to prove me wrong."

Something snaps inside me, the years of restraint and brewing anger boil over. "Wrong? I'll tell you exactly what kind of a man I am. Right now, even with your ankle shot to hell, the house burned down, unknown men after us, and the memories of your assault fresh in your mind, there is nothing I want more than to fuck you until you moan my name."

Her mouth curves into a tempting capital O, and I imagine fucking those pretty pink lips, too.

"Does that sound like something a good man would want?"

"Good is highly overrated, Toni."

And her mouth crashes into mine.

CHAPTER 31
DON'T STOP

Serena

My tongue pushes past Antonio's clenched teeth, and a growl vibrates the back of his throat as his hand curls around my nape. His tongue meets mine, hungry and savage, matching me stroke for stroke.

Dio, I needed this.

After Otto left me feeling so out of control and helpless, I need my power back and Antonio Ferrara is just the man to give it to me. To bring this powerful man to his knees will be the ultimate revenge against that coward who wanted to take advantage of me.

I'm in charge now, and I want this man.

Could it be the pain meds mixed with the alcohol talking? Maybe, but I don't give a fuck. I need this.

Antonio's hands clamp around my hips, and he drags me onto his lap. My towel barely still hangs around my waist, and with nothing but the cotton fabric between us, I can feel his thick cock between my legs.

I grind against him, lost in the heated moment before a flash of white catches my eye. "Your wound!" I squeal.

"I'm fine. I don't feel a thing."

My eyes lift to his, to ferret out the lie. I've been watching him since I finished sewing him up, and there's no doubt he's in pain. "Are you sure?"

"I'm sure." He silences all further objections with his mouth.

His hands roam across my back, unraveling the towel I wear as a top, and my breasts spring free. His arms tighten around me so my nipples brush against his warm skin, sending jolts of pleasure through the highly sensitive tips. My head falls back as I stifle a moan. There's no way he earns one of mine before I get to hear him breaking apart for me.

His mouth moves down my jaw line, tongue tracing the curve before finding my sensitive lobe. He draws it into his mouth and nibbles, and heat races to my pussy. Fuck, I can't remember the last time I've wanted someone so badly.

Ever since the moment I saw Antonio Ferrara all those months ago outside the nightclub, I hadn't been able to get him out of my mind. There was something so tempting about the dangerous mob boss. And maybe, the fact that he was Raf's brother had something to do with it too. Because clearly, I'm insane.

"I thought you told me never to kiss you again." A wry grin curls his lips.

"I did. I kissed you so it's not the same."

"Ah, I see." His tongue flicks my earlobe, and goosebumps ripple across my arms.

From my ear, he licks his way down my neck and collarbone, and I arch against him, my hips grinding against the towel between us. I'm so soaked there's going to be a huge embarrassing wet spot in a second. He draws my nipple into his mouth, and the moan I've been trying so hard to hold back, bursts free.

The corner of his lip tips up as he continues to suck and lick, the heat of him seeping into my own skin and heightening the building flames.

"Mmm, *tesoro*," he murmurs against my breast, "you taste just like I imagined, strawberries and sweet vanilla." His hands wrap around my ass, fingers digging into my flesh in a punishing grip. My towel unravels and now only the one haphazardly slung across his hips remains.

With each desperate rock of my body, it slides farther down. My hand roams his chest, tracing the dips and valleys of his perfectly carved torso. I stay well away from the bandaged wound, keeping one wary eye on it, despite the overwhelming need overtaking all rational thoughts. My fingers trail further to the sharp V that disappears beneath the towel.

"Careful, *tesoro*, if you keep that up, I'm going to lose all restraint."

"Good. I want you at my mercy."

"Oh, Serena, you've had me for days." His eyes smolder, the velvety black ablaze.

My fingers dip beneath the towel and find his silky hard length. His head falls back on a groan as my hand closes around him.

"Fuck," he hisses. "Just your hand feels so good…"

"Wait till you feel my pussy."

He laughs, his chest rumbling beneath me, and his bandage grazes my right breast. I stiffen, the roll of my hips freezing on the spot.

His eyes snap to mine, the hunger in that dark gaze stealing my breath. "No, don't stop. I'm not in pain, I swear it. The only thing that would kill me right now is if you stopped." His hand slides from my ass and curves around my thigh, running over the spring of violets tattooed to my skin. If he notices the tattoo, he doesn't mention it. Maybe he's too caught up in the heated moment like I am. He finds my clit and desperate need unfolds. "Now let me feel that sweet pussy." He slowly draws his finger through my wetness, then begins to circle when he reaches the apex. Tantalizing heat courses through my veins, and I'm powerless not to arch to into his touch. "Do you like that, *tesoro*?"

"Mmm, yes," I rasp.

"If the circumstances were different, I would have you coming on my finger, then my mouth and finally my cock, all night long."

I slow the maddening grinding of my hips just long enough to meet his eyes. "You're a tease, you know that?"

He chuckles again, the smooth, warm sound only intensifying the roaring pleasure. "Oh, don't worry, *tesoro*, I'm still going to make you come, just not as many times as I'd like."

"You're pretty confident, huh?"

Antonio nods and with my hips working like mad, the towel slips from beneath me, exposing his hard-ass cock between my legs. Damn, he's huge. Anticipation tightens my core as I take him in, a bead of cum glistening on his thick head. I can already imagine it thrusting inside me, hitting my clit with each powerful drive of his hips.

I grind against his length, the hot feel of him only heightening the building heat below. I'm so wet I could take all of him in, right now. My eyes drop to the bandage on his chest, to the crimson stains just below the gauze. Fuck, we should not be doing this right now. Too bad my tipsy pussy isn't getting the message. All she wants is that big, gorgeous cock inside her.

As if Antonio has heard my lust-fueled thoughts, he dips a finger inside me. *Holy shit.* My teeth graze my bottom lip to keep from moaning. The sensation of his thick finger plunging in and out, his thumb circling devastatingly slowly as I grind on his cock already has me on the brink of orgasm.

Which is just insane.

I'm never this easily aroused.

His free hand toys with my nipple as his mouth devours my neck, tongue dragging across the sensitive skin. There's so much of him everywhere. And yet, it isn't enough. Raw need throbs between my legs, aching for that fullness only one thing can provide, I need that cock inside me.

Again, I hazard a quick peek at the wound. Would I be able to control myself and go slow?

Probably not.

The raging heat burning up my core is ravenous, and gentle lovemaking is not really my thing.

His thumb circles faster, putting just the right amount of pressure on my needy clit and a second finger drives inside me. This time I can't contain the gasp of pleasure at the sudden, unexpected fullness. The walls of my pussy constrict around his fingers desperate to ring out every ounce of pleasure.

"Come for me, *tesoro*," he whispers against my lips, capturing my mouth like it's his to claim.

He quickens his tantalizing thrusts, drawing nearly all the way out before plunging even deeper, fingertips curling to reach that elusive spot. That raging inferno grows to uncontrollable levels and flames lick across my veins, sucking the breath from my lungs.

"Oh, fuck, I'm going to come," I rasp out.

"Good girl." He draws my nipple into his mouth, a growl vibrating his throat and pleasure explodes from my core, rippling out to every inch of my being.

My head falls back and raw energy tingles across my flesh, diving down to my toes and leaving me breathless. He continues to suck on my breast, tongue flicking at the super-sensitive tip of my nipple until the wave begins to subside.

I'm panting, my legs boneless as I hang on his neck, balancing across his lap. Finally, as the last tremor falls away, I drop my forehead to his, my breathing still uneven. That was the best orgasm from only a finger that I've had my entire life. Now as he watches me from beneath hooded lids, I can't stop imagining what that would feel like on his cock.

"Well?" He arches a dark brow.

"Well, what?" I take the bait, knowing fully well where he's going with this.

"I told you I'd make you come even without full use of my faculties."

"Faculties? Is that what you call this monster?" My hand drops between us, and I stroke his hard length. He's straining beneath me, his balls tight. That cannot be comfortable.

With a frustrated sigh, he brings his hand up to caress my cheek. "Next time, will be more... everything."

"Who says there will be a next time? I'm not in the habit of fucking my kidnappers." Still my hand curls around the back of his neck, fingers trailing the soft hair at his nape.

"Hopefully by tomorrow, I will no longer be your kidnapper and you, my hostage."

"Then what will we be?"

His shoulders lift nonchalantly but the tendon in his jaw spasms at the movement. Shit, the wound. I hope it didn't tear when I was coming from that mind-blowing orgasm. "I suppose we'll see by then," he whispers.

I nod slowly, my eyes now focused on his strained expression. His jaw is clenched tight, and the faint lines between his brows are furrowed. "Are you sure you're okay?"

His hands curl around my hips, and he gently deposits me on the lounger beside him. "Yes, I'm fine. I'm only pissed I can't coax out another few orgasms from those tempting lips. If this really is our only time, it seems a terrible waste."

I grin up at him like an idiot. "Like you said, I guess we'll see what happens tomorrow." Testing out the weight on my ankle, I slowly rise and stagger the step to my own lounge chair. Re-wrapping myself in the towels, I settle in on the soft cushions.

Antonio eyes me from across the small divide, an indescribable longing in those smoldering irises. *"Buona notte, tesoro,"* he murmurs.

"Yeah, goodnight." I force my lids to close, despite the unease ricocheting through my chest.

CHAPTER 32
LOST CAUSES

S*erena*

Something wakes me from a fitful sleep, a feeling I can't even name. Dragging my heavy lids open, I roll over on the narrow lounge chair and take in my surroundings. With the haze of sleep still weighing me down, it takes me a minute before memories of the night before flash to the surface.

Shit. I let Antonio finger fuck me to oblivion.

And damn, it was amazing.

Flipping over to face the mob boss, I feel the burn of embarrassment tingeing my cheeks. He's rolled over to his side, facing away from me. Thank goodness. I need a minute to get myself together. It's a damned good thing he was injured because if he hadn't been, I would have done more than just come on his fingers. I wanted him so badly last night. *Dio*, what is wrong with me?

My gaze settles on the canvas of tattoos across his back, lit up by the warm glow of the rising sun. I've never had the opportunity to get such a close-up look. I can't help but stare at the collection of art inked up and down the hard planes of his flesh. The largest one in the middle catches my eye, a snake wrapped around a dagger with scales hanging from each side of the hilt. Beneath it, in big bold letters, it reads "*Lex Talionis*". My Latin is pretty shit, but the motto is a familiar one in our world. "An eye for an eye" is the law my father and uncles live by. Who are you trying to get revenge on, Antonio? The answer right now is obvious, but who inspired this particular tattoo? I'm tempted to trace the dark lines but squeeze my fingers into a fist instead.

A patch of puckered skin catches my eye, a raised scar bleeding into another, then a noticeable angry red mark. I follow the line, looking past the dagger and scales. I barely restrain the gasp as I finally understand what I'm looking at. Beneath the tattoos lies destroyed skin, puckered, red, burned... Oh, *Dio*, I can't imagine how badly one must have been burnt to leave those scars.

My thoughts flicker back to the story Isabella told me of the day she and Raf escaped his father's compound. The whole thing had been set ablaze. Had Antonio been there? Neither of them had mentioned him at all that day. It had only been a few months ago. And to have the broken, scarred skin tattooed so soon after? It had to have hurt like hell, pure torture. Why would he have done that to himself?

And it would mean that the revenge he sought was against his own brother...

The more I think about it, the more horrific it all sounds. An unexpected wave of pity washes over me. *Dio*, what is wrong with me?

I should be planning my escape, which in Antonio's current state, would be as easy as taking candy from a baby. His gun is just sitting there on the counter, waiting to be stolen. But I can't move. I can barely breathe after this discovery. Antonio was right last night. I could have easily walked away from this disaster yesterday and left him to die. So why am I still here?

Fuck. The answer is so obvious it's embarrassing. I'm a sucker for lost causes, for fucked up men. And now, I just have to know how he got those scars, those burns. What hell had he gone through? Falling for the man who kidnapped you is the worst of all cliches. And here I am *that* girl. I guess it happens to the best of us. It is how my Aunt Stella and Uncle Luca got together...

Pressing my fingers to my temples, I force my thoughts to stop their endless rambling. If I am staying with Antonio until this is over, I need to get him to a doctor. Forcing myself up, I slide to the end of the lounger and reach for his bare shoulder. The bandage he'd insisted on securing across his back has bled through. *Shit.* "Antonio," I whisper. "Antonio, wake up."

I give him a little shake, but he doesn't move. My fingers clutch onto his shoulder a little tighter, and his skin scalds my palm. Oh, no, he's burning up.

"Antonio!" A shrill cry laces my tone as I jump off the lounge chair and hover over him.

Peeling off the bandage, I find the wound at his chest. There's inflamed, red, infected skin rising around the thread I used to sew him up. Ugh, I'm such an idiot. Why did I ever think that would work? I'm not Bella, I'm not a fucking doctor. His breathing is labored, his chest rising and falling much too sluggishly.

"Why won't you wake up?" I shout at him, slapping his face a little too forcefully. "Please, wake up."

He's going to die. If I don't get him to a hospital, it's inevitable. I don't have antibiotics and clearly that wound is infected. I glance at my watch and hiss out a curse. It's barely seven. Should I risk driving him into town on the boat? And if whoever sent those men are still around, I will have condemned us both to death.

Shit, what else can I do?

Antonio's phone is probably at the bottom of the lake by now and every damned person I know in Como is dead. Except for...

Elena, the doctor. Damn it, what was her last name? Bergamo, no, Barga—Bergamaschi! I jump to my feet, letting the towel fall away and scramble for my clothes. I could get him on the boat and—shit, he's so heavy and even if I do get him on the boat, I can't just leave him tethered to some dock. No, I can leave Antonio here, take the boat into town alone and ask around for the *dottoressa*. If Como is like any typical Italian town, someone will know where to find her.

Still, I hate the idea of leaving him here alone and completely unprotected. *Suck it up, Serena.* There is no other option.

As I slip on the sweats, Antonio's musky scent somehow still lingers on the material. The fact that it brings a smile to my face only confirms I've lost my damned mind. I spot the gun on the counter and slide it into my sweatpants. Just in case.

The logical part of me says I'll keep it in case I get a chance to escape, but the other demented part knows I won't leave him, not like this. I glance at Antonio's form sprawled out on the lounger and for a second, I freeze. I'm terrified of what will happen if I fail. Grabbing one of the discarded towels, I pour some bottled water I found in the cabinet on one end and press the cool towel to his forehead.

Dio, his skin is on fire.

Dousing the towel in more water, I cover his entire body, hoping it'll help with the fever. If I had more time, I'd drop him into the lake, but I doubt I'd be able to move the giant myself. Pressing a quick kiss to his forehead, I squeeze his hand. "I'll be back, hold on."

A groan purses his lips, and I freeze again. "Antonio? Can you hear me?" I wait an endless moment.

Nothing.

"Please don't die." Something I never thought I'd say to Antonio Ferrara.

Before I lose my nerve, I shove my feet into my sneakers and race out of the boathouse.

The air is brisk as I pull up to the small dock around the cove. I don't dare leave the boat so close to the center of town where anyone could stumble across it. At least here, it's partially covered by the sprawling trees. Cutting the engine, I prop the old fisherman's hat I found among the tattered tarps on the top of my head, hiding my long, blonde curls. Then I leap out of the old Riva and pat the gun hidden in the oversized pocket of Antonio's sweatpants. *Dio*, if Santi saw me now, he'd never recognize me. Which is exactly what I'm hoping.

I dart across the creaking wooden boards of the weather-worn dock and step onto the sidewalk that rims the scenic views of Lago di Como. Dozens of tourists mill about, taking pictures with their families, and I easily weave in and out of the pedestrian traffic. Now, the question is: where do I go to ask about Elena?

I eye the quaint old town center with the cobble-stoned roads and bright pastel storefronts. There's a *gelateria*, a fresh fruit market, dozens of restaurants and… a post office! I dart across the street, nearly getting run over by a bike rider, and rush inside over the sounds of his Italian curses.

Inside, it's nearly empty, with just one elderly woman hunched over a counter licking stamps to place on a tower of envelopes.

"*Buongiorno*," I call out to the man behind the counter.

The gray-haired, middle-aged man gives me a toothy grin. "*Buongiorno, signorina.* How can I help you?"

Clearing my throat, I tip the wide-brimmed hat back and steel my nerves. "I'm sorry to bother you, but I'm afraid I've gotten lost. I'm supposed to be on my way to see *Dottoressa* Elena Bergamaschi, but I've lost my cell which had her phone number and address."

"Ah, I see." The man's lips curve into a frown, and he rubs at his mustache. "*Mi dispiace*, but as a government employee, I can't give out the personal information of a resident. I wish I could, but you see, my hands are really tied."

"Please, it's urgent. Couldn't you make a special exception this one time?" If I had cash, I'd throw a few Euro to sweeten the deal.

"*Mi dispiace*, I'm sorry," he repeats.

The tiny flicker of hope dissipates, and fear strangles my lungs in a vice grip. If I don't find her, Antonio could die. I shouldn't give a shit, but damn it, I do. And I can't even tell these people what's happening in case those guys are looking for us. Tears prick at the corners of my eyes, and my throat tightens. I bring down the sloping brim of the hat to hide my face before the tears spill over.

The mailman starts to mumble more apologies in Italian, but it does nothing to fill the sprawling void opening up in my chest. A tears spills over, then another and another, and there's nothing I can do stop the waterfall. It's a combination of weeks of pent-up fear, anger and frustration.

I'm so caught up in the whirlwind of unexpected emotions I barely notice the old woman beside me. She slips a piece of paper in my clenched fist and offers a reassuring smile. I startle at her touch, then whirl around to meet a pair of kind, pale gray eyes.

"*Fortunatamente per te, io non ho fatto alcun giuramento del genere.*" Lucky for you, I've sworn no such thing. A smile starts to threaten. "*Auguro tutto il meglio al tuo caro,*" she whispers before depositing her envelopes on the counter and turning for the door.

"*Grazie!*" I shout behind her before I have time to explain to her that he's not a loved one at all, but it was so kind of her to wish him well.

I stare at the crumpled paper in my hands and the dark scrawling of a phone number and address. Those embers of hope burn brightly once again. Glancing up at the postal worker, I sweep away the tears. "Can I at least use your phone?"

His head bobs up and down. "*Si, certo, signorina.*"

CHAPTER 33
INEXPLICABLE FEELINGS

Serena

I pace the short length of the boathouse so quickly I just end up making my head spin. Elena has been working on Antonio for the past hour, and I haven't been able to sit still. His wound was so infected that even unconscious he'd cried out when the *dottoressa* had removed the thread. The thread that I'd insisted on using.

Dio, I'm an idiot.

This is why Bella is the doctor, not me.

What feels like an eternity later, Elena props her glasses on the top of her head and glances up at me. "I've removed all the thread, along with the infected tissue around it. I cannot close the wound now for fear of a secondary infection. All we can do is keep it open and clean and hope it will heal itself from the inside out. It will take longer and the scarring will be worse, but at least he'll live."

"This is all my fault…" I murmur.

"No." Her eyes narrow, lips twisting in disgust. "You did not choose to be dragged into this situation, Serena. The guilt here lies with Antonio, and only Antonio."

"But if I hadn't sewn him up—"

"He would have bled out and died, as he almost did from the wound on his back which was left open. There were no good options. You did the best you could." She speaks matter of factly, and with no nonsense. She isn't trying to coddle me or consider my feelings.

I don't dare bring up the fact that I came all over his fingers last night. The exertion, sweat, and all the rest could not have possibly helped the situation.

Digging into her bag, she places a pile of bandages, disinfectant spray, and a bottle of antibiotics at the end of the sunbed. Then she rises and exhales a long breath. "Now, I suggest you take advantage of his current state and find your way home."

"And just leave him like this?" Guilt and something else zips through my chest, spearing at my heart at the idea.

"I've already given him pain medicine and a dose of the antibiotics. The fever will subside soon enough. Once it does, he'll wake and be more than capable of caring for himself. I've left him everything he needs." She pauses, sharp eyes fixed to mine, on the oversized sweats I still wear. "Go, Serena, your freedom lies just beyond the door." The *dottoressa* signals toward the old timber, but my feet are rooted to the spot.

"I—I..." What? I can't even come up with a single logical excuse that would keep me here. Whoever set fire to the villa must be gone by now. "Can I use your phone to contact my father?"

She nods. "Of course." Drawing it out from the inside of her jacket, she hands it to me. "I'll wait outside so you can have some privacy."

"*Grazie.*" I offer her my best smile as I clutch the phone to my chest. "Elena," I call out before she slips out. "If you hate Antonio so much, why did you come when I called?"

"I did it for Maria Graziella, in his mother's memory." The tight set of her jaw softens. "If she had been here, she would have begged for his life, despite all the terrible things he's done with it."

"It wasn't his fault he turned out this way." I don't know why I find myself defending my abductor, but here we are.

"I know." She nods slowly. "But it's never too late to change, to start over."

"And you don't think Antonio will?"

"I hope with all my heart that he does, but I've found that it's easier to remain on the same familiar path than to forge a new one." She turns toward the door, and I don't stop her this time.

I glance over my shoulder at Antonio, sprawled across the lounge chair. A clean, white bandage stretches across his bare chest and curves around to his back. Despite his wound looking better, his expression is pinched, even in sleep. Am I completely insane to even consider staying with him until he wakes?

Blowing out a frustrated breath, I turn my attention to the phone in my palm. *Papà* is going to lose his shit when he finds out what happened. I hold my breath, waiting for that familiar voice. It rings and rings but no answer. I try two more times before I leave a message.

"Pa it's me. I'm okay, but things kind of went to hell at Antonio's place. The villa has been burned down, and he doesn't know who's behind it. He took a bullet in the back, and we're hiding out until this blows over. We're not sure if they came for me or him. It's gotta be that Sartori guy, right? Anyway, neither of us have a phone so I'm not sure when I'll be able to call you again, but I'll try soon. We're in Como, and I'm going to head back to Milano the first chance I get. I'm safe with Antonio so don't worry too much." I hang up, purposely being vague about the whole hostage situation. If *Papà* knew I had the opportunity to run and didn't, he'd be really worried about my sanity. And rightfully so.

Before I relinquish the phone to Elena, I make one more quick call. *Please pick up. Please pick up.*

"*Dottoressa* Bergamaschi?" Raf's voice echoes across the line and unexpected emotion tightens my throat. I never thought I'd have a reaction like that to Bella's bodyguard.

"No, it's me, Serena."

"Serena, what the fuck? Where are you? Isabella's been going nuts—"

His voice cuts off, replaced by a much more pleasant, if not high-pitched one. "Sere!"

"I'm okay, Bella. I'm safe."

"What? Why wouldn't you be safe? I thought you were ghosting me because you were scared I'd yell at you for not telling me about your permanent move to Milano."

"What? No… I was abducted the night of your welcome home party and dragged back to Italy."

"What?" she screeches across the line. "Abducted?"

"*Papà* didn't tell you?"

"No, I haven't heard from your father since that night. Even my dad has been MIA besides an occasional text message. What is going on?"

"It's Antonio Ferrara."

"Raf's brother?" She shrieks again and now Raf's back on the line.

"I'm going to murder that fucking traitorous—" His voice echoes across the speaker.

"Stop, Raf. He was shot, almost burned alive at your family's villa in Como."

"Why the hell did he bring you there? He vowed never to return—"

"It doesn't matter," I cut him off. "All that matters is that I'm okay, and I think he's going to be."

"I don't give two shits about that *bastardo*," Raf growls.

"Sere?" Bella interrupts. "Are you still with him?"

"Umhmm."

"Put him on the phone," Raf barks.

"I can't. He's still unconscious."

"Then what the fuck are you still doing there?" I can hear the venom in Raf's tone, and a twinge of sadness rears up. I just told him his brother almost died, and he didn't even flinch.

"Sere, are you okay?" The concern in Bella's voice is palpable.

"I am now."

"Then why are you still with him?"

"I—I don't know."

"Oh, for fuck's sake, Serena," Raf grumbles. "Bella said you had bad taste in men, but—"

"Shut up!" Bella hisses, then there's the sound of a scuffle and the speaker shuts off. "Sere, it's just me. Are you going to explain what is happening or will I have to jump on a plane to Como and drag your ass back home?"

"No!" I blurt. "It's not safe for you, Bella. You stay right where you are. We have no idea who was behind the fire and they could still be in the city, which is why we're lying low."

"We?"

"Huh?"

"You used *we* in that sentence twice, Sere." She pauses, heaving in a breath. "What is going on with you and Antonio?"

"It's complicated..."

"Oh, shit. Raf's right, isn't he? You fell for your kidnapper?"

"No..." *Dio*, it's not like I'm in love with him. I just have inexplicable feelings. "Look, he came to my rescue and now I feel like I owe him, okay?"

"Rescued you from what? After he kidnapped you?"

Elena's head pops into the boathouse, and she signals to the watch on her wrist.

I nod quickly. "Bella, I can't explain everything right now, and I have to go but try to get a hold of my dad. Tell him I'm safe and that I'm going to return to Milano as soon as I can."

"Why won't you let me come for you?"

"I already told you, it's not safe," I hiss.

"Then I'll send Raf."

"Absolutely not." He'll kill Antonio before he has a chance to explain. "Raf needs to stay with you and keep you safe."

"Fine then, how about Matty or Alessandro?"

"I've got this under control, I swear." But do I really? I blow out another breath, giving me just another second to think. "Okay, tell Alessandro to meet me at the airport in Milano in three days. If I don't show, tell him to call the cavalry."

"Three whole days?"

I glance over at Antonio, at the blood already seeping through the pristine bandage. "Yes, three days, Bella. And don't you dare come with him or tell my father or anyone else for that matter, or I swear to *Dio*, I'll never speak to you again."

"You're crazy, Sere, but I love you. Please be safe."

"Same here, cuz." I jab my finger at the call end button and walk over to Elena who still stands by the door.

She throws a disapproving glare in my direction. "You're not leaving."

"I'm not leaving. *Yet*."

Her head dips with a frustrated sigh. "If you insist on staying, make sure he rests for the next twenty-four to forty-eight hours. It's crucial he doesn't exert himself and reopen that wound. Do you understand?"

My head dips quickly.

"Maybe *Dio* sent you to him for a reason." Her brow lifts, assessing. "Or maybe it was Maria Graziella herself." With a shrug, she spins to the door and marches out.

CHAPTER 34
SO LONG SUCKERS

Serena

The next day drags on, and I spend most of it just watching the sluggish rise and fall of Antonio's chest. Why isn't he awake yet? I run my hand over his forehead which is cool to the touch. The fever is gone, and I've unwrapped and wrapped the bandages twice now, making sure there's no further sign of infection.

Every time I get a glimpse of the scars on his back, I wince. Now he'll have another one to add to the collection. I just hope he doesn't attempt to tattoo over this one until it's fully healed.

After fiddling with his bandage again to ensure it's comfortable, I flop back down on the lounger. I have Elena's contact information but no way of actually reaching her. I've debated going back into town to buy some supplies for hours. My stomach is growling, close to the point of eating itself, and even the bottles of water I found in the cabinets are about to run out. And I need a phone. After the *dottoressa* left yesterday, I rifled through Antonio's clothes and almost cried like a baby when I found his wallet. The cash had been soaked and destroyed from our walk through the river, but the credit cards seem to be in good shape.

Using the credit card is risky, in case someone is tracking Antonio's financials, but at this point, I'm willing to take the chance. Being cut off from the rest of the world won't be feasible for much longer. Besides, we'll need money once he wakes up so we can get the hell out of here.

The musky, salty scent of the boathouse is already permanently embedded in my nostrils, and I'm not sure how much more of this I can take. My stomach churns, queasiness setting in from the lack of a proper meal in over forty-eight hours. I'd been so worried about Antonio, I'd totally forgotten about my basic needs.

Shit… was Bella right? Have I fallen for Antonio Ferrara in only a week?

Nope, not possible.

Only a complete psychopath would fall in love with a man like Ferrara.

It's just the chaotic situation we've been forced in, the near-death experience, and the amazing mind-blowing orgasm. My poor head and heart are just confused.

With that thought in mind, I force myself off the lounger and grab the wallet beside me. It's time to go into town and plan for my next move. If Alessandro is meeting me in Milano in two days, I need to make damned sure I'm there for the extraction or Bella will have the entirety of the Kings forces descending on northern Italy.

Lacing my sneakers, I shove the wallet in my pocket and head for the door. *Dio*, I'd give anything for a change of clothes and a shower. With Antonio's credit card, I could have both of those things but the moment the store owner runs the card, it's only a matter of time until we're tracked to Como. The boathouse is secluded enough, but for how long will it be safe?

I stand at the door, willing my feet forward, but my head

swings back all the same. Antonio is just where I left him, eyes closed, fast asleep. *Move.* I urge my feet forward. *He's fine. He'll be fine. Damn it, Serena, you are not allowed to fall in love with your kidnapper!*

Reaching for the fisherman's hat by the door, I drop it onto my wild nest of hair. Then, twisting the old door handle, I march out, forbidding myself to look back.

Dozens of tourists fill the cobblestone streets of the old town, and I try my best to remain hidden within the masses, clutching my bag of groceries in one hand and the new pre-paid cell in the other. I'm so hungry, I can't help myself but bite into an apple as I head back toward the dock where I'd left the Riva.

I pass by a little boutique, the mannequin dressed in a cute flowy top and jeans calling to me, but I force my legs to keep moving. Maybe Antonio woke up and for some inexplicable reason the idea of him finding himself alone tugs at invisible strings around my heart.

Shaking the stupid out, I turn down a quieter side street that leads back to the lake. Only a few pedestrians line the road, a woman with a child and another man walking half a block behind me. I hazard a quick glance back and meet a pair of dark eyes. Coincidence. We're in Italy, lots of men check out blondes. Even with the oversized hat and sweats, my long locks are a beacon to the roving eye. I draw in a breath, reminding myself to stay calm. The woman disappears into a store just ahead, leaving only me and the other guy. I quicken my pace, matching the accelerating footfalls behind me.

Turning another corner, I start to move faster, the swishing of the plastic bags against my thighs echoing the manic beats of my thundering pulse. I glance back again, and he's there, slowly shrinking the distance between us.

I have Antonio's gun, but I can't just open fire in the middle of downtown Como without attracting attention. Just to test my theory, I stop in front of a boutique and spend minutes staring at the mannequin. I wait for the guy to pass by me, but he never does. Shit. This is not a coincidence.

"*Buongiorno.* May I help you?" A sales lady appears in the doorway, and I release the breath I didn't realize I'd been holding.

"Yes," I murmur as I point at the display window. "I'd like to try that on."

"*Certo,* come right this way."

I follow her inside the store and instantly, my wild pulse begins to slow. Guess I am going shopping after all.

I take an excessive amount of time trying on clothes, then modeling them in front of the mirror in the main part of the store. Each time I emerge from the changing room, I catch a glimpse of the man lingering just across the street.

Damn it. It has to have been Antonio's credit card. Tracking someone's financials like that is no easy feat. Whoever is after Antonio is still here, and they have deep pockets and eyes everywhere. How the hell am I going to make it back to the boat without being followed? Or worse…

When I disappear into the changing room, I take an extra-long break, trying to figure out my next move. I could call Elena with my new phone. She's the only person I know in Como, but I hate dragging her into this again. She's already made her feelings about Antonio clear. And if reaching out puts her in danger, I'd never forgive myself. Rifling through the pile of clothes I've amassed, I feel slightly guilty for the sales lady. I've worked retail before and cleaning up the dressing rooms at closing is the worst part of the job.

That guilt forces my hand to pick up a cute top and jeans, something that'll be easy to run in. I shove Antonio's sweatpants and gun into the plastic bag with the new phone in it, and finally, push back the linen curtain.

"Have you made your decision?" the saleslady asks.

"Yes, I'll take this." I signal to the new outfit I'm already wearing. "I came on foot so unfortunately I won't be able to carry everything I loved back, but I'll be back with my husband for more!" *Husband*? Where the hell did that come from?

"Of course." She smiles and starts to pull the tickets off the clothes.

Once I've paid, I tick my head toward the door I'd seen at the back of the store. "Can I go out the back? It's a little closer to my walk home."

"Yes, of course, *signorina*." She leads me through the changing room to the metal door in the back. "I hope to see you again soon."

"I hope so too."

As soon as I register the slam of the door behind me, I race down the cobblestone street, sending a thank you up to Mariuccia for getting me these sneakers. If it had been up to me, I would have been in high heels which would have made this escape impossible.

Rushing down the back alley, I emerge onto the main street two blocks later. Pausing at the corner, I glance down the avenue and heave out a sigh of relief when my stalker is nowhere in sight.

You've still got it, Sere. I smile as I cross the street and head toward the lake in a quick, but not breakneck, pace. My stomach grumbles again, reminding me the apple wasn't enough to tide me over. I consider reaching for another one but decide against it just in case. That guy could be anywhere. I can't wait to be back in the safety of the boathouse. *And near Antonio.*

I mentally slap myself for the traitorous thought.

I'll eat, feed him, if he's awake, then tomorrow we go our separate ways. I'll be back in Milano just in time to meet up with Alessandro, and I'll head back to Manhattan for a few weeks while the dust settles. Hopefully, I'll still have a job when I return to Dolce & Gabbana.

The narrow street widens, giving way to the glistening lake beyond, and I quicken my pace as I cross the busy street.

"There she is!" A shout echoes from my right, and I twist my head over my shoulder in the middle of the crosswalk just in time to see the guy from earlier racing toward me. There's another man running up behind him, only a few paces away.

Shit.

I dart across the street, and the shrill blast of a horn thunders across my eardrum as a truck screeches to a halt not even a foot in front of me. My hands slam down on the front bumper, my heart leaping up my throat.

Another crash resounds from behind, metal crushing against metal.

The driver shouts curses in Italian, but I don't stop to apologize for the three-car pile-up I've just caused. Instead, I weave through traffic, thanking all the gods and saints that ever lived for the cars blocking the path of the men sprinting after me.

Clutching my bags, I race across the dock, the Italian flag of the Riva waving on the breeze. Antonio's gun beckons from the shopping bag, but I don't dare pull it out. Nothing like calling more attention to yourself than revealing a gun in a crowded street. Pumping my arms to move faster, I dart across the worn wooden floorboards and leap onto the boat.

The two men are only yards behind me now and gaining as I stab the key into the ignition and twist. *Come on, baby.* The engine revs, but much too slowly. *Come on.* It finally flares to life, and I jerk it into motion, turning the steering wheel to maneuver out of the dock.

The two men barrel toward the end of the marina, barely stopping before plunging into the lake. I turn around, then offer a wave and a cheeky smile. "So long suckers."

One of the men pulls a gun from his jacket and points the barrel at me. *Merda!* I draw in a breath before diving for cover, my heart battering my ribcage. Pinned to the floor, I rifle through the shopping bag and clutch Antonio's gun in my fist. Then, I wait for the longest minute of my life, but the shots never come. Interesting... Maybe they were told to bring me in alive. My frenzied breathing slows, my racing pulse following soon after. Once I'm sure I'm beyond shooting distance, I poke my head up.

They're gone.

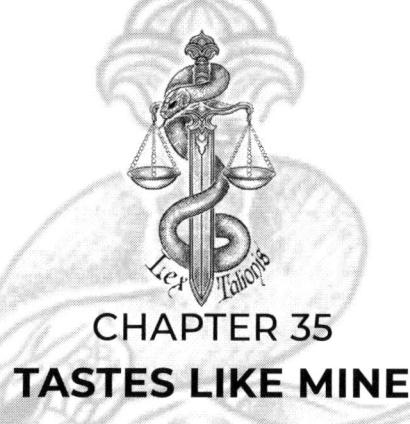

CHAPTER 35
TASTES LIKE MINE

A ntonio

My lids flutter open, a crushing weight on my chest. Fuck, that hurts. Exhaustion weighs on me, heavy and almost unbearable. *Serena*. I force my heavy lids open and meet the dimly lit room. The boathouse. Slowly, memories muddle their way to the surface. I force myself to sit up, and my head spins. I reach for the empty lounge chair beside me, and a tangle of emotions crash across my insides.

Serena's gone.

Good.

Yes, she did the right thing, the smart one.

So why is the thought of never seeing her again more painful than the bullet wound and the terrible fire I'd endured all those months ago combined?

"*Merda…*" I grit out.

Then my gaze lands on the supplies strewn across the lounger to my right. Antibiotics, bandages, disinfectants…

where had these come from? And how long have I been out for? I glance at my wristwatch and stare at the tiny number in the corner. Muttering a curse, I try to stand and fail, as I process the fact that I slept through two entire days. What else had I missed?

Raking my hands across my face, a familiar strawberry scent laced with vanilla fills my nostrils. I bring my fingers to my nose and inhale Serena's intoxicating natural fragrance still clinging to my skin. At least, I hadn't dreamt that part. *Dio*, the sound of her coming on my fingers was like a forgotten symphony that would forever be emblazoned in my mind. Even half delirious from pain and infection, it had been unforgettable. And I hadn't even had the chance to come myself.

I hadn't even cared to. It was all about her.

And now, she's gone.

Rightfully so, Tonio. After what you did to that poor girl. *Mamma*'s voice is exceptionally clear as it bounces across my skull. Which makes me wonder if I'm not still a bit feverish after all.

With the hollow in my chest only growing deeper, I attempt to stand for a second time, and now, I manage to remain on my feet with my hand brushing the sunbed to steady myself. My wet clothes from two days ago hang from a hook on the wall. They smell like the lake but at least they're dry. I rifle through the pocket, searching for my wallet, but it's gone.

I was certain I had the wallet two days ago, didn't I?

Scanning the boathouse, I glance at the countertop where I'm certain I left my gun. It's gone too. Good. At least she'll be armed. As I continue scanning the empty space, I find the remnants of the bottle of Sambuca and my ribs tighten, my lungs constricting from the pressure. Heated memories surge to the surface, those puckered pink lips, the way my hand perfectly fit her breast, her body molding to my own as she ground her hips against my cock. Smoldering heat races beneath the towel, and my cock thickens at the vivid images.

Dio, the things I wanted to do to her… More than that, it was the onslaught of long buried emotions she elicited. I never thought I could feel that way again. She stayed when anyone else would have run away screaming. She came back for me, risking her life to search for me in that blazing inferno. Her teasing smile fills my vision, but I blink quickly to chase it away, the wounds too raw. Maybe in another lifetime, Serena Valentino.

The door whips open, and Serena barrels in, her brilliant blue eyes wild. My breath catches, all the air siphoning from my lungs at the sight of her. *Cazzo*, am I hallucinating? "Serena…"

She drops her shopping bags on the floor, then throws her arms around the back of my neck and her mouth claims mine, devouring my lips. It doesn't matter that I'm dizzy and barely standing because right now all that I know is that she's here, her body flush against mine, her breaths as ragged as my own. My hands cup her ass, in a pair of jeans I don't recognize, and I tug her firmly against my cock which has now gone painfully hard.

"I thought you were gone," I murmur against her lips as she draws back to catch her breath.

"And I thought you were dead." The fear in her eyes has an unfamiliar sensation sparking in my vacant chest. Her lips capture mine again, leaving no room for further discussion.

I run my hands down her thighs and lift, twining them around my waist. Only I forget how weak I am, and the room shifts, the floor coming up to greet me. I whirl around to take the brunt of the fall and hit the wooden floorboards with a smack. Serena topples down on top of me, her legs tangled with mine. She's laughing, her lips parted against my own.

Everything hurts like hell, but I don't utter a sound, too scared to ruin this moment. She straddles me, the towel around my waist coming undone as she wriggles over me. It's impossible to hide how excited I am to see her. Her eyes drift down to my cock, and a smirk crawls across her perfect mouth.

"Someone's definitely feeling better."

"I am now that you're here." Which reminds me... "Where did the medicine come from? And your new clothes?"

Her slender fingers throttle my cock, and she slides down my legs, eyes glittering with lust. "Fuck now, talk later."

"Whatever you say, *tesoro*."

Her tongue flicks at the tip of my cock, and I nearly crumble at the sight as she licks and nibbles, teasing me for an endless moment until she takes all of me in her mouth. "Fuck, Serena," I groan, "you look so good with your lips wrapped around my cock."

Long, blonde locks cascade across her shoulders as she watches me, head bobbing. She runs her tongue down my shaft as her free hand plays with my balls. They're already tightening, seconds from release.

"You are the most exquisite woman I've ever seen."

She comes off my cock with a wet pop, lips curving into a grin. "I think you might still be under the effects of the pain meds."

"No. The sight of you with my cock in your mouth is a work of art. Your lips, your eyes so full of heat and desire, *merda*. Just one taste and you've ruined me, *tesoro*."

Serena laughs, the sound vibrating through my dick, and I draw in a sharp breath to keep from coming too soon. She continues bobbing, licking and sucking until raw, powerful heat rushes my veins. But I'm not ready yet...

Sitting up, I frame her face with my hands, despite my cock cursing at me and draw her mouth to mine. She tastes like me, tangled with her sweet flavor. "It's your turn," I whisper against her mouth.

Her eyes light up, pupils dilated, and a sexy grin has my cock straining against the denim of her jeans. Before I flip us over, I lay the towel out beneath her, then gently place her atop it before I get to work on the zipper.

As I drag the crisp denim down her legs and find new silk panties beneath, I'm beginning to understand where my wallet disappeared. And I couldn't care less. This woman could rob me blind, and it still wouldn't begin to make up for the hell I put her through.

My hungry gaze catches on a flash of purple ink decorating her inner thigh. I'd noticed something the other day, but I'd been too ravenous and delirious to focus. It's the tattoo she mentioned. My thoughts fly back to our conversation...

I'll let you see it when you let me go.
You said I'd be dead soon after...
Maybe it'll be the last beautiful thing you see.

And in this moment, I'm perfectly alright with that. If I'm about to meet my end, at least it'll be between the warmth of her thighs.

Her eyes catch mine, focusing on the direction of my gaze. "I guess you lucked out. You got to see my tattoo earlier than expected."

"I hope this doesn't mean I'll die tomorrow." A rueful chuckle escapes, but it's not entirely far from the truth.

Her expression darkens, and I hate that whatever I've said has upset her. So I slide my fingers beneath the lace waistband of her panties and brush my tongue across the seam of her thigh, then run the flat of my tongue along the dainty flowers. She wiggles beneath me, her back arching off the floor. "I'm honored for the opportunity," I murmur against her skin.

Her smile returns, and I vow to keep my mouth closed unless it's to devour her. I breathe her in, reveling in that familiar perfume. "Mmm, *tesoro*, your scent is exactly as I remembered it." I pause, fixing my eyes on hers. "You know, when I woke up and you were gone, I was certain I'd imagined the tantalizing sight of your tight little pussy wrapped around my fingers." I bring my fingertips to my mouth and run my tongue over each, one by one.

Her eyes widen, then her lips part, a breathy sigh escaping as I suck them into my mouth.

"Mmm, absolutely perfect."

Unable to control myself for a second longer, I push the silk fabric to the side and dip my tongue into her sweetness. A groan vibrates my throat as I devour her slick heat. She's so wet, her arousal coats my tongue, the faint scent of strawberries and vanilla clinging to my nostrils.

A moan squeezes through her lips as she watches me feasting between her thighs. "Do you like to watch, *tesoro*?" I whisper against her clit.

"Yes." Her breathy pant is so damned sexy.

"You like to see my tongue disappearing into your tight pussy?" I make a show of it, drawing the flat of my tongue through her wet folds before plunging it inside. *Dio*, she tastes like sin and salvation all rolled into one, and I'm ready to face heaven or hell, whatever it takes to spend the rest of my days buried inside her.

"Mmm, yes, I love it, Toni."

I smirk at the new nickname. It was jarring at first, but now I like the sound of it on her lips. Any sound really. I glance up at her from over her bare mound, replacing my tongue with a finger. I stroke slow, languid circles around her clit as she writhes in pleasure. "Tell me what you want, *tesoro*. I'll do anything."

"I want to come," she breathes, eyes glittering with need as she toys with a nipple.

"How? On my tongue or on my cock?"

"Both." Mischief flashes across those smoky sapphire orbs. "If you're up to it, of course."

"Your wish is my command." I run one hand up the smooth planes of her torso and find her breast, kneading the soft flesh while the other parts her legs, baring her completely. Then I graze her clit with my teeth, and she bucks beneath me, another moan escaping. Using my finger to circle the taut bundle of nerves, I focus my tongue on her entrance, licking and thrusting, imagining my cock claiming every inch of her.

Cazzo, she tastes like… *mine*.

Now that I've had her, I don't think I will ever stop wanting her. Worse, I don't want anyone else to ever touch her again. The idea of any hands on her that aren't mine sends wrath surging through my veins.

"Get ready to come, *tesoro*," I murmur across her clit, and her back arches in response.

I increase the steady circling of my finger, ramping it up to a feverish pace. She pants and moans, her hips grinding against my face as I drag my tongue through her soaked slit, then thrust again and again. The walls of her pussy clamp down around my tongue, and I know she's close. Replacing my tongue with two fingers, I drive deeper inside her, and her head falls back on another moan.

"Oh fuck, Antonio," she groans. "Don't stop."

I have no intention of stopping. I plan to have this woman coming and crying out my name for the next twenty-four hours straight, until I'm well enough to walk out of here. And then, fuck my promises, I'm never letting her go.

Her pants come in ragged spurts, each one more devastating than the last. I'm so hard it's painful, desperate to sink inside her. But it's not my turn yet, though I promise myself it will come.

I draw her clit into my mouth and suck at the same time as I thrust my fingers inside her, deeper, harder, faster. Curling the tips until I find *the* spot, another moan echoes across the boathouse as her pussy clenches around my fingers, wringing out every last ounce of pleasure. "Yes, Antonio, yes..."

My tongue continues to move across her, stroking and teasing until her body stops trembling and her legs fall open, utterly spent. Only then do I withdraw and glance up to meet a pair of shimmering, bejeweled irises.

A smirk, along with her arousal, coats my chin. "Was it as good as I promised?"

"So much fucking better."

CHAPTER 36
A SUCKER

S*erena*

I'm a boneless, quivering mess as Antonio stares up at me from between my legs. No one has ever made me come that hard or that quickly in my life. I saw the moon, the stars, the whole fucking solar system in that never-ending moment of raw pleasure.

"Get on your hands and knees." His voice is rough, filled with need as his hands curl around my hip and spin me around.

I can feel him thick and hard as he settles over me, and fuck, if I'm not ready for more. He runs his head through my soaked center and those tiny nerve endings light up again.

His body blankets mine, chest rubbing against my back. The bandage skims my shoulder blade, but I convince myself to ignore it. He said he was fine. But then again, he said that last time too…

"Are you sure this is okay?" I spit out before my own selfish motives prevent the words from slipping out.

His thick crown prods at my entrance. "Does it feel like I'm okay, *tesoro*?"

"Yes," I moan as those sensitive nerve-endings go haywire.

He moves higher, his warm breath spilling over my ear. "Are you on the pill?" he whispers.

"Sure as shit." From the ripe old age of sixteen. There is no messing around with unprotected sex.

"Good, because I can't wait to sink inside you and watch as my cum coats that beautiful pussy, then dribbles down your thigh."

Anticipation tightens my core, and I arch my back, baring my already throbbing pussy. "I'm ready," I rasp.

"That's my good girl." He rubs my back, then his hand climbs higher, fisting my hair. He twists so that my neck cants over my shoulder and he takes my mouth, hard, biting my lower lip.

Another round of need pulses low in my belly, and I'm aching for him. With his mouth still pressed to mine, his thick head pushes inside me, and another groan breaks free. It's only the tip and I'm so hungry for more. I press my ass into him, willing him deeper inside.

"More," I pant.

"Are you sure you're ready?"

"Yes," I hiss. "I want all of you inside me."

He thrusts, completely sheathing himself in one go. A cry purses my lips at the sudden fullness, the intense pleasure muddled with a streak of pain from being stretched so hard so fast. Then nothing but raw pleasure unfolds.

"Oh, Serena…" He pumps inside me, then draws out, almost to the tip before sinking in all the way again. "Fuck, you feel so good around my cock, *tesoro*. So tight and wet, you were made for me."

It's like he stole the exact words from my thoughts. I've never had a man so deep inside me, fitting perfectly into every contour, hitting every spot just as I need it.

He draws back before filling me again and again, his balls smacking against my ass and only intensifying the pleasure roaring through me. I could do this all day, all night and never have enough. His hand reaches around my waist and his fingers find my aching clit. Instantly, I give into his maddening touch, the feel of his cock thrusting in and in and in and those devastating fingers endlessly circling.

I'm raw sensation, fiery pleasure and need.

Antonio's lips brush along my spine, each thrust punctuated by a lick or a teasing nibble. "So good," he murmurs against the shell of my ear.

I can barely put together a word let alone an entire sentence. "Mmhmm," I mumble.

"Are you going to come for me again?"

"Yes," I groan. "Soon…"

"Take your time, *tesoro*. We have all the time in the world."

I freeze at his words, memories of the conversation with Bella rising to the surface. Shit. We don't have unlimited time. I have to meet Alessandro in Milano, or all hell will break loose.

He thrusts harder, reminding me I'm on the brink of climax, and I let my mind go blank once more. I'll deal with explanations later. Right now, I just need this.

Antonio's arm encircles my waist and before I can blink, I'm on my back again, staring up at intense smoldering onyx orbs. "What's wrong?"

"Nothing…"

His cock sinks back inside me and the delicious heat rages again, but his eyes remain fixed on mine, a wary expression sharpening his jaw line.

"I'll tell you when we're done, okay?" I run my hand along the hard planes of his back and pause, my fingers stilling, when I meet the raised, scarred skin.

His eyes darken, and I can practically see the icy mask falling back into place. His maddening pace slows, and I barely suppress the groan of disappointment. "We're done." He jerks out of me, and I whine my disapproval.

"Antonio!"

He sits up, his erection thick and angry between us. It doesn't escape my attention that he's made me come twice now, and he has yet to climax once. "Just tell me what's on your mind. I can't focus now."

I suck my bottom lip between my teeth as I regard him. "When you were unconscious, Elena came."

"How?"

"I went into the city and found her contact info."

A flicker of a smile curls the corner of his lip before it morphs into a scowl. "Wait. Why would you expose yourself like that? Why would you do something so risky?"

"I thought you were dying," I hiss.

"So you should have let me," he growls.

"You can't be serious."

"I'm not worth saving, Serena. When are you going to get that through your thick skull?"

"Oh, fuck you, Toni."

"I was trying to, but then you froze... And you wouldn't tell me what happened because clearly something did happen."

"It's nothing."

"Is it because of what Otto did to you?"

"No!" I hiss. "This has nothing to do with that piece of shit. I want this..." I motion to his dick, which still stands erect and pulsing between us.

"Then what?"

"I'm meeting my cousin Alessandro in Milano in two days. When Elena was here, I used her phone to call Isabella."

"Raf knows?" His brows arch, his voice rising a few octaves.

I nod slowly.

"*Cazzo*, Serena."

"I couldn't get a hold of my parents, and I had to tell

someone what was happening." A twist of anger coats my words, bubbling up inside. "I have been more than a good hostage. How could I not contact my family when you were at death's door?"

"You shouldn't have just contacted them, *cazzo*. You should have left me!"

"It's not as easy as it sounds. I ran into some guys in town and—"

"What?" he roars, his eyes widening to twin pools of looming darkness. "Why didn't you tell me that when you got here?"

I shrug. "You were all half-naked and alive and I don't know… It must have been the adrenaline of the chase and—"

"The chase?" His eyes turn murderous as he tosses me a towel. "Explain now."

"So we're really not going to finish?" Yes, I'm fully aware of how desperate and needy I sound.

"Not until you tell me exactly what happened in the past two days since I've been unconscious."

I blow out a frustrated breath and toss him back the towel. "You need it more than I do. I have new clothes." Tossing him a cheeky grin, I search the floor for my discarded panties and jeans.

He's growling curses as he wraps the towel around his waist. I almost suggest putting on the clothes I hung for him to dry, but his lethal expression stills my tongue. Once we're both mostly clothed, we settle on the floor across from each other and I recount my story from the moment I woke up finding him burning up to a few minutes ago when I raced back into the boathouse.

When I finish, he just stares at me for a long moment. "Why did you come back?"

Ugh, not this again. "I don't know, okay? I guess I'm just a sucker for half-dead men with huge cocks."

The ghost of a smile flickers across his face, but he shuts it down before it really shines. "You did the right thing contacting your family," he finally breathes out. "And I'll be sure to get you back to Milano in time to meet with your cousin."

"I'm not sure it'll be that easy now that I've been spotted." I point at the shopping bags by the door. "At least we have food and a phone though."

"I'll find a way to get us out of this mess, I swear it."

CHAPTER 37
AFRAID OF THE TRUTH

A*ntonio*

Chomping down on the apple, I tear the soft pulp to shreds before forcing it down my throat. I'm not the least bit hungry but Serena insisted I eat. Lingering anger still pulses through my veins knowing Serena was nearly captured while I lay here like a useless *stronzo*. *Dio*, if something had happened to her when she went into the city alone... I grit my teeth to overpower the ache in my chest. And this ache isn't from the healing wound, no it's far deeper than that and ten times more frightening.

I watch her from the lounge chair as she upends the shopping bag and my sweatsuit along with my gun crashes onto the floor. I was right, she had taken it. Smart girl. "I'll hold onto this for now." She places the gun on the counter and in my current state I'm pretty useless to do a damned thing about it.

"As if I could stop you."

Serena tosses me a grin before she begins to rifle through the grocery bag, plucking out ripe peaches and a container of strawberries. Instantly, I'm hard again as the sweet scent of the berries fills my nostrils, reminding me of her tempting taste. And with only the towel slung across my hips, it's painfully obvious. Willing my stupid dick down, I focus on the canoe hanging from the opposite wall, the pills thrown on the lounger, anything but those lips closing around the ripe red fruit and the soft moans spilling out.

"Serena," I finally hiss as my dick thickens to uncomfortable lengths.

"What?" She glances up at me, all blue-eyed innocence as she pops yet another strawberry into that perfect mouth. That mouth that's just begging to be fucked again. I squeeze my eyes closed and chase away the torturous images.

"Can't you eat in silence?" I growl, shifting so the tent across my lap isn't quite so obvious.

A wicked grin curls her lips as she takes another bite, this one excruciatingly slowly before she runs her tongue across her bottom lip. "Oh, does this bother you?" She teases the tip of the berry with her tongue before she unlocks her jaw, and it disappears into that tempting mouth. She's torturing me now, and I'm well aware of it. She's still angry I didn't let her finish earlier. It was the least punishment she deserved after risking her life by going into town to save me.

"Yes," I hiss.

Putting aside the bag of fruit, she crawls over on her hands and knees, mischievous blue orbs staring up at me. She's only wearing that new blouse and those tiny panties she bought. Her back is arched, and she moves closer, perky ass in the air. *Dio*, it would be so easy to pick back up where we left off.

Serena finally stops just a hairsbreadth before she reaches me and rises onto her knees, placing a hand on each one of my legs. Sweet strawberry juice still coats her lips, glistening beneath the dim lighting. Her thumbs trail my inner thigh as her gaze latches onto my blatant erection. "You did say we could finish after I told you..."

"No," I rasp out, my rough voice betraying me.

"Seriously?" She cants her head to the side.

"Think of it as your punishment for disobeying me." She releases my knees, slamming her hands on her bare hips.

"How did I disobey you? You never told me not to leave the boathouse."

"I told you to leave *me*!"

"And I clearly told you to fuck off."

"It was a poor decision."

"You're a poor decision," she bites back, and she couldn't be more correct on that count.

"You're right, so leave."

"An hour ago you promised to get me to my cousin in Milano."

"I've reconsidered. I think you'd be safer without me." I hiss out a breath and lean back on the sunbed. She's got my head so twisted I don't know what to do anymore. "I'm nothing more than a liability. And anyway, I don't know that I'll be well enough to travel by tomorrow."

She glances at my cock again, narrowing her eyes. "You seem just fine to me."

"It's just a physical reaction I have no control over." It's a lame excuse, and I'm not surprised she sees right through it. Clearly, if I'm well enough to fuck her, I can manage to get my ass on that boat and get us across the lake. From there, it would be easy enough to steal a car and drive to Milano in a few hours.

Her lips screw into a pout as she continues to regard me while I remain stubbornly mute. "And besides, Elena said you'd be okay in a few days."

I wasn't certain I would ever be okay again. But Serena was right, we—no, I—couldn't stay here forever. With the phone Serena purchased, I could easily call Pietro and have him come for us, but I can't risk the shade of a chance that she's right, and it is someone within my organization who's behind this. If those men found her because they'd pinged my credit card, then my every move is being watched. Until I know for certain who that person is, I won't risk it.

"Well? Are you going to keep your word or not?" Her light brows furrow, and the disappointment in that gaze is worse than the one my father used to shoot me.

"Yes," I finally mutter. "I may not have much anymore, but at least my word should still mean something."

"Good." Grabbing my knees, she pulls herself up to stand, practically shoving her cleavage in my face. Now, I'm the one being punished. And I deserve it. "I'm going to try *Papà* again."

Those words shouldn't sting as much as they do. Still, my head snaps back as if she'd slapped me. Of course she'd want to speak to her father, to assure him she's okay. I don't dare consider what Dante and the Kings will do to me once this is over, once I've safely delivered Serena to her cousin.

Which of course I will do, despite my comments to the contrary.

I'm so damned torn. A part of me wishes she would simply leave me, but the other half can't bear to see her go.

I watch her from the corner of my eye as she unwraps the pre-paid phone and fires it up. Raw emotions wage a war in my gut as she brings the phone to her ear and waits. By now, Isabella must have informed her father and her uncle of the situation. I can practically see my time on this earth slowly dwindling.

Serena better keep her word and make my death a quick one. No doubt Dante would like to drag it out to agonizing lengths. And I can't even blame him. If Serena were my daughter, I would do the same.

"Pa?" Her voice is so filled with hope its piercing. "Yeah, I'm okay."

Dante's shouts blare through the phone in a stormy symphony, but I can't make out the exact words. He's probably cursing me and everyone I've ever met.

Serena marches to the door, then slips on her jeans, waving a hand in my direction as if I would stop her. She knows I would never use my gun on her, or at least I hope she does. Once the door slams behind her, I stretch out on the lounger, awaiting my sentence.

I must doze off while she's gone because I'm awakened minutes later by the sharp crack of the door smashing against the wall. My lids snap open, and I attempt to sit up, but a streak of pain has me laying back down like a pathetic idiot. Serena marches in, irritation carved into her jaw.

"What's wrong?" I mutter.

"Nothing, my dad is just a domineering, overprotective, stubborn asshole."

A grin starts to form, but I thin out my lips when her expression turns murderous. She flops down onto the sunbed beside me and exhales a frustrated breath.

"What did he say exactly?" I hedge.

"Mostly that I'm no more than a naïve child incapable of making my own decisions or handling myself."

"Let me guess, he wanted to come get you and you told him to fuck off."

"Exactly." A glimmer of amusement sparks within those brilliant sapphire orbs. "Alessandro will be here the day after tomorrow, there's no need for him to launch a full scale attack—"

"On me?"

She nods.

"Serena, I don't need you to protect me—"

"This isn't about you," she snaps. "He wouldn't even consider the possibility that this Sartori guy could have double-crossed him. The great Dante Valentino is too untouchable for that, and no one in their right mind would ever dare mess with his daughter. He's convinced this is all your fault."

"He's not wrong," I murmur, eyes cast down to the slight space between us. I hadn't even noticed that her legs were now between mine, her outer thighs pressed against the insides of mine. "Did you at least assure him I would get you to Milano safely?"

"Yes," she snaps. "He didn't buy it. He thinks you're just playing me, and I'm too trusting to see it."

"You, trusting?" I barely suppress a laugh.

"I know, right?" She shakes her head. "I already told him you were half dead, and I had your gun."

I eye the sleek weapon sitting on the counter by the door. I could have taken possession of it when she walked out, but instead, I'd fallen asleep like a baby. Obviously, I'm the one that's too trusting.

"So what excuse did you give him for choosing to remain?"

"It wasn't an excuse," she grits out. "Ale is almost here so there was no point in *Papà* coming or knowing anything about my cousin's involvement. Besides, the town is still crawling with mafia goons, and I'm hoping another day will buy us some time."

"Us?" That one word brings more satisfaction than an orgasm. Which reminds me if I don't get a release soon, it's very likely my balls will explode.

"Yes, *bastardo*, me and the mouse in my pocket."

"I'm sure your *papà* loves that you've stayed with me despite giving you every chance to escape."

"Yeah, well, he'll just have to deal with it." She lifts her hand before I can respond. "And don't you dare ask me why I stayed with you again."

I lean in, dropping my hands to the back of her thighs. "Because you're afraid of the truth?"

"Because I want to punch you in the face every time you ask." She smiles sweetly before prying my fingers off her legs and freeing the phone from her pocket. "Anyone you want to call?"

I pause to consider for a moment before shaking my head. "No, but I would like to find out who the hell burned down my mother's house."

"How are you going to do that?"

"I have an old college friend, not in the business, who can hack anything. If he can get into the security system at the villa, he'll be able to provide faces to our arsonists. Once we have that, it's only a matter of time until we find out with certainty who was behind it."

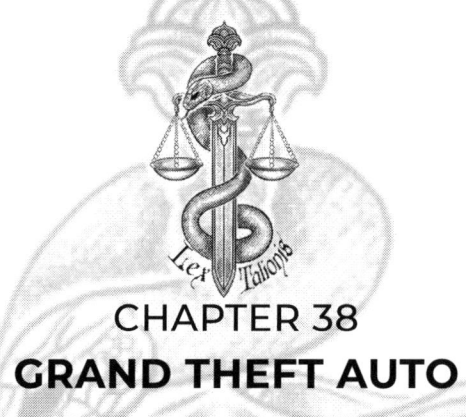

CHAPTER 38
GRAND THEFT AUTO

S*erena*

Antonio grits his teeth as he carries the container of gasoline toward the banked Riva, its glossy hull protected by the boathouse we've been hiding in for days. I'm shocked he's keeping to his word to deliver me to Alessandro in Milano. He hasn't said more than two words to me since yesterday, and he's waited until the absolute last moment to leave the confines of our little wooden cabin. In some ways, it feels like a lifetime has passed since the day Antonio snatched me off the streets of Manhattan, and other times it feels like it was only yesterday.

A vein pulses across his forehead as he lifts the cannister and tops off the engine for our trip. The wound on his chest has barely had time to heal and since he's forced to keep it open because of my stupid attempt at sewing it with a needle and thread, he's clearly in a lot of pain. But of course, he's too stubborn to admit it.

"You sure you don't want me to help you with that?" I call

out, leaning against the exterior wall of the boathouse, the wood worn and warped from the moisture in the air.

"No," he rasps through clenched teeth. "I can handle it."

"Sure, if handling it means you're going to pass out any second now."

He swings a glare in my direction as he fits the nozzle into the tank and the gasoline gushes out, the distinctive noise muffling his ragged breaths. He doesn't even bother to tell me he's fine for the hundredth time, only continues to ignore me.

Tipping my head back, I pretend to watch the stars winking overhead, while keeping one eye on the stubborn Italian who's attempting to single-handedly drag the boat back into the water. At this rate, he's going to bleed out before we make it to the other side of the lake.

Instead of arguing with him, I stomp toward the stern and give it a good shove, so it dislodges from the sandbar.

Antonio glances up over the windshield and shoots me a pointed glare. "I told you I could handle it."

"And you're no good to me if you're bleeding out or dead," I hiss.

Before he can answer, I give it another good shove, and he has no choice but to refocus on the task at hand or risk getting run over by the Riva. By the time I hear the waves lapping against the hull, I'm dripping in sweat and cursing myself for ever offering to help. Who knew that thing would be so heavy?

But at least we're finally almost on our way. By this time tomorrow, I'll be sitting on Ale's jet heading back to Manhattan. As much as I would love to ignore *Papà*'s wishes altogether, I know that if I don't at least make an appearance back home, he'll completely lose his shit and drag me back himself.

Antonio leans against the side of the boat, wiping the beads of sweat from his brow. He's back in his clothes, the canvas of scars and tattoos across his back once again hidden. I'm so tempted to ask what happened, but given his current mood, I don't waste my time.

Toni lifts his eyes to mine, the pain clearly visible in the clench of his jaw and the deep furrow of his brow. "Grab the supplies from the boathouse, and I'll get her ready to sail."

"Yes, captain." I bring my hand to my forehead in a salute, but all I get is a half-smile in return.

Damn, what has gotten into this man?

Even when he first captured me, he wasn't this quiet. Sullen and angry? Yes. But this? This was ten times worse. He seems... sad. As I march back to the boathouse, I can't help but analyze the last forty-eight hours.

Because I'm psychotic, my mind keeps going back to the mind-blowing sex and somehow, I lose my train of thought every time. Which reminds me, I'm supposed to be angry at him for withholding that last orgasm.

Okay enough, Serena, focus. Rifling through our remaining paltry supplies from the wooden cabinets, I fill the bag with the first aid kit, bottles of antibiotics and painkillers the good *dottoressa* left, and the remaining fruit. I'm shocked to find Antonio's gun still lying on the counter. Either he's certain I'm not a flight risk anymore, or he wants me to run and take his gun with me.

I don't think I'll ever understand this man.

Either way, I pocket the gun, then grab the bag with our measly supplies before saying a quick goodbye to our temporary home. "You weren't much, girl, but I'll *never* forget the sex. So thanks for that."

"Are you talking to the boathouse?" Antonio's voice echoes from behind me, and red-hot embarrassment races up my neck, blanketing my cheeks.

I spin around to find him propped against the doorframe, the ghost of a smile twitching at his lips.

"Did you just thank this pile of old wood for the incredible fuck *I* provided?"

I force out a laugh, but it's so fake it grates on my own ears. "Oh, you thought I was talking about you?" I shake my head and wave a dismissive hand. "Since you refused to let me come, I had to take matters into my own hands while you were asleep last night."

The corner of his lip kicks up. "Oh, really?"

"Yes, and it was the best I'd ever had. I even came twice."

"With me sleeping right next you?"

I nod because I'm just too far down this rabbit hole already to even try to get myself out. "Pain meds must have knocked you right out."

Antonio creeps closer, smoldering dark gaze fixed to my mouth, then travels up to meet my eyes. He leans in so his lips are only a breath away and whispers, "*Tesoro*, I'd have to be dead not to wake up from the irresistible sounds that spill out of your mouth when you come."

A chill skates up my spine at the rough edge to his tone. The way he's looking at me like he wants to devour me has heat racing south. *Dio*, this man's mood swings are making my head spin. First, he refuses to speak to me, and now, I'm not sure if he wants to fuck me or murder me.

Before I can string together a coherent thought, he spins on his heel and marches toward the door. "Let's go," he calls out over his shoulder, and finally, free of that hypnotic gaze, my feet begin to move.

This is going to be a long twenty-four hours.

Antonio's master plan of navigating the boat north along Lago di Como instead of directly to Como which would be the most direct route to Milano, seems to have paid off. When we reach Bellagio, a smaller town along the lake a few hours later, the streets of the downtown are quiet.

It's also almost midnight now, so not many tourists still linger along the banks of the quaint lakeside town. Still, Antonio circles for a few minutes, sharp eyes on the dimly lit shore before finally cutting the engine alongside a small dock.

"Are you ready?" His eyes chase to mine. It's the most he's said to me since that awkwardly hot moment back in the boathouse.

I hug the shopping bag to my chest and nod. The feel of Toni's gun hidden beneath the waistband of my jeans gives me a sense of comfort I haven't enjoyed in weeks. I noticed him eying it about an hour ago as we traversed the waves of the sleepy lake, but he never said a word.

"So what's the plan exactly?"

The boat glides up beside the dock, and Antonio ties it to the wooden piling in an expert knot. "The plan is to find a car and drive the rest of the way into the city. At this hour of night, we should be back in Milano in just a little over an hour."

"And by find a car, you mean steal one?"

He nods, the hint of a spark back in those midnight irises. "Exactly, *tesoro*." Then he offers a hand, and I surprise myself at how easily my fingers wrap around his palm. He crosses the gap easily then turns back around to help me.

I'd been so worried about his wound, I'd forgotten all about my ankle. For the first time in days, it doesn't hurt when I land on it. As if he's remembered too, Antonio's eyes meet mine, unease in those bottomless orbs.

"I'm fine. I can barely feel the sprain anymore."

"*Grazie a Dio.*"

Thank God is right. If I'm about to add grand theft auto to my rap sheet, I better be ready to run.

"There." Antonio ticks his head at a two-door Alfa Romeo. It's sporty but not too showy, and definitely a common enough car not to attract unnecessary attention. Best of all the window is open just enough to slip a hand through. "Can you—"

Before he finishes his sentence, I slide my hand through the opening. *Papà* didn't only teach me how to handle a gun. I'm also damned good at picking locks, and I know how to hotwire a car.

I can feel Antonio's weighty stare over my shoulder as I stretch my fingers to reach for the interior door handle. Just a few more inches... The driver's side door pops open, and I take a step back, offering the spot to Antonio. "Do you want to do the honors or should I?"

He watches me, mouth curved into a grin. "You can hotwire a car too?"

"Of course I can. Only one of my many talents. Maybe someday if you're lucky, I'll show you more."

"I only wish I would be so lucky." He smirks before taking my hand and tugging me to the passenger's side and opening the door like an actual gentleman. "The least I can do is start the car. If I don't make myself useful, then you won't have any reason to keep me around."

"That is true." A stupid grin flashes across my face before I can stop it.

As I settle into the car, Toni gets to work on the wires beneath the steering wheel. In less than a minute, the rumble of the engine breaks the silence of the quiet street. He turns to face me, an unreadable expression on his face, then he leans in, and his lips are suddenly only inches from mine. His eyes dart down to my lips, and tension thickens the air as anticipation tightens my core. Slowly shaking his head, he heaves out a breath and stretches his arm out, reaching for my seatbelt.

I sit there, barely breathing, as he draws it across my hips and snaps it into place.

Merda, what is this man doing to me?

CHAPTER 39
POWERLESS

Antonio

The silence in the car is unsettling, pervasive like the darkness stealing in through the windows along the quiet road. I hazard a glance at Serena from the corner of my eye, and I can practically feel her biting her tongue. It's unlike her to be silent for so long.

Though I'm certain her reaction is in response to my foul mood, a part of me wishes she would give in already so her bubbly laughter would fill the car. It would certainly make the drive much more enjoyable and go by faster. As to my dark mood, I can't even explain it. I should be happy to be done with this business, but the idea that my time with Serena has finally come to an end has my cold, dead heart raging.

I'm not stupid enough to think I've fallen in love with this woman in a matter of weeks, it's not possible. Right? *Of course not*, stronzo. My father's voice interrupts my mental musings, further souring my mood. Just focus on the damned road. I hit the gas, anxious to arrive to the city already. I need distance from this intoxicating woman. The day she dropped into my life, I lost myself.

Or maybe, it's the complete opposite, and she helped me find the old me. The one who had been lost to the darkness. Turmoil rages in my gut, and I process the past week and a half with Serena, then the turbulent weeks before. The demise of *Papà's* precious territory, the kidnapping, the ransom, the attempted rape, the burning down of the villa, losing Mariuccia... Fiery anger and pain war in my gut, and my foot presses harder on the gas. We zip across the winding highway, going faster and faster. Everything blurs as raw emotion bears down on me, suffocating.

"You might want to slow down there, buddy." Serena's voice cracks through the downward spiral.

I glance at her from the corner of my eye, and she offers a tight smile. I heave in a breath and glance down at the speedometer. *Merda*. Two hundred kilometers per hour. My hands grip the steering wheel so hard my knuckles are white. I let loose on the gas pedal just as flashing blue and red lights wash over us.

"*Porca miseria*," I mutter.

Serena twists in the seat, glancing out the rearview window as the *carabinieri*'s siren grows louder. "Well, shit, now we're in trouble."

I consider for only a moment before I slam the sole of my shoe to the gas pedal once more. My neck whips back from the momentum as the Alfa's engine roars to life.

"What are you doing?" Serena squeals.

"I can't risk getting caught right now."

"What? Why? So you'll get a speeding ticket. It's much better than going to jail for resisting arrest."

I cock a dark brow at her, shaking my head. "Oh, trust me, *tesoro*, we're not getting caught." The speedometer jerks to the right, then steadily rises.

"But why risk it?"

"Because if it is the Salernos or the Sartoris behind this,

they'll have our location within minutes. Both families have bought off more of the Milanese carabinieri than I can count. Getting caught is not an option, not until you're safely aboard that jet with your cousin."

The engine of the Alfa Romeo roars as I slam the gas pedal down before she has a chance to respond, the lights on the dash blurring as we shoot down the dimly lit road to Milano. Cool air whips in through the slightly open window, mixing with the smell of pure adrenaline.

Sirens wail behind us, and flashing lights are a steady reminder of the *coglione* on our tail. I shoot a quick look at Serena. Under the flickering red and blue, her face is tight with worry. "Hold on," I shout, gripping the steering wheel even harder.

She nods, her bottom lip trapped between her teeth, and even with the chaos unfolding, that look has a direct link to my cock. Shoving down the completely inappropriate thoughts, I refocus on the road.

The winding highway ahead is just a dark strip with only a few scattered streetlights. I swerve left, barely squeezing past a slower car—their horn blares, lost under the roar of our engine and the chaos behind us. My heart's hammering, syncing up with every surge of the car as I push it harder.

Up ahead, the highway splits. Go straight, right into the city, or take the right onto a narrower, more winding road around Milano. I make the call in a split second, jerking the wheel to the right. The tires scream, and I'm thrown across the seat as I switch paths. I hazard a quick glance at Serena before I gun the engine again. It's a riskier road, but the tight lanes might just work for us.

"You okay?"

She nods, clinging to the handle over the window.

The *carabinieri* is stubborn, its lights a constant annoyance in my rearview. Muttering curses, I downshift and the engine growls, finding new life as we tear down the winding road. Trees blur past, turning into a dark swirl overhead.

A sharp curve comes up and I take it way too fast, the car skidding dangerously close to the edge. "Hold on!" I shout again as Serena gasps and grabs the handle above the door, her nails digging in. The police lights lag, then disappear for a second—lost in the curve. It's now or never.

I take a deep breath and swing into an almost hidden dirt track, covered by overgrown bushes and trees. We plunge into darkness, the car's belly scraping against the rough ground. I kill the headlights, and we roll in silence, the sound of gravel under the tires mixing with our heavy breathing.

"You think they saw us?" Serena whispers a second later.

"We're about to find out."

Time stretches out. The sirens fade away, swallowed by the distance and the night. I hold my breath, not daring to believe we're clear until the heavy feeling lifts and the rearview mirror shows nothing but the dark path behind us.

"We did it," I hiss, releasing a breath.

Serena stretches across the console and squeezes my hand hard, grounding me. "Surprisingly." She smirks and the tightness in my chest wanes.

"Let's wait a few minutes to make sure we're clear."

She nods.

"We might have to ditch the car before we reach the city limits. That *carabinieri* likely called in our plates."

"Okay." She rests her head back against the seat and releases a sharp breath. "Now what do we do to kill some time?" Blue eyes sparkle as they regard me, a hint of mischief in that gaze. I know the look, it's the adrenaline that sparks after the thrill of the chase. It unlocks other base instincts…

As if my cock has come to the same conclusion, I feel myself harden against my zipper. Not now, *stronzo*. But it's too late, somehow Serena's gaze has tracked my traitorous dick. Her eyes sharpen as they trail over the bulge, and her tongue darts out to slide across her bottom lip.

A deep growl vibrates my throat as memories of that tongue on my cock surge to the surface. Her hand stretches across the console again, only this time it isn't my hand she wants. Her fingers curl around my upper thigh, only inches from my throbbing dick.

"Serena..." I warn. I have zero willpower around this woman, and if her hand gets any closer to my cock, I will lose my fucking mind.

"You still owe me, Toni, and I am not the type of woman you want to owe a favor to." Her grin lights up those brilliant eyes, and it's not only my dick throbbing now. My stupid heart bashes against my ribs at the beautiful sight of her.

Her hand closes around my cock, over my jeans, and I let out a hiss. With the adrenaline still pumping through my veins, I don't even feel the wound in my chest, nor do I consider the consequences of my next words.

"Take off your pants."

Excitement illuminates her expression, and she shimmies out of her jeans in seconds. Beneath the cover of the trees, she's blanketed in shadows and still I can make out every sexy curve of her body.

"Now the panties." Already my voice is rough, ravenous with desire.

She does as she's told, and I'm honestly shocked.

"Good girl," I whisper. "Now touch yourself. Are you already wet for me?"

Her head dips on a groan as she runs her finger through her slick heat. "Yes, I'm soaked."

"And I haven't even touched you yet."

"Must have been the thrill of the chase." Her voice is laced with desire, and it only makes me harder, my erection straining against the zipper.

I reach beneath the car seat and slide it as far back as it'll go, then I release my cock from the tight constraints of my pants. Serena's eyes go wide as she takes me in, a faint gasp pursing her lips.

Dio, I could come from that sound alone. It's like her voice has a direct line to my cock.

Her fingers wrap around my shaft, and she's not the only one who's already wet. Precum glistens on my tip, moistening my length as she starts to stroke. I'm helpless to her touch, spineless in her hands. My hips start to rock and thrust into her palm with each sweep.

I slide one of my hands beneath her blouse and find her breast, tugging away the soft lace of her bra to feel her warm flesh. I toy with her nipple, rolling it between my thumb and index finger and she releases a satisfying moan. Then my free hand sweeps up her thigh, and she trembles when I reach her apex.

I run a finger across those sweet wet folds, and pounding desire thrums across my cock. "Mmm, *tesoro*, I think you are ready for me." Gripping her hips, I drag her across the console and lift her, so she's straddling my thighs, her pussy hovering right over my cock. Then I lift my gaze to meet hers, pupils pulsing with desire.

A thousand words sit poised at the tip of my tongue, but I don't have the balls to say them. This woman has ruined me. I've become soft for her, completely powerless against her siren's spell. I wish it was only her pussy I was addicted to but it's so much more.

My cock glides across her center, teasing her clit before prodding at her entrance. Before I rock my hips up, she sinks down onto me, taking all of my cock in one go. We groan in perfect sync, fire racing through my veins at the feel of her so tight around me.

"Oh, fuck, Toni," she murmurs as her hips begin to roll. "Why do you feel so good?"

I was about to ask her the same thing. I've been with more than my fair share of women, but there's something about her pussy that feels so right. "Because I am that good," I rasp. It's a stupid answer, but it's all I can manage when I'm focusing all my attention on not confessing something I'll surely regret or worse, coming in seconds like a horny teenager.

My fingers dig into her hips, lifting her then driving her down on my cock harder and harder. She moans against my lips as I devour her mouth. As much as I would love to drag this out all night, we're too exposed out here on the side of the road. I need to get us somewhere safe for the night, and I know exactly where.

As I continue to thrust into her in a maddening pace, I release her hip and bring my thumb to her clit. I start to circle, and I can feel her pussy tightening around my shaft. *Cazzo*, she feels so right.

I nibble on her lobe, running my nose across the shell of her ear. "I'm going to make you come, are you ready?"

"No, not yet."

"Yes, *tesoro*. Now." My thumb exerts more pressure, circling faster until she's panting. My hips take up a relentless beat, pounding into her, harder, longer, wilder. She bounces against my balls with each rise and fall, and fuck if she doesn't come soon, I will.

"Come for me, Serena, me and only me." I whisper the words against her ear, and her head falls back, the silky walls of her pussy clenching around me.

"Oh, Antonio," she groans. "Fuck, yes, yes."

She shatters over me, grinding her hips against me until I finally find my own release. Raw waves of pure ecstasy crash over me as she continues to ride my cock, milking every last ounce of pleasure. It's been so long since I've had an orgasm with anyone it feels like my soul is splitting in two. My breath escapes in ragged pants, my chest heaving from the effort. I spill into her, my cum dribbling down her inner thighs with each maddening thrust.

Dio, this woman is perfect for me in every way.

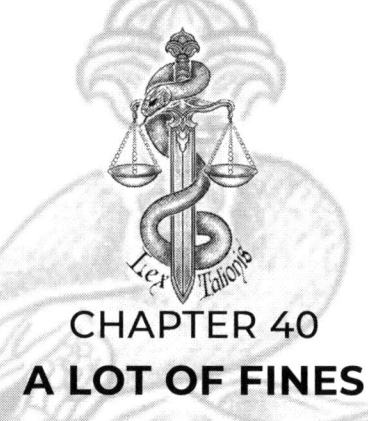

CHAPTER 40
A LOT OF FINES

S*erena*

My entire body is still tingling from the orgasm as I lift off Antonio, cum spilling down my legs. Damn, I've never seen so much come out of a man at once. Either he's been saving up or he's a beast. Either way, I'm suddenly so relieved for birth control.

I flop down on the passenger's seat, and I can feel Antonio's gaze burning into the side of my face. He digs through the glove box and hands me a tissue, a smile etched into his handsome face, then watches as I sop up his arousal from my inner thighs.

"*Dio*, I like how you look with my cum all over you."

I like it too, but I don't dare admit it. Instead, I don't say a word as I slip into my panties, then jeans once I'm relatively clean. This thing between us is insane. It's not like anything I've ever felt with another guy. And it's got me scared shitless.

"Are you ready?" He eyes the seatbelt I still haven't put on.

"Oh, right."

Then he revs the engine and pulls out of the heavily wooded area onto the highway. A truck whizzes by, sending my heart jolting up my throat, but besides the big monster, the road is quiet, no *carabinieri* in sight.

"With that little unaccounted rest stop," Antonio murmurs, keeping his eyes fixed straight ahead, "I don't think we'll have time to swap out the car. I'll stick to the side streets and hope for the best."

"Okay."

We lapse into silence once again, and this time keeping quiet is almost impossible. A part of me needs to know if he feels this weird connection as intensely as I do, but the other half is terrified to ask. Mostly because I'm sure he does. And I don't know what that means for either of us.

So I spit out the first thing that comes to mind instead. "Where are we going to sleep tonight?" Really, I want to know if we'll have another chance to fuck before he drops me off with Alessandro. Because it's only been a few times and I'm already hopelessly addicted to that cock, to that man's fingers, to his tongue…

I blink quickly, trying to chase away the heated thoughts before I work myself up again. Hell, who am I kidding? I could go again right now. I'm tempted to reach across the console and slip my hand into his pants just to feel his silky hardness again.

I'm so wrapped up in the idea, I don't realize he's already answered me. "Huh?"

"I said we can't stay at your apartment for obvious reasons, but I have a friend in the city, the one who is a genius hacker."

"Oh, right." I glance down at the purse between my feet. "We should probably check if he's responded to your messages."

"Yes, and I'm going to need you to send him another one informing him of our arrival."

"Or we could stay with my friend, Santi."

"Not a good idea. The smaller number of people we involve the better. Otherwise, there are too many possibilities for leaks."

"Santiago is one of my best friends," I hiss. "He would never betray me."

"How well do you really know him? Do you know anything about his family? How long have you known him?"

Well, shit, maybe I don't know that much about Santi. "Four months now," I mumble. That's the only answer I have.

"We'll stay with Valerio."

Fine then. I reach for the phone and pull up the most recent messages, easily finding Valerio. Antonio hasn't reached out to a single soul besides him. Me, on the other hand, I'm twitching to send out a few more messages to Bella, Matty, and the whole cousin crew, not to mention my mom. Even though *Papà* is being an overprotective dick, I know Mom would understand.

"Tell Valerio we'll be there in twenty minutes."

"That's it? You're not even going to ask if we can stay?"

He shakes his head. "He'll understand it's urgent."

I type out the message and wait for a response. Despite the late hour, it comes almost instantly in the form of two letters. *OK.* I guess this Valerio guy is a man of few words. Then again, I'd be pretty grumpy if someone woke me up in the middle of the night and told me they were coming over.

Before long, we're pulling into an underground garage in a modern apartment in the center of Milano. It looks a lot like mine, only a few floors shorter, made entirely of tinted glass windows and heavy security along the perimeter.

What exactly does this Valerio guy do for a living anyway?

I'm about to ask when we're stopped at the gate and a scary looking tattooed guy bends over the driver's side window and stares into the car. "I.D.," he barks, clutching a tablet to his barrel chest.

Antonio shakes his head, steely determination in his eyes. "The name is Giovanni. I'm here to see Valerio Palermo." His dark brows furrow but before he can open his mouth, Toni barks again, "Just check the damn list for *Signor* Palermo."

"Listen—"

Toni raises a hand, moving so fast my head spins. He has the guy by his necktie, using it as a noose around his throat. He jerks him into the driver's side window and tightens his grip. "Don't make me kill you for no reason. Just search the list, *stronzo*. You'll find my name along with detailed instructions."

He tries to nod but with Antonio choking the shit out of him his head barely moves. Finally, he releases the security guard and the man coughs and splutters, catching his breath before he scans the tablet. "Ah, here you are, *signore*."

He flicks a button on the screen, and the gate opens. Antonio offers a tight smile before driving through. "*Coglione*," he mutters.

I nearly choke on a laugh. "Him? He's just trying to do his job. You were the asshole who tried to suffocate him for it."

He shrugs. "I'm not showing anyone my I.D., not until you're safe and sound, flying thousands of miles away from here."

I don't even want to consider the obvious here... Antonio may be dead well before that. My father is a loose cannon and there's no telling what he'll do now that he knows who I'm with. He could be on his way here right now, ready to burn Milano to the ground just to find me. And Antonio is going to be his number one target.

As much as I'd like to believe *Papà* wouldn't kill him if I asked nicely, I'm not stupid. And the idea of Antonio dead has an invisible noose tightening around my throat. I'm so lost in the grisly image, I don't emerge from the bleak thoughts until the engine cuts off and Antonio is leaning across me trying to open my door.

"I can open my own door," I tease.

"Just wanted to prove chivalry isn't dead."

But it might be soon.

The stupid thought streaks across my mind before I can stop it, and heat pricks the corners of my eyes. *Dio*, what is wrong with me? I must be PMSing or something. Finally opening the door, I find Antonio waiting with our meager belongings.

Glancing around the quiet garage, I notice the sleek elevator we're parked in front of. Unlike the others around the large space, there are no buttons, only a biometric scanner of some sort.

Antonio exhales a labored breath, as if he's been running for days, and a hint of fear lances through my chest. Shit. It was the sex, wasn't it? It was too much for him... "Are you okay?" I inch closer, and my palm instinctively moves to his chest, but not close enough to the wound to jostle it.

"Yes, I'm fine. The wound is fine."

"That's a lot of fines..."

A wry grin curls up the corners of his mouth. "It does seem like I've been saying that a lot lately, haven't I?"

I nod, but I could say the same for me. And yet somehow, I don't think anything will ever be quite fine again for either of us.

"I want to talk about what happened in the car—"

I press my fingers to his lips, cutting him off. Because whatever he's about to say I'm not ready for. Especially not right now, in this garage. "There's nothing to say," I blurt. "It was just fun, right?"

"Mmm." His head dips, an indecipherable look flashing across the tense set of his jaw. "I only wanted to say that if you want to talk about it, we can."

"I'm good, but thanks." I'm so *not* good. I don't think I'll ever get that orgasm out of my head. The craziest thing is that it was completely vanilla... sex in a car is not something that typically rocks my world. And yet with Antonio, it was the hottest thing *ever*.

The elevator doors glide open before I say anything stupid, and a man in pajamas and glasses leans against the metal wall. He runs his hand through tousled auburn locks, grinning ruefully. "After years of not speaking to me, I get an emergency text a few days ago, then you appear at my door at three o'clock in the morning, *amico*?"

Antonio shrugs, the closest thing to embarrassment I've seen streaking across his face. "I'm sorry. I hope you know I wouldn't have done it if there'd been any other choice."

"I figured." His gaze chases to mine, a slow, steady perusal. "I assume *she* is the reason for all of this."

Antonio's head dips, and now I'm the one almost blushing. It takes a lot to embarrass me, but there's something about his look that feels too personal. Like he knows things about me…

"Follow me."

CHAPTER 41
MAKE IT GOOD

S*erena*

The elevator doors open right into Valerio's penthouse loft, showcasing a stunning view of downtown Milano. It's no Manhattan skyline, but it's not bad. The apartment is pristine with white leather couches and sleek, minimalistic furnishings. He ushers Antonio and me into the great room, the vaulted ceilings soaring with no end.

"Nice place," I murmur. After the last few days of sleeping on a sun lounger, I am so looking forward to a real bed. And I can already bet the mattress is going to be heavenly.

"*Grazie.*" Valerio tips his head, and his chic retro glasses slide down the bridge of his nose. "Please, make yourself comfortable." He motions to the impeccable living room, but after days without a proper shower, I'm scared to sit on the spotless leather. Apparently, Antonio is too because he remains at my side.

"I'm good standing. Long car ride and all." I perch beside the oversized marble island, dropping my purse on the barstool.

"I appreciate this, Val," Antonio whispers.

"I'm sure you do." He grins, but there's something not entirely friendly about it. I can't help but wonder about his earlier comment. Why hadn't Antonio talked to his friend for years?

My abductor, turned I-don't-even-know-what, inches closer, his hand sliding onto the small of my back. I hate how much comfort that faint touch brings. And I despise the fact that I can't keep my body from leaning into him.

Valerio eyes me, then the hand on my back, and a chill snakes up my spine. "A glass of wine perhaps?"

I'm weirdly awake considering the time of night, and a bottle of Chianti to settle my nerves sounds perfect. "Yes, please."

"Are you sure?" Antonio's dark gaze settles on me. "We have to be awake early to make it to the airport."

Shit, that's right. Ale is already mid-air, on his way across the Atlantic. He sent me a text message on the drive over. And still, I nod because the idea of all of this finally being over doesn't bring me the peace it should. "Yeah, I need a drink."

Antonio ticks his head at his friend, or whatever he is. "Just one glass for her, none for me. I need to speak to you about a few things."

"Of course." Valerio moves toward the kitchen, gliding with preternatural grace. Who is this guy? I watch, oddly enthralled, as he pulls a bottle from a wine fridge under the counter and begins to decant it. From the looks of the bottle, it's vintage and expensive. I almost open my mouth to tell him not to bother. It seems like a waste, but it's too late now as the fruity tannins fill the air. At least he grabs two glasses, filling one for himself, then hands me the full one.

Clinking his glass to mine, he offers a smile. "*Cin cin*, to your health."

"I'm going to need it, *grazie*."

He glances at Antonio then back at me. "No luck will be needed, I'm certain you are in good hands."

My escort clears his throat, then runs his hand across his nape. "If you're quite ready, Val, I'd like to go over the footage you've uncovered."

"*Cierto.*" Then his gaze flickers to mine. "Shall I show you to your room on the way?"

"Yes," I groan. "That would be amazing."

We follow Valerio down the hallway, the squeak of my sneakers on the marble embarrassing. I should have bought some sandals while I was at that shop in Como. Antonio's shoulder grazes my side as we walk and it's oddly comforting, just like his hand on the small of my back.

Our host finally stops in front of a door and twisting the knob, swings it open. Much like the rest of the apartment, it's impeccable with a clean, modern design that had to be created by a professional. "I hope it's to your liking. I didn't exactly have time to prepare for your arrival."

"As long as there's a bed and a shower, it's more than enough."

He offers a smile, then turns to his friend. "And your bedroom—"

"I'll stay with Serena." Antonio cuts him off before he finishes his sentence.

I spin at the bold insinuation, knitting my brows as I regard him. "That's pretty presumptuous."

His gaze sharpens, those bottomless orbs daring me to contradict him. "I'm not assuming anything, but I also won't risk you out of my sight all night long."

"Neither of you will be in any sort of danger at my home. But still—" Valerio backs up a step, lingering in the threshold when Antonio shoots him a narrowed glare. "I'll leave you two to discuss."

I take a sip of the wine, and the floral notes burst along my tongue, distracting me from the glaring beast in front of me. Mmm, this is amazing.

"I'll sleep on the floor if that makes you more comfortable."

Glancing up to meet those piercing orbs, I focus on his words, and a pang races across my heart. "Relax, Toni, I'm messing with you. I spent the last few days sharing a tiny boathouse with you. I'm fine with you in my bed."

Something unreadable sparks across those midnight irises, and the ghost of a smile hitches the corners of his lips. "Good."

"Good," I echo.

"Do you need anything before I go?"

"Nah, I'm just going to draw myself a hot bath, drink my wine and pass out."

His eyes darken, and a trickle of heat kindles at the sight. "I wish I could join you."

"You could," I whisper, stepping into him. If this is our last night together, we may as well make it memorable, right?

A groan vibrates his chest and his hand snakes out, cupping the back of my neck, drawing me closer. "Then I'd never want to leave." He huffs out a breath, shoulders sagging in frustration. "And I must discover who burnt *Mamma*'s villa to the ground."

I nod slowly as the smolder in his eyes intensifies with anger, instead of lust. "Guess I'll see you in the morning then."

His head dips, and he releases me, taking a measured step back. "I'll wake you when it's time to leave."

"Perfect." I force a smile, but it feels all wrong. Keeping it firmly in place until he walks out, I'm proud of my incredible acting skills. *Dio,* what is wrong with me? I should be thrilled that this whole kidnapping debacle is almost over. Instead, I'm dreading the end.

The bed dips beside me, and the scent of warm amber and musk consumes me. I'm instantly awake, my eyes snapping open. Antonio sits hunched on the other side of the enormous king, taking off his shoes I imagine. Then he straightens and peels off a shirt I don't recognize, revealing the map of tattoos along his back. The scars they hide are permanently emblazoned in my mind, so much so that even in the dark room, I can make them out. *Lex talionis...*

That pit of dread tightens my gut as I continue to watch him when he strips down to his boxers. My brain isn't the only thing awake anymore. Now, my lusty pussy is on full alert, as if his scent has triggered her somehow.

His head twists over his shoulder, and I squeeze my eyes closed like a big fat chicken. I can't even explain why I do it. Probably because I don't want to seem like a weirdo stalker who has been watching him undress this whole time.

The mattress dips again, closer now, and that familiar scent grows stronger. Antonio's breath dusts my hair, and it takes all my willpower not to open my eyes. Again, I'm not sure why I don't, but I remain completely still. His lips brush my forehead, and something deep inside me just shatters.

"Sweet dreams, *tesoro*," he whispers against my skin, and my heart raps out a manic drumbeat against my ribs. "I'm sorry for everything."

My breaths come more quickly now, and I'm surprised he can't hear the roar of my pulse which thunders across my eardrums. It's so loud I'm certain Valerio can hear it way across the penthouse wherever his bedroom may be.

Antonio curls up beside me, lacing his arm across my belly and his forearm brushes the underside of my breasts. A damned breathy sigh slips out, and he freezes.

Shit. What do I do now?

Slowly, I open my eyes, doing my best to look like I just woke up. I even yawn, drawing it out far longer than normal. "Hi," I whisper.

He unlocks his arm from around my waist and puts some space between us. And my traitorous body screams at the sudden distance. "Sorry, I didn't mean to wake you," he mutters.

"It's okay. It's probably almost time for us to get up, isn't it?"

"Not yet. We still have a few more hours. You should get some rest." Antonio starts to roll to his side of the bed, but my hand snakes out, fingers interlacing with his. An endless moment passes between us, neither one of us moving or speaking. Maybe even breathing. Then he turns back, eyes wide and fixed on mine.

"I'm too wired to sleep," I blurt out in a rush. Then I roll onto my side, tugging on his arm, and pull him beside me so our bodies are flush. "And I can rest on my flight back to Manhattan."

Starlight sparks across those velvety orbs, and the hint of a smile kicks up his lips. "Are you sure?"

I lace my free hand around his back and slide it down to his ass. "Yes. Now fuck me like you mean it because if it's the last night we're spending together, you better make it good."

CHAPTER 42
VILLAINS

A*ntonio*

Those brilliant sapphire eyes sear to mine, and I'm powerless to deny her the very thing I want more than any other. Despite the consequences. This woman already has me by the balls and another night of devouring her will only serve as the final nail in my coffin. But if I'm going to die, I might as well enjoy my damnation.

And sinking my cock into Serena Valentino is like savoring a slice of paradise.

"Get on your knees and put your hands up on the headboard." Raw desire laces my tone, and my pulse skyrockets as she stirs beside me.

When she sits up, I catch a glimpse of her bare pussy beneath my undershirt. *Cazzo*, this woman will be my absolute ruin. And I'm about to jump off the ledge just to get there sooner.

I drag my boxers down, and my cock springs free, already hard at the sight of her splayed out on the bed. Then I lift to my knees and move behind her. I run my nose across the back of her neck, inhaling her intoxicating scent, then I lick my way to her earlobe. She melts into my touch and fuck, it's the sexiest thing I've ever seen.

Serena is as feral for me as I am for her.

What that says about our sanity is questionable, but tonight, logic gets thrown out the window.

I press my body flush against hers, my cock straining against her ass which is still partially covered by my t-shirt. That will not do. I reach for the hem and lift it up and over her head, exposing perfectly tanned skin beneath. There's something about tan lines that drive me crazy, as if getting to see the patches of milky white flesh is reserved only for me.

Now that she's completely bare, I lace my arm around her middle, drawing her back so my cock fits between her ass cheeks. Her body trembles with each sweep of my crown, and she pushes her ass against me, begging for more. Cum glistens on my tip, and from the feel of it, she's already soaked for me.

But I need to know for certain.

I slip my hand between her legs, forcing them apart and trail my finger up her inner thigh. Slick heat coats my fingers, and her head falls back on my shoulder.

"Mmm, Antonio," she groans.

"Do you like that, *tesoro*?" I run my fingers across her wet folds, and she grinds into my palm.

"Yes, so much."

"Do you want me to fuck you with my fingers?"

"For starters." She cants her head over her shoulder and grins.

"That's my greedy little girl." I thrust two fingers inside her, and a gasp fills the air between us. I start to pump and her hips rock into the demanding pace. She removes a hand from the headboard and tries to reach for me, but I cluck my teeth. "Uh, uh. Keep your hands still or I'll stop. You can't touch me yet."

She mutters a curse but returns her hand to the velvet

bedframe, and I'm thankful for another pass. It's only a matter of time before she asks about the scars on my back. I know she's seen them or at least felt them. And I'm not ready to relive that nightmare just yet.

"This is all about you, *tesoro*," I murmur.

As my fingers work her inside, my thumb circles her clit just like she likes it. Then I slide my cock through her arousal, finding her asshole, and tease the delicate nerves. Just a little pressure...

"Oh, fuck, Toni, that feels good."

"I'm going to fill you up, *tesoro*, with my cock, my fingers, my tongue. You'll have all of me, and I'll have all of you." *One last time.* The bitter thought is suffocating.

"Umhmm, yes..."

I thrust harder, my fingers diving deep inside her sweetness, and my cock is so hard it hurts. I'm not sure I'll be able to wait much longer to sheathe myself inside her. I can't decide if I want to take her in the ass or the pussy first. I want to claim all of her tonight. She's right, it's our last chance, and I won't miss out on any of it.

With my free hand, I find her breast, then her nipple, and she arches into my touch as I tease the sensitive tip. My head dips to the crook of her neck and I lavish her skin, devouring that sweet strawberry taste. I want to mark her as mine. Even if this is the last time, I need everyone to know. If I die tomorrow, at least she'll have something to remember me by.

I draw her flesh between my teeth and bite, gently at first. She moans, her hips moving more quickly now, begging for release. "More," she pants.

I toy with her clit, alternating between fast and slow circles, my fingers curling inside her to reach that mystical spot. "I want everyone to know you're mine."

"I'm yours, Antonio."

I lick the spot I just bit then increase the pressure. "Is this okay?" I mumble against her skin.

"Yes." She thrusts her hips to meet each of mine, my cock nudging at her back entrance.

I've found that sometimes just the tip is enough to bring a woman to orgasm, a precise combination of stimulation between both holes and the clit.

"I'm going to come... don't stop."

I bite harder, circling her clit faster and she cries out, her pussy constricting against my fingers but I don't let up the pace, driving harder still until the waves of pleasure consume her.

"Oh fuck, Antonio, yes, yes." Her pussy grinds against my palm, her ass against my cock and I don't stop until the torrent of ecstasy completely subsides, and she's boneless in my arms.

Her head falls back on my shoulder again, and she glances up at me, the haze of satisfaction glittering across those beautiful eyes. "Not bad for round one." She smirks.

"Turn around and spread your legs for me, *tesoro*. I want to watch this time as I fuck you, as my cock sinks so deep inside you, I kiss your spine. I want you to see *my* face when I coax this next mind-blowing orgasm out of you. So that you'll never forget how good this was. Even long after I'm dead and buried."

Her expression darkens, the excitement and lust from a second ago waning. "I won't let you die, Antonio. I would never allow *Papà* to do that..."

I nod slowly, pressing a finger to her lips because I don't want to ruin this moment. I'd rather we both pretend until the sun comes up because our future is inevitable. Like the moon, our paths are bound by forces beyond our control.

Taking her hand, I lie her back on the bed and wedge myself between her thighs. It's a perfect fit, as if we were actually made for each other. If I believed in all that soul mate shit, I would be certain she's the one. But this isn't a fairy tale and villains like me don't get happy endings.

But I can have a happy now.

Her hands drift to my neck, then down my back and I tense as she glides across the puckered skin. Her eyes lift to mine, and

I see it. Pity. *Dio*, she knows. She has seen the scars hidden beneath the canvas of tattoos.

"What happened?" she whispers.

I heave out a breath, dreading this conversation. "Fire..."

"Well, I guessed that much." Her hand dives deeper, gently massaging the sensitive flesh. "But how?"

"I went back into *Papà*'s villa after Raf and Isabella—"

"You were there that day?" Her eyes widen as they regard me.

My head dips slowly, as I draw lazy circles across her bare shoulder. "They didn't see me. I arrived as they were running from the blazing inferno." Leaning my chin against Serena's chest, I lock my gaze to hers. "I went in to look for my father. That's how much of a hold that man had on me. He fucked up our whole lives, and still, I ran into a burning building to try to save him."

"But he was already dead?"

I nod again. Clearly, she'd heard the story from my brother.

"I carried his body out..." I shake my head, the weight of the confession pressing in on me. "Then I got the *lex talionis* tattoo, so I'd never forget."

"Kind of like the violets I got for my Nonna." She squeezes her mouth into a tight line. "Shit, Antonio, I'm sorry, that was a really shitty comparison."

"No... it's sweet. And anyway, I'm not sorry. It had to be done." A rueful grin tugs up the corners of his lips. "And if it hadn't been for that hellish escape from the fire, in which I cursed my brother and his Isabella every step of the way, I never would have found you."

A soft laugh escapes through Serena's lips. "So you're saying you're glad you endured a horrible fire because it pushed you to the edge of insanity and forced you to abduct me?"

"Well, when you say it like that, I do sound crazy." A chuckle vibrates my own chest. "But I guess you must have already known that."

"And still, here I am."

I guide myself to her slick entrance with those mesmerizing orbs still staring up at me. "Everything will work out as it's supposed to, *tesoro*," I whisper against her lips before I roll my hips back and thrust, sheathing myself to the hilt.

Our moans echo in unison across the room, and for the first time I can remember since being with a woman, I keep my eyes locked to hers the entire time. I drive into her deeper, longer, slower, and with every part of my being. Until I can no longer tell where I end and she begins.

And the longer it lasts, the more terrified I become.

Because suddenly, I don't want to die, and I don't want this to be the last time with Serena. I want to spend the rest of my life fucking her, claiming her, maybe one day even loving her.

Dawn breaks, spilling light into the dark room, and overwhelming dread fills my chest. Serena lies on top of me, her soft breaths escaping in time with the rise and fall of my chest. Our time is up. I didn't sleep all night, or what little was left of it after we'd had enough of each other. Well, that isn't entirely true as I don't think I'd ever have enough of Serena.

Four times and we were spent. She was too sleepy to keep her eyes open, but still she held onto my cock like it belonged to her. And I think it does.

With her laying on top of me all night, I'm ready for round five, despite the exhaustion. I don't need sleep, I don't need anything but that hot, wet pussy welcoming me home. Worse, it's more than just my physical desire for her. She's all I think about, her safety, her happiness, all the shit I've put her through. I can't get any of it out of my head.

I'm completely fucked.

What if I don't take her to the airport? What if I force her to run with me? This all started as an abduction anyway. How much more could she hate me?

She stirs above me as if she's heard my thoughts or maybe she feels my raging erection poking her in the stomach. Her head lifts and hooded lids meet mine as her lips slide into a smile. "Morning."

"*Buongiorno, tesoro.*" Only there's nothing good about this morning.

"Is it time to wake up?" She yawns and stretches out on top of me, grazing my cock. Her eyes brighten, and the hint of a smile flashes across her face. "Or do we have time for one more quickie?"

I can't help the chuckle from rumbling my chest. "I wish we did, but unfortunately, we'll have to leave soon, and if I have you just one more time, I'm not certain I'll ever let you walk out of here again."

The slight line between her brows deepens. "It doesn't have to be the last time, Toni. I'll be back in Milano before long and maybe—"

I shake my head. "Let's just play it by ear, okay?"

She must misunderstand my reluctance, and her lips screw into a pout as she rolls off me. I want to explain, to tell her it's not that I don't want to see her again, it's that I can't bear to disappoint her. How can I give her hopes of a reunion I'm certain won't ever happen? The moment she's safe aboard that jet with her cousin, I'm a dead man.

CHAPTER 43
UNDER DIFFERENT STARS

S*erena*

Staring at my weary reflection in the mirror, I huff out a breath and pull out my phone. *It's over, Serena, it's time to move on.* Sure, the kidnapping was fun and all, and the sex was ah-mazing, but clearly nothing more will ever come of this thing with Antonio. And I'm crazy to even want more.

Despite knowing all of this, there's still something I have to do.

I type out a message to *Papà* before I lose my nerve. For all I know, he could be on his way here right now with Alessandro. Bella swore our cousin to secrecy, but I know *Papà* has his ways.

Me: *I need you to promise me something.*

Pa: *Anything,* cuore mio.

I'm surprised the response comes so quickly and now that pit of dread in my stomach expands to twice its size. Is he here in Milano already? My fingers fly across the keyboard.

Me: *Swear to me you won't kill Antonio when this is over.*

Those little blue bubbles dance across the screen for an endless moment, my pulse escalating with every second that passes.

Pa: *I can't promise that.*

I stare at the words, my heart lodged in my throat. I won't let Antonio die because of me. Did he royally fuck up by kidnapping me? Yes. But the thought of the starlight in those piercing irises going forever dark is suffocating.

Me: *You can, you just don't want to.*

Pa: *He stole you from me, Serena! My only child! How can I allow him to live after that?*

I can practically see him fuming across the line, hear him shouting curses at the phone.

Pa: *I will not make a promise I cannot keep. We can discuss this when I see you in person.*

Me: *No, I need the promise first.*

The phone rings, his number flashing across the screen. I send it to voicemail because I'm in no mood to listen to him scream at me.

Pa: *Answer the phone.*

Me: *No. Not until you swear on Mom's life that you won't kill him.*

Pa: *You cannot be serious about this.*

I am deadly serious which is why I mention Mom.

Me: *Antonio saved my life. I owe him.*

Another long minute passes, and I'm sure he's thrown his phone out the window in a fit of rage.

Pa: *Fine...*

Me: *Thank you. I'll see you at home tonight.*

More bubbles, then nothing. The tightness in my chest wanes slightly, and I draw in another breath. At least I know Antonio will be safe once I step on that plane. And for now, that's good enough.

With one last glance in the mirror, I run my hand through my hair and turn for the door. It's time to head to the airport.

When I step into the guest bedroom, Antonio is already

dressed, in what I imagine are Valerio's clothes. They're a little tight on him, clinging to the broad expanse of his chest and highlighting his muscled abs. *Dio*, he's beautiful in a tortured, savage way.

He watches me as I approach, shadows etching his features. His smoky eyes lock onto mine, then hold in an endless, tension-fraught gaze. A thousand unspoken words linger between us, yet neither of us dares to break the silence.

Antonio finally clears his throat, blinking so I'm free of that hypnotic stare. "We should go." He reaches for a jacket slung across the bed.

My head dips, and I grab my purse from the chair. I feel the weight of Antonio's gun still inside, so I slip my hand in to return it to him. "I guess I should give this back now."

He shakes his head, lips pressed in a hard line. "No, keep it. I owe you for the one Otto lost in Manhattan."

I eye the big, clunky gun in my palm and scowl. "Dolce was my favorite, you know. She was the perfect size for my hand."

"I owe you a Glock then, but for now, she's yours."

"I'll hold you to it." I turn the Beretta around in my palm, comforted by the familiar feel of a weapon in my hand. "I'll call *him* Toni."

A chuckle parts his lips, but the mirth doesn't quite reach his eyes. "Whatever it takes for you to remember me."

I don't dare speak the traitorous words. That I'll never forget him. And it's not just because he gave me the best orgasms of my life. No, the real reason is much scarier. So I keep the truth tucked away behind my teeth and force a smile.

The sound of approaching footfalls along the marble echoes through the corridor a moment before Valerio pokes his head in. "*Pronti?*"

Antonio nods. "Yes, we're ready. Thank you again for everything."

"Don't mention it. Or rather, you can wait for the return favor to be called in." That wicked grin has the hair on the back of my neck rising. "My driver is already waiting downstairs in the garage."

"Then let's not keep him," I blurt.

With a quick goodbye to Antonio's intimidating friend, we find his driver in the garage, in the spot we'd parked the Alfa in last night. It's gone. What a waste of a perfectly good car. It's probably up in flames or swimming at the bottom of a lake by now.

The driver gets out of the car, tips his hat at us and opens the back doors of the oversized Mercedes sedan. "We will be arriving in Linate in a quarter of an hour."

"*Grazie*." Antonio dips his head at the man, then ushers me into the backseat.

I glide across the smooth black leather and lean up against the opposite door. A rush of cold air blows from the air vent, sending a chill up my spine. I must shudder because the next thing I know, Antonio is peeling off his jacket and draping it over my shoulders.

"Thanks," I murmur as the engine turns over, and we speed out of the underground garage.

The early morning light is blinding, even beneath the tinted windows, so I scoot closer to the center of the seat to avoid the harsh sunlight blasting in through the glass. My leg brushes against Antonio's and our eyes meet. Tension thickens the air, all those unspoken words dangling on the tip of my tongue. A flurry of memories rushes back, igniting a storm of emotions that threatens to shatter the calm facade I'm barely holding onto. In the silent standoff, it's the words we don't say that speak the loudest, echoing the last painful week and a completely uncertain future.

When the silence grows oppressive, I blurt the first thing that comes to mind. "Were you able to identify the arsonists from the security camera footage?" I'd completely forgotten to ask last night.

Antonio rakes his hands across his face and huffs out a

breath. "Yes, but it was nothing useful, unfortunately. As expected, they're mercenaries. Anyone could have hired them for the job."

"So, we're back to square one."

He grunts in response.

"Well, it wasn't the Kings. *Papà* swore to me when we spoke the other day from the boathouse, and I trust him."

"Of course you do."

"For your sake, you better hope my trust is well-placed." The damned words spill out before I can stop them.

He cocks his head at me, dark eyes scrutinizing. "What does that mean?"

"Nothing," I mutter. I have a feeling Antonio wouldn't be pleased if I admitted to forcing my father into sparing his life. It wouldn't sit well with his pride.

The ride to the airport passes much too quickly and before long, the roar of an airplane landing echoes over our heads. I glance at Antonio, and my chest tightens at the thought of never seeing him again. Unexpected emotion constricts my throat, and I can barely swallow it down.

Merda, this was not the plan.

I was never supposed to develop actual feelings for this man.

And yet, here we are.

Hot tears prick my eyes as the driver steers the Mercedes to the security entrance. Averting my gaze out the window, I blink quickly to keep the traitorous tears from spilling over. The gate opens and we roll through the entrance, heading for the private hangars at the end of the runway.

My phone buzzes, jerking me from the startling onslaught of emotions. Thank *Dio*. I glance at the screen and find a message from Ale. He's landed and waiting for me on his father's jet.

"It's hanger number four," I call out to the driver.

"Very well, *signorina*."

He swings the Mercedes to the right and pulls into a parking spot just behind the row of enormous white structures, then cuts the engine. Oh shit, this is it. My stomach twists, knotting into a pretzel, and a wave of nausea crashes over me. *Dio,* what is wrong with me?

"I'll accompany Serena to the jet," Antonio says to the driver, distracting me from my downward spiral. "Wait for me here."

"*Si, signore.*"

Antonio slides out of the car then comes around to my door, opening it with a flourish, then offers a hand. The silly move brings a smile to my face, and grim realization sets in. I'm totally fucked. I *have* fallen for my kidnapper. What type of a stupid cliché am I?

I glide across the car seat and fit my palm in his. The touch is electric, sparking a wave of longing and desire that surges straight to my heart. He closes the door behind me and tugs me forward, but I grind my heels into the tarmac.

"What's wrong?" His eyes widen, that faint line between his brows furrowing.

"I—I..." Ugh, just spit it out. But what exactly can I say without sounding like a complete nutcase?

His fingers tangle with mine, squeezing as he brings our interlaced hands between us. Then he leans me back against the car, and his mouth captures mine. The fire behind it has my toes curling inside my sneakers. His free hand snakes around the back of my neck, angling my head to deepen the kiss. Each stroke of his tongue is punishing and ravenous, filled with heat and promise. It's as if he knows this will be the very last time, and he's committing every second to memory.

The understanding sends ice through my veins, and I jerk back, pulling free of those fiery lips.

"I'm sorry, *tesoro,*" he whispers, agony etched into his beautiful features. "There's so much more I wish I could say, so much I want to tell you. There simply aren't enough words in the English or Italian language to encompass it all. If only we had met in another life, under different stars, I know I could have made you happy. Just know that every moment spent with you was a treasure I will carry with me to the end."

My throat thickens, roaring emotion making it impossible to breathe. He thinks he's going to die. He believes this really is the end for not only us, but him.

"*Papà* swore to me he wouldn't kill you, Toni," I blurt. "I made him swear it."

A rueful smile spreads his lips, and he nods slowly, almost begrudgingly. "Thank you."

"You don't believe me?"

"No, I don't believe Dante, *tesoro*." He squeezes my hand again before tugging me off the car and leading me toward the awaiting jet, our fingers still intwined. "And I don't blame him. If I was in his position, I would do the exact same thing."

The jet door glides open only a few yards away, jerking my attention to a scowling Alessandro. "Did you just fucking kiss Antonio Ferrara?" he shouts from the top of the steps.

Well, this is going to be a long trip back to Manhattan.

Ale stomps down the steps as a luggage transporter drives by, toting a dozen suitcases. His foot hits the tarmac, and an explosion rockets across the airstrip. Flames burst from the luggage cart, engulfing the front half of the jet. A scream lodges in my throat as Antonio throws his body on top of mine, and I hit the ground with a bone crunching smack.

CHAPTER 44
WRECKAGE

Antonio

"Ale!" Serena shouts, but it sounds like nothing more than a whisper over the deafening whistle ringing in my ears. She struggles beneath me, but I hold her down as a ball of crimson fire consumes the plane. "Let me go! I have to get to him!"

Flames engulf its fuselage, starting at the engines where a furious, fiery roar drowns out all other sounds. The fire quickly spreads, consuming the wings and licking up towards the tail, painting the sky in a horrifying spectacle of orange and black smoke.

My heart is a manic drumbeat pounding against my ribs as darkness edges into the corners of my vision. The familiar scene threatens to pull me under. The smoke, the destruction, all of it is much too similar.

"Alessandro!" Serena cries out again.

"There's nothing you can do," I murmur against her ear. Or

at least that's what it sounds like to me. I could be shouting for all I know. Still, she squirms beneath me, trying to shove me off. Pressing my body against hers, I scan the chaos, the flames erupting from the luggage cart, another burst racing across a line of jet fuel.

Squinting, I scan the wreckage for a body but it's impossible to make anything out through the storm of brilliant orange and sooty black. *Merda*, there is no way Serena's cousin survived that.

Who the fuck did this? And more importantly, who was their target, Serena or me?

The possibilities are few, and as far as probabilities go, it must be one of my enemies. Unless her cousin caused some shit I'm not aware of. The Rossi's aren't a family you'd want to mess with, but to my knowledge they have no business in Milano. There is always their affiliation with the Kings but—

Sirens blare, and my muffled hearing goes in and out. In a second, the tarmac will be crawling with *carabinieri*. We have to get out of here. The intense heat warps and blackens the metal of the jet, windows burst from the pressure, and what was once a symbol of the Rossi empire becomes a devastating inferno.

"We have to go." I curl my arm around Serena's middle and haul her off the tarmac. She's still struggling against me, kicking and wriggling. "Please, Antonio, I need to find him."

I glance at the wreckage again, and a pit of dread consumes my gut. "There's no way he made it out of that alive, *tesoro*."

"But he wasn't inside the plane." Her desperate gaze glances around the charred remains, the columns of thick black smoke making it impossible to see much around the jet. "He could have jumped out of the way like we did."

I don't mention the obvious, that he was much closer when the jet exploded. "Maybe," I whisper against her ear. "But right now, we must go. If he survived and you don't, then it will all have been for nothing."

Tears glisten in her eyes, a few slipping free and gliding down her cheeks. And fuck, I hate this feeling of powerlessness.

"Please, Sere, we must go. Now." I hold her tight against my body as the approaching sirens grow louder. "Whoever did this could still be here." I only hope Valerio's driver is still nearby and didn't flee with the explosion.

I drag her a few feet, but her head remains twisted over her shoulder staring at the charred skeletal ruins of the sleek jet. Without thinking, I bend down and haul her into my arms. My wound screams from the tug of still-healing flesh, but I ignore it and race through the billowing smoke.

I blink quickly as the dark memories rise again, threatening to consume me. No. This is not *Papà*'s lifeless body I'm carrying today. It's Serena and she's so full of life and love, and I will not let her die today. Chasing away the darkness, I focus on the hangar only a few yards away and the bumper of the Mercedes peeking around the corner.

Thank *Dio*, the driver hasn't left yet.

"Wait!" Serena hisses as her gaze focuses on the black car. "What if he's the one who sold us out?"

"Valerio? No way."

"And his driver? Are you a thousand percent sure you can trust him?"

I pause, yards away from the car, my heart bashing a frenzied staccato against my ribcage. Serena's not wrong. At this point, it could have been anyone to betray us. "Fine," I growl. "This way." I spin us around and take off toward the chain link fence surrounding the hangars.

The driver beeps his horn, throwing his hands up. I whirl around just quickly enough to wave him off, then sprint toward the fence. An employee parking lot stretches just beyond, the answer to our escape.

When I reach the chain link barrier, I lower Serena to her feet and hook my fingers around the metal post. "I'll give you a leg up."

"Or we can just go that way." She signals toward a door a few yards away, a thick chain with a padlock around it. Then she pulls out the Beretta I gifted her this morning. "I think Toni can handle this."

I can't help the smile from curving my lips as she takes off toward the opening. With the sirens blaring and the pandemonium from the fire, no one is going to notice a gunshot. I watch as Serena points and shoots, the bullet ringing true and slicing the padlock in half. It hits the cement with a smack, and she's already looping the chain through by the time I reach her.

Dio, this woman is incredible. That gaping hole in my chest, hollowed out from the idea of never seeing her again, feels full again. *Cazzo...* I am so fucked.

Serena jerks the gate open and another alarm blasts, but with the commotion, not a single member of the emergency crew spilling across the runway turns in our direction. "Come on, move it!" She holds the gate open, ushering me through.

I race toward her, grabbing her hand as I pass. Because I need to hold her, I need the feel of her flesh pressed against mine after almost losing her forever. And the second we're out of this mess, I'll admit what a *coglione* I've been and beg for her forgiveness. Then I'll sink my cock inside her, claim her as mine with each orgasm I steal until she forgets she ever wanted to leave me in the first place.

And this time, I will never let Serena go.

"This is a mistake," I growl.

"You've already said that, and you've been overruled." Serena shoots a scathing glare in my direction. "What other choice do we have? I, for one, refuse to spend the night under the stars at Parco Sempione as you suggested. We can't use your credit cards, and I don't have mine. You made me dump my burner phone so I can't exactly call my family, and I need to find out if Alessandro is okay. We need cash, and I can get that from Santi."

"Fine," I hiss as I follow Serena toward the wooden double doors of the courtyard entrance. "But we make it quick, and you don't give him any details we can avoid."

"Deal." She presses her finger to the buzzer, and a moment later a voice crackles across the speaker.

"Hello?"

"Santi, it's me, Serena."

"Serena! Girl, where have you been?"

She glances across the quiet street along the outskirts of downtown. "Open up and I'll tell you."

A sharp buzz rings out, and the lock clicks open. I reach for the handle but don't open it all the way. I drop my gaze to meet hers. "You're sure about this?"

"Yes. Santi was my first friend in Milano. I trust him with my life. And besides, I'm not going to start spilling all your dirty little secrets." She throws me a wink, and *Dio*, that flirty look has my dick twitching. "I'll just ask him for a loan, and we'll be out of here in under an hour."

I dip my head, knowing I lost this battle long ago. Serena needs to know what happened to her cousin, and she's right—we need some sort of connection to the outside world. Again, my hand reaches for hers as I tow her inside the walls of the courtyard apartment. Despite the dismal state of our current situation, the fact that she allows me to take her hand brings me a ridiculous amount of satisfaction.

And *merda*, I cannot wait to be alone with her. Which only proves what a *bastardo* I am because I should be more concerned with her cousin's wellbeing. If he's dead, she'll be devastated. If there's anything I've learned about Serena Valentino, it's that her family means everything to her.

The door to her friend's apartment swings open, and a tall male fills the doorway. I bristle at the sight of the attractive young man who reaches for Serena, her eyes lighting up at his appearance. She never mentioned how good looking he was…

"Eeek!" he squeals, jerking her into his arms.

But I keep a firm grip on Serena's hand, keeping their bodies far from flush. Her head spins at me as she tries to shake free of my hold. "Um, let go, please," she hisses as she struggles to hug her friend with one arm.

"No," I snarl through clenched teeth.

"What do you think is going to happen if you let go of my hand?" she bites back, keeping a forced smile firmly in place.

Santiago glances between the two of us, his brows nearly reaching his hairline as he watches the show. "Oh, my, goddess, this is where you disappeared to? You've been shacking up with a hot Italian daddy?"

"Excuse me?" I growl. I'm not that much fucking older than she is.

"Relax, daddy." Serena throws me a shit-eating grin, her palm resting on my chest before she turns back to her friend. "Yes, I've been with Toni for the past few weeks." She cups my cheek, staring into my eyes like she means it. "It all happened really fast, and it's been super intense."

"Well, come in, come in, and tell me all about it."

Serena squeezes my hand, and I follow her through the entryway. Unease flickers in my gut, but I ignore it, reminding myself we're not walking into the home of a rival family, but rather simply a friend of Serena's. It's been so long since I've lived beyond the chaos of our dark world, it's easy to forget how to behave with a civilian.

"We don't have much time, Santi," Serena rattles on as he leads us to the sitting room. "We're kind of in a rush to catch a train."

"A train to where?"

"The Amalfi coast, of course." She grins at me adoringly. "It's a long story, but *Papà* turned off all my credit cards. He doesn't approve of the measly age gap between Toni and me. And this poor guy had his identity stolen so all of his cards are blocked. It's just been a nightmare."

I watch in absolute awe as she spouts out a story with incredible details that has me buying into our tragic Romeo and Juliet tale.

"So basically, if you could just lend me a few hundred bucks to get down there, I'll owe you big time and I promise to pay you back by next week the latest. Toni's got family down south that will fund the rest of our trip. He's just too proud to ask for help…"

Santiago watches her wide eyed, mirroring my own expression.

"I'm good for the money, you know that. I just don't want my father harassing you if I schedule a transfer from my trust. He's desperate to find us, and I want him to sweat it out a little longer."

"You are a devious little thing." Santiago smirks. "Of course I'll lend you the money. You just have to promise you won't ghost me like that again."

"Never. I'll get a new phone, and I promise to text you." She runs her finger across her chest in the sign of the cross.

"I'll do you one better." Her friend twists toward the coffee table, opens a drawer and reveals an iPhone box. "It's brand new. They sent me the wrong model, and I was going to sell it online, but it's yours. You can add it to my bill."

"Santi, you are the best!" Serena throws her arms around her friend, and I barely restrain the urge to pry them off his cold, stiff body.

Instead, I slide closer to her, wrapping my arm around her shoulders so she's forced to release him. His eyes dart to mine, a knowing grin on that perfect jaw line as he wags a finger at me. "Oh, he's a jealous one. I can't blame him though, Sere, you are one of a kind."

"And mine," I grit out, unable to stop myself.

Serena's head cants in my direction. "Behave," she scolds. "I know you can't get enough of me, but we'll have plenty of time for that when we're cruising down the coastline."

"Of course, *tesoro*." I force a smile, but I tuck her more tightly into my side all the same. If she wants me to act like we're together, I'm more than happy to indulge her.

Maybe even for the rest of our lives.

CHAPTER 45
BEFORE YOU WERE MINE

S *erena*

Sprawled out on the small bed at the *pensione* we found just outside of town, I watch as Antonio paces the tiny room. It's all we can afford with our meager allowance from Santi. The pissed off Italian stalks across the minute space, his shoulders bowed, deep lines furrowing his brow. We've been debating our next move for the past hour, and we're at an impasse.

Worse, I haven't been able to get a hold of Isabella, so I still have no idea if Alessandro is all right. A pit of dread has taken permanent root in my gut, the ache in my chest unbearable. I've searched all the media sites, but it's like the explosion never happened. I don't dare call *Papà*. *Dio*, if something happened to Ale while he was on a mission to save me, it could cause a third world war between my dad and uncles. For decades, the Valentinos and Rossi's have edged the fine line of a stalemate, only the shared blood running through our veins preventing crimson spilling across the streets of Manhattan.

No, he has to be all right.

I would never forgive myself for dragging him into this mess. My chest hollows out, and I wrap my arms around my middle to keep myself together.

"Tomorrow, we go to Rome."

I glance up to find Antonio looming over me, that unsettling look in his eye. It's not anger or fury, no that I could handle, it's something much worse. Utter defeat.

"I wanted to avoid returning home as anyone with half a brain would realize it would be the first place I'd go, but with my credit cards compromised, we have no other option." He drags a hand through his disheveled hair. "I have a stash for emergencies at the train station. It has enough cash to last a few months, a fake I.D., new phone, all of it."

"And then what?" I slide to the edge of the mattress and tip my head back to meet that wary gaze. "We can't just keep running." I blow out a breath, my ribs too tight from worry. "Besides, I'm not leaving Milano until I know what happened to Ale."

"It's not safe for you here, Serena. Can't you see that?" He drops to his knees, hands closing around my thighs. "I'm not running. I'm trying my damnedest to keep you alive. It's clear there's a traitor within our ranks, but is it on your side or mine? There's no way to know right now." His eyes latch onto mine, anguish darkening his features. "I know my brother, and that man is much too paranoid to ever allow Isabella's phone to be compromised. It's the only reason I've allowed you to contact her. But anyone else? It's much too risky."

The phone on the nightstand vibrates, jerking my attention from the paranoid mob boss, and I lunge at it. Antonio is at my side before I scan the number on the screen. "It's Bella," I breathe.

He nods, and I jab my finger at the green button.

"Please tell me you've heard from Alessandro," I blurt.

"I have," Isabella murmurs, a hitch in her voice.

"He's alive?" I barely get the words out.

"Yes, but he's not in good shape. He was badly burned by the explosion at the airport. What the hell happened, Sere? I was so fucking worried about you." She falters, a sob echoing across the line, and my chest tightens. "When I heard about the jet, I tried calling you a thousand times. I thought you were dead." Emotion cuts her off, her voice trembling. "Please, just come home, Serena."

"I'm so sorry, Bella. I'm trying I swear." I stand and move to the small, attached bathroom. "I just can't leave Antonio with this big mess to sort out," I whisper, dropping down onto the toilet, and heave out a breath.

"Who the hell cares about Antonio Ferrara?" she shouts across the line. "He's the reason you're in this crazy-ass situation, and he's the reason Alessandro is fighting for his life in the hospital."

I glance at the doorway and find Toni leaning against the frame. His brows furrow as he regards me and with the way my cousin is screaming, there's no doubt he can hear every word.

I draw in a sharp breath, my heart kicking at my ribs. "How bad is he?" I mutter.

"It's bad, Bella. Uncle Marco and Aunt Jia are on their way to Milano now. They should be arriving in the next few hours. From what *Papà* told me, they have no idea why he was there or anything about your involvement."

Damn, Ale stuck to his word and kept my secret even after I almost got him blown up. Fuck, this is all my fault. My stomach churns, nausea creeping up my throat.

"You better get your ass on that plane back to Manhattan with the Rossi's, Serena, or I swear to *Dio*, I'll never speak to you again. And if you get yourself killed, I won't come to your fucking funeral."

"Geez, Bella, way to go dark on me."

"I'm serious. I don't care what is going on with you and Antonio, but you need to get your ass back home."

"Okay," I rasp, standing to continue my pacing.

"Promise me."

"I promise to come home."

"Okay, good." She heaves out a breath, the tremor in her voice subsiding. "So you're really okay?"

Moving to the sink, I stare at my reflection in the mirror. "Yup, not a scratch on me." Thanks to Antonio. But I know better than to let that part slip out right now. Clearly, my cousin thinks I've lost my mind, and she's not wrong.

"Thank *Dio*." Muffled voices resound through the line before Bella cuts in again. "Raf wants to talk to his brother."

My gaze swivels to Antonio, still braced in the bathroom doorway, but his head whips back and forth. *Coward*.

I hand him the phone, but he mouths an adamant, "No."

Ignoring him, I shove it in his face and press the speaker button. "He's on."

Raf shouts across the line, a chaos of Italian curses mixed in. Then Antonio's hand latches onto the phone and he starts in on his younger brother. I squeeze between him and the open door, my best effort at giving them some privacy.

It's time Antonio hashes this thing out with Raf. Their family feud has been going on for too long and with only the two of them remaining from the once great Ferrara empire, it's now or never. With their asshole of a father gone, it's their chance to start over again.

I slump down on the bed, burying my face in my hands. Antonio's furious shouts are muffled in the distance, drowned by my own swirling thoughts. How the hell am I going to get out of this?

Now, not only has Antonio kidnapped me, but he's also nearly cost Alessandro his life. As if he didn't have enough trouble with my father, he's now incurred the Rossi's wrath as well. My Uncle Marco is a fairly reasonable man, but his kids are everything to him, and Aunt Jia… she's more ruthless than he is.

A long minute later, the crash of the bathroom door smashing into the wall jerks me from the dismal inner musings. Antonio stalks out, anger carved into his jaw, and a furious vein pulsing across his forehead.

"It went well I take it?" I shoot him a cheeky smile.

"Yes, it's extremely pleasant to be verbally crucified by your holier-than-thou younger brother. Thank you for that." His fists clench at his side as he nears.

"No problem."

He blows out a frustrated breath. "I'm sorry about your cousin."

Clenching my teeth, I will steel into my veins. *I will not cry.* If I let the dam burst, there will be no stopping it. "Alessandro is strong. He'll survive this."

"I'm sure you're right." He moves in front of me again, then crouches, onyx eyes smoldering. "Raf made it clear that my life would be forfeit if I don't return you to the Valentinos safely. That said, my little brother also agrees that getting you out of the city for a few days is the best option. As soon as your cousin is well enough to be transported from the hospital, I'll deliver you to the Rossi's and you can all fly home together."

"So you plan on dumping me in some safehouse in Rome until then? And then what? Are you going to run off by yourself and play the hero?"

"Yes," he grits out, "if that's what it takes to keep you safe."

"Well, I'm not okay with that. Just like you don't find it acceptable that I risk my life for yours, the same holds true for you." I'm not exactly sure when that happened, but it has. The idea of Antonio dying is unbearable, a thought that chills me to the bone and leaves my heart aching.

"You have no say in the matter," he growls, rising so that he towers over me.

I jump up, climbing on the mattress and gaining a foot on him. Jabbing my finger into his chest, I hiss, "You may have taken me hostage, kept me in a comfy cage for weeks, but I do *not* belong to you. I am more than capable of taking care of myself. I have been for years."

His eyes flash, the fury I much prefer to the utter defeat, surging to the surface. "I don't give a fuck what you did in the past. That was before—"

"Before what?" I snarl, leaning into his space. The air thickens between us, my world narrowing to only his breath and my own.

"Before you were mine." His hand snakes around the back of my neck and his mouth claims mine, punishing and ravenous, as if he needs to prove that I belong to him with this fiery kiss.

And in this moment, I want to.

CHAPTER 46
BLISS

A *ntonio*

Wrapping her legs around my waist, I drop us onto the bed. I kiss her like I need her breath to live, to survive. As if these next few moments will determine everything. A few hours ago, I was prepared to say goodbye to her forever, but each time I'm forced to be selfless grows more difficult. Taking her to Roma will only make matters worse. Every day that passes, I become more obsessed, more captivated by her.

Her lips part for me, and I sweep my tongue across hers. Now that the immediate hunger to claim her has lessened to manageable levels, I take my time, savoring, nibbling, exploring every corner of her mouth.

I may have been the one to steal her away, but she's the one who stole my damned heart and revived my soul. The idea of losing her now is unacceptable. Which means I have to find out who has targeted us and why. Once I kill the son of a bitch, Serena will be safe, and she can remain here in Italy.

With me. Forever.

The traitorous thought bounces through my mind as I tangle my fingers into the hair at her nape. "I need you," I whisper against her lips, the admission slipping out before I can stop it.

"I need you inside me," she counters.

"All you had to do was ask, *tesoro*." Releasing her mouth only long enough to unbutton her jeans and drag them, along with her panties, down her legs, I have her bare in seconds.

Arousal already glistens within the folds of her pussy, and I'm feral at the sight. Either the fighting from earlier got her going or she's wet from just that fiery kiss. Either way, it only proves how perfect this woman is for me.

She paws at my pants, her fingers fumbling with the button and zipper. She strokes my cock with one hand as she releases me from the denim restraints.

"Do you feel how hard you make me, *tesoro*?"

She draws her bottom lip between her teeth and groans as her hand glides up and down my length. "Only for me, right, Toni?"

"Only for you."

Serena guides my thick head to her entrance, and anticipation coils low in my gut. I've never had her this quickly before, usually the foreplay drags out the expectation and my restraint, and I'm worried I'm going to come the moment I sink inside her.

"Are you sure you're ready?" I whisper against her lips, running my tip through her slick heat.

"Mmm, yes, I'm ready. I want you to fuck me, Toni." She reaches between us, toying with my balls, and already, I can feel them tightening. "Please, I need to feel you inside me, to forget about everything else for a few blissful moments."

Cazzo, I'm such a *bastardo*. Of course she does. All I've brought her is misery since I captured her.

I throw her legs over my shoulders, and she gasps, spreading her wide for me. "*Dio*, you have the most beautiful pussy I've ever seen."

She throws her head back and cackles as I line myself up at her entrance. Then I thrust my hips, filling her to the hilt. Her back arches up off the bed, our moans echoing through the small room in perfect unison.

"Merda, *tesoro*, your pussy feels so hot and wet, so tight around my cock. It's absolutely perfect." I drive into her, my balls smacking her ass with each thrust. With her legs over my shoulders, I plunge deeper than I've ever been, my thumb circling her clit as I rail into her.

Her free hand toys with her nipple, her mouth curved in a perfect O. "More, don't stop," she pants, her hips lifting to meet each of my thrusts.

"Oh, I'm not planning on ever stopping. Not until you come so hard you'll be feeling it for days." I scoop her into my arms, wrapping her legs around my hips to drive deeper. Her arms curl around my neck, hands drifting down my back. I usually avoid any position where her hands have access to my scars but driven by the overwhelming need for her, I slip up. She doesn't say a word as her fingers run across the puckered skin. After a moment of panic, I give into the pleasure instead. On my knees, I crawl across the bed to the cushioned headboard. Holding her up, I pin her against the soft fabric and thrust, again and again.

I'm in so deep, so completely sheathed inside her heat, I can feel every inch of her. Her pussy walls tighten around me, constricting with each manic thrust. I withdraw to the tip then plunge again, earning a breathy moan.

"Again," she rasps.

I do as I'm told because fuck, I would do anything to hear those moans from her lips. Withdrawing until I'm nearly completely unsheathed, I drive back in again and again. My crown hits her clit, driving her closer to the edge. I can see how close she is to unraveling by the rosy hue of her cheeks, the wild look in her eyes, and the steady pulse of contractions around my dick.

"I want to live inside you," I grit out. "I want to wake up every morning and fill you with my cock."

"Mmhmm." Her arms tighten around my neck, and I grip her hips more firmly, forcing her up and down in a feverish rhythm. "I'm so close," she pants. "I'm going to come."

I pick up the pace, my muscles burning from the effort of lifting her again and again to maintain the frenzied stride, but I couldn't care less. I'd let her ride my cock all day and night until I couldn't feel my arms if it meant I could remain inside her.

Serena is it for me.

I may have lost my home, my entire family, but I would have enough if I could simply have her.

The thought opens flood gates I didn't know existed and a surge of emotion runs straight to my cock. *Merda*, I'm going to come.

Whirling around, I splay her out on the bed, her head falling over the edge, breasts bouncing with each wild drive. "Come for me," I command, my voice a ragged symphony in tune with her rasping breaths.

Her eyes meet mine, so full of lust and fire, and something shatters inside me.

"Oh, Toni," she cries out an instant before my cock twitches inside her.

We come in perfect unison, her eyes rolling back as her perfect lips curve into a tempting O. Just seeing her break apart for me has a tremor rolling through my body. I come inside her, fire surging through my veins at the powerful release. I can feel the warmth spilling down her inner thigh.

And *cazzo*, I love the sight of her filled with my seed. One day, I want that belly full of it.

Fuck, where did that come from? I blink quickly, chasing away the much too vivid image of a very pregnant Serena.

"You okay?" She stares up at me, pupils blown with lust and crimson coating her cheeks.

I'm still inside her, semi-hard, and I'm pretty sure I could go again in another minute, despite the startling image floating around my mind. "Yes, *tesoro*," I finally manage, "I couldn't be better." I drop a kiss to her forehead and as I move, her pussy constricts.

And just like that I'm hard again.

I roll my hips, and her arms encircle me, hands gripping my ass.

"You're ready again?" She smirks.

"I am if you are."

"I could use a few more minutes of bliss."

"How about a lifetime?"

Her eyes widen as she regards me.

Panic stills my tongue as I realize what I've implied, and I freeze inside her, nearly losing my erection. "I meant sexual bliss, not marital bliss…"

The smile returns slowly, and she tilts her hips to meet mine. "That was a close one, Ferrara. For a second, you had me worried you'd fallen in love with me." She digs her fingers into my ass cheeks, urging me into motion.

I force out a fake chuckle as I drop down on top of her and begin to thrust in earnest. Right. Because falling for this incredible woman would be completely insane. And yet, I'm afraid I've done just that.

Still half asleep, a noise draws me from a deep sleep. Heated memories flit across my mind from the amazing night of sex. I'd had Serena across the hotel room, coaxing orgasms out of her with my finger, tongue, and cock. She'd reciprocated enthusiastically until we'd finally fallen asleep from utter exhaustion.

I blink, the numbers on the digital clock atop the nightstand blurring. Just past six o'clock in the morning. Rolling over in the small bed, I reach for Serena. The mattress is still warm from where she lay. My eyes snap open, the haze of sleep completely vanishing as I search the dark room.

"Serena?" I call out.

Maybe she's in the bathroom. I jump out of bed and dart to the door, whipping it open.

Empty.

Fear's claws lance into me, tearing at my insides. Did someone take her? No. There's no way I would have slept through that. I stalk straight to the chair in the corner where I'd seen her purse earlier. It's gone. Along with the gun I'd given her and the phone.

Where the hell could she have gone at this hour?

CHAPTER 47
THE BEST NURSE MAID

S*erena*

The heavy scent of antiseptic lingers in the air as I cross the quiet corridor of the hospital, the buzz of the halogen lights overhead the only sound besides my steadily increasing heartrate. The idea of escaping to Rome without seeing Alessandro first is unacceptable. I know Antonio would never approve which is exactly why I didn't ask.

I tug the cap I bought from a street vendor further down over my eyes, hoping desperately not to be recognized. With my blonde locks tucked underneath the hat and wearing Antonio's oversized sweatshirt again, I don't look a thing like the real Serena Valentino.

Not that I know who exactly that is anymore.

I've always been reckless and had shit taste in men, but this thing with Antonio has absolutely flipped my world upside down. I've fucked lots of guys, but it was *never* like this. Amazing sex is one thing, but the part that has me messed up in the head are the unexpected feelings I'm catching. And I don't think I'm the only one. Already, I've felt the shift between us.

The sight of a uniformed guard sitting in front of a room ahead draws me from the jumble of thoughts. I pause, muttering curses. Of course there'd be a guard. Did I really think I could just stroll in? Even if Uncle Marco hasn't arrived yet, he probably hired some local guys to keep an eye on Ale until he lands.

Throwing my shoulders back, I saunter up to the guard and flash him a smile. "Do you know who I am?"

The young guy's eyes widen, dropping his phone on the floor. Before he can reach for it, I press my foot down on the screen. Not hard enough so that it breaks the glass, but firmly enough so that he knows I mean business.

"I'm Alessandro's cousin, but no one can know I'm here. Do you understand?" I slide my hand to the gun at my hip, hidden beneath the oversized sweatshirt. It's a good thing we aren't in the U.S. There's no way I would have been able to walk into a hospital armed.

"Yes, *signorina* Valentino. I know who you are."

"I just need a few minutes with him, then you can call whoever you have to."

"Let her in." A rough voice echoes from inside the room, and my heart rockets up my throat.

"Ale!" I barrel by the guard and race in, eyes locking on the familiar form of my cousin stretched across the hospital bed. Oh, *Dio*. I stiffen my upper lip as I take him in, the entire left side of his torso covered in bandages that run all the way up to his hairline. He's never going to forgive me, that perfect face of his must be ruined.

I resist the urge to throw my arms around him just to ensure he's alright.

"No smart remark, Sere?" he whispers, his voice nothing like its typical cocky timbre. "I must really look like shit."

"Nah, you look good, Ale, really good for someone who just got blown up."

The hint of a smile lifts the corner of his lip before he winces. "Fuck, I'm sorry."

"Don't be. I could use a little humor in my life."

I fold onto the bed beside him, careful not to jar the mattress or tangle the wires and tubes coming out of him. "Not for the comment, *bastardo*. I'm so sorry I got you caught in this mess."

"Not your fault. I volunteered for the rescue mission."

"Why would you do something so stupid?"

"I don't know, Sere, maybe I missed your face."

I chuckle, finding his hand beneath the bandages and squeeze. "I missed you too. I miss all of you."

"Then it's a good thing you're coming home with me as soon as the doctor gives me the all-clear to fly."

I nod, but my face must give something away because his dark brows furrow.

"You are coming home with us, right?"

"Yup. Just as long as Pa sticks to his word."

"Which is?"

I blow out a breath, shifting on the small bed. "You don't want to know."

"Listen, you already dragged me into this shit, so I deserve to hear the whole story. I'm guessing it has something to do with you making out with the asshole who captured you?"

"It's complicated…"

A rueful chuckle slips out, and again, he winces. "It always is with you, Serena."

"I made *Papà* promise not to kill Ferrara, but I'm worried he won't stick to his vow."

"Of course he won't. The man stole you from us, held you hostage, then tried to use you as leverage against Dante. You have met your father, right?"

Rolling my eyes, I let out a grunt. "I see Bella caught you up on everything." *Traitor.*

"I wouldn't have volunteered without being privy to the whole story."

"Fair enough."

"Please don't tell me you've fallen for this guy?"

"No, of course not," I blurt, a little too quickly apparently because Ale's brows arch incredulously.

"Holy shit, you have!" His nostrils flare as he eyes me before his lips twist in disgust. "Oh, damn it, Serena, you're fucking him, aren't you? I can practically smell him all over you."

"I'm glad the explosion didn't do anything for your sense of smell," I snap, crossing my legs, then my arms over my chest. The man has always had a weirdly sensitive gift for tracking scents.

"Oh, *merda*, it's more than just fucking, isn't it?" His worried gaze rakes over me, and the irritation lessens a bit.

"I don't know…" I mutter. "All I know is that I don't want him dead."

"He didn't hurt you?"

I shake my head. "He saved me—a few times."

Ale lets out a low whistle before laying his head back on the pillow. I can see the exhaustion carved into his face, and I feel like a total asshole going on and on about my problems when he's lucky to be alive.

"None of it matters." I squeeze his hand again. "I'm just glad you're okay and that all of this will be over soon."

He nods. "My parents should be here any minute. The jet landed just before you got here. If you don't want my dad handcuffing you to the chair to ensure your departure in a few days, I'd get out of here ASAP."

"Thanks for the heads up."

"Don't make me regret it, Sere. Figure out your shit with this guy and get your ass back home. From what the doctors say, you'll have two or three days max. And you know I'll be itching to get out of here as soon as possible."

I jump up, irrational fear of my uncle and aunt arriving before I can escape suddenly overwhelming. "I swear I'll be here." I grab a piece of paper from the nightstand and jot down my number. "Just call me when it's time and please don't share this number with anyone. If my dad asks, tell him you haven't seen me, okay?"

"That's a big ask, Sere."

"I know."

"Dante's going to kill me if he finds out…"

"He won't." I tick my head at the guard by the door. "Just give him some cash to keep my secret. I would, but I'm kind of low on funds."

Alessandro rolls his eyes before motioning toward a clear plastic bag on a chair across the room. "My wallet is in there. Grab whatever you need."

"Seriously?"

"Yes, seriously. I can't have you running around with some mobster without cash for a quick getaway." His gaze drifts down to the gun at my waist. "I'm assuming he trusts you since he's letting you carry a gun. The guy must be as batshit crazy for you as you are for him." He grins and man, it feels good to see it. "Maybe it's a Ferrara thing."

Now I'm the one smiling. Maybe he's right. I can't help but think about Raf and Bella and how happy they are together. The man worships the ground she walks on.

Rifling through the bag of my cousin's belongings, my thoughts suddenly take a dark turn, chest hollowing out. What if he hadn't survived? What if this had been all that was left of Alessandro? I swallow hard, forcing down the fear. *Dio*, I never would have forgiven myself. "I'm so glad you're alive."

"Yeah, me too."

"And I'm really sorry about everything."

"Don't be sorry, just don't fuck up again, okay?"

I nod, stuffing a few hundred-dollar bills in my pocket. "And when we're all back in Manhattan, I swear I'll be the best nurse maid."

"Don't fucking lie to me, Serena." He chuckles, amusement

dancing across his dark eyes. "You'd be an absolutely awful caretaker."

"You know me too well." I close the distance between us and gently wrap my arms around his head, the least injured part of him, and squeeze. "Love you, asshole."

"Same, Sere." He holds my gaze as I turn to walk out. "And if you don't show up when I call, I will personally hunt down Antonio Ferrara until I find you."

Twisting my head around my shoulder, I throw him a smile. "Thanks, cuz."

CHAPTER 48
THE L-WORD

S*erena*

I hug my arms around Antonio's sweatshirt as I walk through the sliding doors of the hospital and into the busy streets of Milano. The quiet from earlier has given way to the hustle of morning activity. My steps are quick, anxious to get back to a hopefully still sleeping Toni, as I thread through the bustling streets lined with age-old buildings and modern shops. The mix of old and new is one of the things I love most about this city. I'm not looking forward to leaving it.

A sudden prickling sensation creeps up my spine, a whisper of instinct that I've learned never to ignore.

I glance over my shoulder to confirm—there's a man in all black a few paces too close, matching my speed, his gaze a bit too focused beneath his baseball cap. My heart kicks up its pace, thudding loudly in my ears. I tell myself it's nothing, just nerves after days in hiding, but the feeling doesn't fade.

How did they find me? And who the hell is this guy?

Focus, Serena. Right now, all that matters is losing him. I make a sudden turn into a busier street, weaving through a group of tourists snapping photos of a grand cathedral. He follows. I cross the street without waiting for the light, mingling with a crowd of locals that flows around a cluster of street vendors. He's still behind me, now dodging through the same crowd, his eyes locked on mine.

Panic tightens my chest, but I force it down, replacing it with cold strategy. I palm the gun at my hip, its presence bringing me a measure of comfort even if I can't use it in the middle of a crowded street.

Instead, I duck into a small café, the warm scent of espresso and baked pastries hitting me immediately. I don't stop; I head straight through to the other side, exiting through a back door that leads into a narrow, less populated alley.

My steps quicken, soles smacking against the cobblestones. The alley opens up to another street, this one lined with high-end boutiques with brightly lit windows. A tram barrels down the street, wheels squealing against the track. *Yes!* It slows at the stop and I quicken my pace, slipping into the crowded tram just as the doors are closing. Once I'm in, I press myself against the back and peer out the window.

The guy is there, on the platform, scanning the departing tram with a frustrated scowl. *See ya, sucker.* Relief floods through me, my breath coming out in a shaky laugh. As the tram pulls away, I watch him disappear, a dark figure swallowed up by the city's shadows. Fuck, that was too close.

Safe for now, I lean against the cool metal of the tram, the adrenaline slowly ebbing from my veins. Antonio is going to kill me when I tell him.

If I tell him...

I gnaw on the inside of my cheek as the tram meanders down the busy streets. Just a few more stops, and I'll be back to the *pensione*. My heart flutters in anticipation, but I quickly smack my palm to my chest, slamming down on the ridiculous sensation.

No man makes my heart flutter.

It must be his magical orgasms that have me in a fluster.

I spend the remainder of the ride with my thoughts in chaos, juggling between the overwhelming guilt over Alessandro and the inexplicable new feelings for Antonio. Pressing the call stop button, I weave between the passengers and hop off at the stop only a block from the small hotel.

As the tram pulls back onto the track, I glance down the street in search of the man in black. Dozens of locals and tourists fill the busy avenue, men in suits, women in designer dresses, but no stalker. Drawing in a steadying breath, I wait for the light to turn before crossing the busy street.

A few minutes later, I'm twisting the knob to our hotel room, a mixture of relief and anticipation building at the thought of seeing Antonio. The door swings open, and I find him half-dressed, dragging his pants up his legs. Wild eyes find mine, and the surge of emotions flashing across the dark abyss nearly takes my breath away.

"Serena!" He lunges at me, curling his muscled arms around me and pinning me to his firm chest. "Thank *Dio* you're alive." His lips are at my ear, kissing and nibbling. "I was so fucking worried."

"I'm fine," I whisper into his shirt, allowing myself a minute to revel in his familiar scent.

He holds me out to arms' length, anxious gaze scouring over me. "Where the fuck did you go?"

My spine stiffens at the change in his tone. "Where do you think?" I bark, brows furrowed.

"I have no idea!" He throws his hands in the air, the fear from a second ago, morphing into something darker. "I thought I knew you, but I guess I was mistaken. I thought for sure you would never be reckless enough to visit your cousin in the hospital. Please tell me I'm not wrong."

Clenching my jaw, I grit out, "You are wrong. I am that reckless and of course, I went to see Alessandro."

"How could you do that?" he howls. "Do you have any idea how dangerous that was?"

"I don't care!" I shout right back. "He's my cousin, my blood, and one of my best friends. I couldn't just run away to Rome without seeing him."

He erases the distance between us, his hand curling around my throat. He jerks me against his body, his chest heaving against mine. "You could have been killed." There's a tremor in his voice that has my anger slowly melting away despite the punishing grip. "*Cazzo*, Serena, I could have lost you forever."

"But you didn't," I rasp.

"But I could have, and after mentally preparing to say goodbye to you twice now, I don't think I could handle a third. Especially not if it meant never seeing you again, never breathing the same air as you, never looking into those brilliant blue eyes. Fuck, Serena…" His hands slide to my cheeks, firm fingers framing my face.

"What are you saying?"

"I was so damned scared." Raw emotion glistens across those midnight eyes, forcing the air from my lungs. "I thought I could let you go, but I can't. I—I'm so fucking in love with you I'm terrified."

Love? I blink quickly, trying to process that four-letter word. The one that I've been running from my entire life. The one that makes all of this much too real.

"*Merda*," he curses a long moment later, and I realize I've remained silent for too long. "I shouldn't have… It's insane I know but—"

"Toni, relax, it's okay." My fingers curl around the collar of his shirt, my heart tapping out a manic beat as I completely ignore his earth-shaking confession. "I'm safe; we both are. We'll go to Rome just like you said, and we'll figure it out."

"I don't think you understand. I cannot let you go; I'm physically incapable of it. The idea of spending even a day without you is impossible." His lips crash into mine, so full of hope and a promise of so much more.

I'm helpless but to give into the rush of emotions. To the thrill those three words provoked. My stupid heart doesn't just flutter, it full-on skips a beat then takes up that maddening rhythm.

It's the sex. It's just the mind-blowing, best orgasms of my life fucking. To drill the point home to my traitorous heart, I start to unfasten his pants as he kisses me senseless. I brush his cock, already hard and ready for me, and focus on the lusty sensations heating my core because focusing on that is much safer than even considering the horrifying truth.

That I've fallen in love with Antonio Ferrara.

That damned L-word echoes across my mind as Antonio thrusts into me, again and again, pushing me closer to oblivion. His arm encircles my waist, hand buried between my legs, thumb stroking my clit as he pounds into me from behind. My bare breasts are plastered against the window of the private train car, the verdant Tuscan countryside racing past us in a blur. I groan at the growing embers of intense pleasure. It's so hot, knowing that at any moment someone walking along the train tracks could see me getting fucked by the powerful man draped over me.

The man who claims to love me.

His free hand fists my hair, twisting my head back so that his tongue can lavish my neck. He nibbles at my skin, teeth grazing the sensitive flesh that grows more feverish with each maddening drive.

Once we reached the safety of the express train's private

compartment, we picked up right where we left off at the *pensione* with his cock balls' deep inside me. Reveling in this intense pleasure feels much safer than discussing the L-word or everything that will come once we reach Rome.

And at this rate, we'll be there in no time, the entire trip spent riding multiple orgasms. I can't get enough of him. The icy glass sends a tremor across my heated skin as he picks up the pace, his thrusts growing wilder with each roll of his hips. I match him stroke for stroke, so hungry for him.

"I'm going to come," I pant.

"Wait for me, *tesoro*." His warm breath spills across the shell of my ear, then he takes the sensitive lobe into his mouth and bites.

A wave of goose bumps pebbles my skin, drawing my nipples into tight peaks against the glass.

"Look, Serena, look at the rolling hills, the deep green valleys, the vineyards that stretch for miles. Isn't my country beautiful?"

I murmur a yes, lost in the building orgasm.

"And still, it pales in comparison to you. You, Serena Valentino, are exquisite." He sucks on my neck, nibbling on the sensitive flesh, and my entire body preens at the compliment. "I wish we could stay like this forever." He pounds harder, the slap of his hips against my ass echoing in an erotic harmony. "*Dio*, I must have done something right in my life to end up here with you."

His heartfelt words break that final wall, obliterating all restraint. "I can't wait any more," I pant. I mutter something incomprehensible as the dam crumbles and pleasure roars through me. Fire singes my veins, ripping a cry from my lips, my knees wobbling from the overwhelming sensations. Antonio's arm locks around me, steadying as he drives into me one last time.

I feel his cock twitch inside me an instant before his lips are at my ear, moaning my name as he comes. We ride the wave of ecstasy together, both still grinding against each other, squeezing out every last ounce of pleasure as the Italian countryside blurs by.

CHAPTER 49
ALMOST HOME

A*ntonio*

The Roman countryside zips by, the gentle rocking of the train lulling my churning thoughts. Running my fingers through Serena's hair as she lays across my lap, I glance down at the woman I *love*. I didn't think I was capable of the emotion, and yet, now that I've given up fighting it, the truth of it swirls deep within the marrow of my bones. She's still naked, we both are, and my cum slickens her thighs. It's the most glorious thing I've ever seen.

Her eyes are closed, breaths soft.

She's my *tesoro*, my real-life treasure. I will never let her go now. *Whether she likes it or not*. That monster that lives in the dark recesses of my mind growls that last bit. Ignoring the truth of his words, I draw in an incredibly sated breath. I can't remember the last time I came so many times. And the craziest part is that I could do it again. Just the thought of Serena has desire igniting in my core and my cock twitching.

I never knew sex and love could be so intrinsically intertwined.

For the first time in years, I actually sympathize with Raffa. I finally understand what he did and why. Because only a few weeks with Serena and I can honestly say without a shred of doubt that I would destroy anyone who came near my *tesoro*. I'd raze the entire country if that's what it took to keep her safe.

And I will… as soon as she is tucked away in my safehouse in Roma.

But that would mean leaving her alone and the thought of that is suddenly unacceptable.

It wakes a fiery rage in my gut and has heat pummeling my veins. My instinct to protect her seems innately tied to my desire to fuck her. It's as if when my cock is nestled deep inside that warm pussy, I know that no harm will come to her.

The train begins to slow, and a pit of dread unfurls in my stomach. Our blissful reprieve has come to an end.

Serena must also sense the deceleration because her lids open, and she stretches across my lap, the haze of deep satiation across those mesmerizing sapphire orbs breathtaking. "Are we there yet?" She smirks.

"We'll be arriving in Roma in minutes. We should probably get dressed."

Her lips purse, and it brings me an inordinate amount of pleasure. "Ugh, do we have to?" She's just as obsessed as I am. Only she completely ignored my confession of love.

It should irritate me more…

It does, but then again, our relationship hasn't exactly been conventional. But I remember someone telling me the best love stories never are.

Dio, what has this woman done to me? I'm daydreaming about love…

"Yes, we have to." Leaning over her head, I reach for her discarded clothes and offer the bra and panties first.

With a growl of frustration, she sits up so that I'm finally free to move around the compartment. Maybe she's as nervous for what's to come as I am. Crouching down to pick up my pants off the floor, I dig through the pocket for the cell phone gifted to Serena by Santi. In the ultimate show of trust, she'd given it to me to hold. It's a fair trade since she still has my gun.

I glance at the screen, my fingers frozen above it. I've known Pietro my entire life and still, my faith in him falters. After everything that's gone wrong since stealing Serena away, I can't help but question everyone's loyalty.

"Just make the call," Serena whispers as she tugs her top over her head. "At least we'll know where we stand one way or another."

I nod. We discussed this part of the plan briefly before reaching the train, before we could keep our hands off one another. My fingers fly across the keyboard using the emergency code we'd developed years ago. If Pietro is alive and still loyal to me, he would meet us at the safehouse.

The train grinds into the station, the brakes squealing in protest, and Serena stumbles into me. Curling my arm around her waist, I hold her close, my heels digging into the floor to keep us steady. I press a kiss to the top of her head, then brush another one on her temple. A breathy sigh escapes her lips, and that familiar fire starts to rage.

Tamping down on the sensations, I give her one last chaste kiss to the cheek as the train finally halts. "I love you, *tesoro*," I whisper against her ear. The confession is so quiet, I'm not certain she'll hear it. But the way her body stiffens against me confirms that she does.

Begrudgingly, I release her, unable to keep the damned hurt from rising at her rejection. No, a rejection I could understand given the circumstances, but she's completely ignoring me. For some reason, it's a hundred times worse.

A chime sounds and the train doors glide open, the sudden flurry of movement jerking me from my pity party. "Let's go," I mutter and unlock our private cabin. She nods, swings her purse over her shoulder and follows me without a word.

We weave between the hordes of people flooding the *binario* of Termini Station and despite that damned ache of uncertainty, I reach back for Serena's hand. Her fingers easily entwine with my own and I tug her down the platform and across the congested terminal until we reach the storage lockers. Moving quickly through the space, I head straight for the locker on the end of the row. Within minutes, we're equipped with my go bag and on our way to the taxi stand outside.

The cacophony of horns, shouts and revving engines feels like home, and in spite of the polluted air the tightness in my chest subsides. I wave down the first taxi I see and usher Serena into the backseat. Glancing over my shoulder through the rearview window, I scan the busy streets for a tail. None that I can make out, but the avenue is much too crammed with vehicles to be sure.

Over the chaos, I shout the address to the driver and settle in beside Serena, releasing her hand. As the taxi darts into mid-day traffic, my phone buzzes, and relief floods my system at Pietro's response.

With my righthand man on board and headed to the security of the safehouse, I'm certain we'll finally be able to piece together who is behind this.

The small stretch of land nestled on a quiet street in the outskirts of Rome comes to view from down the road. Tall hedges and a wrought iron fence line the perimeter, keeping most of the house from view. It isn't much, a small three-bedroom house I bought from the money I earned at the first café I worked at in college. It was well before I'd become entangled in *Papà*'s illegitimate operations but not before I understood how things worked in our world.

I'd purchased the property under an assumed name to be sure it would never be entangled with the Ferrara family. Over the years, there were countless times I was thankful for my foresight.

"Almost home," I whisper to Serena.

She nods, her gaze far away as she stares out the window.

The car ride has been spent in a semi-comfortable silence, each of us caught up in our own thoughts. I can't help but wonder where hers lie. Twice I've admitted to loving her and still, she remains silent on the topic. It stings like hell.

The terracotta tiles of a familiar rooftop peek over the towering hedges a block down, and I lean forward to the driver. "You can stop here."

He twists his head over his shoulder, eying the vacant surrounding fields. "*Sei sicuro?*"

"*Si*, I'm sure."

With a shrug, he pulls the old Fiat over, and I hand him the cash. I slide out of the backseat, offering Serena a hand and we wait along the edge of the field until the taxi has turned around and disappeared down the dirt road.

"How far do we have to walk?" she asks, the first words she's spoken since the train. I hate how my pulse quickens at the sound.

"Not far." I tick my head to the looming hedges at the end of the street. "That's it over there."

"Good, because I'm suddenly exhausted."

"Probably from all those earth-shattering orgasms." I offer a tentative smirk, and she rewards me with a smile in return.

"Maybe." She snorts.

We reach the gate moments later, and I punch in the security code. The old wrought iron squeals as it heaves open. It's been just a bit over six months since I've been here. When *Papà* informed me of his plans to move in on the Kings' territory in

Manhattan, I figured it wouldn't be long until this place would come in good use.

I couldn't have been more right. I just never thought I would be coming here with one of the princesses of the King's empire.

Serena is unusually quiet as I guide her into the small house. The furnishings are sparse but enough to get by. Though I haven't been here in months, I have staff who keep it stocked with necessities. There should be enough food and water to last for a month at least. I'd had it equipped for three at the time. Who knew in only six months I'd be the only Ferrara left in the business?

"Where's my room?" Serena asks as she follows me down a bare-walled corridor.

I whirl around and she stops in her tracks, her palms smacking into my chest. "Your room or *ours*?" Even I can detect that hopeful twinge at the end of the word. *Dio*, I've become soft for her. Father must be rolling over in his grave, but maybe *Mamma* is rejoicing in it.

Serena's lips twitch as she regards me. "I thought you were going to leave me here to go track down the assholes after us?"

Right. I did say that. Then why does the idea of being away from her for even a few minutes have panic rising? I nod, choosing to ignore her question much like she's been doing to me. Instead, I lead her down the hallway to the master bedroom at the end.

Much like the rest of the house, it's simple but functional with a king size bed, full closet, dresser and well-equipped desk. The security system is top of the line and with a VPN that's completely untraceable set up by my friend Valerio, I'm certain I'll be able to track down exactly who's behind this.

Serena drops her purse on the bed and turns to me. "I'm going to shower."

My nostrils flare as memories of my cum slickening her thighs surge to the surface. "Do you have to?" I rasp, my voice already rough just from the vivid thoughts. "I love the idea of you covered in my cum."

Her grin turns wicked as she tugs the top over her head, revealing her breasts through that lace bra. "You've been throwing that L-word out a lot lately." Her jaw snaps shut as if she hadn't meant to say it out loud.

But I won't let her out of it that easily. I erase the space between us, framing her face with my hands. Her eyes are wild as they lock on mine, chest suddenly heaving. "I did not simply throw the word 'love' around. Much like I've never thrown my actual *love* around. To anyone." I suck in a steadying breath, steeling my feelings for yet another rejection. "When I said I loved you I meant every word. You've become a part of me that I didn't even know was missing. If I lost you, you would take a piece of me with you—it's as simple and complicated as that."

Raw emotion glistens across those lively sapphire irises. Her lips purse, and a tear slips down her cheek. I sweep it away with my thumb, completely speechless. Is she crying from happiness? Is she upset with me? I can't for the life of me tell.

A loud chime rings out, breaking the spell between us, and I mutter a curse, whirling back toward the door. "I'm sorry," I mutter. "That must be Pietro." I press my thumb print to the digital scanner by the doorframe and the video surveillance system turns on.

Pietro's full face fills the screen. "It's me, *capo*."

I press the button, granting him entrance, then turn back to Serena. "I'm going to let him in. Hold that thought, I'll be right back."

She nods and spins toward the bed. "Wait," she calls out and I watch as she digs through her purse and reveals the gun I gave her. "Take little Toni with you. Just in case."

The hint of a smile curves my lips. She may not love me yet but at least she's proven time and again that she doesn't want to see me dead. I'll take it for now. "There's a safe in the closet.

There are guns, fake I.D.'s and enough cash to take you around the world. The code is zero six two nine."

Mamma's birthday.

"Got it."

I move toward the door, turning back with my hand strangling the knob. "Stay in here and if anything happens—"

"Nothing is going to happen," she blurts. "We still have to finish our conversation…" A full smile flashes across her face and *Dio*, it's the most glorious thing I've ever seen. With foolish hope kindling in my chest again, I toss her a smile and close the door behind me.

Holstering the gun at my waistband, I look through the peephole when I reach the entrance. Again, Pietro's familiar face fills the circular frame. Unlocking the door, I whip it open, and my heart catapults up my throat.

A man holds a gun to Pietro's head, just outside the field of the camera's vision. Tears stream down my friend's cheeks, his face bruised and bloody. *Merda*. Then another familiar face pops up behind my righthand man.

Santiago.

CHAPTER 50
TRAITOR

S*erena*

"Run!" Antonio's panicked voice sends ice rippling through my veins.

What the fuck just happened?

I dart toward the bedroom door and twist the deadbolt, my pulse skyrocketing. Muffled male voices leech through the thick timber, but they're too warped to make them out. I tap the screen by the door, but I'm locked out, the system requesting a fingerprint. Shit. Pressing my thumb against the reader, I pray for a miracle, but no luck. *Access Denied* flashes across the screen in bright red.

Wait a second... maybe there's a manual override option.

I jab my finger at the screen again and again until a keypad appears. "Insert override code now or the alarm will be triggered," a robotic voice drones.

Either option could be good. I tap out the code Antonio just gave me, again praying to all the gods it'll work.

"*Access granted,*" it hums in response, and the screen flares to life.

I stare at the grainy image of the doorway, and fury pours through my veins as the familiar face coalesces. "Santi?" I blurt.

No, it can't be. I've known him for months, told him everything. He's been my best friend from day one at Dolce & Gabbana. Betrayal cuts deep, a knife carving out my insides. How is this happening?

Worse, how could I have been so stupid to trust him? *Papà* is right; I am just a naïve child. Or at least I was...

I squint trying to get a better view of another guy standing behind Pietro and just out of the camera's view. Santi shoves Antonio's man inside and the other male's face flashes across the screen. Federico Sartori.

"I knew it!" I hiss.

A gunshot echoes through the monitor and panic claws its way up my chest until I see Pietro fall.

Shit.

Santi and Federico barrel inside, slamming the door behind them, and I grit out another curse. A furious tangle of betrayal and anger rush my insides. The two of them were working together all along. But why? Federico was in line to inherit the Sartori territory from his father, but Santi? What does he have to do with all of this?

Shoving the pointless thoughts down for now, I spin toward the master closet. There is no way I'll let those two assholes kill the man I love.

What the actual fuck?

I freeze before my fingers finish typing out the code on the safe. My heart stutters, then kicks up into overdrive. Did I just say love? Holy shit. I love Antonio... Damn it. I do. My breaths come out faster, echoing the ragged tempo of my heart as realization sets in. It's the last thing I wanted, the absolute worst thing for me, but I *love* him.

And I will *not* lose him today.

My fingers fly across the keyboard and the safe clicks open, revealing an assortment of weapons. I take the Glock, relishing in the familiar feel of the weapon in my palm, then I tuck a knife into my pant leg. Beside the weapons sits a burner phone. I hesitate a moment before powering it on, typing out a quick message and then shoving it into my jeans pocket. Just in case.

Moving silently, I unlock the bedroom door, holding my breath. The world narrows to the barrel of my Glock as I step into the hallway, the sound of my footfalls nonexistent. My heart pounds in my ears, adrenaline surging through my veins like wildfire. Antonio is somewhere in the foyer, held by Santi and Federico, and desperation claws at me with icy fingers.

I haven't heard his voice since he shouted what seems like forever go. He didn't really expect me to run, did he? If so, this relationship is never going to work out.

Turning the corridor, I force my thoughts to focus. The nervous rambling is not helping. Drawing in a steadying breath, I creep around the final corner and spot them before they see me. Antonio is bound and gagged, blood dribbling from a gash across his forehead. Santi and Federico stand on either side of him, my friend pulling his arm back for another blow. Fury flows like lava through my veins. How dare they try to take him away from me? Their laughter cuts through the stale air as Santi lands another punch to Toni's face, and the sound of cracking bone only fuels my rage. I don't hesitate.

"Fuck you, asshole!"

"No, Serena, don't!" Antonio's desperate muffled cry falls on deaf ears.

My finger squeezes the trigger, sending a bullet flying toward Santi. He dives behind the couch, but the shot grazes his arm. Federico returns fire, his bullets slicing past me, too close, dinging the wood planks at my feet. I duck behind an oversized chest in the living room, barely catching my breath, steeling myself for the next move.

"Surrender, Serena! You can't win this, sweetie." Santi's voice echoes through the space, mocking and confident. Nothing like the friend I'd spent countless *aperitivi* with over the past few months. The hurt threatens to erupt, to bowl me over, but I grit my teeth, my thoughts only on Antonio. Now is not the time to get sentimental. Santi is a traitorous bastard, and he deserves to die. Shaking my head even though they can't see me, I shout, "Go to hell, you *pezzo di merda*." Surrender isn't in my vocabulary, especially not when Antonio's life hangs in the balance.

I peek around the corner of the wooden chest, and Antonio's frenzied eyes meet mine. Somehow, he's gotten the gag off. He's only a few yards away; I can almost touch him. "Go!" he mouths, but I shake my head.

"I'm not leaving you," I hiss.

He mutters a colorful array of expletives, cursing my stubbornness, and I toss him a good eyeroll before ducking under cover again. The movement presses the cool blade tucked in my pant leg against my skin, triggering an idea. If I can just get the knife to Toni maybe he can use it to jimmy the handcuffs. Now, I just have to figure out how to slip it to him undetected.

Six feet of open living room lie between us.

From behind my cover, I fire two quick shots toward where Santi's voice had come from. There's a satisfying shout of pain, and a grin splits my lips. *Gotcha, traitorshit.* I don't waste a second to leap out from behind the chest and dart by Antonio, dropping the knife between his cuffed hands before sliding along the floor and ducking behind another couch.

Federico, now bleeding and furious, charges at me, firing wildly. I roll to the side, the heat of the bullets much too close to my skin.

"Serena, watch out!" Antonio shouts.

I scramble to my feet as pain sears through my shoulder. *Son of a bitch!* That bullet must have grazed me. Damn it. Blood trickles down my arm, and I grit through the pain. The room spins slightly, but I push through the dizziness.

Antonio's eyes meet mine, wide with fury and desperation.

"Serena!" He kicks and squirms against the restraints, the knife hidden in his fist, but he's no match for the metal handcuffs. "Leave her alone or I swear to *Dio*, when I get loose, I'll rip your heads off and parade around the city wearing your skulls as hats."

The gruesome threat is enough to reignite the fury and focus within me.

With a fierce cry, I rush Federico, dodging his clumsy attempts to grab me. I'm close enough to see his surprise as I land a solid punch to his jaw, followed by a quick kick that sends his gun skittering across the floor. But before I can celebrate, a sharp pain explodes across the back of my head. *Shit, ow!* Santi looms behind me, and I curse myself for letting my guard down for a second.

The gun drops from my numb fingers as Santi's arm locks around my neck, pulling my back against him. "Thought you could outgun us, Sere?" he hisses in my ear, his breath foul against my cheek. "I'd heard you were good, but this was pathetic." I struggle, trying to break free, but the world begins to blur, his grip tightening like a vise.

"How could you, Santi?" I choke out.

"It was easy. You were so desperate for a friend, to have someone at your side that you never once questioned anything."

His words spear me in the chest, each one cutting deeper than the last. "Why? Why are you doing this?"

"Your father and his brothers killed my mother," he hisses. "Does the name Blanca Alvarez ring a bell?"

My thoughts swirl back in time to Pa telling an animated story around the dinner table. Before any of us were born, he and Uncle Luca flew to Puerto Rico and got into a high velocity, mid-sea shootout to save Alessandro's dad, Marco, from *La Sombra Boricua*, the Puerto Rican mob. Shit! How could I have been so blind? Did that mean the fire to Alessandro's jet was another part of Santi's revenge plot?

"Just let Antonio go," I manage to rasp out, my vision darkening at the edges. "I'm the one you want anyway, right? This is all about me and my family."

Santi laughs, the sound harsh and foreign to my ears. "Oh, this isn't even close to being over, Sere. You're only the first piece of the puzzle."

Shit, my cousins. My breath hitches as realization hits, wasting the final remaining air in my lungs. Santi's hold tightens, and my knees buckle as darkness encroaches into my vision.

"Serena, no!" Antonio's voice, screaming my name, echoes across my subconscious as he struggles against the cuffs.

"I love you," I mouth, hoping he understands over the chaos.

His panicked, furious face is the last thing I see before the ominous black consumes me.

CHAPTER 51
YOU SAVED ME

A*ntonio*

"*Porca puttana. Maledetto pezzo di merda!*" The avalanche of curses erupts from my clenched teeth as I watch Serena collapse, and there's nothing I can do but struggle uselessly against the damned cuffs biting into my wrists. I've been trying to force the lock open with the tip of the knife but so far, my efforts have been in vain. My gaze dips to her motionless form splayed across the floor, and a wave of fury crashes over me.

Then a ray of light erupts from the darkness…

Was I imagining it or had she told me she loved me right before she blacked out? *Dio*, I have to know.

"When I get loose, I'm going to fucking annihilate both of you," I growl. "Then I'll drag your flayed corpses across the entire city of Roma for all to see what happens when you fuck with what's mine." I glare at Santiago then Federico. "And just so that we're clear, Serena Valentino is mine."

Her friend barks out a laugh, but the strain across his features gives away the true state of his wound. "Maybe in the afterlife. You two can live happily ever after together in the hell you deserve."

"I'll gut you with my bare hands before I ever let you touch her again." *Dio*, I just need to get to her. Drawing in a steadying breath to still my manic heartbeats and frantic movements, I position the knife's edge into the locking mechanism. If I can just disengage the ratchet...

"You'll both be dead long before you ever get the chance." Santi smirks as he folds down onto the couch.

"Take me instead then. I'll surrender and let you do whatever you want to me. Just let her go."

"I already have you, Ferrara." He grins, and I can't wait to rip that cocky smirk of his face. "Besides, I just need to keep Serena alive long enough to lure Isabella, Matteo and Alessia here. I've heard Alessandro is barely alive as it is. His arrival was a happy coincidence I couldn't pass up. The Valentinos and Rossi's stole my mother's life, so now I'll have their children's lives as payback."

He's a lot of talk considering he could bleed out at any moment.

"You're such a cliché." A harsh laugh bubbles out as I eye the *bastardo* while furiously working on the manacles behind my back. "You killed my mommy, and now I'm going to kill you," I scoff in a whiny voice. Then I tick my head at Federico. "What's your excuse?"

"I hate you." He shrugs, pressing a towel to the wound in his upper arm and wincing. "Always have. There's just something about you that irritates me."

"I appreciate the honesty." I wiggle the tip of the knife, and something clicks. Hope kindles deep in my gut, and I cut a quick glance toward Serena. Her chest rises and falls slowly, the slash on her head still dribbling blood.

"And with the old man retiring," Federico continues, his breaths ragged, "taking over the crumbling Ferrara empire is the perfect way to cement my position as the new capo of the Sartoris."

"How very ambitious of you, Fede, and here I thought you were simply a spoiled brat, cowering behind your father's tremendous shadow." Just one more twist... another click, and the lock disengages. Pain lances through my wrists as I finally slip one hand free from the cold metal of the handcuffs. Gripping the bracelets between my fingertips to keep them from clattering to the floor, I eye the pair then my gun on the floor by the door. It's a little too far to reach, but both men are nursing gunshot wounds thanks to Serena's sharp shooting skills, and I'm just a little banged up, plus I have a knife they know nothing about.

I like my odds.

I'm on my feet in a heartbeat, adrenaline masking the faint ache in my joints from the time spent bound and immobile. Federico and Santi are hunched over on the couch, their focus on tending to their wounds instead of me. Their guns are splayed across the coffee table just within their reach.

I fist the knife, its handle fitting snugly in my palm, a familiar and comforting weight, and inch closer.

Santi's head snaps up, his eyes widening in a mix of shock and fear. "Antonio, you—" he starts, but his words cut off as I step closer, the blade catching the light.

"I think we've had enough talk," I interrupt. Federico fumbles for his gun, cursing under his breath as his injured arm slows him down. I don't give him the chance to aim. With a swift move, I kick the weapon out of his reach, sending it sliding onto the floor.

Santiago lunges at me, his larger frame a weapon in its own right, but not as good as mine. I sidestep, using his momentum against him, and he stumbles past. Then I lunge again, and my knife finds its mark, a shallow cut across his thigh. He howls and staggers back, hitting the wall.

"You should have stayed down, *imbecille*." I circle him, clutching the knife, my other eye on Federico as he tries to prop himself up against the wall. "No, it wouldn't have mattered, I'm going to make this painful for you either way."

Federico makes another grab for his gun, desperation etched into his features. I close the distance between us, my kick sending sharp pain up my leg but knocking the breath out of him. He collapses with a groan, clutching his side. I kick him again, this time going for his head. No mercy for anyone today. Not when Serena's life is on the line. His head cracks against the wall, spattering blood across the pristine white. His body immediately stills.

Spinning back to Santi, I catch the *bastardo* staggering across my peripheral vision. I follow his line of sight to the gun sitting at the edge of the coffee table. I lunge for it at the same time he does, and we crash midair, the hit squeezing the breath from my lungs.

I pound into the floor with a smack, but somehow, I find the cool metal of the gun clenched in my fist. Santiago rushes me, reaching for the gun with his injured arm. Wrapping my fingers around his bicep, I squeeze, crushing the wound, and a stream of crimson pours out.

"Motherfucker!" he grits out as I stab my finger into the bullet wound again.

"I'm torn here, Santiago," I hiss as I flip us over, so he's flattened against the floor. I bring the knife's blade to his throat, the gun clutched in my other hand. "I would like to fulfill my promise of a long, torturous death, but the other part of me just wants to kill you so I can get to Serena." I hazard a quick glance over my shoulder to ensure she's still where I last saw her.

"Fuck you," he snarls.

"Not in this lifetime or any other, *figlio di puttana*." I slowly drag the blade across his throat, leaving a thin line of crimson. "The only person I'll be fucking is Serena Valentino. For the rest of my life, if she'll allow it. So you know what? I guess I should be thanking you. Because if you hadn't burned down my house and interfered with the kidnapping, I'm not sure we would have ended up here."

I twist the knife, following a path down his throat, then carve into his chest. The pressure is light, only enough to sting but not enough to kill. Fuck, I really do want to draw out his torture. The monster I've kept locked up since Serena fell into my life is ravenous. Santiago hisses out a curse, squirming beneath me. "You betrayed her, *testa di cazzo*, then you tried to kill her, not once, not twice, but three times. And that is unforgiveable, a punishment worthy of the most gruesome death."

"I hope you and Serena burn in hell," he rasps.

"Antonio…" That whisper of an angelic voice has my head spinning over my shoulder.

"Serena!" My weight shifts, my entire body helpless but to move toward the sound of that melodic timbre. And I realize my mistake an instant too late.

With my attention diverted, Santiago rips the knife from my hand and jabs it into my thigh. I bite back a scream and level the barrel of the gun at his head and squeeze. The trigger jams, and he squirms out from beneath me, crawling across the floor on hands and knees. I spot Federico's discarded gun under the coffee table a second before Santiago's fingers curl around the grip.

Merda.

The next few seconds move in slow motion.

Serena's cry echoes from behind me, and the pain in her voice is worse than the gunshot that I know is coming. Kneeling on the floor, Santiago points the gun at my chest. The air thickens, everything narrowing to this one moment. All my regrets, all my fears, all my mistakes rush to the surface. Then I see her face, Serena. Despite all the shit, she made the last few weeks worth it. With a sense of peace settling over me, I wait for the searing pain of the bullet.

"I love you, Serena," I shout.

Piercing shots ring out in an angry symphony. *Bang! Bang! Bang!*

All the air siphons from my lungs, and I'm numb, ice running through my veins. Santiago slumps back, blood blossoming in rivulets across his chest. I run my hands over my own, searching for the warm crimson liquid, only there's nothing.

I whirl around and meet a fearsome blue-eyed gaze peering over the barrel of a Beretta. Beneath the wild tumble of blonde hair, dried blood stains her forehead, but the hint of a smile curves the perfect bow of her lips.

"Serena…" I whisper as I crawl toward her.

She throws her arms around me, tugging me into her chest. "You're okay," she murmurs against my mouth.

"You saved me, *tesoro*."

In more ways than I could ever imagine.

CHAPTER 52
IMPERFECTLY PERFECT

S*erena*

My head feels likes someone took a jackhammer to it, but I crush Antonio to my chest all the same, ignoring the throbbing ache in my temples. "You're okay," I repeat, more to convince myself than him. His lips brush mine, softly, but the gentle touch only lasts for an instant. He grips the back of my neck, and the sweet kiss becomes fiery and demanding, distracting from the ache across my skull to the one already developing between my legs.

Our tongues entwine in a scorching dance, teeth gnashing as we devour each other. Every stroke of his tongue is demanding, insistent and all-consuming. It's everything. *Dio*, for a terrible moment I thought I'd lose him. And before having the chance to tell him how I really feel…

I rip my mouth from his, my chest heaving from the building fire that always rages between us. "Wait," I murmur, his breath still mingling with my own. "I need to tell you something."

His dark eyes sear to mine, hands gripping my face in desperation. "Anything, *tesoro*."

"I should have said it before... I was just scared because—"

"Because this raging inferno between us isn't exactly conventional?" A smirk tips up the corners of his mouth. And I just want that mouth all over me.

I nod.

"You don't have to say anything if you aren't sure."

"No, I'm sure. That's the terrifying part." My eyes chase to his, then hold for an endless moment. The tempest of emotions surging below the sleek surface only amplifies my resolve. "I love you, Antonio Ferrara. You are probably the worst decision I've ever made, but I can't seem to regret it. You're as perfectly imperfect as I am."

He chuckles, the smile setting those onyx orbs ablaze in starlight. "No, you're wrong, you are perfect in every way, *amore*." His hand cups my neck, bringing my lips to his again. I'm dizzy from blood loss or maybe it's his ravenous kiss, but I don't dare pull away. Not when we were so close to losing each other forever.

The front door whips open, wood cracking against plaster and Antonio leaps up, gun trained at the entrance. My eyes nearly pop out of my head when I take in the familiar form darkening the doorway, and again when the other three figures appear behind him.

"Raffa?" Antonio mutters, lowering his gun.

"Who the fuck else did you expect, *stronzo*?" Raffaele keeps his weapon pointed at his older brother.

"Oh, my gawd, Serena!" Isabella barrels toward me with Matteo and Alessia trailing behind, and Raf finally lowers the gun. "Are you okay?" She hauls me to my feet and the entire living room spins.

"I think I will be."

Her eyes rake over me, not the ones of a concerned family

member, but those of a soon-to-be doctor. "Shit, Sere, you're going to need stitches, and you probably have a concussion."

"But I'm alive." I offer a weak smile. Antonio curls his arm around me, and the collective gasp from around the room is deafening. "Largely thanks to him." I throw my thumb in Toni's direction.

"But you never would've been in danger if he hadn't captured you in the first place," Raf snarls.

Antonio stiffens beside me, his guilt pouring off in suffocating waves. "I've already apologized countless times, and I will continue to do so until I've proven myself." He glances at each of my cousins. "To all of you."

"Listen, Raf…" I throw a glare at the righteous *bastardo*, "this is between your brother and me and if I've been able to forgive him for the little abduction thing then so can you."

"But will Dante?" Matteo throws me a wicked grin.

"I'll handle my father."

"Well, you better figure it out quickly because he should be landing in Rome in the next few hours." Bella eyes me then Antonio, and her lips twist. After all the terrible things she's heard about him from Raf, it'll take a while for her to understand. But I'm sure she will eventually.

"Wait, how did you guys get here so quickly?" I eye my cousins, the relief in seeing them all here jumbled with the emotional overload of the past hour. I'd only just texted Bella when Santi and Federico arrived.

"We flew in with our parents last night," Alessia replies, "to see Alessandro."

Of course. So Bella was already on the jet when I spoke to her last. That sneaky little…

"How is he?" I blurt.

"Better," his sister answers, "but it's going to be a long recovery."

The guilt I'd felt bubbling from Antonio seeps into my own

gut. It's my fault he came. I'll never forgive myself for what I put him through.

"And we figured you could use our help." Bella's words interrupt my shame spiral. Then she winds her arm around Raf's waist, leaning against her big bodyguard. "So we took the first train to Rome this morning after checking in on Ale last night."

"Well, as you can see, we had this under control." I motion to the heap of bodies scattered around the living room.

Matty eyes the two motionless figures, dark brows knitting as it focuses on one. The one that still hurts to look at. "Is that your friend, Santi?"

I wave a dismissive hand. "Yeah, it's kind of a long story."

"Holy shit, Sere," Bella cries.

"We all know I've never had great taste in men." I throw Antonio a smirk before brushing my lips against his stubbled cheek. "Until now."

More groans echo across the room.

"That's highly debatable," Raf mutters.

"Thank you, *amore*." He presses a kiss to my temple, and the throbbing subsides a touch.

"*Amore*?" Bella's curious gaze bounces between us. "You guys are in love?" she blurts. "I thought this was just hate sex."

Heat flushes my cheeks as I glance up at Antonio who wears a matching ridiculous grin. "No, it's definitely love."

"Oh man, Dante is going to lose his shit." Matteo throws his head back, chuckling.

Releasing Toni, I jab my elbow into my cousin's gut. "Shut up and keep your mouth closed about all of this. I need to have a serious sit down with Pa when he arrives."

"Maybe you should leave Antonio with me for safe keeping," Raf offers.

I eye his younger brother skeptically. "I don't think so." I'm not sure who hates Toni more, Raf or my father.

"I'll make sure he's safe," Bella cuts in before lancing a glare in Antonio's direction. "I'm going to trust in Serena's rather questionable decision-making skills for now, unless he proves otherwise."

Antonio draws in a breath, then takes a step toward my cousin, but he doesn't make it far before Raf jumps between them. Toni lifts his hands, palms up. "I mean Isabella no harm, Raffa." Then his gaze pivots to Bella. "I only wanted to apologize for all that you suffered under our father's hand. I will spend the rest of my days trying to make up for my sins against you and Serena."

Bella nods and relief floods my system. "Just don't fuck with my cousin, or I'll murder you in your sleep."

Antonio chuckles. "I would never." He draws me into his side, his warm breath spilling through my hair as he plants a kiss to the top of my head. "I love Serena more than I ever thought possible. She's been the light in the darkest of days, the calm in the chaos that surrounds me. Without her, I'd be lost in a world that offers no forgiveness. She's not just my love, she's my whole heart."

Raf snorts on a laugh as the girls *ooh* and *ahh*. "Who knew you were such a poet, Tonio," he grumbles.

"Raffa…" His voice softens as he steps closer to his brother, his words a mere whisper. "I don't think I could ever apologize enough for my behavior over the last ten years." His dark eyes glisten with unshed tears as he regards his brother. "I tried the other day on the phone, but I don't think you were ready to hear it then. Maybe now, you will be. I won't pretend to think we could ever go back to how things once were between us, but I'd like to try. I've done everything wrong over the years since *Mamma* died, but you're my baby brother and I love you. I need you in my life."

Raf stares at him, eyes wide, jaw slack.

"Say something," Bella whispers.

"Okay," he mutters.

"*Grazie.*" Toni makes a move to hug his brother, but he backs out the last minute, tucking me closer instead.

"Not that all of this isn't lovely and all," says Alessia, "but the smell of blood and fresh bodies is making me gag."

I snort on a laugh, shaking my head at my cousin. "Alessia is right. Let's get the hell out of here."

"Do you need me to call a clean-up crew?" Raf offers.

Antonio's expression darkens, and I know he's thinking about Pietro. His righthand man's body is strewn across the floor at the entrance. At least Toni knew his friend had remained loyal until the end.

"I'll handle it," he grits out.

"What about Enrico Sartori?" The question erupts before I can stop it. He's going to lose his shit when he finds out his son and heir is dead. Who would pay the price, just Antonio or would the Kings be in the crosshairs now?

"I'll take care of that too. The Sartoris are my problem."

A whisper of fear streaks through me. "I'm going with you."

Antonio shakes his head, a rueful grin pulling at his lips. "I would try to argue, but I have a feeling there's no point."

"You're damned right, *amore*."

"Smart man." Bella shoots me a wink. "I think I'm starting to understand why you fell for him."

CHAPTER 53
DANTE VALENTINO

A*ntonio*

"Don't be nervous." Serena squeezes my hand as we walk toward the door. The early morning light filters into her apartment, but it does nothing to cast away the icy shadows frosting my veins. There aren't many things in this life that scare me, unless it relates to losing Serena, but coming face to face with Dante Valentino is one of them.

"I'm not nervous," I mutter.

Serena halts midstride and tugs my hand so I spin toward her. "Look, Toni, I'm not going to lie and say my dad is going to be thrilled about this, but he loves me. If there's anything I'd stake my life on, it's that. And I love you… it won't be easy for him to accept at first, but he'll give in eventually. He'll understand."

I force my lips to slide into a smile I don't feel. "How can you be so sure about him?" I thought my father loved Raffaele and yet, what he did to him…

As if Serena has read my thoughts, her expression softens. "Dante is not your father, Antonio. *Papà* would never do to me what he did to Raffaele."

"How can you know for certain?"

"Because I know my father, and I'm one hundred percent secure in his love for me."

"I hope you're right, *tesoro*."

Another knock, this one more forceful than the first resounds across the apartment.

"We better not keep him waiting," I murmur.

"There, you see, you're beginning to get Dante Valentino already." She offers a reassuring smile. "He's definitely not a patient man."

Heaving in a steadying breath, I march the remaining distance to the door, half-certain I'll meet the barrel of a gun when it swings open. Twisting the handle, I hazard a quick glance at Serena over my shoulder and memorize every detail of her face in case it's the last time I see it.

I wouldn't blame Dante one bit for killing me. Without even having a child yet, I feel it with the utmost certainty. If the roles were reversed, I would destroy anyone who ever threatened my daughter.

I can already imagine a family with Serena…

Blinking quickly, I chase away the heart-warming image for now, storing it in my memory forever. If all goes well today, then maybe, but I can't afford to lose myself in visions of a future that may never be.

Serena's hand closes around mine, twisting the knob, and a scowling Dante fills the doorway, his dark presence sucking all the air from the small foyer.

"*Cazzo*, how long does it take to open a fucking door?" he growls, eyeing me with barely veiled disgust. The temperature in the apartment drops to frosty levels, the tension thick in the air.

"Well, hello to you too, Pa." Serena, ignoring his dark glare, curls her arms around his neck and pulls him into a warm embrace.

"I'm glad you're alive," he grumbles, that murderous gaze focused solely on me. For a middle-aged man the King's enforcer is still intimidating as fuck.

"Same." She steps back, an attempt to move by my side, but Dante's big hands remain, fingers curled around her shoulders protectively. "So, this is Antonio Ferrara…"

The scowl only grows deeper, magnified by the now openly savage glare. "I never agreed to speak to that *pezzo di merda*, only to meet with you," he grits out. "After the hell you put me through—"

"Dad…"

Already, this is going wonderfully. Clearing my throat, I prepare to launch into the speech I spent all night writing, but Serena cuts me off.

"Where's Mom?"

"Grabbing some coffee and pastries from the café down the block. I don't know why she insisted, as if this is a social visit." He rolls his eyes. "She'll be here in a minute."

"Oh, stop, Pa." Serena tries to wriggle free of his hold, but he doesn't budge. "Well, are you going to sit down or what?" She ticks her head toward the leather couch in the great room. It's impeccably maintained, her housekeeper must have been coming weekly since I took her. A fresh bouquet of violets sits on the center of the coffee table, my contribution to the inviting room. I'd snuck out of bed earlier this morning and picked them up from a street vendor.

Nothing brings a smile to Serena's face like those brilliant lavender blooms.

With a grumble, she tows her father toward the sitting area, and I move into step behind them, keeping my distance. At this point, I'm more than happy to allow Serena to take the lead when it comes to dealing with her father.

"Sit," she barks.

And to my surprise, the pissed-off, tattooed King's enforcer does.

Maybe she really does have her father wrapped around that cute little pinky like she claims. A twinge of hope sparks, but I smother it before it grows out of control.

Serena folds down onto the couch across from him and I slide in beside her, my arm instinctively curling around her shoulders.

"Get your fucking hands off my daughter before I rip them off." Dante's words are low and deadly, nothing more than a frosty whisper.

I pull my arm back so quickly I nearly hit the back of Serena's head.

"*Papà!*" she hisses.

Dante slides to the edge of the cushion, raw fury blazing across his icy glare. "I agreed to hear you out, *cuore mio*, but I refuse to sit here and watch as the man who threatened to kill my only daughter gropes you right in front of me."

"Gropes? I think you're being a little dramatic."

"Dramatic? No. Dramatic would be me whipping out my knife, cutting Antonio's arms off and beating him with them until his body goes limp."

A shudder races down my spine at the vivid image. I clench my molars to keep the retort from blurting out. He's not the only one who can make threats here.

"*Papà*, if you can't even hear us out—"

"Us?" he roars. "There is no us, Serena! This man captured you, kept you hostage for weeks and tried to use you to regain his territory."

"Territory you stole from him!" Serena shouts back.

"It was just business."

"But for him, it was personal. It was his father's land, his newly deceased father."

"Who was a complete psychopath from what I've heard…"

"You of all people should know you can't choose your parents."

Dante's eyes flash, nostrils flaring. "Serena—"

"No." Her head whips back and forth. "It's time for you to listen to me." Her hand closes over mine, fingers tangling tightly with my own. "I love Antonio, and I need you to promise that not only will you return the rightful territory to the Ferrara's, but you'll also swear never to hurt him."

His jaw tightens, a tendon fluttering like mad. "I can't promise that, Serena."

"You can and you will, or you'll never see me again." She stiffens, her entire body cut from glass. "If I can't trust you to back off, then I'll have to run away with him. He has too many enemies now, and I won't lose him, Pa. So, you'll leave me with no other choice."

"You can't be serious," he snarls.

"Wait." I squeeze Serena's hand, pivoting to face her, my heart nearly exploding from the lengths she's willing to go for me. We never discussed any of this last night when we returned to her apartment. Her family means everything to her, and her willingness to walk away from all of it for me is incredible. But it's more than I would ever ask of her. "I could never allow you to make that sacrifice for me, *tesoro*."

"Finally," Dante grumbles. "Someone talk some sense into this girl."

Ignoring her father for a moment, I pin my gaze to hers, holding both hands between us. "I don't care about the Ferrara empire anymore, Sere. You're all that matters to me. The Kings can have it if it means I get to keep you. I'm getting the far better part of the deal."

Her lips tremble, those brilliant sapphire irises glittering as she regards me. "Are you sure? You fought so hard to keep your father's legacy alive—"

"My father was an asshole, and I don't need anything from him anymore. I'll build something new, something with you." I finally turn to face Dante, prepared to bear his wrath. "I know that what I did was unforgivable, and as much as I hate the pain

I caused you and Serena, I can't bring myself to completely regret it because if I hadn't made such a rash move, I never would have found your daughter. I don't blame you for not believing me, for thinking I'm a piece of shit, but I love Serena with my heart and soul. I will spend the rest of my days on my knees, begging for her forgiveness. And yours, if that's what you want."

Dante just grunts, but the hard set of his jaw softens a touch.

"My territory is yours, all of it. I'll even throw in my men, if there are any still loyal to my family." I lock eyes with the daunting man, injecting steel in my veins. "I will love and protect Serena until my dying breath. There are no lengths I wouldn't go to in order to keep her safe. But I will never walk away from her, *Signor* Valentino. I may have stolen her from you all those weeks ago, but she's the one who ended up stealing my heart. Now, it's hers to keep forever."

Serena's hand finds mine again, fingers entwining with my own. She leans in, soft lips brushing my ear. "I love you," she whispers.

The sharp buzz of the doorbell breaks the spell of the tense moment, and Serena shoots up to answer. Standing, my wary gaze trails her form, fingers twitching for the gun at my hip. I don't relax until the door swings open, revealing her mother on the other side.

Dante hisses out a curse, drawing my gaze across the coffee table. His eyes are fixed to mine, studying, analyzing. "*Merda*, you do love her, don't you?"

"With every part of my dark, broken soul, *signore*." I drop back down on the couch, dropping my gaze to my clenched fingers.

"Just perfect," he grits out. His eyes narrow, still scrutinizing. "You do understand how this will look to my enemies, don't you?"

My brows knit as I regard him, and it only takes me a moment to understand. I've grown up in this world, aware of all the ramifications, of the importance of each calculated move.

"You think Serena will be at risk if you don't make an example of me?"

He nods.

He's not wrong.

"Taking my territory is a start..."

"It doesn't make a statement quite like your dead body hanging from one of the Ferrara nightclubs."

"Fair enough." I consider, gnawing on my bottom lip. "I would never want to put Serena's life at risk again."

"Well, you would be."

A jumble of thoughts race through my mind. The most obvious answer is there, but I'm not certain Dante or even Serena would agree to it.

"What are you thinking?" He eyes me from across the table as Serena and her mother continue their own hushed conversation in the foyer.

Steeling my spine, I look Dante dead in the eyes. "An arranged marriage for the sake of bringing our families together, strengthening both and avoiding bloodshed."

He snorts on a laugh. "Why would I ever choose the Ferraras when there are dozens of more powerful families to pick from?"

"It's a logical option considering your niece's relationship with my brother."

His mouth twists, but already I can see his resolve faltering. "It's a stretch at best." It isn't though. Serena has already told me Raffaele has won over the younger Valentino. It's only a matter of time until my brother proposes to Bella. Our families will be tied together, nonetheless.

"No one will question the Kings, and you know it," I add just to stroke his ego.

Dante's lips curl into a rueful smile. "There's still a more pressing issue." He ticks his head toward the foyer, to the beautiful woman hugging her mother. "Have you met my daughter?

Do you know her at all? She would never agree to an arranged marriage."

"I think she would if it meant keeping me alive and peace in the family."

He smirks, a flash of something unexpected in those dark eyes. "Maybe you know Serena better than I thought."

I certainly hope so, and I plan on spending the rest of my life learning everything there is to know about her.

Serena and her mother walk into the sitting room, and I rise, my body moving toward her as if propelled by gravity. It takes tremendous physical effort not to touch her. Dipping my head to Rose Valentino, I offer a smile. "A pleasure to meet you, *Signora* Valentino."

She waves a dismissive hand before curling onto the couch beside her husband. "Gawd, please don't call me that. It makes me sound so old. Rose is just fine."

"Okay, then, Rose. Now, I see where Serena gets her good looks and sparkling personality."

Dante's scowl morphs into something truly murderous, and I give up on any further attempts at flattery.

Serena plops down onto the couch, and I fold down beside her, my gaze darting between her and her father. Would he bring up the idea, or should I?

A long moment of silence passes, and when he doesn't utter a word, I turn my attention to my *tesoro*. The bright sunlight streams into the windows, setting those vibrant blue irises aglow. Her lips pucker as she regards me, cheeks growing rosy when I don't speak for an endless minute.

"Why are you looking at me like that?"

It only takes me an instant to decide. Since the moment this woman dropped into my life, it's been pure chaos, but *Dio*, I can't remember the last time I was happier. She awoke something inside me, something I was certain had long since shriveled up and died.

I drop to my knees and take her hand, eyes locked to hers.

A gasp squeezes out through her perfect pink lips.

"Serena," I begin, my voice unsteady with the overwhelming weight of my emotions. "From the moment we met, my life has been a whirlwind. A whirlwind of danger, of uncertainty, but also of unimaginable excitement and unexpected love—all because of you."

She shifts on the couch, free hand pressed to her chest.

"You've seen me at my absolute worst, yet somehow, you saw something in me worth saving. You challenged me to be a better man and to love as fiercely as I fight."

I squeeze her hand tighter, my nerves getting the best of me. "Serena Valentino, you stole my heart in ways I never imagined possible. I love you more than I thought I could love anyone. Will you marry me? Will you be the one I wake up next to, fight for, cherish, and protect, for the rest of our lives?"

My gaze remains fixed to hers, vulnerable and hopeful. Everything else fades to a whisper as I wait for her answer, my future hanging in the balance.

"Where's my ring?" she blurts.

A chuckle dislodges the tension in my chest as her sparkling eyes meet mine. "I—I don't have one. Yet."

Serena's eyes dart to her father, brow curved in an incredulous arch. "Did you make him do this?"

"Of course not," Dante grumbles. "You think I want you to marry him?"

Grasping her chin between my thumb and forefinger, I force her wary eyes to mine. "*Amorè*, it might seem sudden, but I meant every single word. And I'll get you any ring you want as long as you agree to marry me."

Her eyes light up, the blue shimmer more radiant than the rising sun. "Sounds good to me." She slides off the couch and into my waiting arms, claiming my mouth with a ravenous kiss.

I may have taken her hostage in a blind quest for revenge, but she captured my heart in return, and now I would make her my wife and spend the rest of my days proving how much I love her.

EPILOGUE

A *lessandro – One Month Later*

The happy laughter, clinking glasses and soft music seeps through the very walls, infiltrating the crevices of the closed door. I roll over on the bed, wincing, and bury my head beneath the pillow. Every movement still hurts, the skin grafts across my body requiring frequent dressing changes. I never should have come to Serena and Antonio's impromptu engagement party. The whole thing was set up to prove to the other powerful crime syndicates that the joining of the Ferraras and Valentinos was a calculated move, not a kidnapping gone wrong.

I'm still surprised Serena agreed to the whole thing. I don't doubt she loves the guy, but I never thought my eldest cousin would get married at all.

And to think, if none of this had happened, I would be the one about to get married. It turns out that the reason my Uncle Dante was initially unavailable to discuss Antonio's ransom demands was because of me. He and Luca were on their way to meet my parents in China to arrange my marriage with the daughter of a rival family. I nearly lost my shit when I found out which was what sent me on that plane to rescue Serena. I'm not sure what would have been better, being forced to marry a stranger or dealing with this.

Footfalls and animated chatter echo out in the hallway, and I tense. *For fuck's sake, I just want to be left alone.* The sound falls away a moment later, and I draw in a breath of relief. After a month in the burn unit at New York Presbyterian hospital, the best specialized facility on the continent according to *Papà*, I thought I was finally ready to face the world again.

But fuck, the sound of all that happiness only magnifies my misery.

Alessia wheeled me into the party in the hospital scrubs which hide the depressing compression garments underneath, the only asshole not in a suit or tux. I refused to come with my live-in nurse; the impossibly cheery woman only makes me feel like an invalid. After quick hellos to my family members, I only lasted out in the great room of Serena's apartment for a minute before losing my twin and ducking into my cousin's spare bedroom.

Still the muddled voices and contented laughter surround me, each happy sound only amplifying the bitterness in my heart.

How did I become this?

How did I fall so fast? From heir to the Gemini throne with women throwing themselves at my feet to this shell of a man with gruesome scars across half my body, barely able to walk, to fuck, to do anything by myself…

The door whips open, slams against the wall, and I mutter a curse for forgetting to lock it when I staggered in. Serena stumbles backwards, Antonio glued to her mouth, his hand palming her ass.

Oh, hell, no, this is the last thing I need.

"Don't you guys have your own room to do that in?" I hiss.

Antonio releases Serena and she whirls around, eyes glassy from champagne and lust as they meet mine. "What the hell are you doing hiding out in here?"

"I needed a minute."

Her eyes widen, the happiness from a moment ago, vanishing. "Are you okay? Are you in pain?" She rushes over to the bed, concern etched into her face.

"I'm fine, Sere, relax." Since the moment I was released from the hospital in Milano and returned to Manhattan, she's been hovering over me like a mother hen. She's always been like that with all the cousins, but never to this extent. I know she feels guilty as hell for what happened in Milano. She thinks it's her fault, that she owes me somehow, but her guilt only makes me feel worse.

And the pity…

That is the absolute worst of all.

It's not only from her, but from all my family, which is why I've been avoiding everyone as much as possible. Seeing the pity in their eyes when they look at me is worse than the pain of the skin grafts, the wound care, the endless physical therapy, all of it.

"Maybe we should give Alessandro some time alone," Antonio offers, curling an arm around her waist.

Smart man. As much as I despised the guy when they first got together, I can't deny he's perfect for her. And oddly enough, I don't blame him for what happened. It was my father who'd been abducted all those years ago and the reason why he and my uncles killed Santiago's mother. I don't hold them responsible either, it's the fucked-up world we were born into.

No, I should have been faster, should have been more aware of my surroundings. If anyone is to blame for me getting burned in that explosion, it's me.

"Fuck that," Serena shoots back at Antonio. "That's not how we do things in the cousin crew." She rushes out the door and shouts down the hallway.

"Oh, fucking hell," I grit out as I hear her call for each of our cousins, one by one.

"I tried," Antonio mutters, lifting his shoulders.

"How do you put up with all of us?" The question pops out unbidden as I force myself to sit up, gritting through the pain. In the past few weeks, I've found it easier to talk to Sere's fiancé than my own family. Maybe it's because he too survived being burned alive, or maybe it's because he wasn't close to his own father or siblings. Lately, they're just suffocating.

A silly grin flashes across his face and instantly, I regret asking. "Because I know how much Serena adores all of you, and I love her."

"Love certainly is a fickle beast," I murmur.

"You'll see one day."

A cold, hollow laugh escapes. "I don't think love is in my future, Toni." Then I motion to my scarred neck and cheek, not to mention all the layers of bandages hidden beneath my loose-fitting clothes. "I look like a fucking monster."

He shakes his head, that familiar flash of pity surging to the surface. But he masks it quickly, and it only takes me a second to remember why. He, too, bears the scars of the fire he survived. They're nothing compared to mine, but still, I almost take back the callous remark. Luckily, he's already speaking before I can figure out what to say.

"We're all monsters one way or another, Ale. It only takes the right woman to look past our darkness, our flaws, physical or otherwise." He offers a smile, and it's a genuine one, not like the ones I receive from random strangers on the street when they stare at my bandages. "You'd be surprised how love can find you when you least expect it."

"Right," I grumble. Maybe I'll find a hot, blind girl at their wedding next year.

Speaking of the bride-to-be, Serena bounds in with Bella, Raf, Matty, and Alessia trailing her. Antonio's hand lands on Serena's lower back the moment she's in the room, the kind of casual, effortless touch I'll never have again. With each of my cousins finding love, our cousin crew is growing exponentially. I should be happy for everyone, but my raging bitterness only swallows it up.

"What are you doing moping around in here?" Bella asks, a glass of champagne in her fist.

It isn't only her gaze pinned to mine now. They're all staring at me, watching, waiting, walking on eggshells. The worst part of all of this isn't the scars, the pain, or the fact that I can't even walk right. It's the way they look at me. Like I'm already half-dead.

"I'm just not in the mood to dance," I finally manage, flashing her a sneer before ticking my head at the bandages poking out from beneath the navy hospital scrubs I live in.

"No one said anything about dancing, grumpy." She takes my good hand in hers, squeezing. Not that I'd ever admit it out loud, but Bella has always been my favorite. There's just something about her selflessness and endless optimism that gets through my thick armor. Or at least it used to.

I don't even recognize myself in the mirror anymore.

"Yeah, just have a drink." Matty pulls a bottle of champagne from behind his back, and Alessia throws him a scowl.

"He can't drink on the pain meds, you idiot," she hisses.

"Aw, come on, let him have one drink. He looks like he could use one."

I'm about to agree with my cousin when the last person I want to see marches through the door.

Rory Delaney roars in, her mane of fiery crimson hair wet and wild across her bare shoulders. She looks like she just jumped out of the shower and raced right over. She probably did when she noticed I'd escaped the four walls of my suffocating penthouse.

"There you are!" She jabs an accusatory finger in the air, the slight Irish lilt seeping through like it always does when she's angry. "How could you just take off like that? Are you trying to give me a heart attack?" She claps her hand to her chest dramatically, and I focus on her skimpy tank top and sleep shorts. This crazy girl ran over in her pajamas.

"Who is this gorgeous woman?" Matteo's mischievous gaze darts between us.

I huff out a breath, the expanding of my ribcage only tearing at my delicate flesh. But I clench my teeth to hide the wince. The last thing I need is my new overzealous nurse proving her point.

"Yes, who is she?" Serena lifts a curious brow in my direction.

"Everyone, meet Rory Delaney, my new live-in—." I can't even force her title out because it's too depressing. As a virile twenty-four-year-old male, admitting to needing a nurse is just embarrassing.

"I'm his nurse," she blurts, marching closer to the bed.

I sit up as straight as the compression garments beneath will allow without tweaking my healing skin and meet her fierce emerald gaze. "And I've already told you, I don't need one." I should hate the infuriating woman, should send her packing with a single word. But for some reason, the way she storms in like she owns the place makes me want to see what happens if I push back.

"Well, that's not what your father said, and he's the one who hired me." She offers a smile, flashing her teeth. "And the next time you leave the penthouse without telling me, there will be consequences."

"You're really going to punish me, Red?" I taunt, watching for a reaction.

She smirks. "Don't tempt me."

I stare at her, brows slamming together in surprise, and she glares right back. At all of five foot nothing, Rory Delancy is a fiery little thing. She looks like she walked out of a Celtic fever dream, all fire and fury. But something tells me she's more than she seems… and that could be dangerous.

Strangest of all, she's not even remotely intimidated by me.

Even the women I used to bring back to my penthouse for a good fuck were. I've never been friendly exactly, and now I'm surly as all hell.

Matteo laughs, the sound cutting through the suddenly quiet room. "Well, Ale, I think you've met your match."

I meet Rory's gaze, bejeweled irises burning with something that makes my pulse spike.

Shit.

I might really be in trouble with this one.

Get ready for Alessandro's story in Brutal Heir, coming in September! You can preorder it now :) Can't wait till then to find out what happens? Join my Patreon and follow along as I write the next story, chapter by chapter!

In the meantime, join my Facebook reader group, Sienna Cross's Heartbreakers or Heartbreaker mailing list to get a sneak peek of the first chapter of Brutal Heir AND the FREE prequel novella from Ruthless Guardian, and get a glimpse at when Isabella and Raf first met!

While you're waiting for Brutal Heir, go back to Isabella and Raf's story in Ruthless Guardian.

She was my assignment, now she's my obsession...

Raffaele

Isabella Valentino is off-limits.
She's young and naïve and most importantly, my new client.
I live by my rules; in my world, everything is about control.
That's why I'm the best at what I do.
And rule number one: Never get involved with the principal.
But the woman is a force of nature.
Ignoring my rules and procedures, she's intent on breaking every single one.
And my tethers of restraint grow weaker by the day.
Worse, I don't want to fight it anymore.
Isabella Valentino is mine.

. . .

<u>Isabella</u>

I'm a mafia princess, heir to the Kings' throne.
My entire life has been spent behind the bars of a gilded cage.
Protected, admired, adored.
Controlled.
I long for freedom.
In one night, everything changes...
Enter Raffaele Ferrara, dark, broody and tormented.
And the most frighteningly gorgeous man I've ever seen.
My new bodyguard is all rules and restraint.
But beneath our clashes, an undeniable attraction simmers—dangerous, forbidden, irresistible.

Click here to devour this steamy, enemies-to-lovers, age-gap, bodyguard mafia romance.

Check out all the novels in the world of the Kings:
<u>Kings of Temptation</u>
Ruthless King
Savage King
Brutal King
Wicked King

<u>Ruthless Heirs</u> (Second Generation)
Ruthless Guardian
Savage Prince
Brutal Heir

ALSO BY SIENNA CROSS

<u>Ruthless Heirs</u>

Ruthless Guardian

Savage Prince

Brutal Heir

<u>Kings of Temptation</u>

Ruthless King

Savage King

Brutal King

Wicked King

ACKNOWLEDGMENTS

I'll let you in on my dirty little secret... Sienna Cross is my pen name, one I've been dying to launch for a while now. I never would've even attempted it if it wasn't for the support of my husband. He's the only one in my family who knows about naughty Sienna. Thanks for pushing me to do all the things, honey!

A special thank you to my awesome V.A., Sarah, who has been such a huge help and also vault when it comes to keeping all of this a secret. And thank you to the incredibly talented Samaiya for the gorgeous art (you really make the story come to life!) And of course my beta readers and Sarah (again!), and my ARC team, you're all amazing! Some of you have been with me for years and I really appreciate all your feedback (thanks for keeping the secret too!)

And the biggest thank you to my readers! I could never do this without you :)
    ~ Sienna

ABOUT THE AUTHOR

Sienna Cross was kidnapped by mobsters, saved by her super-hot step-brother, then forced into an arranged marriage with a billionaire. From there, things got really interesting... She loves to write about dark, morally-gray alpha males and the captivating women that bring them to their knees. For all the inside info, join Sienna Cross's Heartbreakers on Facebook, like her page, and follow her on Instagram and Tiktok. She has a thing for stalkers ;)

www.siennacrossbooks.com

Printed in Great Britain
by Amazon